Tales from the Pit

Archibald Olrig Campbell

GOBLINSHEAD

Musselburgh

Tales from the Pit

First published 2001
© Martin Coventry 2001

Published by Goblinshead
130B Inveresk Road
Musselburgh
EH21 7AY
Scotland
Tel: 0131 665 2894
Fax: 0131 653 6566
Email: goblinshead@sol.co.uk

British Library Cataloguing in Publication Data
A catalogue record for this book is available from the British Library

ISBN 1 899874 17 8

Typeset by **Goblinshead**.

If you would like a full catalogue of our publications, please contact Goblinshead at the address above.

The moon had set.

A dark shape flitted from shadow to shadow. A few torches flared from along the battlements, but the shape vanished against the darkness of the stonework. Two sentries passed within a pace or two. Their watchful eyes saw nothing. The shape waited until they had disappeared from view, then stepped out into the light.

Revile stood back for a moment, peering upwards to the roof of the royal apartments on the highest part of the rock of the Citadel. His hands and face were covered in soot. Only the whites of his eyes were clearly visible in the flickering light. There was a window thirty or so feet above him. He inspected the climb carefully. It did not look too difficult.

Taking a padded grappling hook from a small pack, the assassin again checked the battlements were deserted. Then he swung the grapple about his head a few times, before throwing it towards the roof. It caught on the eaves. Revile tested the hold. Then, with great agility and speed, he scuttled up the rope, and soon stood on the window ledge. The window was shuttered. By slipping a dagger between the shutters, he undid the latch and opened them. He stole into the chamber, retrieving the grapple, coiling the rope.

Shona's room was quiet, quiet as the grave, the only sound her untroubled breathing as she slept. Revile was not troubled that she should awake: she had drunk enough wine to drown a whale. Revile closed the shutters softly, then slipped over to the bed. Although it was dark, he located the princess without difficulty and stood over the cot, peering down. She stirred slightly and sighed – but the assassin hesitated, his daggers left untouched.

He left her bed side, padding across the rugs to the door, listening intently. He heard nothing untoward, then decided to search the room for anything of value. He carefully avoided a stool by the side of her bed; quickly rummaged through her clothing and effects; finally inspected a chest at the end of her cot. It was locked. While Revile had some skill at opening locks, it was too dark for such work. He searched for the key, but it could not be found. Guessing it might be around Shona's neck, he returned to the bed and gently pulled back her blankets and furs. The woman lay quite still. Revile stared down at her naked body. But still he hesitated.

There was a soft click from the door.

The assassin froze, hardly dared to breathe.

Introduction

The origins of this novel are said to go back the Dark Ages, reputedly back to a time not long after the events themselves took place. The story of the finding of the manuscripts is given in more detail below. The novel, or at least the set of manuscripts from which it was compiled, was brought together by Archibald Olrig Campbell in Victorian times. His work was never published, but has been updated and edited for this version of his novel.

Archibald Olrig Campbell was from Argyll and spent his youth, while not away at boarding school, at Ardnasaul (not located), apparently a great house, on the banks of the Firth of Lorn, some miles south of Oban. It was in the old basement of the family home there that he found a set of manuscripts in an old trunk. These manuscripts were written in Latin, seemed to date from around the beginning of the 9th century, and related the adventures of an assassin and adventurer called Revile. Campbell translated these when a teenager, but had not completed the task by the time he joined the British army in the first half of the 19th century. He saw active service, and was promoted to the rank of Major (although he did not use his military rank in his letters and papers).

When he returned from serving abroad some 30 years later, he went back to translating, updating and greatly expanding the manuscripts, adding a lot of his own material. He did not return to Argyll, however, and the work seems to have been undertaken at Blackness Manor House (now demolished) to the west of Dundee. Campbell appears to have been a guest for some years there. He completed his work at Blackness, finishing the first draft of what is now called *Tales from the Pit*. Campbell never married, and although his estate and the draft of this novel were left to a distant cousin, the original ancient manuscripts were not amongst his belongings (they may, of course, have remained at or been returned to his family's home).

The story behind the ancient manuscripts is as follows. They were compiled a few years after the events in the novel: some time in the 9th century. Campbell believed that they were written at Dunkeld in Perthshire. After the abbey of Iona was refounded by Queen Margaret in the 11th century, they were taken and stored there with other records and books. Here they stayed for hundreds of years, indeed until the abbey was dissolved during the Reformation in the 16th century. The manuscripts, along with many other papers, were shipped for safekeeping to the castle of Cairnburg, located on the Treshnish Isles, two miles off the west coast of Mull.

According to Campbell, Cairnburg was besieged and captured by Cromwell's forces in the 1650s, which included a party of his relatives. Many of the books and papers were destroyed during the storming of the fortress, but these manuscripts survived (possibly because they had no religious or Roman Catholic connotations) and came into the possession of the Campbells of Ardnasaul, of whom Archibald was the descendant. Archibald is vague about which family of Campbells this may have been and who exactly he was related to – it has been suggested this may have been because he was illegitimate, or because he actually made up the origins of his work (such as James MacPherson's *Ossian*).

His novel descended through one of his cousins, then to myself in 1983. *Tales from the Pit* is based on his work, and although the language has been updated and some of the structure of the stories changed, the names of people, places and kingdoms have been left largely unaltered, except for consistency. Some appear to refer to real places: Dundonald is very probably Dunadd in Kilmartin Glen, while Alclwyd is Dumbarton. Others cannot be or have not been identified, and the kings do not appear to be those in the king lists of the times. Campbell believed that the Pit itself was located at Bamburgh in Northumberland. Incidentally, the reference to Conan in 'The Assassins and the Princess' appears to be to the early saint Conan, patron saint of Lorn, or his namesake, King Conan.

Iain Martin, Edinburgh, September 2001

Tales from
the Pit

T he bolts of the cell door were withdrawn, and a flood of light suddenly entered the Pit. Two of the tower guards pushed a girl into the cell, manacling her beside the other prisoners. The guards left quickly, slamming the iron door behind them, the clang reverberating down the passages and tunnels.

It was dank and dark in the dungeon. The only light issued weakly from a narrow shaft to the surface. Three other shadowy figures sat there, chained by the wrists, manacled in the condemned cell.

The prisoners peered at their new companion. Silver thread and gems glittered from her dress, but little else could be seen in the gloom.

"So," said a cold voice, "you, too, have come to join me dancing at the end of a rope."

The girl choked, and then broke down and wept.

The Pit was now as black as a coffin buried deep in the bowels of the Earth. Out of the cloying and claustrophobic darkness came a long deadly cry of fear and anguish, rising like an evil spectre, then dying suddenly.

The girl tensed, then broke down afresh.

The cold voice muttered and cursed her.

"Peace," said another voice to the girl, that of a woman. "Please don't cry any more. Please. You must try to be brave."

The girl struggled to control her sobbing.

"Forgive us for our companion here," the woman went on, "I'm sure he meant nothing hurtful. We're all to share the same fate so we might as well be friends."

"I'm sorry ..." started the girl.

"Well don't be," replied the woman. "Not on our account. I am Margaret, daughter of Kenneth, of this town. This is Fergus of Duncreag, and this friendly fellow is Revile of Llaith, a stranger in these parts – or so he says. What's your name?"

"I'm Alwyn nic Whiteadder," the girl said a little proudly. "My father is the Lord of South Caerwinnion."

"So you are of noble birth then?" said Fergus.

"In a manner of speaking," said Alwyn, "my father and mother were never married."

"Well, we've that in common as well," he said. "What did they do you for?"

"I'd rather not talk about it," replied the girl.

"Very well," said Margaret. "For my part, I robbed a burgess of a little trinket, a ring. He was furious when he found out, and had me arrested. God damn his soul to hell!"

"And I," said Fergus sourly, "stole a loaf of bread."

"They will hang you for that?" asked Alwyn in surprise.

"Indeed," Fergus replied, "and they've as surely damned my wife and children to death."

"I'm sorry," started Alwyn.

"Forget it," muttered Fergus, "it's not your fault. It was that pig of a baker. And the loaf was stale, stale I tell you, hard as a stone! I can't believe he would do this to me. I've known him all my life. Bastard! Bastards!"

"Shush," said Margaret, "we're all in the same boat."

Alwyn paused for a moment, then said slowly: "I'm to be hanged because I refused Prince Bregorin, because I would not lie with him. He wanted to take me as a mistress. I couldn't ..." Her voice tailed away and fell silent, her body shaking.

"I see," said Margaret softly, then nodded. "Yes, we've all heard the Prince is a difficult man, that it is he who wields the real power in Bamburg. Anyway, not to worry. I hope he didn't hurt you?"

"No," replied Alwyn in a whisper, "he never touched me, thank God."

"Good," said Margaret more brightly, "I'm glad. As for our other friend: he's been here for two days already. I guess that helps to explain his foul mood: that and being hung in the morning. Fergus and I have only been here for a couple of hours. Anyway, Revile here murdered old Rule – you know, the furs merchant – in his bed. Him and his wife and servants."

"O really?" said Alwyn, "I'd heard he'd been assassinated."

"Killed them in their sleep," continued Margaret, "although I don't know why, to be sure. Rule was as slippery as a serpent, and twice as nasty: but to be slaughtered in such way. Why did you do it?"

"I was paid," said Revile shortly.

"Really?" said Fergus. "How much, I wonder?"

"Ten gold pieces," replied the assassin.

"My God!" said Fergus in wonder. "That's a fortune! How were you caught?"

Revile shrugged slightly: "I was betrayed by the man who employed me."

"Where are you from?" asked Margaret. "You said you were a stranger."

"I'm from here and there," replied Revile with a sigh. "I travel about a lot, although I've spent too many hours in the taverns of Llaith, in Lothland, to the north. Have you ever been there?"

"No," said Margaret, "I've never been far from Bamburg."

"Same with me, except during the war," added Fergus. "Duncreag is just outside the town walls."

"How about you?" Margaret asked the girl. "Alwyn was it?"

"Me?" Alwyn replied. "I lived happily at my father's house at Caerwinnion until a few years ago. Since then I've worked in the tower here. I've never had the chance to travel. And I so wish I'd never left my home, that I'd never come to the court here, and that I'd never heard of Prince Bregorin."

There was a pause. The drip of unclean water ticked away the seconds into the darkness.

"So, friend Revile," said Margaret eventually. "What is your profession? Or is killing helpless merchants and their wives and servants all you do?"

"I'm an adventurer," he replied. "What *did* you do?"

She laughed. "Well, I suppose we need no secrets now," she said. "I am a whore. I make money selling my sex."

Revile grinned. "So," he said, "I am an adventurer and back-stabbing assassin, Margaret is a whore, and Alwyn a servant in the tower, despite – or even maybe because of – her noble blood. That just leaves you, Fergus. I reckon you were a farmer, and a poor one at that."

"I am," said Fergus, "although I am a freeman, and held some land. It wasn't really enough to make much of a living, though. Poor. Stony. Your could hardly grow a thing."

"O, that bad," said Revile.

"We're a mixed bunch, to be sure," said Margaret. "Strange we should all go to the gallows."

"What time do you reckon it is?" said Fergus. "It feels late."

"About ten o'clock," replied Revile.

"And the hangings take place about ten tomorrow," said the farmer sadly. "We've about twelve hours altogether. Not very long really."

"It'll seem it," said Margaret, sounding gloomy.

"It could be worse," said Revile. "At least we are only to be hanged. In Thule they are less kind. They flay all the skin from your body, then boil you slowly in salted water. It is said that the screams can be heard from the mainland."

"Hush," said Margaret sternly as Alwyn choked. "There's no need to be talking that way."

The assassin smiled crookedly.

"What exactly does an adventurer do?" asked Fergus in a less-than-friendly manner.

"Depends what's on offer," replied the assassin easily. "Thievery and murder, peril and adventure. Boring stuff. Not like being a brave farmer: fighting the elements, the soil, the wayward frolicking sheep. Just robbing tombs, killing noblemen, fighting endless wars. Dull stuff."

"Tell us about it, anyway," said Margaret. "Waiting for the morning is hard, even if it is really just a short time."

"If you're sure," laughed Revile.

"Yes," said Margaret cheerfully. "What else would we do but worry about the morning."

"Very well," said Revile, not at all displeased.

An Epic Feat

Revile the assassin was very drunk. This was obvious to anyone with half a brain who cared to glance in his direction. However, as the rest of the revellers were hard put to muster a serviceable brain between them, not one of them was aware of his condition. The tavern was packed with as many brigands as it could hold, and one more sozzled adventurer was hardly worthy of notice. Lewd singing and laughing filled the steamy chamber. Tankards of ale and pots of wine were constantly refilled only to disappear again into the merry drinkers.

Revile was very drunk, slouching on his bench, and tried to focus his mind on his drink. This proved impossible as his mind was away on some business of its own. He concentrated again – but no matter how hard he tried he could not see his mug of ale. In desperation he leaned forward, flailing about the table in front of him. He discovered a tankard. His hands clasped it tightly and tested its weight. The tankard was full to brimming. Sighing with relief, Revile pulled the drink towards him.

A massive hand clamped itself about his wrist.

"That's my drink, friend!" said a disembodied voice from somewhere far far away.

Revile was very drunk. Yet he had a vague notion these words were addressed to him. Struggling uselessly against the vice-like grip, he heaved himself to his feet, staggering a bit.

"Sit down, friend," said the distant voice.

Revile did not know what to say. He focused his bleary stare on the fist, then followed it to a thick forearm, passed a veined biceps, up to a massive shoulder, on to a bull neck, then finally arrived at a pair of unusually cold and violent eyes.

Revile was very drunk – but considered his next move very carefully. The owner of the fist and the eyes was a massive Highlander from the mountainous North. Even seated, he was only inches smaller than Revile. The Highlander's friends were sitting all around him. There could have been six of them, there could have been twelve, even twenty four. But they were definitely very big and very nasty. They were all staring at Revile. The situation called for a measure of prudence and tact. The assassin could not fight a legion of Highlanders.

Revile paused, searching for some joke or play on words that might retrieve the situation.

"Bugger off, you Gaelic woolly-back sheep-shagging git!" he said with a warm, winning smile.

Revile was never sure what happened next – something most likely hit him. When he regained consciousness, he was lying in thick mud, very smelly unpleasant thick mud – mud to be found in a cesspool.

The assassin rolled over and staggered to his feet, a little of the noisome mud seeping up and over the tops of his boots. Lights flickered and flashed before his eyes. Wading out of the stagnant pool, he struggled to firmer land. Revile turned and gazed back.

He wondered how he had come to end up in the burgh's cesspool.

"Must have been something I said," he concluded, then headed for the nearest tavern.

He wandered about for a long time, but never did find a tavern.

The dark warren of closes which burrowed the burgh were all but deserted, the windows lightless, the dingy facades looming over the narrow streets.

Revile dearly wanted a drink.

The moon was full and cast dim pale fingers over the mounds of refuse, down the open sewers, disturbing a few rats.

Revile felt ill.

The closes would have been quiet but for the scrape of Revile's boots on the cobbles, the drip of unclean water, Revile's uneven breathing.

Revile was violently sick all over his boots.

When he had finished emptying the dearly-bought contents of his stomach, he straightened up, still spitting the last of the bile from his mouth. He tried to wipe some of the mess from his fouled breeks.

Then the assassin thought he heard voices. Recovering a little, he headed off in their direction with the hope of finding more drink.

In the near distance three people appeared in the light of an uncovered lantern. The assassin hurried towards them, an eager fire burning in his eyes. But he tripped over a gutter and sprawled into shadows by the road. Lights appeared before his eyes, the world began to spin.

"Listen," said a gruff voice, unaware or uncaring that Revile could hear. "Listen good! You know the bargain. Either bring us the Bull of Heaven, or it will go ill for your sister. Constantine has spoken. He has sent us this last time. What do you say?"

"I can't do as you wish," said a girl forlornly. "I don't know where this Bull of Heaven is kept. It is hidden and I have never heard word of it. I'm a novice in the Order of the Cross – but even if I was a priest I couldn't do this. You must understand!"

"By Mithra! Your words are as nothing. You have no choice but to follow our orders. Either do as we command or suffer the consequences. And this last thing Constantine bade us say: There are many ways to die, Margaret of the Cross. Some are peaceful, some are painful, some are terrible torture. Disobey me in this and your sister will be familiar with every suffering of death. But she will not die. When we have broken her, she shall be returned to you, maimed and twisted. You shall know that you caused her destruction. Think on it. The choice is yours – if choice there be!"

There were the sounds of receding footsteps, then the anguished weeping of a young woman.

Revile regained his unsteady feet. Weaving over to where the girl wept, he put a comforting but noisome arm about her trembling shoulders. She broke down in his embrace, unwisely burying her head in his fouled tunic.

The assassin considered for a moment. "Have you any wine?" he asked her tenderly. "Or do you know of any taverns which are open at this hour?"

A little while later the two new-found companions were seated in Margaret's small well-furnished apartments, not far from the Great Church, not all that much further from the cesspool.

They sat at opposite sides of a table, an earthenware bottle of good wine and a foul smell between them. Revile had suggested that a goblet of wine might ease her distress, then companionably joined her.

In truth, the young woman was too upset to refuse.

Gradually Margaret regained her composure and took more than hesitating sips of her drink. And whether it was this – or the closeness of an apparently sympathetic human being – she unburdened her troubles, and told Revile her sorry tale.

The girl was called Margaret, the daughter of a prosperous merchant. She had tired of a life of indolence and failed love affairs – and had sought a more satisfying vocation. Nothing suited and at last she despaired and joined the Order of the Cross: a small fanatical cult based at the Great Church. She had entered the Order as a novice, and progressed no further, no matter how hard she worked in the fields and gardens, and attended the teachings.

Then this final calamity had struck. Her sister, her beloved sister whom she loved above all else, had been abducted by the wicked Constantine. He was the High Priest of an opposing cult, a secret religion which had once been popular in the South. The cult worshipped the bull.

Constantine was always making trouble for the Order of the Cross, but had little support except amongst a dedicated few. He had devised the abduction so he might gain possession of a powerful talisman, the Bull of Heaven, an object so mysterious it had not been seen for a generation. Reputedly it was kept at the Great Church. However, Constantine had chosen the wrong target for his schemes: Margaret had no idea where – or even what – the Bull of Heaven might be.

Finally the girl fell silent, and Revile the assassin was hard put to stifle a yawn. Margaret composed herself again, then said after a pause: "I am without hope, unless, well, a brave adventurer might steal the Bull of Heaven for me. Then this unhappy situation might be redeemed and my sister saved."

Revile had to admit that Margaret had a very fetching smile. "Very well," he replied, "I will steal this Bull of Heaven for you. But I will need to know more about it."

Margaret quickly told him all she knew about the Great Church, which was not much, and then Revile decided to ask her one or two intelligent questions.

"I'm sorry if I'm being slow," he apologised, "but what does this Bull of Heaven look like and where is it kept?"

"I don't know," admitted his companion. "As far as I'm aware only the head of our Order does. It has been hidden for a long time. I can't even guess where it is kept. I'm sorry – that's not much help, is it?"

"No, it's not much to go on." The assassin thought for a moment. "Who is this Constantine? I've never heard of him. Is he a Southerner?"

"His father was a Southron soldier, or so he claims, and his mother High Priestess of Mithra in some temple. Constantine is supposedly a wizard, but has few followers. Yet with this Bull of Heaven who knows? It is his last hope or the Cult of the Bull will become extinct in the North."

"I see," said Revile, draining the last of the wine from the bottle. "That would be a terrible shame."

14

A little later, the assassin left Margaret's apartments and struggled down the steps to the street. He turned at the bottom of the stairs, gazing back at the young woman illuminated in the doorway.

"My hopes go with you," she said down to him.

"Never fear," he replied and waved back, nearly falling over. He stumbled off towards the shadowed buildings of the Great Church, Margaret's promise clutched to his heart.

II

Margaret sat forlornly in her apartments with little hope of ever seeing her would-be saviour again. There was no grief in that itself, perhaps, but with the coming of the dawn her dear sister would be horribly tortured.

Margaret's heart was frozen by a frost of despair. Her sister, Matilda, was the only person for whom she had ever cared – and it only emphasised the futility of Margaret's existence that she could do nothing herself to help. All her hopes rested with a strong-smelling drunken adventurer she had met searching for a tavern. The chances of him stealing the Bull of Heaven would be minimal. It was far more likely that he was lying in an inebriated stupor somewhere close by. And she had made her promise, and it would not be easy to fulfil.

Gradually the eastern sky lightened, and a few shafts of light glimmered through the closed shutters. The new day was dawning, all the too soon, yet in great splendour. Margaret's mood darkened. Her mission to save her sister had failed, and it would only be a short while before she met her final torment.

And, as the sun rose out of the eastern hills, there was a pounding at her door. Margaret started then hurried to answer it. She flung the door back, her heart thumping in her chest.

All hope withered.

On her doorstep stood the servants of Constantine.

"We have come for the Bull of Heaven," one said.

Margaret staggered back as if she had been struck and they entered her apartments.

"Where is the Bull, by Mithra!" cried the other one.

"I don't have it," moaned Margaret. "I don't have it."

The two men did not seem surprised by the news.

"Then," said one of them, "in time we will return to Constantine, and tell him of your disobedience. But first, since our master will have no more use for you, we will say good-bye properly, unbeliever!" He drew a dagger. "By Mithra! We'll show you!"

"Unhand her foul oaf!" cried a noble voice. "Or you will feel the bite of this troll's bane!"

Revile leapt through the doorway into the chamber, brandishing a shining sword. His old garb had been replaced by fine garments of dyed wool and a shining breast plate – which glinted in the morning sun and was only muddied by a few hand-prints. The assassin must have bathed for a disgusting smell did not follow him into the house. Indeed, he was quite impressive in his new attire, despite the fact he lurched slightly. "Unhand her, oaf!" he reiterated. "Or you will feel the bite of this wolf's bane!"

"Who are you? By Mithra!"

"I am Dourhand, son of Felleyes," replied Margaret's redeemer proudly. "Also I am Deathshade the Cleaver, of the House of Assassins. Here is The Sword-that-was-Notched! Do you wish to test its razored edge against your innards? Be swift in answering! Or I will trim your finger nails to your sweaty armpits!"

"We are disciples of Constantine," they answered swiftly. "We are on an errand for our master. He is a mighty wizard, wise in all lore. Will you be foolish enough to hinder us? For if that is your purpose you will feel the sharpness of the Bull's horns!"

"Indeed?" laughed Dourhand, son of Felleyes, recklessly. "Do not make me scoff, you heathen scum! You are fortunate that it is not my purpose to hinder you – far from it indeed!" And he uncovered a shining silver bull, rearing on its hind legs. Its back was encrusted with glittering jewels, and its eyes were ruby and evil. "Where is this girl's sister?" he went on. "For that was the bargain: her safe return. Bring her to the steps of the Great Church for there you could not risk treachery. There we shall trade this mysterious talisman for Matilda. Do you understand? Or are these orders too complex for your dull wits? Be gone and return swiftly! We will await you at the church."

The two servants hurried from the apartments, running down the stairs into the street.

"But how?" asked Margaret in surprise. "How did you manage ..."

"It is a long story," interrupted Revile. "Too long for the telling here and now. And we must hurry to the Great Church."

The huge daunting edifice of the Great Church of the Order of the Cross stood behind them. Its many walls and fortifications were etched against the blue sky; for the Church was not just a temple, but also a fortress and town for the acolytes, novices and priests. The roof of the Church shone gold in the sunlight, two tall spires reaching towards the heavens. It was quiet at this hour, and there was no sign of either priests or guards. The theft of the Bull of Heaven had not yet been discovered.

Margaret gazed at the massive structure of the Great Church as if for the first time. She wondered how her companion might have breached the defences and stolen the Bull. There was apparently more to him than met the eye. She searched for some sign of bravery in his face, but found nothing noble or daring. Frowning slightly, Margaret realised Dourhand, son of Felleyes, was thoroughly enjoying himself.

"What is your name?" she asked softly.

He regarded her for a moment. "I am Dourhand, son of Felleyes," he replied with a crooked smile. "I am also named Deathshead the Beaver ..."

"No, I meant your real name."

"Is it important?"

"Perhaps," she replied. "I might have heard of you – such a brave fellow."

"I have many names ..."

"So you've said!" she told him, becoming a little irritated. "I am being serious!"

"So was I," he said with a smile. "And you won't have heard of me. And considering what I've just done, and am about to do, it's better it remains that way."

"So what do you do when you're not saving damsels in distress?"

"Depends," he replied, with an exaggerated flourish. "Sometimes I drink wine, and other times I earn money so I can drink wine."

"You're hopeless," she said. "Won't you tell me anything about yourself?"

"We noble heroes have to retain an air of mystery."

"I see," she replied wearily.

Their conversation was interrupted by the appearance of a small party of people entering the square between the burgh and the Great Church. Two men dragged a girl from one of the streets. Behind them walked a man of impressive girth and appearance. He was cloaked in a bull's skin, and carried a staff fashioned from horn. The staff was shod with silver and carved with many mystical devices. The man's beard was full and black, his eyes wild like a mad bull's. This was Constantine as legend had reported him.

Margaret could not help but be impressed.

If Dourhand was similarly minded he gave no indication.

"Hail and well met," greeted the son of Felleyes, "I am Sourhand, don of Feelies ..."

"Yes, I know," replied Constantine as he approached. His voice was deep and booming. "Have you the Bull of Heaven?"

"Of course," replied Dourhand, uncovering the talisman. "This," he continued proudly, "is the fabled Bull of Heaven as engraven in the hidden temple of Mithra. Many wise men have guessed as to its likeness, but no one has seen it for a generation. Is that not true, my noble wizard? Few can imagine its secrets. And, yet, I have risked the most deadly peril – the Seven Secret Watchers of Hanuman – to steal it for you. I alone have walked those entrapped and fatal roads and returned to tell the tale. I hope the pain and fear I endured have not been in vain – for then you will know my wrath! Is this woman Matilda?"

"Yes," breathed Margaret.

"Give the Bull of Heaven to me!" demanded Constantine. "Give it to me!"

"In a moment," replied Dourhand, son of Felleyes. "First release Matilda!"

"Very well," said Constantine. "Let her go, my disciples."

Matilda was freed and fell into the arms of her sister. The two young women embraced tightly.

"Are you all right?" asked Margaret. "Did they harm you?"

"No," sobbed Matilda, through tears of relief. "I was treated tolerably well. At least, so I'd guess. I'm so dazed. You stole the Bull of Heaven from the Great Church? I had not thought such a thing possible! I didn't dare hope you would save me."

"Now the Bull!" said Constantine. "Give it to me!"

"Very well," said Dourhand calmly. He handed the talisman to the priest, then his hand strayed to the hilt of his sword. "Guard the Bull well," he advised. "For if I could steal it from the very fortress then others may seek to wrest it from you. And this last caution I would give: the uses of the talisman are many and subtle – and its possession can be deadly! Use it wisely lest it

17

destroy you!"

But Constantine hardly heard the warning. He was simply overjoyed to possess the Bull of Heaven. Clasping it tightly to his chest, he no longer took heed of friends or foes. Now he had the talisman, now he had the thing for which he had always wanted – and with it power and glory. In a moment, he turned from Revile and hurried out of the square, followed by his two disciples.

And that was the last Dourhand, son of Felleyes, ever saw of Constantine. Which was perhaps as well under the circumstances.

The three companions returned to Margaret's apartments, and were soon seated around the table. Revile opened a new bottle of wine, then lounged back on his stool, stretching out his legs before him. The two women eyed him intently, with some little awe, but he was content to grin inanely, supping his drink.

"How can I ever thank you?" asked Margaret at last. "Words are not sufficient to express our gratitude."

"Have you forgotten our bargain?" replied Dourhand, son of Felleyes.

"Of course not," she grinned, "but what use will you find for a hundred casks of wine?"

Revile grinned back, a dreamy look on his face: "I'm thinking of having a party."

"I must ask," said the girl after another pause. "How did you steal the Bull of Heaven? I had not thought it possible."

Dourhand, son of Felleyes, also named Deathshade the Cleaver of the House of Assassins, began a lengthy and embellished tale of heroic content. He had fought sorcerous priests and envenomed serpents, walked devious corridors of fire and deadly traps, solved intricate puzzles and esoteric questions, had finally come to a maze, a maze inhabited by some monster which was half-man, half-bull. And – at last – escaped through fear and peril, emerging alive and unscathed with the Bull of Heaven in his possession.

Revile was very drunk. His story was rambling and entirely inconsistent. But, nevertheless, the two women believed every word. They looked on him with admiration and gratitude, showering him with praise.

It was some time later when the truth of the matter emerged – by then Dourhand the brave adventurer was long gone.

Constantine raised a small army and marched on the Great Church of the Order of the Cross. He brought with him the Bull of Heaven and with the talisman, he thought, victory. Constantine's army was soundly defeated by the Church garrison. Constantine was captured. In his possession was found the Bull of Heaven. Only it was not the mysterious talisman Constantine thought it was. It was a rather expensive piece of costume jewellery, which had been stolen from a local tavern called the Rearing Bull. There had been several robberies that night, and two violent attacks on rich burgesses. It was not clear why Constantine had taken the bejewelled bull – although there was considerable amusement in the burgh.

And it was rumoured the famous wizard, the last priest of Mithra in the North, took his own life because of the humiliation.

Revile did not learn of his death for some weeks after the event. In truth, the assassin was not aware of much. It took several weeks to finish the wine – and several months to recover from the hangover.

And so, Revile achieved an epic feat: an epic feat of drinking.

***

Revile fell silent.

His companions said nothing for a moment yet, despite their fear and unhappiness, had listened to his story.

"That was silly," said Margaret at last. "You've quite destroyed any illusions I had about you – Revile the mysterious adventurer. Yet I can't help thinking your tale was a little unlikely."

"Strangely enough," replied the assassin, "it's actually true. It was brought to mind because you are also called Margaret."

Fergus snorted. "Well, I don't believe it for one," he said. "If this Constantine was such a great wizard he would never have believed you had really stolen the Bull of Heaven, would he now? I think you jest with us. I may be a poor farmer, but I'm not stupid!"

Revile laughed. "Maybe you're not, and believe what you will. Anyway, you shouldn't believe everything people say about themselves. Constantine may have claimed he was a wizard, but I don't think he was. He was just a fat pompous fool with delusions of grandeur. Anyway, does it matter if it's true or not?"

"Yes, it does," answered Fergus. "I don't want you to think we're impressed by your story!"

"Well, you've set me right on that score," replied the assassin. "Perhaps you could tell us a tale or two: maybe about the weather, or the growing of crops? I always enjoyed those rustic sort of stories – you know the ones – about dung-covered udders and the amusing sexual antics of chickens."

"By the Rood!" cried the farmer. "You've got a damn cheek! Who, by Hell, do you think you are? You ..."

"Peace, Fergus," said Margaret. "He's just joking with you."

"O aye!" continued Fergus angrily. "That'll be right! He thinks he's better than us, the murdering swine with his stupid story."

Revile laughed at him, and Fergus cursed.

"Stop it!" ordered Margaret sternly. "That's enough! We're in a bad enough fix without you two fighting like children. What does it matter whether the story is true or not, Fergus? If you can do better then we'll listen to you."

The farmer continued to mutter under his breath, but said nothing audible.

"Anyway," added Margaret, "we should be friends."

"O very well!" conceded Fergus. "I suppose I'm just worried about my family. I over reacted."

"Who cares?" said Revile tiredly.

"You don't seem to take this very seriously," said Margaret, suddenly getting angry herself. "It's just a bit of a laugh getting hung."

"Is it?" said the assassin softly. "I reckon you're wrong. I just don't see any point in worrying about it. And we're not hanged yet. Anything might happen."

"Like what?" said Fergus hotly.

"There might be an earthquake," replied Revile. "A legion of dragons might invade Bamburg. There might be an amnesty for all prisoners. I don't know. Why worry about the future?"

"Here we go again," muttered the farmer, "the brave, noble, fearless adventurer, who makes his living by slaughtering others."

"Don't laugh at me Fergus," said Revile coldly, "not when I'm trying to be nice to you."

"If this is you being nice," said Margaret, "I'd hate to see you horrible."

"You don't know the half of it," said Revile grimly.

"Phooey!" said Fergus.

"Stop it!" cried Alwyn suddenly. "Just stop arguing for God's sake!"

"O don't start weeping again!" said the assassin in irritation.

"You really are a bastard," Margaret told him. "A cold conceited bastard! I don't know what kind of life you've led and maybe you do think this is all a big joke. But we are going to die. They're going to hang us in the morning, and we've each done nothing to deserve it apart from you! And not only that, but there is the shame of it, the shame of being hanged as a common criminal with all the town coming to see us executed. It's all very well for you to laugh at us!"

"I wasn't laughing at you," replied the assassin, "but I don't give a shit what any of you or your stupid town thinks. I've been sitting here for two days now. I've fouled myself. I've had nothing to eat. My arse is so numb I can't feel it. I am cold and bored. Plain bored. Bored to tears. I'm bored listening to Fergus moaning on about his precious family. I'm bored with you moaning on about how small an item you stole. I am bored with Alwyn blubbering. If I'm to die then it will be with dignity. I'm not going out on to the scaffold weeping like a baby – I'm going out like the bastard I am. If you want to die like frightened sheep, that's up to you. The last thing you'll hear is the jibes of the crowd, your precious townsfolk, as they taunt you, smirking at every whimper, laughing at every tear."

An uneasy silence followed.

"I suppose you're right," said Alwyn at last.

Margaret turned to the young woman in surprise.

"Yes, you're right," continued Alwyn. "What's the point of worrying? They're going to hang us, there's nothing we can do about it. I've worried most of my adult life – and look where it's got me. I'm sorry we're weak, weak and undignified. I'll try not to weep again."

"Good," said the assassin. "I'm glad to hear it. You at least show some courage." He paused. "But," he added, "I can't help wondering why you of all people are here. What on earth did you do to Bregorin? Can't your father help you with the prince?"

"My father is ill," replied the girl, "and what could he do anyway? Like Fergus, I've probably doomed my family as well as myself. Prince Bregorin will use this as an excuse to seize my father's lands and forfeit his title. As for what the prince did? In truth, he did nothing. He wanted to take me as one of his mistresses. I tried but I couldn't. I even knew what would happen to me but it made no difference."

"The prince has the pox," mentioned Revile.

"Really?" asked Margaret.

"O yes, definitely," replied the assassin brightly. "There is much talk. He caught it from a mistress. She from the captain of the guard. I'm surprised you of all people hadn't heard."

"I'd heard," said Fergus. "We laughed about it in the tavern. It was the baker who told me."

"The baker who turned you in?" said Margaret.

"The very same," said the farmer. "We laughed together." He shook his head.

"What were you doing in a tavern if you had no money?" asked Revile.

Fergus chose to ignore that.

Revile nodded. "Anyway, Alwyn," he said, "I think you're being silly. You should let Bregorin have his wishes. Not even the pox is something worth dying over – although sometimes I've not been so sure."

"I know," said the young woman. "I know. I tried but I just couldn't"

"Well, you can still change your mind."

"I hate Bregorin as well," said Fergus. "He was the judge at my trial. He didn't even listen to me, and sentenced me to death."

"He was the judge at my trial too," said Margaret.

"You can never get revenge on these kind of people," muttered Fergus. "They're too powerful, surrounded by guards in their strongholds. He'd be too difficult to murder," said Fergus thoughtfully. "Far too difficult."

"You'd be surprised," said Revile. "All you need is money and to know where to look. After all, Bregorin is just a man like any other. Even a prince shits, eats, screws and dies like any beggar."

"Don't tell me," Fergus said sourly, "you've killed a prince?"

"No, just the odd king or two," said the assassin modestly.

"Very well then," said Margaret, "tell us about it."

Blood Moon:
The Assassins and the Princess

I t was deepest, darkest night. The white moon, which was nearly full but shrouded in a pale halo, shone out from the black clouds for a moment, casting silver fingers onto the broken setting of tall standing stones. The setting consisted of a line of stones with outliers, one of which was a prominent monolith with a hole piercing right through the stone near its top.

By this holed stone, a small fire hissed and sparked, shedding its shifting light on two huddled figures warming their hands. Both had dark cloaks wrapped tightly around themselves, both shivered as the chill wind sought out every seam and opening in their garments.

"Will he come?" asked a muffled voice.

"Yes, he will come, my lord king. He has but been delayed."

"I fear he may betray us."

"I think not – he would have nothing to gain. With our aid he may reign again in Strathclwyd; and that is his sole ambition – if I am any judge of men. As I have said: he has but been delayed. So be at peace, my lord king."

The king nodded at his companion, then hid his hands in the folds of his robes. "Yes, I suppose he does have much to gain," he whispered. "But you? What do you have to gain? I do not think the rule of any realm would interest you. So why do you help us?"

"Revenge, my lord king," replied the other quietly. "I would have revenge on the murderers of my people. These Feni hunted us down, slaying all they could find, until all my people were dead, left rotting where they had fallen. I, alone, am left – the last. The Light has left El-Firion forever. Life and Death, Destruction and Creation, are the Word and the Weird of the Earth. By Azzchzog, I will restore the balance in the many names of my Dead. I would rid these unbelieving murderers from the land they desecrate and defile. Is that sufficient reason?"

"I know not for I do not understand. Your speech and words are strange to me. Although I am not of the Feni, I am of one of their kindred people, one of the Seven Families that crossed the sea from the west. I share the religion you call unbelief. What say you now?"

His companion eyed him for a moment, filled with reflected fire, but made no reply.

"Nechtan the Old, I must trust you," continued the king tightly, his hand searching for the hilt of a dagger concealed within the folds of his cloak. "It will be of little use and comfort to me that you pull down the House of Lord Donald by destroying mine. Do you understand my concerns?"

"Only too well, my lord king. And in answer all I can tell you is if I sought your destruction, and not your help, then we would not be holding this council. By Azzchzog, you would be dead!" And the fire flared up for a moment, the tall standing stones looming over them, the holed monolith staring back at him with a dark eye. The king hastily removed his grasp from his dagger.

"I am sorry," he managed to say without sounding afraid. "I do not mean to offend."

Nechtan waved the apology away. "Your distrust is wearying," he muttered, "but remember not all have my patience. One approaches now who is quick to anger."

The king had heard nothing and listened for a while. There was the dull clink of armour and soft footfalls of a man. Into the setting of stones strode a tall figure, a billowing cloak flapping in the gale, a sword held before him.

"Hail, my friend," said the king, jumping to his feet. "Greetings, my lord, Eocha ap Gawain, rightful King of Strathclwyd. I hope this ill night finds you well?"

"Well enough," replied the stranger lowering his sword. "And you, my lord, Malcolm of Lornland? How are you?"

The King of Lornland shrugged in answer, then introduced his companion. "This is Nechtan," he said softly, "Nechtan the Old."

"Nechtan the Old?" exclaimed Eocha in surprise. "Nechtan the Slayer? I have heard of you!"

"Indeed," said Nechtan, still seated by the fire. "Then does my presence displease you?"

"No, of course not," replied Eocha hastily, licking his lips. "It is just that I had not expected you in our, ah, conspiracy. Think no ill of me, I beg."

"I do not," muttered Nechtan. "For we are all friends here – if not by choice then by necessity. This night is running out, we have much to discuss. Come, my lord Eocha, and be comforted by this fire, small and meagre though it may be. Let us set our minds on how we may achieve our desires: the restoration of the crown of Strathclwyd to you, my lord, Eocha; the restoration of the stolen lands of Carndubh and Blackwater to you, my lord Malcolm of Lornland; and the restoration of a little honour and peace for my murdered people. But simple ambitions each, my good lords."

The mage smiled, but his expression was without humour.

"Indeed!" said Eocha ap Gawain, still ill at ease. "And I do not see how we may achieve these desires."

"Then, perhaps, I can help you," said Nechtan. "For have I not thought long on this matter? The long years have concealed me, and soon my plans and plotting will come to an end. By Azzchzog and the Blood Moon, know you then that King Donald has contracted a bitter wasting disease to cripple and maim his last days alive. He has endured untold suffering these past months – it was the least I could do for him! But he will not live much longer and on the Eve of the Last Day, the Eve of the Blood Moon, he will die in torment. His World shall be left on the barren mountain with only my Dead for company; to Azzchzog I will send him where the chill shall pierce his soul and shrivel his being. For such is the cruel end I have planned for him!"

"The Eve of the Last Day?" asked Malcolm. "The eve of the Blood Moon? Forgive me, but I do not know when that is or what you are talking about."

"I forget," said Nechtan wearily. "I have outlasted my world – light has been robbed from El-Firion. Your religion is new to me but still the stranger. I will not explain – for to do so would be blasphemy to your ears, and such things are beyond the knowledge and wisdom of men of a later age. All I will tell you is that King Donald will die four days from now, that the moon will be eaten slowly until it turns red. The cycle is complete and a new time shall dawn."

"How can you be sure of this?" asked Malcolm.

Nechtan shrugged.

The King of Lornland nodded. "I am not saddened by this news," he said, "whether or not it is true. And, may I say, I hope his death is as unpleasant as possible. But how can it help us?"

"Ah, my lord, Malcolm of Lornland," answered Nechtan with a quizzical smile, half mocking, half sympathetic. "Take no offence, I beg, but that is why men fear the name of Nechtan the Slayer, and laugh at Lord Malcolm of Lornland who lost half his kingdom in a wager."

Malcolm seemingly took no offence.

"For see you," continued Nechtan, "Lord Donald will die, and his only heir is an unwed daughter, a daughter who will inherit not only the lands of the Feni but also the ancient Kingdom of Strathclwyd and half of Lornland. And that is what should concern us, I reckon. So how may your lands and titles be restored?

"Well, we will see won't we? As soon as King Donald dies, his daughter, the Lady Shona, will become a ward of the High King, Lord Duff MacDuff MacAiden, Father of Dalria, and overlord of all these lands – chief scum floating on the sewerage. I need not tell you that you will never see you property again. Rather, the High King will marry this Shona off to one of his allies with all your lands as dowry."

"I am newly returned from the High King," said Eocha evenly. "I asked if I might be considered as a husband for this Shona."

"What did he say?" asked Malcolm.

"Need you ask?" said the other gruffly. "He insulted me, calling me a low-born upstart of a rude and defeated people, little fit to marry a tinker's daughter, never mind a Dalrian princess. Fine words from a king whose people are little more than interloping pirates and back-stabbing brigands. Little matter that now! Princes must sometimes bow to robbers. Yet I would hardly have joined this conspiracy if the High King's answer had been to my advantage."

Lord Malcolm of Lornland pondered Eocha's words and frowned.

"Yet," said Nechtan, "all is far from lost. For see you, King Donald of the Feni might yet be persuaded to change his mind and leave his two closest friends all his lands and titles, dividing his wide kingdom between you both."

"How?" asked Eocha. "He despises both of us."

"It could be done," said Nechtan. "It would please me greatly if he gave his lands into the hands of his bitterest enemies, knowing full well what he did but unable to prevent it. Now you know why I need your help."

The two kings wondered at that, but kept their peace.

"But there is still one obstacle remaining to the throne of the Feni." Nechtan paused for a moment. "The Lady Shona. She must die."

"Why?" asked Malcolm.

"Donald could not leave his possessions to you whilst she yet lived. Shona would inherit these titles and lands for she is the only heir – or at least the only one of consequence. It would not matter that her father had contrary wishes. No, she must die. Of that I have no doubt! True, it would also take the dagger I have conjured in Donald's guts and give it one last turn!"

Malcolm looked about. "Could you not," he whispered softly, "use one of your sorceries to destroy her?"

"Perhaps," replied Nechtan, "but I would only do so as a last resort. And such things take time and energy. I have been patient all these years, and I would not have my plans cheated now. Not all of the Feni are fools. By Azzchzog and the Blood Moon, many still remember Nechtan the Old, Nechtan the Mage, Nechtan the Slayer! There are already mutterings his illness is caused by sorcery. No, we still have a little time. This can be done without resorting to magic."

"It would be madness if either me or lord Eocha attempted to kill Shona," said Malcolm. "It is well known we have much reason to hate King Donald's House. And we are virtually prisoners in his fortress. I was hardly able to slip away unnoticed"

"It would be folly to do this deed yourselves," agreed Nechtan. "I do not ask it of you. But you must know of men who would willingly commit such a murder. A cut-throat, a murderer, a man of the baser sort who does not mind getting his hands smeared with virgin's blood." And the mage smiled coldly, as if he saw some joke his companions could not understand.

"And yet," said Malcolm, "such a killer might not be easy to find at short notice. He would have to have the cunning of a fox, the honour of a sewer rat. His greed for gold would have to be greater than his love of life. This would be dangerous, difficult murder. We would need to find the most callous assassin in all this land."

"I know of such a man," said Eocha.

"Who?" asked Malcolm.

"A character who calls himself Worm, a pale villainous creature. I know for certain he is staying at Aodh's Tower on the border with Cowlsmark. I have been told he is efficient and discreet."

"Good," said Nechtan, "have you gold?"

"Of course," said Eocha, "quite enough to employ him."

"Then contact this Worm with our proposal," continued the mage, "and if he will not accept make sure he does not talk. You must tell him of our urgency. By Azzchzog, Shona must die tomorrow – or the day after at the very latest. I need not tell you he must not know nor guess of our involvement. And you should arrange to have this assassin caught after he has completed his foul work. As you have said: both of you are living at Dundonald. You should capture this assassin yourselves. Do you understand?"

"Aye," said Malcolm.

"Yes," replied Eocha ap Gawain. "I will see to this matter without delay. Well, I have suffered this cold long enough. I will leave you now and send a messenger to Aodh's Tower with all speed." He stood up and eyed his fellow conspirators. "Farewell for this time, Nechtan the slayer. Farewell, Malcolm."

Eocha strode to edge of the setting of standing stones, then vanished into the gloom.

"Come," said Nechtan, looking at the pale moon. "There is still much to do."

II

The trees rustled gently in the morning breezes, the sun shining weakly through the mist which hung and curled in the valleys. A muddy path led through the midst of the open forest and forded a swollen burn by two massive hewn boulders. The air was heavy with moisture: the slender branches of the silver birch dripped and the grass stalks were wet with dew.

Along the track, from the east, came a rider on a shaggy pony. He was a pale jolly fellow with short black hair and merry blue eyes. An adventurer, mercenary or some other brigand, he was dressed in a leather tunic and breeks, his trousers tucked into the tops of his sodden boots. A sword lay across the shoulders of his pony. Its sheath was tattered and cracked, but the sword was as sharp as a razor. Several daggers of various sizes were strapped to the front of his tunic; and amongst his other possessions were a bow and a quiver of arrows, a skin full of blood red wine, and a large bag of gold.

It was this last item that was the cause of Revile's excellent humour.

The assassin leaned back a little and unstoppered his wine-skin, taking a long drink. Then, spurring his pony on through the water, he forded the stream by the two mighty rocks and climbed up the far bank.

Revile rode eagerly on down the forest track, towards the town and stronghold of Dundonald, which was also known as Dunadd, brooding on its rock.

Revile met nobody on the long journey through the forest of Carnmor, and the miles passed without company. In the late afternoon, he climbed one last slope out of the trees and gazed down on Dundonald, the fortress of Lord Donald of the Feni, shielding his eyes from the glare of the westering sun. The wide glen ran back to the north, the meandering river wandering lazily to the sea in a haze to the south-west. The bottom of the glen was flat, marshy and featureless – except, that is, for the large rock and fortress of Dundonald.

Dundonald was a sprawling place of earthworks and fortifications, of ditches and palisades surrounding the rock. Within the fortress proper – within the Citadel – were halls, storerooms, apartments, kitchens, brew-houses, butteries, and other buildings the use of which Revile could not discern. The Citadel with its Great Hall was built on top of a large steeply-sided rock, and could only be a reached across a narrow bridge which spanned a chasm hewn from the hill, then through a steeply enclosed entrance, carved from the natural rock and defended by several gates. The highest part of the rock was crowned with the rich but precarious dwelling of Lord Donald and his daughter, Lady Shona.

A road led to the bridge and entrance, leading through the mass of cramped houses and dwellings confined within the high wooden palisade and deep ditch. Sentries paced the walls and guarded the gates into the Dundonald: the north and south entrances were the busiest with wains, riders and walkers thronging the wide roads to the capital of the lands of the Feni.

There was no traffic from the east, from where Revile sat on his pony, a day's ride from Aodh's Tower.

The assassin peered down a moment longer, then encouraged his horse into a canter down the track towards the gently reeking fortress.

Dundonald was a sprawling place indeed – and it had the most sprawling midden and cesspool upon which Revile had ever set eyes.

Revile reached the eastern gate, and pulled his pony to a halt. He was watched by a small group of soldiery guarding the eastern entrance. The palisade loomed over him, the ditch was filled with sharpened stakes. A thin log bridge crossed the ditch and led to the open, iron-spiked gates. The assassin dismounted and led his pony to the bridge.

"Greetings," shouted one of the guards, and hurried across to Revile. "Greetings, stranger." Revile waited for the guard.

Two other guards followed the first from the gates, their flaxen braided hair streaming from their polished helmets, dressed in fine clothes and dangling earrings. They were all tall men, much taller than Revile, and had sea-grey eyes and proud faces – the assassin seemed small, dark and shabby beside them. These were men of the Feni, the most noble of the Seven Clans of the Dalria – although many men might have called them proud and arrogant. Impressive and lordly, almost, the noble Feni might have appeared to lesser men.

Revile, a lesser man, was less than impressed.

"Welcome to Dundonald, sir," said the first of the Feni, friendly enough but towering over the assassin. "I hope you find your stay here pleasant. But first it is my duty to delay you a little. For I must ask you your business and name." The Feni had a strange sing-song accent, which Revile, despite his good humour, found irritating.

"Of course," said the assassin, brightly in response. "My name is Maggot, a traveller from Mannan to the south and east. I have a little gold and heard the repute of Dundonald from afar. I thought to visit your fortress during the Festival of the Last Battle: I was told one day's travel would be worth the miles – that the celebrations should not be missed."

"You were not mistaken," smiled the guard.

"Then I'm not too late?"

"Indeed not. This is the first day of the festival and the celebrations are only just beginning."

"Then I'm glad," said the assassin with enthusiasm. "Are travellers welcome? I would not intrude."

"All are welcome," replied the guard. "You may enter the fortress presently. But this one favour I would beg: no weapons are to be drawn within the walls – no matter what the cause – and none, at all, are to be carried in the presence of the Lord Donald or the Lady Shona."

Revile nodded. It was not an uncommon custom. "All right and proper," he said.

The assassin was led across the bridge, through the gates, and into Dundonald. The streets were already filled with celebrating people; colourful banners were draped across the otherwise rather shabby buildings. Revile followed the guard along and then up a winding road towards the Citadel, peering at the many houses and revellers. The Feni he chanced upon were merry – drunk anyway – and many danced and greeted him with kind words. Revile smiled back, taking a drink or a friendly kiss, his pony plodding behind him.

Never had the assassin been made so welcome in any town – and never with less reason.

Revile and his guide approached the chasm that separated the rest of the town from the Citadel. Here, he searched the massive grey walls and the many clustered buildings with his eyes. The stronghold was built of stone, roofed with dark stone, defended by ramparts of grey stone. Many towers and battlements and turrets looked north and east and south. It was a mighty fortress, not to be reduced or breached by a host of enemies if properly provisioned and garrisoned – except, perhaps, by treachery.

Almost despite himself, Revile was impressed by the stark grandeur and dark strength of Dundonald.

The assassin smiled at the sinking sun and the long shadows. It would be a grand night for a murder, despite the almost full moon.

III

It was very much later before Revile remembered his reason for visiting Dundonald, later still before he considered making a move in its furtherance. He had been given a small but clean apartment in the very Citadel; his pony had been housed in the large stables. The Feni were a courteous people, and he had been given everything for which he had asked. After having washed and eaten well in his chamber, he went out, as night fell, to explore the many slypes and alleys and passages that formed a maze around the huddled Citadel. As the very last rays of the sun disappeared behind the hills to the west, Revile returned to his room to wait for fullest night.

To his surprise, he was invited to a banquet to be held in the Great Hall to celebrate the 'First Night': a commemoration of the great battle when the Old People, the Ing, were finally vanquished. That war had been bitter, and the Feni had ruthlessly exterminated all that remained of their enemies: old men, pregnant women, children, babies – everyone. To the Feni, the Ing were sorcerous low-born heathens who reputedly practised human sacrifice and collected the severed heads of their enemies. Little better than vermin they were: rats inhabiting the bleak glens and rude fastnesses of Lornland and Fenis. And no more did the Feni fear the night or the Ing, fear the silent unexplained murder that visited the securest fortress – dark murder summoned by the Ing warlocks. Only a few of the Feni still remembered Nechtan the Mage, Nechtan the Old, Nechtan the Slayer: that his body was never found, that nobody knew what became of him.

Revile knew the story, and might have sympathised with the Ing for he had no love for the Feni. Indeed, he cared little for the feast: the assassin was unimpressed by victory celebrations for one-sided battles. He agreed to attend because he guessed the Lady Shona would be present – her father was too ill – and it would certainly have been suspicious not to have done so. The assassin was taken to the Great Hall and followed the many other guests – Feni and visitors – into the lofty, sound-filled chamber. He smiled at every one he met.

He was taken to a table near the back of the Hall, given a mug for his wine and a platter for his meat. He sat himself down between two other visitors: a wandering monk from Bernecia, and a heavily built, brooding individual, who called himself Conan. Revile made conversation with the cleric, but soon tired of his other companion who was boring and prone to exaggeration beyond even the assassin. Revile eventually changed places with the cleric, who was called Wilmund, when Conan became totally unbearable after a mug or two of wine, claiming he was actually a king or descended from a saint, or some such nonsense. Revile fingered the edge of a dirk, thinking of one or two places where it might find a home.

After about an hour, Conan fell unconscious under the table, and Wilmund and Revile drew a large sigh of relief. The two companions chatted quietly about all the places they had seen and visited. The cleric had travelled almost as widely as the assassin and they talked of southern deserts and the pyramids; the east and its fabulous cities and civilisations; the north, the mighty Kings and Jarls; the west and the kingdoms of Bernecia, Dalria, Pentland, and Strathclwyd. Revile spent some time quizzing Wilmund about possible enemies of the Feni, and learnt of the ceding of Strathclwyd from its native king – and the ridiculous tale of how Lord Malcolm of Lornland had lost half his kingdom in a wager. To be precise, on the role of two dice: two dice, the cleric assured Revile, which were weighted in Malcolm's favour. The King of Lornland had forgotten the roll. The assassin laughed. Their conversation turned to trivialities as they drank more wine, and finally degenerated into joke telling. Wilmund, as a cleric, knew the crudest and dirtiest jokes: soon they were roaring with laughter.

Just after midnight, Wilmund decided to retire for he was due to leave the next day, continuing a journey to the holy monastery on I, an island by Mula just off the coast. Revile bade him good night, then got down to the serious business of eating and drinking.

He leaned back for a moment, looking for someone new – preferably female – to talk to, a mug of wine in one hand, half a roasted chicken in the other. Peering forwards to the High Table, he searched for a glimpse of the Lady Shona. Finally he found her, surrounded by a press of worshipful nobles. She was a handsome woman: athletically built with broad shoulders, long flaxen-coloured hair streaming about her neck, and clad in a leather jerkin and rough shirt. No shrinking violet or blushing maiden, the Lady Shona joked and brawled with her nobles and other menfolk. Revile grinned as she drained her goblet to the dregs and then ordered more wine in a mighty bellow. She was like no princess he had seen before.

Some instinct prompted the assassin to sit up straighter. He had a niggling sensation something was wrong. Shona ordered more wine again, but her servants had vanished and did not attend her. The Lady looked around in bewilderment.

Revile stood up awkwardly, cursing the amount of drink and food he had consumed. And as he rose to his feet, he searched in his tunic for a dirk. A side door into the Hall was thrown back, and a party of heavily-armed men burst into the chamber. They were smaller and darker in colouring than the Feni. Revile guessed they were from Strathclwyd.

They ran towards the High Table, cutting down any who barred their way. The Feni fell back before them. All except Shona herself. She grabbed a carving knife from a joint of meat, then leapt forward into the fray. Revile sprinted up the Hall.

And things went from bad to worse for the Lady Shona. She fought unaided; the men of Strathclwyd surrounded her. There were seven assassins – but two had already fallen to her

30

knife. Revile had never seen any weapon more effectively handled.

An axe was raised high above her head. The stroke would have cloven her head in two had it been completed. At that moment, Revile launched a dagger at the axe-wielder. It flashed past Shona's head – narrowly missing her – and sank to the hilts in the axe-wielder's throat.

Shona disembowelled another, fighting with skill and ferocity and little care for her own safety. Her eyes shone with blood-lust.

Only three of the assassins remained.

With little thought for his own safety, Revile jumped on top of the High Table, launching himself into the struggling group. Another dirk appeared in his hand, a man died with an opened throat. The Lady Shona almost beheaded another.

The last assassin turned and fled. But Shona leapt after him, followed a moment later by Revile. The last man was cut down as he fled, daggers driven again and again into his back until he lay still, still that is apart from his twitching limbs. Shona checked the rest of the assassins were dead by stabbing them in the throat. A large pool of blood oozed from the corpses.

"We have not met, I think," Shona said to Revile when they had completed their butchery. Her voice was husky, she was perspiring and splattered with gore, but seemed well content. She wiped blood from her hands on the tunic of one of the assassins. "What is your name, friend?"

Revile mopped his brow. "I am called Maggot," he said with a grin. "You, I guess, are the Lady Shona of the Feni."

She smiled back. "Indeed I am," she said, taking his hand, "although I wasn't blessed with such a pretty name as you – apt though it may be. Come, Sir Maggot, join me at my table. I must thank you for saving my life." She decided not to mention that he should not have been carrying any weapons, nor should he have drawn them in her presence.

"Thank you, my lady."

"Shona will do," she said a little curtly. "Have a place set!" she ordered, "have the bodies of these treacherous dogs removed and spike their heads on the gates! Clean up their blood. Come you cowardly swine! Come now! The danger has passed! You need no longer fear for your lives! And bring me more wine!"

Men hurriedly dragged the corpses from the Great Hall, washed the gore from the floor, and more wine finally arrived.

"Why are you all silent?" the Lady Shona cried in a loud voice. "This is a feast – not a funeral!"

Gradually talking and laughing resumed, and in a few minutes it was as if nothing had happened. Revile sat down at the side of Shona, helping himself to a goblet of wine. The wine was certainly better than the drink served at the lower tables.

"Were they of Strathclwyd?" he asked her. "Or are all your guests so friendly? Perhaps the sourness of the wine angered them."

"They were men of Strathclwyd," she replied, turning towards him. "I have no doubt of that. Treacherous dogs! Where is Eocha? I should have him boiled in oil for this!"

"Has he reason to hate you?" said Revile in an innocent voice.

"Yes," she said softly. "We have stolen lands from these Stratchclwydians? ... Strathclwydans? ... Strathclwydui? ... damn them! I can't even say their name. We have stolen land from the men of Strathclwyd, stolen their ancient kingdom; we have imprisoned their king, forced him to swear allegiance to the High King of Dalria. What do you think, Sir Maggot? We the Feni, the interlopers and foreign raiders from across the sea that we are, have defeated and enslaved them, an ancient and proud people. Do they have reason to hate us?"

"Perhaps," he replied, "but surely killing you wouldn't help either this Eocha or his people."

"How do you mean?"

"Well, if they had murdered you," he said thoughtfully, guzzling wine between muses, "what would have happened?"

"My warriors would invade their stinking land and waste it from Alclwyd to Caerisle."

"That's what I guessed."

"Ah, Sir Maggot, all that would happen except for one thing: I am an only child and my father is near death. If I was murdered, my people would be left leaderless and quite possibly divided. Who knows what would happen then?"

"Perhaps what you say is true," said Revile, "although I think your people would stay united even if it was only for long enough to devastate Strathclwyd. The Strathclwydians? ... Strathclwydus? ... Strathclwydruns? ... people of Strathclwyd could gain nothing just by your death. There must be some other reason."

"Perhaps you are right," she said, sounding bored, "but what does it matter? Politics, plots and the machinations of princelings and kinglets are quite tiresome. I am still alive at present. No doubt they will try again. Let us hope they have not poisoned the wine!"

Revile helped himself to some venison: the fighting had left him hungry again. "You fight well," he told her. "I hadn't thought it possible for a royal princess, if you won't take offence."

She favoured him with a sour expression. "My father had a son, Osric," she said softly, "but my brother left Dundonald when I was still a child: he was different, whatever that means. I needs do although I'm the weaker sex." Revile grinned at that. "And, may I tell you," she went on, "I have no wish to play the role of the weak and fragile princess. That is a part for a simpering girl, parading before men until one asks for your hand. But I will not be sold off like some chattel, married to the highest bidder!"

Revile shrugged. "Then you don't need to be," he said. "You are the heir to wide lands and powerful armies. Who could force you?"

"The High King," she replied softly. "He could and he will. I am a pawn in his games, but a pawn with lands and property. How can I refuse him? Pawns have no power."

"On a chess board perhaps," said the assassin. "But in this world the High King would risk war. Wouldn't your people follow you?"

"I hope so," she whispered, "but I could not plunge Dalria into a war. It would be brother fighting brother. Our enemies would use it to destroy us, drive us back into the sea like the pirates they believe us."

Revile shrugged. "Then pack a sword," he said, "some provisions, take a little gold. Ride out into the wide world. Someone who fights as well as you would get on fine."

"Thank you for saying so, but you misunderstand me, I think. I do not crave freedom; I am well content here. But I wish to rule in my own right, not as the servant of some man, however noble he may be. But I have said enough on the matter, Sir Maggot. Come, tell me something of yourself."

"There's not much to tell."

"So you'll be mysterious, will you? Where are you from? What do you do?"

"Very well," he said, feigning reluctance, "I suppose you'd call me an adventurer. I go wherever I think there will be gold or silver. As for where I come from? In truth I have no home – or nowhere I could call home. Such is an adventurer's sad life!"

"And very tragic it sounds," she said in a solemn tone, but there was amusement in her eyes. "You don't seem too depressed!"

"I hide it well, I think."

"Come then, tell me of your adventures."

Revile laughed, for he was not a man who quickly tired of talking about himself.

The assassin and the princess talked and jested and drank well into the long autumn night. Revile enjoyed her company: it was with some surprise he realised he liked her. This was unhealthy for an assassin, akin to the butcher caring for a lamb he was about to slaughter. In the end, to him anyway, it mattered little.

Finally, however, the celebration began to break up, and the Lady Shona retired to her chambers, wishing Sir Maggot sweet dreams.

Revile walked thoughtfully to his own small apartment.

It was a shame he had to kill her.

IV

The moon had set.

A dark shape flitted from shadow to shadow. A few torches flared from along the battlements, but the shape vanished against the darkness of the stonework. Two sentries passed within a pace or two. Their watchful eyes saw nothing. The shape waited until they had disappeared from view, then stepped out into the light.

Revile stood back for a moment, peering upwards to the roof of the royal apartments on the highest part of the rock of the Citadel. His hands and face were covered in soot. Only the whites of his eyes were clearly visible in the flickering light. There was a window thirty or so feet above him. He inspected the climb carefully. It did not look too difficult.

Taking a padded grappling hook from a small pack, the assassin again checked the battlements were deserted. Then he swung the grapple about his head a few times, before throwing it towards the roof. It caught on the eaves. Revile tested the hold. Then, with great agility and speed, he scuttled up the rope, and soon stood on the window ledge. The window was shuttered. By slipping a dagger between the shutters, he undid the latch and opened them. He stole into the chamber, retrieving the grapple, coiling the rope.

Shona's room was quiet, quiet as the grave, the only sound her untroubled snoring as she slept. Revile was not troubled that she should awake: she had drunk enough wine to drown a whale. Revile closed the shutters softly, then slipped over to the bed. Although it was dark, he located the princess without difficulty and stood over the cot, peering down. She stirred slightly and sighed – but the assassin hesitated, his daggers left untouched.

He left her bed side, padding across the rugs to the door, listening intently. He heard nothing untoward, then decided to search the room for anything of value. He carefully avoided a stool by the side of her bed; quickly rummaged through her clothing and effects; finally inspected a chest at the end of her cot. It was locked. While Revile had some skill at opening locks, it was too dark for such work. He searched for the key, but it could not be found. Guessing it might be around Shona's neck, he returned to the bed and gently pulled back her blankets and furs. The woman lay quite still. Revile stared down at her naked body. But still he hesitated.

There was a soft click from the door.

The assassin froze, hardly dared to breathe.

The door opened a fraction, a little light entering from the corridor. Noiselessly, Revile sank to the floor, hidden by the bed.

He heard the door creaking slightly, a soft footfall, then a click as it closed.

Somebody else was in the chamber. Revile wormed his way to the foot of the cot.

"At last," whispered a voice with a southern accent. "Sleep soundly, Lady Shona of the accursed Feni – so soundly that you never awake." There was a short laugh. "We have failed once tonight, but not again."

There was a faint ring of metal.

Revile the assassin leapt soundlessly to his feet. His eyes were fixed on a darker shape stooped over the bed. With the hilt of his dagger, he clubbed the figure from behind.

Shona moaned in her sleep.

The assassin dragged the unconscious man from the bed, then sat astride him. His dagger was held to the man's throat, the other hand over his mouth. Revile gently tried to revive him.

"Who are you?" whispered Revile into his face.

The man groaned softly.

"Who are you?" repeated Revile, pressing the dirk tighter, looking to see if Shona stirred.

"Gareth ap Uther," moaned Gareth, shaking his head slowly from side to side.

"What are you doing here?"

Gareth said nothing more, but he opened his eyes. His stare was wild and bleary.

Revile drew blood from his throat.

"I was sent to kill the Lady Shona," Gareth managed shakily.

"Who by?"

"The King."

"The King of Strathclwyd?"

"Yes," he grunted, focusing his stare.

"Why does this Eocha want Shona killed?"

"By the Dragon, they stole our kingdom, forced us to swear allegiance to Dalria."

"How would killing Shona help you?"

"I don't know. Nechtan ordered it," whispered Gareth. "I don't know why. You must believe me."

Revile looked puzzled. "Nechtan the Mage?" he said softly. "Nechtan the Slayer?"

"Yes."

"This is a strange alliance of old enemies," said the assassin. "Is there anyone else in this conspiracy?"

"Malcolm, the King of Lornland. That is all."

"I don't understand," said Revile. "Do you know me?"

"Yes, you are Worm."

The assassin sighed. "Is it they who pay me?" he asked. "Eocha and the rest?"

"Yes."

"You're sure now? O well," the assassin fell silent. He clamped one hand over Gareth's mouth and nose – then sank his dagger into his heart. Gareth tensed, let out a sigh, then went limp. Revile released him. "Sorry, Gareth, son of Uther," he told the corpse.

He returned to Shona's bed, his dirk dripping blood. "Well, my lady," he thought, "lost in your dreams, eh?" He sighed. "No," he said out loud, "not this way. It's too dangerous."

Revile uncoiled the rope from his pack, padded across to the window, opened the shutters. The cold wind blew on his face. "Am I going soft?" he asked the night. "I wonder."

He climbed onto the window ledge.

V

Revile slept late the following morning.

He had spent some time washing the soot from his features, blood from his dagger and tunic. His small room was frosty cold. He shivered under his thin blanket until he had finally fallen asleep.

An instant later – it seemed – there was a knocking on his door. He started and jumped out of bed, drawing his sword before he could check himself. The knocking came again, but this time the assassin relaxed, put away his sword, and answered the door. The Lady Shona stood there, looking as fresh as a mountain spring. She was dressed as if for hunting: only the fullness of her breast and fairness of her features betrayed her for a woman.

"Greetings, Sir Maggot," she said with a gleam in her eye. "How are you this fair morning?"

Revile yawned and scratched at a flea bite under his tunic. "Suffering a little," he admitted. "Your hospitality was too generous. You have a strong constitution, my lady. Stronger than Maggot's to be sure."

"Perhaps," she replied. "It might interest you to know I had a visitor in my bed chamber last night."

"Really?" said Revile. "I didn't think you'd tell me all your secrets. Do you try to make me jealous?"

She smiled thinly. "I did not invite him," she said. "The poor fellow tripped over his own feet and stabbed himself through the heart – or so it seems."

Revile raised his eyebrows. "How inconsiderate of him," he yawned again. "Perhaps he chose death rather than failure under your furs." But then he added, in a more serious tone. "Or maybe he was a Strathclwyduthian? ... Strathclwydtutute? ... Strathclwydussian? ... mmm ... a man of Strathclwyd."

"Perhaps he was. How did you know?"

"I was his accomplice – but seeing the error of my ways, I repented and killed him in remorse. You have found me out."

"Hmmm," considered the woman. "Perhaps. It would not surprise me. You are a strange one, Sir Maggot. Anyway, it is not important. I am going on a spot of hunting. Would you care to join me?"

"Why not?" Revile slept fully clothed, including his boots. Quickly belting on his sword, he collected his bow and quiver of arrows and said: "Lead on, my lady, and if you have some wine I'd bless you!"

"As it happens," she replied, "I do." She gave him a half-full skin. "And my name is Shona."

"You are an angel amongst women, Shona," said Revile.

"Hush," said the woman.

Shona led the assassin down from the Citadel to the stables in a wide courtyard. A large number of nobles were gathered there, waiting for the Lady Shona. The Dalrian lords threw Revile some rather ugly and ill-favoured looks. It did not seem right that their princess should be so familiar with a low-born adventurer – no matter how bravely he had saved her life.

The assassin ignored them. He might have laughed himself. The nobles were seated upon garrons, mere hill ponies, and they looked ridiculous in their armour and painted shields and flaxen hair and golden earrings, like over-sized children on toys too small for them. Revile climbed onto his own sturdy beast with a grin. Only the Lady Shona and Eocha ap Gawain had proper horses; they towered above all else.

"Well, Eocha," declared Shona, "it seems that once again your people have tried to murder me. I think I should hold you responsible. I hope I never find out you a hand in this."

"Of course not, my lady," protested Eocha. "Why would I wish you harm? I have only affection for you and your father. Some of my rebellious and hot-headed people believe – wrongly, I have often pleaded with them – that you Feni have harmed them, that you treacherously stole their ancient kingdom, that you are back-stabbing stinking thieves, murdering scum-sucking brigands." The Feni muttered angrily. Eocha ignored them. "I am prevented from returning to Alclwyd. If I was allowed, I would seek out these villains and deal with them, the scum!"

"I doubt it not," said Shona lightly, "but have a care to loose your arrows in the right direction."

With that, she nudged her horse into a trot, followed by her nobles and lords. She rode out of the north gate, passing many town's folk and fortress guards. Revile trotted along behind

36

her, an idea suddenly springing to mind. But he kept his thoughts to himself.

The body of horsemen rode along the northern road for some miles, then veered to the east into the higher and drier ground; and they entered an expansive, open forest, which covered the rolling hills and sheltered glens before the glowering mountains. It was warm for the time of year, the sun cast green and golden shadows on the turf. The forest was teeming with life: deer, bear, wolves, wild boar, otter, beaver, salmon, birds and many other creatures. Winter was rapidly approaching, but its touch had not yet been felt in this corner of the world.

The riders gathered in a large clearing, and after drinking from a horn of mead, they set out into the woods after the luckless prey that roamed the wilderness.

The Lady Shona, Eocha ap Gawain and two servants rode off in one direction along a wide forest track. Although their horses were larger and swifter than the garrons, they were less adept at negotiating rough terrain. Revile spurred his own pony across country, hoping for a quicker, straighter and yet more devious route.

VI

The Lady Shona and Eocha ap Gawain thundered down the track, followed some distance behind by the princess's two servants. Shona had managed to convince the King of Strathclwyd that she did not really suspect him of plotting to murder her. Consequently, Eocha seemed in a happier mood, and he charged along the path in abandon, a long spear before him. Shona was armed with a hunting bow and a dagger, and she led the small party, bow in one hand, reins in the other. She spurred her horse on to greater speed, enjoying the feeling of rushing air against her face.

Her horse suddenly gave out a troubled neigh, stopping its gallop so suddenly Shona was nearly thrown. Eocha was hard put not to spit the stricken horse with his spear. The princess leapt lightly from the saddle and examined the beast. It limped, and the woman sighed bitterly.

"Ah, my friend," she told the horse, stroking its neck. "I have ridden you too recklessly. No more hunting for you today."

The horse nuzzled her neck and whinnied.

"Take my horse," said Eocha gallantly. "I will ride one of these garrons."

She shook her head. "No," she told him, "your beast has an evil gleam in its eye." Her two servants came riding up at that point. "I will take one of these garrons. They will suit well enough – and teach me not to be so foolish again."

She sent her servants back to the fortress with the injured horse, then sprang into the saddle of her new mount, a rather plump but sure-footed pony. Shona continued the hunt. Eocha ap Gawain trotted after her, a dark and calculating expression on his face. He rode behind the princess, his spear lowered to the height of her back. Spurring his horse on, he slowly gained on Shona. After all, hunting accidents were all the too common, and by the time this one was discovered he would be half way back to Alclwyd. The Feni would hunt him but it was worth the risk: Shona was getting more and more suspicious. "Let Nechtan deal with Lord

Donald," he thought grimly. "Let the old mage plot on with out me!"

But the Lady Shona was not as trusting as Eocha had imagined. She wheeled around in the saddle to find the King of Strathclwyd bearing down on her. Without slowing her pony, she twisted in the saddle and loosed an arrow in his direction.

The arrow missed by a hair, the flight scoring Eocha's cheek, but was sufficient to give her a few more strides of a lead.

But Eocha grinned again and chased after her. The princess swallowed and struggled to fit another arrow to her bow. Eocha was only a short distance behind, his spear only feet from impaling her. She frantically dug her heels into the belly of her pony, but the poor beast was galloping as fast as it ever would. She swept out her dagger and hewed at the spear point, but her blows had no effect on the iron barb. Shona leaned as far forward as possible, but she could no longer avoid the keen tip of the spear between her shoulder blades.

There was a dull snap like the breaking of a dry branch, and Shona heard a crash behind her. Eocha's horse stopped short and slithered to a halt.

Shona pulled up her pony, and gazed back down the trail.

Lord Eocha ap Gawain, King of Strathclwyd, lay sprawled in the old leaves and dirt of the track. His shivered spear lay beside him and his sweating horse stood over him. He was dead. His head was looking back over his left shoulder. His neck had been broken.

She rode back to where he lay and stared down at his corpse. Apart from his neck, there was no other sign of violence and his horse was not harmed. She examined the branches above her head and discovered a thin rope had been tied tightly between two trunks, stretching across the track. It was this that had killed the treacherous Eocha. She smiled grimly, then started the ride back to the clearing.

A short time later she reached the opening in the trees where other nobles and servants awaited her. Revile sat there, a newly killed deer across the shoulders of his pony. Other riders still emerged through the trees.

"Hail, my lady," greeted Sir Maggot, jumping gallantly to the ground and helping the princess dismount. "No luck, eh?" he said, then hesitated, regarding his hand. It was red with blood. "Are you wounded? Where is Eocha?"

"It is a scratch merely, Sir Maggot," said Shona sadly. "My lord Eocha mistook me for a deer and would have spitted me if he could."

"I see," said Revile, examining her back. "It is not deep. You were lucky, I guess."

"I would say!" said the woman. "And in more ways than one. I won the race by a neck. At least I no longer fear my lord Eocha."

"Why? Is he dead?"

"Very," said Shona, "and I will have his head spiked. I should have done it earlier."

"A delightful adornment to any gate," said Revile, "but I, for one, am saddened by his death."

"Why?" demanded the Lady Shona.

"Well, we'll never find out how to say the name of his people, you know, the Strathclwydwhatsits. Have you any wine left? All this death makes a man thirsty."

"So that's why you drink so much!"

VII

Lord Malcolm of Lornland was dismayed by the demise of his fellow conspirator, although he had no love for the King of Strathclwyd. It was so bizarre. He sat with his back against a standing stone, pondering this new turn of events, not sure that he should remain part of the plot. He was worried. It should have been so easy to murder Shona.

"Do you think he talked?" Malcolm asked Nechtan.

The old mage peered at his companion. "No," he said, looking away, "he would not have had a chance. That much I am certain." He sighed. "By Azzchzog and the Blood Moon, but I wish I knew why he took matters into his own hands. I do not know how things could have gone so wrong. Is this Worm, or Maggot – or whatever he calls himself – to be trusted?"

"How can a man ever tell?" replied Malcolm. "Eocha believed so, but now he is dead and Shona is still living. And this Worm has the favour of the Lady Shona, or so it is said. He saved her from the men of Strathclwyd. Yet maybe this was just to get closer to her. I do not know."

"Eocha should not have interfered," muttered Nechtan. "We had made our plan."

"I know," said the King of Lornland wearily.

"Perhaps I should take I hand," said the mage, sounding just as tired. "By Azzchzog and the Blood Moon, the old king will die tomorrow. I think I will risk my sorceries this second-last time. I judge I have the strength, and this is a powerful time of the year when magic is at its strongest. Let us forget this assassin, this Worm. Let him keep the gold – I will deal with him later. He has done naught but get in the way. No, my friend, I can no longer do this alone. You must help me." And he sighed again. "I am getting too old for all this. My ancient bones need that long rest in the final sleep. Aye, Malcolm, Nechtan the Mage has lived too long."

VIII

Revile and the Lady Shona walked the battlements together, taking the brisk evening air. A wind had got up and clouds rushed away to the west. The full moon was hidden. They had left the second night of feasting early, and wandered aimlessly about the Citadel, talking and looking at the bright stars and the full moon. Both appeared to be quite drunk, but the assassin was sober and still committed to his mission. He was patiently waiting for a moment to push her from the battlements. Shona's inebriation was caused, at least in part, by some clear liquid he had poured into her goblet.

"What do you do, Sir Maggot?" asked Shona again.

"I have already told you," replied Revile, "I am an adventurer."

"Then why did you come to this fortress?" she asked. "There is not much adventure to be found here. I, of all people, know that too well."

"I heard about your Festival at Aodh's Tower, and having nothing better to do I thought I would give Dundonald a visit. In truth, I had become quite bored and would have done much to relieve the monotony. I have enjoyed myself more here."

"You still have not satisfied my curiosity," she said. "You say you are an adventurer. What exactly does that involve? Thievery? Murder?"

"Depends," said the assassin, "what's on offer at the time. I have thieved, it is true. I have also been a mercenary but I didn't like that much – too many rules, fat men giving orders, being thrown into the most dangerous of battles. I have worked as a bodyguard, but it is impossible to know who to trust. I prefer the life of a wanderer, making a living where I can. Anyway, I came into a little money and thought I would take a little rest up here in the north. But generally I just do what ever comes along."

"Do you never become tired with your kind of life?"

"Yes, sometimes," he replied, "but if I settle down for a while I quickly become restless. Adventuring is just a way of life, a profession. Nothing else would suit."

"Have you slain many people?" she asked.

"This is a strange question to ask me again!" he replied, sounding a little irritated. "But yes, I have killed the odd one or two. As you have yourself, no doubt. But only when there was no other way."

"Is there no other way now, I wonder? I suppose you are going to add me to this odd one or two." The woman regarded him closely. "That is what they paid for you, is it not? You see, I am not as trusting as you might have thought. I had my men go through your possessions. They found much gold. I can not believe you earned it honestly."

"I don't know how you can believe this of me," said Revile in a hurt tone. "I saved your life, remember. Why would I have bothered if I intended to murder you myself?"

"Because you knew you would not be paid the rest of your blood money."

The assassin shook his head as if trying to clear it.

"It is strange," the Lady Shona went on, "very strange. The one man I have any regard for in this whole world is only in my company so he can kill me. Three times you have saved my life unwittingly."

"My lady," he told her, "you are very drunk."

"My name is Shona," she replied, "and in the morning I will still be telling the truth."

"You don't know what you're saying," said the assassin uncomfortably.

"Do I not?" she said, her words slurred. "Do you take me for a fool? It was you who set that rope across the track and so killed Eocha. I believe it was you who was in my chamber when the assassin came visiting. Come on then, Sir Maggot, do what they paid you to do. Cast me from the walls and have done with it."

Revile could find nothing to say.

"What do you say to that?" said Shona, and she staggered. "Eh?" And she prodded him in the chest with her finger. "Eh? You feigned friendship so you might murder me the more easily."

"That's not true," said Revile tiredly. "And why would I have needed to bother? I could kill you easily enough as a stranger."

She lurched against him, said something incoherent. Mumbling as if in her sleep, she fell into Revile's arms and went limp. The potion had finally taken effect.

Revile sighed. The princess was unconscious, her head lolled. The assassin lifted her easily into his arms and carried her to the battlements. He held her out over the wall, his arms trembling with her weight.

Then he saw the moon, emerging into a break in the clouds, and his jaw dropped. It was unnaturally dim and was red in colour. He placed the Lady Shona carefully on the ground, and rubbed his eyes. There could be no mistake: it was a blood moon. He shook his head. Gathering himself, he once more took Shona in his arms and carried her to the parapet.

But then he heard a strange scraping sound. The noises were coming from the wall below him. "What by Helgard?" he muttered: it was proving to be a extremely strange night. He put Shona down again and leaned out, staring down into the gloomy chasm.

His eyes opened wide in surprise and fear. Several things were climbing the wall. This was impossible in itself for the courses of masonry were laid without crevice or hold, and the rock below the walls was shear.

The assassin peered down again, not quite able to believe his senses. There were four climbers. The climbers were skeletons, fleshless and bony, clad in rusty armour and rags, clutching notched weapons.

Revile looked about wildly, completely at a loss under the strange wan light of the blood moon. "Helgard!" he muttered. "Ganish, Thor, Hanuman, Mithra and all the saints protect me!" He staggered back from the battlements.

But then, like an arrow loosed from the bow, he scooped Shona up in his arms and ran for the nearest door.

A bony hand appeared over the wall.

Revile tugged at the latch frantically and finally got the door open. He leapt inside, slamming the door behind him, dropping Shona untidily on the floor. But his luck had deserted him. The entrance could not be barred; he was cornered in a small roof-top storeroom. The chamber was filled with arrows and weaponry, casks of oil and piles of stones, for the defence of the fortress during a siege. There was no other way out. His only hope was the Dead had no business with him or Shona; but then he thought of Nechtan and all hope withered. He searched for some weapon with which he might defend himself – but what use were weapons against the Dead? He shuddered slightly and swallowed.

There was a pounding at the door, then another.

The timbers protested and splintered. The assassin saw patches of night sky as bony fists hammered through the wood. He retreated to the far wall, dragging Shona with him. Fumbling with tinder and flint, he tried to light a torch so that he might, at least, see. Finally he succeeded and placed the torch in a brazier by his side. The darkness was thrown back, but the light did nothing to improve Revile's spirits.

The door held for a moment longer, then shivered and crashed inwards. A tall skeleton stood there, peering in with eyeless sockets. It advanced across the threshold, turning its skull from side to side as if it could smell their life-blood. It carried a shield decorated with the painted devices of Fenis and Dalria.

The assassin looked at the skeleton, his expression grim. Not really expecting to be able to do anything, he picked up a halberd and, in the same action, brought it crashing down on the outstretched skull. The skull was split asunder; bones scattered over the floor. The three other Dead stepped over the remains. Revile cleaved all three and they disintegrated into chaos. He grinned.

But the smile died on his lips. Hideously slowly, as if there was no reason to hurry, the fragments and bones started to move back together, pulling themselves along the floor. The bones reformed and the joints snapped back together. It was like some terrible nightmare. And in a while, the skeletons reformed and picked up their weapons. They stood at the door, then shambled into the storeroom.

Revile took another step back, nearly tripping over a small cask of oil. The Dead shuffled, their lifeless jaws working as if they tried to speak. The assassin looked at the cask. He threw down the halberd, then unstoppered the small barrel, kicking it over. The viscous oil ran under the feet of the skeletons. Grabbing Shona, he snatched the torch from the brazier. The Dead were only a short distance away, flailing with their thin arms.

The assassin jumped atop the other barrels, his muscles straining, and leapt towards the door. Something caught at his arm and did not let go. Revile tore away with all his strength, letting out a cry of pain, dead fingers ripping his tunic and gouging his flesh. Stopping at the door, Revile wheeled round. The Dead had turned towards him. The assassin grinned, then tossed the torch into the storeroom.

Momentarily nothing happened. But then there was a great whoosh and flames sprung from the door. Revile ran along the battlements, carrying Shona.

There were three massive explosions, then a fourth. The assassin and the princess were thrown to the ground by the force of the blasts. The building shook, fire flared from the roof.

Revile picked himself off the ground and sighed, looking at his handiwork. He caught his breath for a moment longer, then hurried off to tell the Watch what had happened.

It would not be easy to explain why he had decided to burn down the fortress.

IX

Revile woke about midday. He moaned in his sleep, then sat up in his furs, coming out of some evil dream. He stared about the room, but there were no skeletons lurking in the shadows or sneaking in through the shuttered windows. Relaxing, he lay down again and rubbed his arm. There were four deep wounds there: he examined them carefully, searching for any sign of infection. But they appeared to be healing, so he scratched his head in a thoughtful way and yawned.

He had not got to bed until very late, or early anyway. The fire had been quickly brought under control. But it was the moon that fascinated Revile: slowly he had seen it return to normal. It was a strange time, but he had no way of explaining it.

He decided to forget it, and he yawned again.

Dragging himself from his bed, and shivering a little in the cold, he padded across to the window. He threw open the shutters and peered out into the courtyard. The morning was chilly and crisp, a thin covering of snow lay on the cobbles. The assassin groaned. Grey clouds rolled down from the north-east, a few snow flakes fluttered past the window.

Later, as Revile still watched the snow, there was a soft rap on his door. He answered it: again it was the Lady Shona. She appeared both bright and cheerful, and smiled at him.

"Greetings, Sir Maggot," she said huskily. "How are you this chill morning?"

"Weary, my lady," he replied. "Very weary. This is a most tiring climate you have. Yesterday it is sunny and warm; today it is cold and snows. I am very weary with it."

"I would guess your weariness is due to too many late nights, my friend. Anyway, what are you doing?"

"I am watching your snow and thinking of the South."

"Then again I am not surprised you are weary," she said. "Perhaps I could find you some thing more exciting to do ..."

"I don't doubt it," said Revile evenly.

"I may find you one presently," she went on, "but it seems I am in your debt again. And, so, I must thank you. But have a care not to burn the rest of my House. Anyway, I am grateful, Sir Maggot."

The assassin nodded slowly. "You weren't so sure last night," he told her, "you were convinced I intended to murder you."

"I was drunk – or whatever."

"Perhaps," he replied, then turned back to the window.

"I had not expected," the woman said softly, "to find myself alive this morning."

Revile gripped the edge of the window sill; his knuckles went white. "You have naught to fear from me, my lady," he said, "of that be sure."

"I do not doubt you, Sir Maggot," she said, more seriously. "Now, how is your fencing?"

"Fencing, my lady?" he said, grinning at her. "Would you have me out in the snow fixing your pig-pens?"

"Fool!" she snorted. "I meant your sword-play!"

"I know. I'm competent, I'd guess."

"I've a mind to test you."

"Very well."

Shona led him from the apartment to a narrow flight of stairs, and climbing these, took him to a large chamber. The room was empty except for a table, chairs, and several racks of different weapons: swords, axes, spears, maces, polearms, and all other types of bludgeons and cleavers. Revile had brought his own sword and – he reckoned – there was not a weapon there to match it.

"You have a good sword," Shona commented. "How did you come by it?"

"It's a long story," he replied, "but it is the hardest and strongest steel I have ever chanced upon. Even so, the edge is notched."

"Perhaps it has seen too much use?" she said with a smile. "Too many foolish innocents have thrown themselves on it?"

"That again," said Revile wearily. "I thought you might have grown tired of such questions. Anyway, a sword is not an assassin's weapon."

"I never said it was," she replied. The princess unbuckled her cloak and rolled it up, placing it on the table. She shivered a little in the cold for there was no fire in the chamber. Selecting a sword from one of the racks, she tested its balance and cutting edge. "This will do," she said, and sent the weapon whistling through the air.

"No armour, my lady?" asked Revile. "Is that not dangerous?" She was dressed only in a woollen tunic and leggings.

"My name is Shona," she said absently, "and I have no need of any armour."

"Very well, then," said the assassin. "When you are ready?"

And they fought. The Lady Shona proved to be as expert a swordsperson as Revile had ever met. Her technique and stance were faultless; she was as strong and skilful as any man. Shona was full of tricks, feinting and ducking and weaving, her sword flashing hypnotically in the torch-light. She made no allowances for any stumble or mistake by her opponent. Revile parried and battled as if for his life: he only narrowly avoided a sweep of her blade that would have disembowelled him. He wiped sweat from his nose and grinned.

For they were quite well matched. The Lady Shona had the greater skill and strength but less experience of real combat. Revile's reactions defied sight, his stamina seemed endless, and he had survived countless fights. He had beaten many men who were superior in technique simply because of his patience, speed, and because he fought in a very cunning, devious way.

They struggled round the chamber, sometimes Revile winning the initiative, sometimes the princess. In one melee, the assassin took a shallow cut on his shoulder; as they joined blades again, he slipped under her guard, slicing through her tunic, nicking her stomach.

Then the battle shifted out of Shona's control; the assassin assumed the initiative. Soon she was retreating to defend herself. And she was tiring fast, or so Revile believed. He forced her back towards the table.

But just when he thought he had the victory, he found she was toying with him. With a dexterity Revile had not thought possible, she whirled out of his reach and his last slash went wide. She caught his sword with hers and, with a flick of the wrist, sent his weapon from his grasp, spinning through the air. Shona grinned and wiped her forehead.

It was the assassin's turn to back towards the table, the point of her sword held to his throat. Shona forced him over the table, grabbing the front of his tunic with one hand, holding her sword across his neck. He could feel the sharp blade against his throat; did not even dare swallow. A drop of sweat rolled from the princess's chin and landed on his forehead.

"I enjoyed that, Sir Maggot," she told him, breathing heavily, "and all the more because I have won in the end. I fear you underestimated me."

"I fear I may have," he panted, "but I'm not the only who is stupid."

Shona felt a tickling against her belly. She glanced down and found Revile held a long dirk to her stomach. She laughed and said: "This is a pretty pickle. What should we do?"

The assassin shrugged, still bent over the table. "Resume the battle?" he suggested. "I've no desire for a slit throat, and I guess you don't want your stomach opened to the spine."

But she remained pressed against him. "I think I would prefer to die this way," she said, "taking my assassin with me. So much better than a hunting accident, or a knife in my sleep, or poison in my wine. What do you say? Would that not be better, Sir Maggot?"

"My lady, you have nothing to fear from me. Haven't I already saved your life on two occasions? If it wasn't for me, you'd already be dead. Think on it."

She shook her head. "You take me for a fool," she told him, "a poor, blind, foolish woman. I would rather die this way."

"Listen," he said a little angrily, "don't be so stupid! You have all your life stretching away before you. There is always risk – that can't be avoided. But it is not from me. I promise you. Helgard, after all that has happened you must trust me now!"

"You fear that you will die, that is all!"

"Do I?" he said. "Yet I don't think you would murder me – not like this, not now. In the heat of battle you might, in combat. But you're no assassin!"

"And you, Sir Maggot?"

"I am an adventurer only," he said. "I promise you. You are in deadly peril perhaps. But you must trust me. Helgard, what do I need to do convince you?"

She grinned, then released him. Turning from him, she examined her stomach and the thin cut there. Revile stood up, the dagger still clutched in his hand. He loomed over the stooping woman, his arm raised high – but then the weapon dropped from his hand and clattered to the floor. His eyes were fixed on a point over the princess's shoulder; but his stare was vacant.

The Lady Shona whirled around on her heel, but the smile died on her lips. Revile was as motionless as a statue.

"Greetings, Lady Shona of the accursed Feni," said a strange voice. "Greetings and well met."

The princess froze, then spun quickly, her sword held before her. "Who are you?" she demanded. "How dare you enter this room without knocking!"

The hooded figure smiled grimly. "I do not come or go at your bidding," he told her. "I am Nechtan the Old, Nechtan the Mage, Nechtan the Slayer!"

She gripped the hilt of her sword more tightly. "What do you want with me?" she asked, her knuckles whitening. "What is your business here?"

"By Azzchzog, can you not guess?" he replied in a voice of death.

"What have I ever done to you?" she angrily replied.

"You ask?" he thundered, yet taken unaware by the sharpness of her tone. "You of the Feni ask? What have you been celebrating these days? Your glorious victory, the noble war you fought against us? You murdered my people to the last child – you slaughtered them all – stole the light from El-Firion! Except me, you forgot about me, and I will have my revenge!"

"I am sorry," she said. "Truly sorry about your people. I understand how you must feel."

"Do you?" he cried. "Do you? By Azzchzog, how could you?"

"But I do," she said with feeling. "I know what it is like to be alone and without friend or lover."

"Pah!" spat Nechtan the mage. "You do not know! Have you seen your loved ones slain, seen women and children violated and tortured, heard their last cries of agony? Do you know what happened – what your people did – to my wife, my beautiful wife? When they had finished using her they cut her open with a heated knife and took my half-formed child from her womb! By Azzchzog, I will destroy you" he added coldly, "I will destroy you all!"

"So how did you escape," she asked, "when your family, when your whole people were massacred?"

"What?"

"Why did you not die with them? How did you escape Nechtan the Old?"

"I saved myself," he said. "I could not save them."

"So you left your wife to be tortured?" replied the princess in a tone of scorn. "You left them to die while you ran for your own safety? You did nothing to help them?"

"What could I do?" replied the mage. "I could have done nothing but die uselessly."

"Who can say?" she said coldly. "Why did you leave? Were you afraid to die, old man? Was that it? You coward, you craven, stinking yellow coward!"

"You reproach me?" he cried in bewilderment. "You?"

"Yes," she hissed. "Yessss! Maybe the war against you was unjust, maybe it was. But do you know what they did to my mother, my dear mother that I never knew. She died just as horribly as your wife. My father was devastated, he has never recovered from the anguish. I was left alone, just a child, robbed of affection and love. Was that just?"

"It was war!"

"Exactly, you craven! Your people were no better than us. Your people were just as savage, just as cruel. But we were not cowards. My father did not desert my mother in her need. He rescued her from your savages even though she died a little time later from her injuries. But you? You left your wife! You left her, you cowardly dog!"

"I don't need to listen to this!"

"Silence!" she commanded. He was so stunned by the compunction in her voice that he faltered. "What have you done to my friend?"

"He is under a simple spell," replied the mage before he could check himself. But then he recovered, his voice became hard. "But by then you will be dead! Your words are as nothing. No matter how cowardly my part was, you people still wronged us. You will pay for your arrogance and conceit! For tomorrow, your father will die – in agony – and he will leave his lands to Malcolm of Lornland. There will be a bloody war with Strathclwyd which will consume your people. By Azzchzog, I have seen it! It will happen, have no doubt of that. I tell you this so you go to your death in despair. My revenge will be complete ..."

Revile saw and heard everything that was happening. He knew he should do something to help the princess, but his thoughts were vague and imprecise: he could not concentrate. He tried to move his muscles, but they would not respond to his will. There was a pain that seared him as if a heated dagger was turned in his stomach. The assassin would have cried out if he could. His vision swam; the world reeled.

But he was Revile the assassin. Stubbornly he had fought against many terrors, stubbornly he fought against the spell, no matter how much it cost him. To be dominated by anything was unbearable. He had too much pride to submit. He was in agony but he battled with the compulsion until his muscles trembled and his fingers twitched. Slowly his hand balled into a fist and moved jerkily towards the front of his tunic.

"... I will have my revenge. Prepare to die, Lady Shona, prepare to die!"

Nechtan the Mage started to mumble a few strange words, and the air crackled with energy at his spell. The Lady Shona stood defiantly before him, bracing herself for the attack. "Come on you, craven," she cried, "come on, Nechtan the Bold!"

But the mage did not hear her. He began to wave his hands. A spasm took the princess as he clenched his fist. Dropping her sword, she bent double in agony. She opened her mouth to scream, but no sound came. Her stomach bulged and bubbled as if her organs were trying to escape out through her belly. Her chest heaved. Blood trickled through her hands. It was as if someone had got hold of her insides and was trying to tear them out.

Nechtan continued his spell in a harsh voice. Shona opened her mouth and green bile spilled over the floor. The bubbling and convulsions became fiercer; blood spurted from her clenched fists.

There was a whirling noise, a thud, the spell was suddenly cut short. Shona went limp, wheezing where she lay.

Nechtan the Mage sank to his knees, a dagger buried in his chest to the hilts. Bright red blood coursed from the wound, soaked the front of his robe. He toppled forward and his head thumped off the stone floor. The mage twitched once.

Shona dragged herself to her feet, still bent with pain. She straightened up slowly and gazed at Revile, blinking the sweat from her eyes. The assassin was soaked, his face scarlet. He sagged back, leaning against the table.

"Helgard," he said. "Helgard."

The princess grinned through the pain. "It seems it is your destiny to save me," she said. "Never mind."

"It is a honour," he replied. "Is Nechtan dead? I would be certain."

But when they looked for the body, it was gone. Only Revile's dagger remained where the mage had fallen.

The assassin and the princess frowned at each other.

X

"Was that true about your mother?" asked Revile.

A great feast was in progress, and the sounds of laughter and merriment all but drowned their conversation. The celebration was triply glad: it was the Last Day, the anniversary of the concluding battle with the Old People, the Ing; Lord Donald had recovered a little from his illness, and his death no longer looked certain; and Nechtan the Mage was almost definitely dead – at last. Everything had turned out for the best. The princess and the assassin sat at the High Table together, laughing and joking. They no longer even received their share of ugly glances. The Feni nobility were too inebriated to care about Maggot's low birth.

"Was that about your mother true?" Revile said again, this time more loudly.

"Ah no," she replied, sounding ashamed. "It was a complete and utter lie. I was not even born when the Last Battle was fought, as Nechtan would have realised if he had thought about it for a moment. My mother died peacefully in her bed two years ago. I thought it was a good thing to say at the time."

The assassin laughed. "You were very convincing," he told her.

"As you are yourself, Sir Maggot," she replied with a half-smile. "A plausible rogue."

"Thank you," he said, bowing his head. "I am honoured by your courtesy."

"It was nothing," said the princess, taking a drink from her goblet. "So," she went on, "what are your plans now? I think your business here is finished. Unless I am mistaken?"

"I'll be around for a while yet," he said softly. "After that, who knows? I have a mind to take passage for the south to escape the coming winter. I need a rest in the sun. There is more there for one with my talents. Besides, I'm getting too well known for my comfort. Anyway, how do we know Nechtan is dead? Perhaps he is only gathering his strength for the next blood moon."

"Then let us hope it is many years away. Anyway, I will miss you, Sir Maggot," she said, "and feel the less secure. For I have not forgotten Nechtan's prediction: he said Fenis would be devastated, that the Feni would be consumed in a bloody war. He told me he'd seen it."

"Perhaps he was lying," replied the assassin. "Why would he tell you the truth?"

She shook her head and shivered. "No," she said in a whisper, "there was truth in his voice. I might have need for one of your talents again."

"Well, if you have need of me, I'll come. Send word to the Wastrel, a tavern in Llaith in Lothland. Ask for Maggot."

"I will," she said brightly.

"Anyway," he said, "what are you going to do in my absence? Will you marry a grizzled greybeard as you feared?"

"I hope not," she said. "It appears my father will survive this illness, and as long as he lives I will be safe. But he will not last forever. I do not wish to look beyond that. Sometimes I wish I was a man, for then they would leave me alone!"

"Don't say that," said Revile, "I think you're fine as a woman."

"Why thank you, my silver-tongued knight," she grinned. "I had not thought Sir Maggot so chivalrous!"

"Is it chivalrous to simply tell the truth?"

"No, probably not," she replied, "but I thank you anyway."

They fell silent – yet shortly they were jesting and drinking again.

Lord Malcolm, King of Lornland, approached the High Table, the very picture of cordiality. In one hand was a goblet, the other a flagon of blood-red wine.

"May I join your company?" he asked, lurching slightly, spilling some of the wine from his goblet.

"If you must," said the princess in a far-from-friendly tone. Space was made; Malcolm sat down between Shona and Maggot.

"Have some of my wine," said the King of Lornland. "It is a truly excellent vintage, all the way from the land of the Franks. It is truly excellent, yes truly excellent."

"That would be delightful," said Shona sweetly, "but I already have plenty."

Revile indicated that his only goblet was full to brimming. The three sat for some minutes without saying anything. Then Shona's attention was distracted by one of her nobles, who was telling an absurd tale about Conan, who had told a ludicrous story about being a king in his own right. The Feni had thrown him out the previous evening when he had started a brawl.

"I must talk to you," Revile whispered to Malcolm. "I plan to poison the princess. Have you got my gold?"

The King of Lornland nodded.

"Good," the assassin went on, "then say and do nothing."

Revile reached across the table and took Shona's now empty goblet and started to fill it with wine from a large jug by his side. He ignored Malcolm's excellent vintage. With a dextrous slight of hand, he emptied the contents of a small phial into the goblet. Only Malcolm saw him do it.

The assassin returned the goblet to the Lady Shona and watched her drink the wine. Malcolm grinned.

"It will take some minutes," Revile told him in a whisper, then drained his own goblet. He refilled it from Malcolm's flagon. The King of Lornland took a sip of his own wine.

Shona was relating the appearance of Nechtan the Mage in the armoury, and there was much jesting and ribaldry at the old wizard's expense. But Revile took exception to something that was said, and shouted an obscenity at one of the nobles.

"What did you call me, you low-born scum?" bellowed the lord, heaving himself to his feet. "You son of a whore!"

"Nothing to your favour, you pot-bellied scum-sucking slime-bag!" replied the assassin, rising unsteadily and knocking Malcolm backwards off the bench. Revile lurched against the table.

"Stop this!" cried the Lady Shona. "Sit down both of you!"

Revile seated himself angrily, then helped Malcolm back to the bench, handing him a goblet of wine.

"Sorry," he said to the King of Lornland. "But the arrogance of some of these so-called nobles! It makes my blood boil, don't you know? I hope you're not injured?"

"No, I am fine," said Malcolm, then whispered in Revile's ear: "How much longer will it be? Shona seems unaffected."

"Patience, my friend," said the assassin. "I know my business." Revile took his goblet and drained it to the dregs.

Suddenly, he clutched at his throat, making several strange gurgling sounds. He gave out one last gasp – then slumped over the table. His goblet clattered away across the floor.

Malcolm feigned surprise. "What is wrong?" he said, shaking the assassin's shoulder. Revile did not stir. "Perhaps he has drunk too much?"

"Perhaps," said Shona, "he's probably jesting with us."

"Very well," said Malcolm, and he took another sip from his goblet.

Revile sat up and grinned at the King of Lornland. "You are perceptive, my lady," he said, winking at Malcolm, but then whispering: "I think your wine is a little too sour for my taste. Too much poison in it, I'd reckon. But I did not wish to waste such an excellent vintage. So you'll be glad to know I swopped goblets with your good self."

"But the princess?" spluttered the King of Lornland. "The gold?"

"Ah, that," he said with a smile. "The phial contained only water. And while that may be a shock to Shona's system, I don't think it'll kill her. And the gold? I'll survive without it."

"You ... treac ... erous ... low ... down ... bas ...," Lord Malcolm staggered from the bench, his eyes wide in terror. A convulsion took him; he stumbled, collapsing backwards with a large crash. Revile moved along the bench and sat next to Shona.

"What is wrong with him?" asked the princess, looking over her shoulder at the prostrate King of Lornland.

"I think he has died," replied Revile. "I fear his wine disagreed with him. I would leave his excellent vintage alone for it is too potent a brew – even for you, my lady."

"Is he the last?" asked Shona.

"I don't know what you mean."

"O well," she sighed. "I think I'll have his head spiked all the same."

Revile nodded. "He'll complete the set," said the assassin. "You'll soon have to build more gates, my lady."

"My name is Shona!"

XI

"Well, farewell, Sir Maggot."

"It's been quite fun," he replied. "I shall miss Dundonald and its lady." He leapt lightly onto the back of his pony. "Good-bye!"

"Fare well, Sir Maggot!" cried Shona.

Revile encouraged his pony into a trot, riding up the track and never looking back. He reached the top of the ridge by the edge of the forest of Carnmor. Stopping just inside the trees, he turned his pony around, peering back down at Dundonald and its walls and towers. There was a group of people by the east gate. One of them waved.

Revile waved back, then rode into the forest. The assassin had gold and wine for the journey east, but his expression was thoughtful and he did not smile.

***

R evile finished his tale, then sat quietly, thinking over the story. He shook his head. The others fidgeted, uneasy there was silence again.

While Revile spoke, their plight seemed diminished, a small affair in the great scheme of things. But as the silence lengthened, they were closed in and left alone in the dark with their doom – and fear and despair filled them.

Alwyn stirred. "Have you seen the Lady Shona again?" she eventually asked. "You seemed very friendly."

"We were – then," he replied with a sigh. "I saw her not so long ago, but we parted as enemies."

"That is a pity," said Margaret. "I'd thought, perhaps, she of all people could have helped you."

Revile sighed. "Maybe she would have once," he said, "but she doesn't know of my imprisonment – the lands of the Feni are many miles to the north. And they have just withstood an invasion during which Dundonald was besieged by the men of Strathclwyd and for the most part destroyed. Yet even if she did try to interfere, Prince Bregorin would take no heed. I'm just one more no-account criminal – too unimportant for the attention of princesses or kings. All of you must have attended the hangings?"

"Of course," said Margaret, answering for the others. "They are something of an event."

"Did you ever wonder," the assassin went on, as was his wont, "why those particular people were to be hanged? For wasn't their deaths – dancing at the end of a rope – not just entertainment to relieve the monotony of your dreary lives? Yet you think your deaths are unjust. What had those others done? Had they stolen a stale loaf of bread? Had they stolen trinkets from their customers? Had they refused to sleep with the prince? Were their offences as great as yours? I fear you didn't care – not one of you."

"No, why should we?" said Margaret coldly. "We were too busy surviving. We have enough misfortune in our lives without worrying about other people's. Why do you attack us in this way? For one thing is very clear: you yourself don't give a damn for them or one tiny bit for us. How dare you lecture us! I have more compassion, care and humanity in my small toe than you have in the whole of your heartless body."

"A whore with a heart of gold," said Revile. "How touching! My faith in people is restored!" And then added: "But I don't care, not a tiny bit. I accept the last walk into the dark, I accept my death, I don't curse or feel ill-done. I have murdered a man, been caught, and am to be executed. Why do you think your deaths so unjust?"

"Because we did nothing," swore Fergus. "Nothing compared to you anyway, you backstabbing pig! My crops failed, my family had nothing to eat, we were starving. Yet we still had to pay dues to the King. The crime was my wife and children would die of hunger while lords in their grand halls stuffed their bellies. What else could I do? I took the only option left to me."

"Do you try to convince me or yourself?" said Revile. "And I don't know of what help you will be to your family for your holdings will be seized and your family evicted. They will have less than nothing, not even a roof over their heads. They will die all the sooner. Don't fool yourself, Fergus."

"Don't accuse me of that!" said the farmer, his voice broken. "It is enough I am to die without my family as well. I am not the same as you! It is ridiculous!"

"Is it?" said the assassin. "You're right of course: you are not the same as me – you are far, far more stupid. Killing a merchant or stealing a loaf lead to the gallows. At least I'd have earned more than one poor meal."

"I can't believe you think that," muttered Fergus. "I have done nothing wrong my whole life. I've paid my dues, gone to war when my lord asked, attended church every Sunday and Festival since I was born. I treat my wife and children well, I have never raised my hand to her. How can you judge me so? I only tried to feed my family. I didn't murder for profit or malice!"

"Yet tomorrow we'll both be as dead," said Revile. "Isn't it strange all you virtue will end with all my wickedness? Did the commandment: 'Thou shalt not steal' not apply to you?"

"Leave him alone!" cried Margaret. "What right have you to judge him? There are degrees of evil and sin – that is what we are taught. Perhaps in this life they are treated the same – but not in the Next! God would not damn Fergus or this young woman – for myself I don't know, my life had not been blameless. But you, Revile the assassin, are as surely damned as I sit here."

"Perhaps I am," he said, "yet luckily I don't share your faith in gods. We'll just have to wait and see, won't we? We'll find out first thing tomorrow."

"What do you believe, then?" said Alwyn softly.

The assassin paused for a moment, then shrugged. "I believe," he said, "that when I die I will be snuffed out like a candle. Then, perhaps, for a few years people will remember me or my deeds – I will live on as long as they do. But eventually I will be no more. My bones will disappear into the earth, and all my deeds, dreams and existence will vanish into the nothing from whence they came. So much for me: Revile the bold adventurer!"

"Aren't you frightened of dying?" asked the girl. "Doesn't it scare you?"

"No," he replied. "I value my life highly but I have always accepted I will die. I've been too close too many times. It is that last release from old age or agony or torture." And he laughed. "What would I do in my old age except end my days starving? My pride would not let me beg or rely on charity. I'm just disappointed it could not have been later, during some great adventure or enterprise." He smiled crookedly.

The others were puzzled for a moment – it seemed a strange admission from a man like Revile.

"What is wrong with growing old?" asked Fergus, forgetting his earlier anger. "I was rather looking forward to it."

"The loss of strength and power and independence," replied the assassin. "If I have wanted something I've gone out and got it – or at least have had the strength and cunning to try. But if I grew old my limbs would weaken, my wits would become blunted, and in the end I would have nothing, not even my pride. If I was to choose to end my life now or to live into an unending dotage I think I would rather die now.

"Mind you," he added, "I might think differently if I was old. Anyway, Margaret, if there is a Hell, as your religion believes, then my torment would be to spend eternity as a doddering old man, but still able to remember what had been."

"You are a strange one," Margaret told him. "You are cruel to us but I can't stay angry with you. You sometimes surprise me. Why should that be, do you think?"

Revile laughed. "Perhaps you realise I don't take myself seriously. Many things cross your mind, alone in the wilderness with an empty purse and belly, every hand turned against you, the howl of wolves in your ears. I am Revile but inside I revile myself as much as I do you or Fergus or Alwyn here. And, in all truth, I am embarrassed to be here. I've done one or two things worthy of note and it hurts my pride to think I will die with the likes of you!"

"Damn cheek!" muttered Fergus. "What's wrong with the likes of us?"

"Nothing," he replied, "you are good honest folk but I despise you all the more. I hoped my death would be more exciting and notable, amongst the company of the Great. I am, as I have said, sadly disappointed."

The farmer swore, but Margaret laughed at the assassin. "You poor lamb," she said. "My whore's heart of gold goes out to you!"

"Could I ask you one thing more?" added Alwyn. "Do you think you are evil?"

"How can a man judge?" replied the assassin. "Let me answer that by asking you a question: do you believe you are evil?"

"No," said the young woman, her voice certain. "I don't."

"I see," said Revile. "Do you hate the prince for what he's done to you?"

"Yes I do," she said equally as certain. "But I have good cause."

"Would you like to see old Bregorin hanging from his own gallows?"

"Yes, I suppose I would," but her voice faltered as if she could see the direction of Revile's argument.

"If I told you I was going to kill the prince would you try to stop me?"

"No," she said wearily, "I wouldn't."

"Would you even pay me if you could?"

"I guess so."

"I suppose," said Revile, sounding pleased with himself, "you think I enjoy killing people. Yet you would all employ me if you could – for whatever reason. Perhaps it is only the idea of murder for profit which is wicked to you – murder for hate or revenge is fine. But I am the only dagger in the hand. So let me ask you this: is the assassin more evil than the person who pays him? The assassin does not have hate in his heart ..."

Ketil Potbelly's Revenge

Ketil Potbelly was very rich. This fact remained undisputed. Indeed, he was the richest man in Stormwall, even wealthier than the Jarl Erik himself. Ketil had made his first fortune trading otter and beaver pelts for wine, spices and pig-iron – and had sold each and all for enormous profit. Silver bred silver, and gold bred gold, and before Ketil was even thirty no one could rival his wealth, opulence, or indeed, his rapidly-thickening waistline.

Money bought position in the small community and an extensive, comfortable house on the edge of Stormwall. If Ketil's home was not actually larger than Jarl Erik's longhall then it was certainly more richly furnished and decorated. Gold-threaded tapestries hung on the walls, rare foreign rugs covered his floors, gold goblets and plate littered his tables, jewels and even more gold circled his fingers and hung about his flabby neck.

Ketil Potbelly was very rich and wanted for nothing – nothing that is except a wife.

Not that the object of Ketil's affections could not be guessed. Many men's hearts and eyes were turned in the same direction. Ketil Potbelly could not be blamed for his desire.

He was enamoured of Ragnhilde Olavdottir, the only child of a prosperous freeman in the pay of the Jarl. She was a lithesome creature, not very tall, but with a pleasing sunny disposition. And for all his baubles and trinkets, Ketil could think of little else but the clinging line of her dress, or the tresses of her red hair, or the gentle curve of her breasts and hips, or the sound of her voice, or the life in her brown eyes, or the smell of her body. Ketil had discovered a treasure more precious then diamonds – and a sight harder to come by. He had discovered something deeper than the love of money.

And it was unbearable, irksome, infuriating. He had not thought there could be anything more desirable than hoarded wealth. But he had been wrong and to his dear cost.

Thinking himself a most advantageous match, he asked for the hand of Ragnhilde in marriage. How could any woman refuse such an offer? How could any loving father not greet the prospect of Ketil as a good son with delight? Ketil Potbelly planned the wedding down to the finest detail. He purchased the most expensive wines for the banquet, bought rare silks and perfumes for his bride-to-be, commissioned a fabulous embroidered blanket for the nuptial bed. Success in this venture, as in any other, was assured to his profit.

And then, when everything was at last prepared, Ketil Potbelly, the wealthiest man in Stormwall, asked Ragnhilde Olavdottir to marry him.

She rejected him. There was no anger or indeed any other emotion on her part: she had just told him – matter-of-factly – she desired, and was betrothed, to another. Ketil was very upset and demanded to know the name of her lover. Svein Erikson, she told him.

But it was then, for the first time perhaps, Ketil thought he could hear scorn in her voice and sense the glint of loathing in her glance. But why? he had asked. And she shrugged as if he had too little wits to understand. So Ketil had pleaded with her, unmanned himself before her.

She rejected him, only adding she was flattered by his generous proposal.

Flattered? Flattered!

Ketil Potbelly could have screamed in rage. How could she! How could she do this to him! The slut! The painted whore! It was crystal clear now. She had encouraged him deliberately so he would make a fool of himself, so he would waste his precious gold. He knew men envied his fortune. What a grand joke it must have been! They would all be laughing now! He could just picture them in the Longhall, hooting and hollering at the funny, fat, comic Potbelly. How could he have been so stupid?

So he went to visit her early the next morning. Perhaps she had been toying with him. He took a jewel encrusted brooch so she might understand how deeply he felt for her.

Her answer was the same, still in the kind manner. But he was sure he could see laughter in those calculating brown eyes. He stormed from her apartment, his face scarlet with rage, his hands trembling.

He returned to his home, but the finery seemed gaudy and worthless, mere baubles to torment him. Stalking around his rooms and corridors, he could not accept her rejection. It was so unfair!

Then an idea came to him. Perhaps it was her father who did not desire the marriage. There was the question of the dowry. Perhaps Olav could not raise the necessary gold. Yes, that was it. Olav did not wish to embarrass himself by admitting his poverty. Yes, that must be it. Ketil would visit Olav and explain the situation. After all, the dowry was not important.

And he had seen Ragnhilde's father. Olav had been quite polite. O yes, so polite, the low-born oaf! Ketil shouted and raged. The bastard! The bastards! How could they do this to me! How could they! He saw amusement on the faces of his servants, even the peasants and carls smirked and pointed their grubby fingers.

And yet, and yet he knew in the end Ragnhilde would change her mind. Then they would all laugh on the other sides of their faces.

And there had been a marriage. Svein Erikson and Ragnhilde Olavdottir had been married on Wotansday past the full-moon. They invited Ketil to the wedding. And he had gone because he knew there was some kind of mistake. But it was true! The reality came crushing down on him. Ketil was struck speechless. When the celebrations were over, he returned to his home, numb to the world about him. He was empty. His apartments were featureless and vague and empty of value.

He remained in this state for a week or more. He shambled about his house as if he was in some unwaking nightmare from which there was no redemption. He spoke to no one, knew nothing, was unfeeling and uncaring. There was nothing to do – except to eat.

This he did with vigour. He consumed everything put before him – no food was too distasteful or unappetising. He ate as if by filling his stomach he might fill the void left by her rejection. There was no solace. The void was bottomless and food too trivial. Nothing could dispel the emptiness, nothing.

One morning he awoke from his nightmare. His hunger had finally been satisfied. Hate filled Ketil Potbelly. He rose from his furs and his expression was almost grim. His deep set eyes were filled with malice. There was a solution.

Ragnhilde Olavdottir had chosen Svein Erikson. So be it! Let them gloat while they may, he thought, staring at the shabby buildings of the Longhall. But I will have my revenge. If I cannot have the woman I desire then no other man shall. Potbelly grinned, baring his teeth, his double chin folding into layers. There was a solution.

Svein Erikson and his lovely wife would die.

It was that simple. Ketil laughed aloud. With their deaths would come contentment.

But how was it to be done? Ketil was not fool enough to imagine he might commit murder himself. Not only was he a weak man but he had no skill with weapons. He was sufficiently honest to admit he was a coward.

So he thought a little more, reaching an answer swiftly. He might hire an assassin, cheaply most likely for he could not envisage any problems for an experienced murderer. But who? Certainly no man of Stormwall. That much was certain. The fools were too attached to their buffoon of a Jarl. No, this needed to be done with subtlety and tact. Ketil had contacts in the ports of the lands of Mannan, Calatria and Lothland. They could arrange the hire of such an assassin. Yes, that was it! He could send instructions through a messenger, in vague terms so his purpose would not be guessed. Yes, that was it. Then Svein and Ragnhilde would learn the truth of Ketil's resolve. Let them have their sniggers for the moment.

So he sent his most trusted courier. And that same afternoon, he visited Svein and Ragnhilde in their apartments in the Longhall. He apologised, telling them he had been a fool and begging their forgiveness. He even gave the couple a small cask of his finest wine to celebrate their marriage. Ragnhilde had smiled and said she was gladdened. Ketil smiled back ruefully.

When he had got home how he had laughed.

And then he waited.

II

It was a full turning of the moon before Ketil heard any more on the matter although he thought about it constantly. Then late one night, there was a knock on his door. Potbelly answered it himself, for he had dismissed his servants, and admitted a pale, unshaven character into his home.

"Welcome," said Ketil, "I have been expecting you."

The visitor shrugged, then followed the merchant to his hall.

"I have brought you here for a purpose," Potbelly went on when they were seated. He did not offer the assassin any wine.

"So I'd imagined," said the visitor. "I've made a journey of some weeks to get here. The miles are many from Llaith in Lothland. I hope I will be adequately rewarded for my time."

Ketil studied the assassin. It was true his visitor had a hard, rough appearance for his dark hair was unkempt and unwashed and an old scar ran across one cheek from eye to mouth. But the assassin did not have the look of an experienced murderer. He was, well, average and unremarkable, and could have been one of a thousand ruffians or brigands who inhabited the seaports and towns throughout the north. The assassin did not seem to have the strength or cunning for Ketil's mission.

The merchant hesitated, then shrugged. "What is your name?" he asked. "What should I call you?"

"I have many names," replied the visitor, "but you may call me Louse, if you wish."

Ketil nodded. "Well, Louse," he said, "I have employment for you. There is a son of the Jarl Erik in this town of Stormwall. He is called Svein. He and his new wife have wronged me greatly to my lasting shame and discomfort. I want them punished, I want then dead. Can you accomplish this discreetly?"

"I dare say."

"Good," said Ketil more eagerly, then told his visitor all he thought appropriate about the situation. "How soon can this be done?"

"By tomorrow night."

"Very good – then there is nothing else to say."

"Not quite," said the visitor. "There is the matter of my pay. I have not travelled all this way to return home without profit. You would do well to remember it!"

"Of course, how foolish of me!" laughed Ketil. "How much do you normally charge for such a job?"

"Fifty pieces ..."

"Of silver," interrupted the merchant. "Very well, although it is a high price to pay."

"... of gold."

"Gold?" spluttered Ketil. "Gold!"

"Aye," said the visitor, "that is my price – fifty pieces of gold. You would not want the job half done."

"This is preposterous!" cried Ketil. "It is a fortune! Surely you are a jesting?"

The visitor's expression was blank. "Do you see me smiling?" he said. "It is my price."

"I will give you ten," the merchant went on. "No more. I am not a man given to haggling or bargaining. If it is too little then return home now. It is my only offer. Take it or leave it."

The visitor shrugged in reply, and Ketil counted out five gold pieces into his hand.

"Five now," said the merchant, "five after you have completed the work."

The visitor weighed the pieces in his hand and frowned slightly, perhaps guessing they were underweight. But he said nothing.

"And one last thing," added Ketil. "They must know before they are punished who it is that does this to them."

The visitor nodded again. Ketil showed him to the door, a feeling of deep triumph in his heart. He returned to the hall when the assassin had gone, and poured himself a large goblet of wine. He drank deeply. Ketil Potbelly did not think he would get much sleep that night. His eyes gleamed with excitement at the thought of his revenge.

Ketil woke late the next morning and yawned. He heaved himself out of the chair with some difficulty after draining the last drop of wine from the bottle. It would be a long day, he thought, but an enjoyable one.

He spent the morning on his accounts. But his mind wandered often and no matter how he tried he could not balance the columns of figures. He gave up and took to wandering about the house, not even noticing the coming, then the passing, of the midday meal. Food and money were of no interest to him now.

Finally, as the waiting became unbearable, he escaped the confines of his house for the harbour and town. He searched the few streets and along the rocky shore for a glimpse of the assassin – and then even the complex of buildings, which formed the Longhall. But he did not find the man who called himself Louse. A few of the inhabitants and warriors spoke to Ketil or waved their greeting, but Ketil hardly heard them and acknowledged them blankly.

As the westering sun dipped into the sea, the merchant retraced his steps to his own doors. He slipped inside, took a new bottle of wine from the cellar, and settled down in front of the cold grate with a goblet of wine and his thoughts.

His face was expressionless but in his heart there was joy.

Ketil Potbelly stirred, then opened his eyes tiredly. Something had woken him and he staggered to his feet.

There was another louder knock at the door.

The merchant's heart pounded in his chest, blood pulsed in his forehead. It must be done, he thought. A wave of satisfaction washed over him as deep as the deeps of the sea. He almost danced his way down the corridor to admit the assassin. He undid the latch and bolts and stood back.

Framed in the doorway was Jarl Erik, silhouetted by torches in the hands of his men. Ketil's visage became suddenly blank.

"My Jarl," he said, trying to dampen a yawn, "I had not expected to see you at this late hour. You must come ..."

"Friend," the Jarl replied, his voice was cracked with emotion, "I have terrible news. Terrible. Ragnhilde has been ..." He faltered. "You must come."

Ketil was speechless but his soul was singing.

"You must come," repeated Jarl Erik. "I must show you."

The Jarl and his men hurried from Ketil's house and the merchant followed as quickly as he was able. They ran through the deserted streets of Stormwall to Erik's Longhall, passed the open gates, and into the complex of buildings. Ketil rushed after them, his breath rasping in his lungs, his legs labouring. The Jarl led him down one last corridor to the door of Svein's apartments. Erik waited a moment and then entered the chamber.

Ketil's heart missed a beat. Ragnhilde Olavdottir was dead. Her naked body was covered in blood. Standing beside the fireplace, with his back to the door, stood Svein Erikson. The young man was weeping.

But it was not this that made Ketil's face go pale.

On the wall above the bed, painted large in Ragnhilde's blood, was the name:

Ketil

Jarl Erik grinned like a wolf. "Ragnhilde and Svein had a visitor tonight," he said. "My son was knocked senseless and when he awoke found Ragnhilde dead."

"What has this to do with me?" Ketil blurted out.

"We found this on the floor," said Erik, handing the merchant a piece of parchment. "It is addressed to you."

Ketil opened the letter and read:

Ketil
You got more than you paid for and
no less than you deserve
Louse

Ketil Potbelly's jaw dropped.

"Aye, friend," said the Jarl, "I hope you can explain this letter, and the explanation better be good. My son wishes to discuss it with you."

Svein Erikson turned towards them, but did not appear disposed to hear any explanation. Ketil Potbelly's revenge had cost him only five gold pieces, but he could be forgiven for thinking it was not a bargain.

***

I didn't enjoy that story," said Margaret, "but I suppose to some measure you are correct: the person who employs the assassin is just as evil as the assassin he employs. But that does not excuse you. You make your living murdering folk for silver and gold. And it is one thing to wish a person dead; quite another to be provided with the means."

"Is it now?" replied Revile. "What you mean is I have the courage to risk my life whereas you don't. I wasn't joking when I said I despised you. For you are cowards – too frightened to take the risk of controlling your own lives. You blame others for your own misfortune. Well we're all here through our own fault. That is enough for me."

"Pah!" spat Fergus. "You've ranted on long enough! You started this conversation and I'm sick to death of it!"

"Yes," asked Alwyn, "why do you turn on us? What have we ever done to make you hate us?"

"Hell's Teeth!" muttered the assassin. "*'What have we ever done to make you hate us?'* I please myself in most things, I'm neither fair nor reasonable. Peasants – you three – I have always hated. Always so ready to compromise and do what you're told. What a way to spend my last hours alive! Gad, it is greater torture than being boiled alive!"

"Not only for you!" retorted Margaret. "You are the most ill-tempered and objectionable person alive! Do you have any friends? God in Heaven, have you nothing good to say about anyone?"

"Certainly not about you, you old hag," said Revile. "I'm not surprised you had to take to thievery to support yourself, but then having sex with an aged crone doesn't appeal to most."

"O shut up!" said the older woman in exasperation. "Stop wasting your breath!"

"As you wish," said the assassin.

"Great God!" moaned Fergus at the same time. "What have I done to deserve this? I'm doomed with my family and this maniac thinks it's funny!"

"Yet perhaps he's the most sensible of us," said Alwyn. "What is the use of bothering?" There was a dull resignation in her tone which made Margaret feel very old. "This assassin is right," the girl went on. "It is my own fault I'm to die. I can't blame even the prince, I could not do any differently. We're weak, weak and foolish and cringing, too weak to make any decision not made for us, frightened what others would think or say about us. We're all too used to doing what we're told." And then she added: "In all things but one."

"Don't be too hard on yourself," Margaret told her. "Surely, you don't blame yourself?"

"It isn't that easy," sighed Alwyn. "It never is. I feel what this Revile feels – or so I imagine. I want to be free, I want to make my own choices and decisions. But I don't know how to. It is easier – safer – to live out my life as a serving wench, attending to every whim and fancy of my mistress and master. Still, I dreamed of far kingdoms, handsome princes, and a time when I'd live as a queen. In the end it has been the death of me. I have nearly a score of years, but in all that time I've done nothing – I was too frightened of the unknown, taking the difficult path, breaking away from Bamburg. I couldn't lose my dream for there was nothing else."

"We all dream, Alwyn," said Margaret. "How else could we live through each day? And each night? But dreams are dreams. They never could come true."

"How do you know?" said the girl. "We've never even been out of Bamburg. We'll both die without ever knowing. At least this man has travelled and adventured. And I would murder Bregorin if I could – and not just for having condemned me to death. I'm just as evil as Revile, I only lack his courage."

"Don't be stupid!" said Margaret with a tinge of anger. "There is no comparison between us. He is here for good reason: he's an assassin, and by the laws of all civilised folk he should be put to death."

"I don't think," said Alwyn slowly, "he is any more evil than the rest of us."

"Phoooey!" said Fergus. "He is by any standards, cruel and callous beyond human measure. We've done nothing wrong – or at least nothing of consequence. We don't deserve to share his fate."

"You don't see it, do you Fergus?" said the young woman. "He wants us to believe the worst of him, it enhances his reputation and that is important to him. Haven't you listened to his stories? He has helped people when they needed it, in a strange was he is honourable. He has the strength to do so. Have you ever helped anyone, Fergus? Do you even have the power to? You have lived your life without responsibility, as I have, caring only about yourself."

"That's not true!" cried the farmer angrily. "I've sown crops and reared beasts so my family would eat! I've spent most of my life supporting my wife and children. Perhaps to one, like you, who was born to luxury, that is not caring. You have a damn cheek!"

"I wonder," said Alwyn thoughtfully. "If your neighbours were starving would you help feed them?"

"Yes, probably!" replied Fergus, becoming heated. "And they would me. If we didn't we would all starve."

"So did they?"

"Yes. Some. As much as they could."

"As much as they could," replied the girl. "As you have pointed out, I've led a life of plenty compared to you – but I would do the same. I would risk little – and especially not my life – to help a soul. Revile is different, he has. He saved the sister of Margaret of the Order of the Cross and in the end he saved Lady Shona of the Feni – and not for his own profit."

"I have the odd failing," added Revile. "I can't always maintain my otherwise untarnished reputation."

"I see," said the farmer sourly, "that you've found your tongue again."

"Do you think we're evil?" asked Margaret. "Alwyn is convinced we are."

"I know," Revile said, "I was listening. But I reckon you're just about normal: uncaring and cold, cruel and callous, interested in nothing but your own rear end and what the gossips at the hovel on the corner are saying. I'm surprised you needed to ask me of all people."

"Why do you lower yourself to talk to us?" said Fergus. "Why don't your keep you peace and leave us alone?"

"I don't know," said Revile. "I would certainly never choose to spend a night in your company. I guess I'm bored and there's not really much else to do. Apart, that is, from knocking all your teeth down your throat, Fergus. We could do that if you'd prefer?"

"Charming!" said Margaret. "I certainly don't know why we bother to talk to you!"

"Do you want me to tell you?" muttered the assassin.

"Aye, go on," scorned the farmer, "astound us with the sharpness of your wit!"

"I'd rather astound you with the sharpness of a dagger," muttered Revile. "I suggest you go back to playing with yourself, friend Fergus."

"Tell us," said Margaret.

"I can't be bothered," yawned the assassin. "Suffice it to say you've not once asked about the time and how long you've left alive."

"No," said Alwyn, "I suppose we haven't."

"What time is it?" asked the farmer quickly. "What is the hour?"

"Hell, Fergus, what difference does it make?"

"Perhaps it will be light soon!" cried the farmer. "How long have we got?"

"Fergus," said the assassin tiredly, "I doubt if it's even midnight."

"Thank god!" said the farmer, crossing himself. "We've still ten hours or so."

Revile made a rude noise.

"So that's what you think," said Margaret, returning to their argument. "You think you liven up our otherwise dull evening. But if we are so uninteresting, why do you bother: why do you talk to likes of us, or argue with us, or laugh at our cowardice?"

"I've already told you I'm bored," he said. "Talking takes my mind off things. And, besides," he added with a laugh, "you listen to my tales and laugh at my jokes."

"What does that matter?" she asked.

"I want you to be impressed by my cunning and courage, my noble and heroic deeds. Few other folk in the whole wide world know as much about me as you three."

"Why does that matter if you truly despise us?" asked Alwyn.

"Let's face it," said the assassin, "what other audience am I going to get now?"

"Your life doesn't sound exciting to me," added Fergus. "In fact your stories are pretty dull."

"Well, I've enjoyed it, o noble dung-shoveller," said Revile. "And my life is not yet over."

The farmer snorted. "I can't believe," he said, "you entertain any hope of escaping the noose."

"I don't," replied the assassin, "but the way I go to my death is a part of how I lived my life. I'll not ruin the end of my tale. Besides, friend Fergus, I've survived tighter corners than this and lived to spin a yarn or two."

"Would I enjoy your kind of life?" asked Alwyn. "I think it sounds quite exciting, going hither and thither, doing what you fancy."

"It's all right," said Revile, "but you would need to be tougher than you seem to survive."

"Perhaps," said the girl, not listening to him "I should have tried your adventuring way of life. It would not have been difficult to have stolen a horse and some provisions." And then she added sadly: "My life has been very boring compared to yours."

"Have you always lived in the Tower?" asked Margaret. "You said some thing about your father's lands in Caerwinnion."

"No, I've not always lived here," she replied, then laughed, remembering happier times. "I was born at my father's Hall in Caerwinnion. He is a lord of the Penti, of whom Ailred, Lord of

Pentland, is the king. Pentland has shrunk north and east, and now we owe allegiance to Sivard, King of Bernecia.

"Anyway, Caerwinnion is half a day's journey from Bamburg and on the edge of a wilderness. I used to wander in the hills and glens for I was ever alone. I wondered what lay beyond the borders of my ken. Was there a dragon's lair? Was there the tomb of some long-dead king? Were there the ruins of a lost temple? I would wander there in my dreams."

Alwyn paused, and the memories quickly faded. "I was ever alone," she repeated, "for my mother died giving me life – I never even knew her. She was my father's woman, but although he loved her dearly they never married. He was a lord and she was the daughter of a blacksmith. Yet my father and I were never close – I think I brought him much grief – although no child ever had more indulgence or freedom. I was spoilt by the folk of the Hall. I wish I was back there."

She sighed. "As soon as I was old enough," she went on, "my father sent me away to Bamburg. He said he wished me to find a husband – but I reckon he wanted rid of me. He took the death of my mother hard, and they say I'm very like my mother. Besides, when he dies I would have had no home for I am a *bastard* and can't hold land in Bernecia. So he sent me here, to the court, arranged I should work for the queen. It has not been hard work but I miss wandering in the hills.

"Anyway, I had some suitors but none to my liking. I was friendly with Bregorin – I suppose I flirted with him. He wanted to take me as one of his many mistresses. I refused. I wanted more. For once I said rather more than I should have. And that is how I ended up here, in this dungeon, waiting to be hung."

"Why on earth did you refuse the prince?" asked Margaret in surprise. "If he offered me the chance I would've taken it full willing!"

"I ...," Alwyn hesitated, "... don't know. I guess I was foolish. I wanted to be more than a mistress."

"You are foolish," said the older woman. "Stupid even. I can't believe anyone values their chastity so highly!"

"Not you certainly, Margaret," said Revile. "A mouldy piece of bread would be the unlocking of it, I don't doubt. But, Alwyn, she's right. The other three of us are hanged as surely as the sun will rise. Only a miracle will save us. But you, you should call for the prince. Tell him you've changed your mind."

"It is too late for that," said Alwyn angrily. "Much too late. I just couldn't! And I have said too much to Bregorin to seek mercy from him now."

"O well," laughed the assassin, "it has a certain style, I suppose. Some things are more valuable than gemstones. But if by some miracle you should escape, I wouldn't set your mind on the real wilderness. It is a perilous place, full of danger and wild beasts, and those that go on four legs the least of your problems. There are outlaws, shunned men, always willing and able to slit the throat of an unwary traveller. There is the cold and rain and hunger, where a full belly and a warm bed become only memories. You are free to wander where you desire, free to choose where to starve, or be lonely, or where to be murdered in your sleep or torn to pieces by ravening wolves. It is a great life, to be sure."

"Then why do you do it?" asked Fergus. "Why do you live that way if it is so awful?"

"I would have no other life, peasant," replied the assassin who had not insulted the farmer for some minutes, "certainly not one where my only pleasure was to be found with the soft, woolly bodies of sheep."

Fergus ignored the insult for once.

Margaret shivered. "It's cold," she said, changing the subject, gritting her teeth. "Very cold. Do you think we'll sleep tonight?"

"Do you want to?" asked the farmer. "I want to savour the last hours of my life. I've never felt less like sleep."

"Yes," shivered Revile, caught by a memory, "it reminds me very much of a time before. I was imprisoned in the black hold of a slave ship. And that was a darker time than even this."

"You were a slave?" asked Margaret. "When?"

"Some years ago," said the assassin. "Aye, I was a slave, taken on a ship by the Men of Thule, by raiding Vikings. I was younger then. I was enthralled for over a year."

"Were you a good slave?" asked Alwyn.

"I guess so," said Revile, "I never got beaten once. I'll tell you about it but it's a long tale."

"What else have we to do?" said Alwyn. "You have a captive audience."

"Yes, tell us," said Margaret, "and I hope it's not as dull as your last."

The assassin grinned. "I'll do my best," he said.

The Jarl's Daughter

It was night, a night that is starless and moonless and as black as the Earl o' Hell's waistcoat. The wind howled like a demented demon and hurled sheets of rain and sleet across the foaming sea, thrashing the small islet known as the Brough. A few twinkling lights, for the most part hidden by the spray of waves, shone out from the fastness of Jarl Thorfinn the Ugly. Yet within the rough stone buildings little of the outside violence made itself felt – the rattling of shuttered windows and drips from the ceiling were all that bore witness to the fury of the storm.

In the longhall of Thorfinn, a great feast was in full progress to celebrate the betrothal of the Jarl's daughter, Ingioborg the Fair. The low chamber was filled with billowing smoke from the hearth. Other less suffocating smells also hung in the air, the smell of dogs that rolled and capered for their masters, the smell of roasting meat slung over the hearth, and the musky smell of revellers and their unwashed bodies.

Many men sat at a table, which ran nearly the length of the longhall, between the dais at one end and the doors at the other. Most of the revellers were dressed in simple robes or furs, but those near the top, those above the salt, were garbed in colourful finery adorned with much plundered silver and gold, and they glinted in the flickering light.

The table was laden with wooden and earthenware platters and jugs, each filled to brimming with food or drink. The men were waited on by slaves, thralls who catered to their every whim and desire. Most of the slaves were young women captured in numerous raids on shipping and on the mainland.

Jarl Thorfinn, quite as ugly as repute reported, sat at a separate table on the dais. He looked down from his position, a huge horn of mead in one hand, a leg of pork in the other. Beside him sat the Lady Ingioborg, quite as fair as repute made her, nibbling at her food and sipping her wine. Both regarded the feast with the seriousness it demanded.

The feast was not a sober affair, and the Jarls, warriors and oarsmen roared, jested and brawled.

Not all found the feast so entertaining as those seated, or slumped, at the tables. One pale slave, a brand burned into the skin of his upper arm, was – indeed – quite miserable.

Revile toiled with steaming sides of mutton and pork that scalded his hands, he struggled with massive jugs and horns of ale that drenched his robe, he danced and pranced in a humiliating manner at the command of his masters. He suffered abuse and insult from all and sundry. An oarsman punched him on the nose, sending him tumbling across the floor.

They all laughed.

Revile was miserable. But that he showed nothing but complete servitude was a tribute to his self-control – and his well-developed sense of self-preservation. He did not even permit himself a sigh.

The feast continued well on into the new day and became wilder as the morning progressed. The Lady Ingioborg had retired for the night, and the celebrations were unrestrained and barbaric.

The young female slaves were dragged from their other duties and ravished on the table top or in the dirt of the floor amongst old animal bones and discarded drinking vessels. Not one of the girls made any protest and seemed to accept the inevitable with a weary resignation.

Other slaves were even less fortunate. One young thrall so displeased a warrior that he was roasted over the blazing hearth like a side of pork. Scorching flesh and burning hair added their own unique flavours to the reek.

Arguments began to develop between drunken and bleary-eyed revellers, and many fought, upsetting goblets and benches as they brawled. That few were seriously maimed paid tribute to the enormous quantities of food and drink consumed. Indeed a few revellers refused to fight being quite content to throw up – only to return to their feasting when they had finished.

Some performers were brave enough to attempt to entertain the revellers. A juggler foolishly claimed that he could juggle anything thrown at him. He quickly retired when a score of axes, a large table, and several benches, came flying in his direction. The juggler needed several pounds of extraneous ironmongery removed from his flesh.

Then a small theatre company appeared in the longhall to the sound of a proud fanfare. The players lasted nearly as long as the juggler. They had just begun their play when a warrior decided interfering with one of the actresses was more entertaining than watching the play. The warrior quite quickly found the actress was in fact a young lad, and was not overly delighted with his discovery. What happened then was not pleasant to behold. Even Revile winced.

The only performers to escape the fray were the mysterious, half-mystical bards. They told the tale of the raising of the House, and the inexplicable doings of the Northerner's warrior gods. When at last the stories were finished, a hush fell over the chamber, and all those at the feast rose to their feet to drink a toast – all those that could anyway.

Jarl Thorfinn the Ugly struggled to stand. He addressed the revellers, but it was impossible to make out what he said – his speech was distorted and slurred beyond the measure of ordinary men. The assembled throng cheered and hooted anyway.

As the morning waxed, the revellers fell asleep where they sat or lay, sprawled on the table or a bench or on the floor in a pool of vomit. There were no more entertainers to hold their interest, their baser desires had been satisfied to the full, their stomachs were bulging with food and drink.

Before too long the only sounds in the longhall were those of men snoring, the crackling of the fire, the quiet conversation of one or two of the most hardy individuals, and the rasp of settling bowels. Revile was as tired as any other, and longed to find his own bed: well, not a bed exactly, more of a corner in a byre or sty. But just as he considered leaving the longhall, he noticed Jarl Thorfinn was watching him.

"Come," slurred Thorfinn, living up to his byname ably, "in my own house I should not have to drink alone!"

66

Revile approached his master cautiously.

"Come closer," said the Jarl, clearing a place at his side by pushing the lord of Birsay from his chair. The lord fell backwards into an untidy heap but did not awake. "Come," went on Thorfinn, "closer so I can speak to you. What is your name?"

"I am called Goat," replied the slave.

"Well, Goat," said Thorfinn, "come sit by me."

Goat the slave climbed onto the dais and seated himself next to Thorfinn. The Jarl handed him a bejewelled goblet, and the thrall sipped at it warily. Thorfinn peered at him, and it seemed to Revile there was intelligence in the ugly stare.

"So," said Thorfinn with a gleam in his eye, "what is your real name? What did they call you before you, ah, joined us?"

"My real name, my Jarl?" swallowed Goat. "It is Goat, I am permitted no other."

"Of course," murmured Thorfinn softly. "Where did we find you?"

"I was travelling from Llaith in the south when a storm blew the ship far off course. I was a merchant but had recently fallen on hard times and this journey was a last attempt to save my business. Anyway, the ship was, ah, liberated by your men. They would have killed me, but I was unarmed and they knew I was also harmless. In their wisdom, they brought me here so I might find a better living, serving at banquets and all other manner of essential duties."

He fell silent, swallowing several times more.

"So you were a merchant, eh?" said Thorfinn. "What did you trade?"

"Hides and pelts, my Jarl," replied Goat. "They fetched a good price in the south, but the supply has dried up. I traded them for wines and rare perfumes, delicious perfumes. I can almost smell them now."

Thorfinn's eyelids half closed and he yawned. "No matter," he said sleepily. "No matter. I grow weary, I think I will sleep now." The Jarl slumped over the table top and began to snore loudly.

Goat the thrall was left alone with his master, wondering what he should do, for Thorfinn had not given him leave to go. Goat turned his head to the Jarl's great axe hanging from the wall behind him. A malicious grin spread across Revile's features. But almost as quickly the expression was gone, and the assassin remained Goat the slave.

Goat sighed, waited a while longer, then wearily left the chamber.

Once the thrall was gone, Thorfinn's eyes flicked open and he raised his head slowly, placing the hidden dagger thoughtfully on the top of the table. He disliked and distrusted the slave called Goat, yet had found nothing to substantiate his suspicion of the man. Thorfinn the Ugly had missed the murderous smile that so easily transformed Goat's normally servile features.

Thorfinn shrugged, retrieved his axe from the wall behind him, and lurched from the longhall for his own apartment.

When it finally became light – a light which could penetrate the still raging storm – those in the longhall began to stir. They suffered terrible hangovers, their eyes vacant and red, tongues grainy and dry, as if they had eaten shingle off the beach. Men staggered about, searching for water to freshen their mouths or faces, or merely sat, holding their heads.

Goat the thrall was more cheery than usual, even singing a few verses of a bawdy ballad. This was due, in part, to the rather foolish thievery committed by the very same man who had blooded Revile's nose the previous evening. It seemed this man had robbed many of his companions during their sleep and the stolen articles were badly hidden about his person. The poor man was set upon by his companions and badly beaten.

But by then, Goat had made himself scarce. The thrall was in the sty, dutifully cleaning out his fellow swine.

II

Several days later, Ingioborg the Fair, and her sizeable entourage, prepared to depart for the south, for the lands of her betrothed, Alfred, Lord of Dunstaneburg, in the realm of Bernecia. Goat was a baggage carrier, and would go on the journey as the obedient slave of Jarl Thorfinn the Ugly.

By midday, the colourful party was ready to leave the Brough. Goat was weighed under by a small cask of ale, his back bent, his face already shiny with sweat, waiting for his master's order.

The Lady Ingioborg sat on a magnificent white palfrey. She was dressed in the softest, finest furs and a magnificent silk robe as her lofty station merited: the cloak and robe were part of the plunder from the ship on which Revile had taken passage. Much gold, too, she wore: around her slim neck and wrists, hanging in cascades from her ears, buckled about her slender waist, laced through the tresses of her hair. Her skin was white and pale, as if the sun feared to touch her; her eyes dark and blue, secure in their command, haughtily gazing at the assembled party.

Ingioborg was as lovely a vision as a man could have set eyes on. She would make even the most powerful and venerable king a worthy wife.

Revile sneered inside. Looks could be deceiving.

Her entourage of warriors matched her for dress if hardly for looks. The party accompanying here was large, both to protect the sizeable dowry and to provide comfort and amusement for Ingioborg on the journey south. Over two hundred captains and men rode or marched behind their Lady. There were nearly as many slaves.

Thorfinn had no wish to leave his island realm, and his parting with his daughter was as brief as it was sweet. The Jarl was in an uncommon good mood, perhaps because Ingioborg had at last found a husband. Thorfinn smiled slightly – Alfred of Dunstaneburg had not met his betrothed.

The party moved off, crossing the causeway separating the Brough from the main island. The weather was fine and crisp, and the sun beamed down from the clear autumn sky. First went a troop of the Lady's bodyguard and the emissaries from Dunstaneburg, riding small shaggy ponies. Then Ingioborg herself, on her magnificent horse, towering above the riders flanking her. And finally, making up the rear, the slaves and wains of provisions and plundered treasure. Goat hoisted the cask further up his back, trudging in the wake of his masters.

Goat the thrall was dripping with sweat by the time the party reached a dingy haven on the southern shore of the main island. People lined the muddy street or stared from their hovels. Some cheered as Ingioborg rode past. She did not bother to acknowledge them.

When they arrived at the shore, the wains were unloaded and their contents transferred to three large longships moored in the shelter of The Flow. Ingioborg's vessel was a huge double-prowed ship with eighty oars and a massive red sail. Goat peered at the longship from under his cask. He supposed it was sea-worthy enough but was not convinced. The thrall disliked the green ocean, and travelling upon it, and to him the longship looked flimsy, a toy to be smashed by whim of wave and weather. Goat toiled with the other slaves, carrying sacks of oats and vegetables, kegs of water and wine, barrels of herring and salted mutton, chests of gold and jewels. Until finally, with many sighs of thanks, the longships were loaded and ready.

To many shouts of farewell, the three longships slipped their moorings and made their way out of The Flow, men straining at the oars. Before too long, the purple hills of the islands disappeared into a silver mist. The ocean was calm, and the vessels skimmed over the water without effort.

Goat the thrall brooded, his mood gloomy. As later events were to prove, his dark thoughts were well founded.

The longships gained the coastline of the mainland the same morning and followed the shore eastwards, sailing just in view of land to avoid skerries and reefs. There was always the possibility of storms, especially in the late season, and the coast was dinted with bays and havens where ships might seek shelter if they could not run for the open sea.

Goat had spent the afternoon emptying the bilges – unnecessarily as it happened for the longship took in little water. It was, however, a disgusting task and the thrall stank even in his own nostrils. The other slaves shunned him, although Goat did not seem to mind.

Later that same day, it was decided to make port at the haven of one of Thorfinn's kin, Ragnir Haroldson. This decision was not made purely for comfort – although it was true Ingioborg had demanded to be put ashore – but also because the captain reckoned there was a storm brewing to the north and east. As night fell, the three longships made the haven with the wind strengthening and veering. The crew and passengers were glad of friends.

The settlement at the haven consisted of a longhall, akin to that of Thorfinn, but not nearly as large. The hall was enclosed by a wooden palisade and built on a rocky rise a short distance from the shore. Surrounding the hall were several other buildings, thatched with turf, where animals were housed, food and drink prepared, and the slaves worked. Standing a little apart from the other buildings was a stone-built tower, round in plan, a broch of the old people. The wall was many feet high, and there was only one low entrance. This was Ragnir's treasury.

Goat and the other slaves were ordered to unload part of the cargo so that another feast might be held in honour of the Lady Ingioborg. Ragnir needed a flimsy excuse to feast even at the worst of times. The dowry was also transferred from the longships to Ragnir's treasury.

As darkness fell, the preparations for the feast were complete, and as the sun slipped into the sea those in the longhall rose and drank a toast to Ingioborg from a huge horn. Goat the thrall served at the feast but afterwards remembered little more about it. Undoubtedly, it was as delightful an occurrence as anyone there could recount. But better was to follow.

Eventually, after hours of merriment, the party broke up, and Goat slept in a corner. The few remaining hours of darkness passed all the too quickly and Goat woke early the next morning. He stretched and yawned tiredly, helped himself to unguarded food from the table, then lay back down in a feigned sleep. The storm which had been threatening the night before had evaporated like the memory of a nightmare.

Sometime after the first heralds of the morning peeked through the holes in the ceilings and walls, a slave ran into the longhall shouting wildly. Some of the dozy revellers stirred and angrily muttered. But the slave would not hold his peace .

"My Jarls! My Jarls," he cried, "the boats are sunk, the boats are sunk! My Jarls!"

Ragnir was called, and he emerged from the bowels of the longhall looking haggard, dishevelled and angry. "What is it?" he demanded. "Why have you woken us?"

The young slave trembled. "My Jarl," he whispered, shaking like a jelly, "the longships are sunk, the crews and sentries gone."

Ragnir said nothing in return. He sprinted the length of the hall, still dressed in his undergarments. Such men as could followed him, snatching weapons from their gear. Goat ambled after them.

Outside the palisade, there was chaos. Warriors, oarsmen and slaves ran about without purpose, as if to a man they had been struck down by some nervous disease. But the longships had gone, gone from the moorings. They had been smashed to pieces. Shattered timbers and pieces of wood were strewn across the calm water of the haven and washed up on the beach. There was much other gear also: barrels, oars, rope, fragments of the sails, other debris. It was as if a mighty wave had risen with the wrath of the gods and unleashed its fury upon the longships.

"What has happened?" cried a man in disbelief. "What could have happened?"

Ragnir Haroldson raised his hand and speculation ceased. Sanity returned for he showed no emotion. "My people," he told them, "a tragedy has befallen us. I cannot explain what has happened. A freak wave must have devastated the haven, perhaps from the storm. The ships have been wrecked in this way. Perhaps those of the watch who survived can tell us what happened?"

"Ragnir, my Jarl," answered the steward of the settlement, Ironhelm, as if he knew his words would displease his master, "my Jarl, the watch are gone, and those of the crew who stayed on the longships. We have found no bodies, although they might have washed out to sea." He faltered. "The treasury has been broken into, much of the dowry stolen, much of our own treasure also taken. There is no sign of a struggle. I think we have been betrayed and robbed by

70

our own folk!"

Momentarily, Ragnir's shoulders slumped. "Has it come to this?" he muttered. "My own men would turn traitor for a few baubles?" But when he addressed his men it was strongly: "Despair not, my people, despair not."

Revile had not realised he was despairing, but took Ragnir's advice.

"This is not a disaster," Ragnir went on, "although many of you may think it is. Our ships are destroyed but they can be rebuilt, the dowry is lost but it can be refound. All we need is some time.

"You," he said, indicating a woman, "the Lady's maid, wake the Lady Ingioborg and tell her what has befallen but make no mention of the lost dowry. Tell her rather that only the ships are destroyed. Go now!

"And you, Ironhelm, take what men as can be spared from the defence of the Hall and search out these thieves. When you catch them, return them to me unharmed if possible. I wish to pay them myself for their betrayal, such wealth of suffering and torture that they will richly regret stealing this treasure."

Men scurried off to do their master's bidding, some to fell trees for the building of new longships, others to arm and provision for the chase into the hard bleak moorland and hills which backed the haven. Ragnir, himself, disappeared into the hall to dress, and then inform Ingioborg of the unhappy news.

Goat the thrall frowned as he peered around the bay. He knew if he had stolen the dowry he would have tried to escape in one of the longships. These men were never too happy away from the sea. It seemed unlikely mariners, burdened with a huge amount of treasure, would flee into a pathless wilderness without food or even four-legged transport, especially when they were certain to be followed. The destruction of the longships and the robbery had to be connected in some way.

But his thoughts were interrupted by the ire-filled Ironhelm, and Goat the dutiful thrall scampered off at his master's bidding.

The rest of the day passed slowly as Goat stripped branches and bark from fallen logs. He worked in a shady copse that clung to a side of the long steep glen behind the Hall. It was hot work in the midday sun, but he had become hardened to such labour since his capture. He would normally have found this work pleasant, a break from the degrading and often perilous waiting at table, but he was worried. His fears took no solid shape, yet they nagged at him like toothache. He could do nothing but wait.

During a quick break for a snatched meal, Revile stood and watched Ironhelm and his men set off into the wilderness. The steward had found a badly-concealed trail, and even one or two pieces of gold. Revile wondered what they would find. It was as if they were supposed to follow the trail.

When Ironhelm and his party had disappeared from view, Revile stripped off his sodden woollen shirt, then resumed his wood cutting. Scars criss-crossed his lean frame and muscles relaxed and bunched with the easy strokes of his hatchet.

A warrior near him noticed the many scars and stopped his hewing to curiously regard the thrall.

"Were you always a slave?" he asked. "If I didn't know better I'd have taken you for a warrior yourself. Did your luck so desert you?"

Revile grinned ruefully. "Perhaps," he replied, "for the Fates are not always kind, even to warriors. I reckon some god has played a cruel joke on me."

"So it would seem," said the warrior, "and not, I think, just on you, my friend."

The two men, slave and warrior, continued their work in silent companionship.

As the light faded, the men left the copse and made their way back to the settlement through the opened gates of the palisade. The warrior who had spoken to Revile handed him a skin of ale and then made his way into the longhall. Goat scrubbed sweat from his tired body and cleaned his robe as well as possible. Finding a quiet spot, out of the way, he sat down against one of the outbuildings, hoping his absence would not be noticed. He breathed deeply of the cool night air, ignoring the shivers which racked his body.

They would help to keep him awake.

The longhall was awash with light from the flickering torches and open blaze. Ragnir Haroldson sat at the head of the table with Ingioborg the Fair to his right and his young son, Bjorn, to his left. Ragnir indulged the Lady in polite conversation as she daintily nibbled at her meal. In truth, Ingioborg heard little of what he said. She, the daughter of one of the most-feared pirate-jarls of the north, found Ragnir dull and uncultured. She had been more than displeased to find her journey delayed. Ingioborg waited as patiently as was possible for a moment when she might leave the feast and retire to her own chamber.

The feast was, anyway, a half-hearted affair. There was little laughter and no tales. The men, slaves and freemen, were exhausted by the day's work. The gathering was about to break up – and Ingioborg had risen to her eager feet to retire – when there was a loud hammering on the outside of the doors of the longhall. The chamber fell silent. Ragnir's face lightened with the thought that Ironhelm might have caught the thieves and recovered the dowry.

"Enter!" cried Ragnir. "Enter!"

The doors creaked open and Ironhelm strode across the threshold and into the chamber. His helmet was of a strange southern design, with a long noseguard and chin strap, and it obscured his face. His boots and cloak were muddied and befouled but he walked up the chamber with a swagger. He approached the head of the table, saluted with one grubby hand, the other fidgeting with the hilt of his sword.

"Greetings, Ragnir Haroldson," said Ironhelm strangely, his voice muffled by the helmet. "I come with tidings, grave tidings of treachery and thievery and death." But he could not conceal the laughter from his voice. "Aye, grave tidings!"

"Did you find the stolen treasure?" demanded Ragnir.

Ingioborg threw Ragnir a surprised and angry look.

"To be sure," answered Ironhelm, "we found the treasure, we found the thieves also and brought them here with us. For was that not your command? Aye, I would do nothing but obey such a noble lord's command!" The tone was mocking. "Such a noble lord!"

"Are you drunk?" asked Ragnir angrily. "Or are you wounded, man? Have you forgotten the Lady Ingioborg's presence? Remove your helmet, Ironhelm, and tell us what has happened?"

"Do not be angry, I beg," replied Ironhelm, sounding aggrieved. "I have undertaken a terrible journey on your behalf. For I only did what you desired, as I do now."

"What is wrong with you, man?" demanded Ragnir.

The steward laughed, removing his helmet.

Ragnir Haroldson collapsed back into his chair in shock. Ingioborg screamed, her eyes wide in terror.

Ironhelm's head had been cloven, his skull spilt to the brain. His features were masked in blood and gore. He slavered in pleasure. For it was not just his hideous wound that made Ragnir gape and stunned those in the longhall to fearful silence.

Ironhelm's eyes were jet black, without iris or cornea or pupil, black sockets in a tortured face. It was as if his skull had been filled with the outer void and his eyes were windows into the black.

The demon dribbled in delight, ignoring Ragnir, savouring Ingioborg's flesh as if he wished to devour it. The Lady could not break the stare until the thing that had been Ironhelm first bowed slightly, then threw back its head in mirthless laughter.

His attention returned to Ragnir Haroldson.

"Well, are you not pleased to see me, my friend?" said Ironhelm, sounding hurt again. "Is this the way you treat your most-trusted companion? No matter. I am sorely grieved but bear the pain well, do you not think? For I have paid a great price in obeying your orders, a great price – none greater, indeed!"

Ironhelm paused for a moment, sneering.

"I would continue with this, mortal," he went on, "but, unfortunately, I have so little time. Maybe we can talk again later when we are alone in the darkness. I have many games to delight you! But my orders must be obeyed. Shame it is! A great shame! For you have much pride, Ragnir, and it would give me pleasure to unravel your arrogance with your entrails. The delay can not be afforded." There was genuine regret in his tone. "A great shame!"

Ironhelm-demon took a dagger from his belt, the weapon glowing at his touch. Ragnir Haroldson could only watch as the dirk was stabbed into the young Bjorn, piercing his chest to the hilt. The lad gurgled and black steam wafted from his nose and mouth and ears, curling lazily to the ceiling. Bjorn Ragnirson writhed in agony, then slithered off his stool to the floor.

With a tremendous wrench of will, Ragnir broke the demon's compunction. In a fluid movement, he whipped the sword from the wall behind him and struck the demon with all his might. The blade of the weapon melted away like butter in a fire. Ragnir's hand was scalded.

Ironhelm gave out a huge bellow of rage which made the walls of the chamber shake. He threw down the dagger and grabbed Ragnir's head, gripping with molten fingers as cold as the abyss. Ragnir struggled uselessly, his hair flaring into black fire, unable to break the hold. Ironhelm increased the force, his hands crushing Ragnir's skull as surely as a man might crush an egg.

73

Finally, the demon's strength was too much for mortal flesh and bone, and Ragnir's head shattered over the floor and table, splattering Ingioborg with charred brains. The girl sat in unmoving fear and silence, not even uttering a cry of terror.

"Do not worry, my lovely," fawned Ironhelm, a reek rising from his palms. "I shall not hurt you, more is the pity. O no, I shall not hurt you. There is much better to come, to be sure!"

Ingioborg reeled back, falling from her chair to sprawl in the ruin of scorched flesh which had once been Ragnir's head.

Other figures entered the longhall, in guise of mariner or warrior or friend. The demons attacked the men and women of the place without regard for their sex or status. Oarsmen and shipwrights, freeman and slaves, were taken with little resistance, struck down by a companion they had once known well, or a lover, or a brother, or someone dear to them. But all their former companions had eyes as black as the deepest pit of Helgard. Bodies were crushed and gouged, beaten with their own detached limbs, trampled underfoot, dismembered – until the floor was wet and sticky with blood and gore.

Not one person escaped from the longhall of Jarl Ragnir Haroldson, kin of Thorfinn the Ugly. Neither freeman nor slave, man nor woman, warrior nor thief, remained alive when the demons had finished their work. Then, with a forlorn wail, the demons left that place and returned to the haunted realms of darkness from whence they came. Forever afterwards Ragnir's haven was an evil place where it was said the shades of lost souls roamed, repeating some grisly doom until the world was ended.

Yet no tale ever reached the Brough of Thorfinn the Ugly, secure in his fortress; or rumour to Alfred, Lord of Dunstaneburg, in the realm of Bernecia. Only one adventurer ever found out the truth of what happened to Jarl Ragnir Haroldson, the last of his House.

III

Those outside the longhall fared better for they were attacked by human foes, and those who did not resist were bound and dragged away to one end of the palisade. Most of the prisoners were too bewildered to understand what was happening. Goat the thrall hid amongst the rest, trembling and shaking as if his bones had turned to jelly.

Then Goat felt a presence, a strong and malign presence which approached the settlement from the haven: a presence which added by degree to the evil that hung over the longhall. The assassin's heart almost stopped. He had never felt anything like it. A figure, clad in a shroud of deepest black, walked through the opened gates and to the doors of the hall. The hairs at the back of Revile's neck rose.

A hush followed and the wind died.

The atmosphere was tense and potent. There was a terrible wail, loud at first, but receding as if to a great distance. The dark figure peered through the doors for a moment more, nodding his head as if satisfied by what he saw, his teeth glinting in a grin. He strode into the longhall, emerging a minute or two later, effortlessly carrying the blood-spattered Lady Ingioborg. He

74

barked an order at a soldier with a plumed helmet. The language was not familiar to Revile who thought he had a working knowledge of most tongues of the North.

The soldier with the plumed helmet hurried over to the prisoners. "Come," he commanded in a harsh accent, "all of you come!"

Goat the thrall relaxed. It seemed he was not to die just yet.

The prisoners were led away, taken from the settlement to a strange ship moored in the haven. They were prodded aboard, shackled together on deck, then manacled in the hold of the vessel. The noisome cabin smelt of death, filth and despair.

The hold was closed and battened, the prisoners left alone with their misery in the dark. Revile smiled bleakly into the gloom and tried to get some sleep.

The journey south was not pleasant for any of those in the hold of the ship. The sea was rough for days on end, the stumpy vessel wallowing like a pig in the swell. Freezing water gurgled into the hold through the hatches, sloshing about the deck as the ship yawed or rolled or pitched or heaved or did all at the same time. The prisoners were neither fed nor exercised although water was provided for those, like Revile, who did not mind the green scum that floated on the surface. The stench of closeted humanity would have been unbearable under normal circumstances but none, now, noticed it.

The prisoners were manacled closely together. Revile sat, crushed between a large warrior and a young lad. His stomach was empty and he had repeatedly fouled himself. He sat, staring forward, his mind far away wandering in kinder places.

The warrior on his right cursed and swore, making empty threats of terrible vengeance against his captors. The lad to Revile's left was mostly quiet.

Revile, himself, made no sounds and he hardly moved – just enough to put life into his fingers and toes, and exercise his limbs. He ignored, as far as was possible, his unhappy plight, concentrating his energies inwards, dwelling on happier memories. He did know where they were headed, how long it would be before they got there, or what fate awaited him when they arrived.

The assassin just did not care.

The days passed into weeks. Time no longer had any meaning for the prisoners in the hold. They slept fitfully but woke to a greater nightmare than their imagination could invent. This had a profound effect on many of the prisoners, especially those men and women who had been free before the arrival of the dark ship at Ragnir's haven. The warrior beside Goat gibbered and muttered all the time he was awake, and he would struggle, crying like a child, while asleep as if he was tormented in his dreams. The slave, the lad, was also poorly and it seemed he would die before too much longer.

The nights were fiendishly cold and Goat and his miserable companions shivered and trembled in the hold. Revile took the young lad in his arms, embracing him tightly, sharing their warmth between them.

One morning the warrior finally died in his sleep. The assassin had grown weary of him. The lad, however, recovered a little. Revile was gentle with him for he was no more than a child.

"What will become of us?" asked the lad.

"I don't know," replied the assassin gently, "Don't worry about it. The future may never come."

The lad died the next night, Revile waking to find him cold.

One afternoon some weeks after the slaughter at Ragnir's haven, the ship made port, and the journey was finally over for the captives who had survived. That was not very many. By this time, surviving did not seem very important. Conditions had become truly appalling. None who lived would regard death in the same way again – many of the less stubborn or more sensible had died rather than continue in torment.

The hatch of the hold was opened, and those with sufficient strength shielded the blinding light from their eyes. Warriors entered the hold, stretching cloaks over their noses, some even vomiting. The prisoners were freed from their chains and then dragged outside, bewildered by the sudden change in events. Goat let himself be helped, rather than needed it, and struggled up a ladder out of the gloom. Turning back for a moment, he gazed at the shadowed form of the young lad. A frown transformed his features into Revile the assassin.

When Goat emerged from the hold, and his eyes had become accustomed to the light, he viewed the surrounding area with some interest. The ship had landed at an island or peninsula. It was a well-ordered place. Men and women, obviously slaves from their garb, toiled in large fields; black-robed priests, with a red eye emblazoned on their backs, marched about the many roads on their mysterious business; merchants and freemen flocked a market in the port; mariners swarmed over many merchant vessels docked in the harbours; troops of soldiery rode everywhere, escorting prisoners or dignitaries. One large body of dusky warriors awaited the dark figure Revile had seen at Ragnir's haven but the assassin did not see them leave.

Goat was taken from the ship down a ladder and onto the quay. It was hot and dusty, and the sea was clear and green. The port swept away along both sides of the bay, rising up the side of a hill towards a stone-built fortress. The buildings were white with shuttered windows and flat roofs, and many shops, stalls and taverns lined the waterfront. Crowds milled through the narrow streets. The slaves were led along the quay, past numerous ships and boats, and into the port.

They were taken to a bath-house, a low building, faced with columns and carved pillars. The slaves were told to wash in the clear, cool water of the many basins. They were given fresh clothing, a simple tunic; then fresh food. Goat ate slowly and with difficulty after his enforced fast, eating only a little. He felt better after the meal and grinned.

His companions were less lucky on the whole, either not having the assassin's hardy constitution; or having been beaten or wounded when they were captured. More than a few were led away, never to be seen again.

The slaves were taken through the bath-house and into another building, a prison. They were put in a large cell with many other slaves and captives. Goat learned from the prisoners that they were waiting to be sold in the following days. They were an unhappy bunch, although for good reason. If a captive was not sold within one week of entering the prison, he or she was sacrificed by the priests of The Black Orb on The Sabbat, or full moon.

Goat proved to be lucky in that he was purchased the very next morning. He went for ten silver pennies and was regarded as one of the best slaves on show. To his satisfaction, he was sold to a very-attractive young noble woman. She, however, regarded her latest purchase coldly. Goat's mobile features were carefully subservient and he took on a fawning manner, walking at her heels like a faithful dog. The young woman had him manacled with her other slaves.

He was delivered to a large estate a few miles inland from the port. The sun shone down and it was hot out of sight of the sea. Goat wiped his forehead. The cart rolled down the dirt road, through orchards and groves of olives and orange trees. Arriving at a villa, the slaves were taken from the cart and into a cobbled courtyard. The villa was a low sprawling building, built of some white stone, fronted with marble statues. Vines grew up one side of the villa on trellises and red flowers lined the edge of the court. The windows were glazed with glass of many colours, or closed with carefully painted shutters.

Goat waited as the others disappeared into the villa. He had been told to wait. Out of one of the doors emerged a large, bearded man. This fellow was Maddog, Goat had been told, the Lady's Master of Slaves. Maddog viewed Goat with distaste. Goat could only wince and tremble in fear at the terrible size of the Master.

"What is your name, slave?" demanded Maddog harshly. "What is it?"

"I am called Goat, sir," the slave replied with a lisp.

"You were, you mean!" growled Maddog, clenching and unclenching his huge fists. "From this day on you will be known as, ah, Worm! I have never set eyes on a more slimy, loathsome, low, spineless creature than yourself. If you take one step out of line – just one, mind you – I will skin you and nail your hide to the barn door! Do I make myself clear? Or shall I have it beaten into you?" He waved a well-muscled finger in Goat's face. "What say you, you slime?"

Revile knew any hint of defiance would result in a beating. "O yes, sir," he replied, "I understand perfectly. I'll do whatever you tell me. I am totally obedient. I would happily debase myself at your feet if that is permitted. I'll do anything you wish."

Maddog spat and a dob of spit hit Goat on the nose and ran down his chin. Goat started to weep, trembling in terror.

"Get this out of my sight!" said Maddog in frustration. "Get this slimy worm out of my sight!"

Goat was gently taken from the courtyard by another of the slaves and into one of the buildings at the side of the villa.

"Pull yourself together, man!" the slave told Goat. "There's no need for these tears!"

"I'm sorry," said Goat, manfully striving with his emotions, "I'm not usually like this. Its just the Master – Maddog was it? – is such a frightening fellow. I expect I'll recover in a minute."

"You were lucky in a way," mentioned the other slave. "Maddog usually has the new people beaten if they show anything but obedience. But, perhaps you knew this already?"

"No, I knew nothing of this," replied Goat, new tears welling in his eyes. "Beaten! Beaten? How bitter is life!"

His companion nodded. "My name is Dunghill," he said with a wince. "I think you did rather better with the Master's choice of names. Maddog has a strange sense of humour. Anyway, this is the estate of the Lady Theogigios of Heraglion. I suppose I should welcome you."

"Thank you, Mister Dunghill," said Goat. "My name is Worm it seems." He pumped the other slave's hand weakly. "How do you do?"

Dunghill did not reply. Instead he gave Worm a strange look, half of disbelief, half of speculation.

"Wait here," said Dunghill at last, "and keep out of Maddog's way if you can. Now and at all times for the Master is a cruel man and enjoys making us suffer. I'll introduce you to the others of the household when I have completed my duties."

Dunghill left. Worm sat by the fire, his head buried in his hands, his mind deep in thought.

Worm was lucky enough to be assigned to the villa to wait on table and do such menial tasks as were needed around the large residence. This mostly involved the preparation and serving of food. He also had to do the chores most despised by the other slaves.

He did not see the Lady Theogigios for several weeks. She was on business elsewhere on the large island, visiting her many estates and enterprises. Not only did Theogigios own groves of oranges, olives and other fruits, but she also had interests in shipping, the mining of iron ore and the making of weapons.

Revile had discovered the land was called Viriggia and at this he wondered. For the assassin had travelled widely in the world and yet had only chanced upon rumours of the infamous Viriggia during his wanderings. But he had not thought them any more than myths, inventions about a fallen civilisation which had perished hundreds of years before. It seemed Viriggia had risen again like the phoenix from the ashes, or an evil wraith from its tomb.

What stories he had heard were not encouraging. Viriggia was the last outpost of a people called the Viri, a war-like evil folk who once controlled a vast empire. The Viri revered the black arts: tales of their sacrifice and slaughter to the terrible gods of The Black Orb were still muttered in the South. Finally, the Viri had been defeated and the last remnant had fled south and west, harried by the barbarians upon whom they had preyed. And there they disappeared from history and legend, only remaining a cloud in the memory to overshadow the past.

That the Viri had appeared again to trouble the world would have caused dismay and panic in the civilised north and east. In truth, it caused the assassin little sorrow. He might prosper in lands beset by war as much as in the relative peace of the last few decades. His only concern was how he might elevate his lowly position and escape the duties of a slave.

Anyway, the work at the villa was reasonably easy although Worm made sure he was always occupied. He found that Maddog despised him – it might have been wiser and safer to have taken the beating – and Worm the slave had no wish to give the Master any excuse to punish him – or nail his hide to the barn door.

A few more days passed until one morning Worm was informed by the cook that the Lady Theogigios was expected home that very evening. Worm was to serve at the feast to be held in her honour on her arrival. He was told of the correct etiquette for such a feast – and he absorbed all such information carefully. He did not want to displease his new mistress. Worm dressed meat and prepared vegetables most of the rest of the afternoon. Then there was the polishing of the silverware, setting the table, tending the fires in the Lady's apartments.

By early evening everything was finally ready and the slaves relaxed in the kitchen with the cook. Maddog had left to escort the Lady Theogigios from a nearby tavern. The staff and servants were merry and they laughed and joked amongst themselves. Worm sat a little a part on a stool by the stove, mulling over his fortunes of late.

Revile the assassin, now Worm the slave, was not content with his lot in life – although this was far from unusual even at the best of times. It was true the last weeks had been an improvement over the time spent in the thralldom of Jarl Thorfinn the Ugly and his minions. But Revile's thoughts could not help turning to escape, or at least to a bettering of his position. He played the cowardly, cringing man, even acquiring a very realistic lisp which fooled one or two people of the weakest intellect. He was not sure how much longer he could maintain his act. Maddog would finally find some pretext to punish him and Helgard alone knew what would happen then. He also had no idea why the Lady Theogigios had purchased him.

Contemplating his situation for a while longer, a glimmer of a smile spread across his pallid features. Leaving the kitchen without a word to anyone, he searched for a friend who worked as a scribe, labouring at the accounts of the many estates and businesses. Revile spent over a hour closeted with the scribe, a man called Indulf, finally emerging from the hut with a phial of clear liquid and a large grin.

As night fell, ten sat down to dine in the hall of the villa. The hall was a grand, imposing room with Eastern rugs on the floor and frescoes covering the walls. A fire burned in the fireplace for it was cold after sunset, and many candles and lanterns lit the chamber. The beams of the ceiling were carved into beasts hiding amongst trees with details picked out in gold and precious gemstones. A table made of marble ran the length of the hall. It was richly laid with bejewelled goblets and plate, servers made of solid silver, candlesticks carved from jet and amber, knives and spoons fashioned from gold. Ten places had been set – although the table had room for many more – with ten dark hardwood chairs padded and sewn with silk.

Worm was dressed in a smart uniform with silver buttons. He had never worn clothes as expensively made as his tunic and trousers. There was even a pair of soft leather boots to match.

Of the ten diners attending the feast, Worm knew only two: the Lady Theogigios and Maddog, her Master of Slaves.

The Lady was a tall dusky woman in her late twenties. Her eyes were so dark they were almost black and her hair was like polished mahogany. She wore a crimson gown, laced with some red metal, finished off with cascades of glinting rubies. Her feet were bare, as were her guests', but around her lower legs were wound two enamelled snakes, striking from her ankles.

Maddog was dressed in a flowing robe of black and turquoise with baggy trousers. He carried a scimitar in a gilded scabbard, decorated with many green amethysts.

Five of the other diners were merchants. They were dressed similarly to Maddog although none of them was so tall or largely built. Each had hair as black as night and beards trimmed into the shape of a triangle as was the fashion amongst the Viri. They were also armed but with curved daggers.

Two of the remaining men were ranking officers in the Viri army. With black cloaks, robes and leggings, they were both martial in their appearance, men who would not shirk at a little murder. The two officers carried scimitars and helmets, plumed with black and red feathers.

The final guest was a priest of The Black Orb. He was soberly dressed in comparison to the others, wearing only a deep-coloured robe decorated with an eye picked out in red. The robe was belted at the waist but the priest carried no weapons. Despite this, Revile had never set his eyes on a more forbidding or cruel-looking man. If men could have black souls, then this priest definitely had one of the darkest tone.

Worm served drinks to the guests as they discussed events in Lasithii, the capital, and the doings of merchants and princes. He listened intently to their conversation, although his grasp of their tongue was not complete, hoping to glean some useful information. Revile learned quickly, but their tongue was strange to him and unfamiliar in vocabulary and structure. Anyway, most of what they said, while perhaps being amusing to the guests, was of no interest to Revile.

As the night lengthened, the conversation turned to a festival to be held on the third full moon, the Third Sabbat, in eleven weeks time. Worm had become bored and only stirred when he heard mention of the events at Ragnir's haven. Ingioborg was discussed. They also called her 'The Chosen' although why Revile was unsure.

Finally in the small hours of the new morning, the party broke up and the guests retired for the night. The Lady Theogigios tarried awhile in the dining room with Maddog. They talked quietly together. Worm refilled their goblets with more wine, emptying the phial of colourless liquid into Maddog's drink. He watched the Master of Slaves sip the wine.

Nothing happened for a few minutes, but then a strange expression passed across Maddog's hard face.

"What is the matter?" asked the Lady Theogigios. "Have you drunk too much again?"

"I think I must have," he replied in hoarse voice. "I feel very strange." He staggered to his feet, almost as if driven against his will. "My lady," he said, "I am consumed with passion for you. I find you desirable beyond all measure. I know you are an important, beautiful woman – and I am not your equal – but underneath I know you desire me."

"Maddog!" the Lady cried in alarm. "Don't joke with me! Stop this foolishness now!"

"My lady, I cannot," he murmured back, lust in his eyes. He took a step towards her. "I need you now!"

"Slave! Do something!" cried Theogigios as Maddog caught her by the arm. Slipping one hand down the front of her dress, his mouth sought her. There was a ripping sound as he tore at her dress.

Worm did nothing but tremble in fear.

Theogigios was pushed over the table, upsetting crockery and goblets as she fought against Maddog. The Master of Slaves pawed at her, pulling at her skirt, groping about her thighs.

At last, Worm summoned enough courage for action. Picking up the nearest weapon to hand, which just happened by chance to be a large carving knife, the slave plunged it into the exposed back of Maddog, burying the weapon to the handle. Blood spurted over Goat's hands. Maddog gave out a terrible cry and then fell silent. The Master of Slaves was dead, Worm had found his heart. Maddog dragged the Lady with him to the floor. Worm extracted Theogigios from the tangle of limbs and helped her to her feet.

"My lady, Theogigios," he began with a shake in his voice, "are you harmed?" But then, noticing the blood on his uniform and hands, he moaned, his bottom lip trembling. Theogigios thought he might burst into tears. Worm, however, managed to keep a hold on himself. "My lady," he said, "what have I done?"

"It is nothing," she said with a slight smile. Her breathing was heavy. "He would have ravished me." She shuddered slightly. "It was as well you were here."

Worm wiped blood from his hands onto the front of his tunic in nervous movements. There was a heavy knock at the door and two guards entered the dining room. They removed the heavy corpse of Maddog at the Lady Theogigios's command, leaving a sticky smear on the floor.

Theogigios poured her slave a goblet of some clear spirits. Worm gulped it down, colour returning to his cheeks.

"What is your name?" she asked, rearranging her clothing and pulling the gown tight across her breasts. "We have not met, I think."

"I am called Worm," he replied, averting his gaze.

"Are you, indeed?" she smiled. "And who called you that?"

"The Master," he swallowed, "Maddog."

"Hmmm," she said, "how unfortunate for him. Maddog ever had a way with names. Well, Worm, I think you and me could perhaps do business. It seems I need a new Master of Slaves. I trust you could carry out the duties? I purchased you hoping you might have some special talents."

"I would guess so, my lady," replied Worm, not sure what to make of that, and bowed.

"You may change your name if you wish," she went on, "for I do not wish to end up like poor Maddog with a knife in my back. If you get my meaning?"

Worm nodded.

She smiled at him. "Be careful," she told him, "my Master of Slaves. Maddog's death has benefited you, and it may be that you can now benefit me: I do not believe you have always been a slave. But if I was less kind I could have you tortured and slain for his murder. That is all. Things could have been different. Remember it well!"

"I will," he said softly. "I am grateful, my lady."

"I will tell you of your duties tomorrow," she said. "Go now. We shall talk in the morning."

Worm bowed again and left the dining room. The beautiful Theogigios let go her gown and sat on the table, a goblet in one hand. Her expression was thoughtful, but then she smiled: the slave called Worm might prove useful.

The new Master of Slaves went to the hut of his friend, Indulf the scribe, and the two men spent the rest of the night drinking wine.

There was some surprise at the events that night but if anyone was suspicious, no one said so openly. Most of the household were content to keep any opinion on the matter to themselves. The unfortunate demise of Maddog brought no tears or sorrow to the slaves. Although Worm was as strict as his position merited, he was well-enough liked and respected by those below him. Worm still assumed his lisping voice. His lisp only slipped once or twice, especially after a bottle or two of the vintage wine from the cellar.

The days passed quickly and Worm enjoyed his new found freedom.

IV

The Lady Theogigios of Heraglion and her entourage prepared to depart for Lasithii, the capital of Viriggia, for the Festival of the Viri, a great celebration which lasted for six days and six nights. The first day of the Festival would be the morning after the full moon, the Third Sabbat. Worm had taken a suite of rooms in one of Lasithii's best taverns. Several estate slaves were to accompany the Lady and her Master of Slaves, including Indulf the scribe. There was business in Lasithii which needed taking care of quickly.

The Lady Theogigios had prospered since making Worm her Master of Slaves. He seemed to have a strange talent for helping customers to find their money to pay off their debts. They both did very well together and she never regretted buying him.

The trip to Lasithii took a few hours. They travelled by covered cart but it was hot and thirsty work. The land about them was fertile and peaceful. There were many streams and rivers running from the mountains and they stopped at a bridge to paddle in the cool water, before continuing on towards the capital.

About midday, the party reached the outskirts of Lasithii, travelling through a region of large villas and country houses. They found the tavern near the centre of the town, a grand building of white marble and flowering creepers. Riding in through the gate to a courtyard, the cart rolled to a halt and the passengers got out. They were met by the taverner who took them through miles of cool corridors until they arrived at their rooms. The Lady Theogigios had a large suite of lavishly-furnished apartments, and Worm's chamber was similarly splendid. Every whim of the guests was speedily attended to – Revile had discovered some very damning knowledge concerning the taverner.

When the Lady Theogigios and her other slaves had gone, Revile sat down in a plush chair in his own room, a goblet of the very-best wine in his hand. Only Indulf the scribe sat with him, but he did not look happy.

"What do you think?" asked Revile of his friend. "We've talked about this before."

"I think you're mad," replied Indulf. "If you really want my opinion, I reckon you could be ↳ powerful enough here if you had the will. Put these stupid notions out of your head! I how the brat of the man who enslaved you can possibly be worth the risk, even if there ↳ance we could rescue her, which there isn't, and supposing he would reward you if

18

you do rescue her, which he won't."

Revile thought for a moment. "Then you're not in favour of my plan," he said at last. "Well, no matter. But can you get me into the Temple? That's all I ask. You needn't come any further than the doors. There is no risk for you!"

"O no!" said Indulf scornfully. "O no, there's no risk for me! What do you know of such matters, what do you know of the Five Magics? When was the last time you went for a wee jaunt around a massive temple brimming with soldiers and priests and demons: when was the last time you visited the Temple of The Black Orb? The moment I work any illusions, the priests will know! Sorcery is their ken, sorcery is their way of life, but all magic has the same source and the priests will sense mine. I don't fancy being a snack for a demon even if you do! The whole idea is insane, completely insane!"

"You dealt with Maddog easily enough," said the assassin, "I don't see what the problem is!"

"Maddog desired the Lady Theogigios, he wanted her," snorted Indulf. "Normally he had the restraint to contain himself but with the potion all restraint left him. It was a simple potion. These priests summon demons, by the Ring of Boggans! I'm out of my league, Worm, way out."

"Will you help me?" asked Revile. "That's all I want to know."

"I guess so," said the scribe tiredly. "To be honest, you give me little option. I am your slave."

"Good!" said the assassin brightly, slapping his companion warmly on the back.

Indulf the scribe eyed his friend with little affection.

V

On the eve of the first day of the Festival, two dark shapes made their way through the streets of Lasithii, hugging the blackest shadows and passing like a breath of wind. They approached a massive building which dominated the skyline of the town with its dome and high-crenellated walls and towers. Lights shone out from windows which peppered the dark facade – it seemed few of the occupants of the Temple of The Black Orb slept that night. The shapes crept to the bottom of a well-worn staircase leading up to the entrance of the Temple, up to the silver and steel gates. Torches blazed from the head of the steps, casting hideous light onto massive marble gargoyles and carvings adorning the entrance. Warriors dressed in black armour paced about, their watchful eyes peering about for any sign of intruders.

"What now?" whispered Indulf. "What happens now?"

"We wait," replied Revile softly, "here, until someone shows up."

"What happens if the bodies of the priests are found?" said Indulf. "They're sure to be discovered. Was there not some other way of getting robes?"

"No," said the assassin, "so relax. They won't be found until all this is over and by then it won't matter."

"I don't know why I listened to you!"

So they waited, for several hours. The moon rose slowly out of the east, a clear silver disc in the black sky. It was nearly full. Still they waited. The moon had almost reached its zenith before anything happened.

Indulf had been just about to suggest again they called the whole thing off when a group of hooded priests, dressed in the same robes as Indulf and Revile, entered the court before the Temple of The Black Orb. The line of men walked with bowed heads towards the stairs. The scribe sighed.

"Now!" whispered Revile, and the two companions joined the end of the long file of priests as they climbed the stair. They ascended without comment or alarm, following the shrouded figures to the top of the steps, passing the sentries and shuffling through the opened gates. They entered the Temple of the Black Orb. Nothing untoward happened.

Indulf breathed a sigh of relief as they slipped down a corridor away from the file of priests.

"I told you it would be easy," said the assassin, well pleased.

"O aye, a real ball of laughs!" snorted Indulf. "The only reason we've got this far is you'd need to be a complete moron even to contemplate entering the Temple. All we have to do now is find this Ingioborg, free her, fight a few hundred sorcerers with a few demons thrown in to make it interesting, then escape past these guards, who are obviously blind, deaf and witless, back through the gates chased by the rest of the Temple garrison! This should really be fun! What a fool I am to worry!"

"Hush," said the assassin mildly, "and remember if we meet anyone, try to bluff it out. Only use your powers as a last resort."

"Fine," muttered Indulf, "I just hope you know where we're going?"

"Ah, not yet."

"Well, I suppose it doesn't matter – after all, they're bound to have her signposted!"

Revile ignored that and headed off down a corridor, followed more reluctantly by the still-muttering scribe. The passed several doors on each side of the passageway as it sloped down into naked rock, below the foundations of the Temple. Fear flowed out of the walls as they padded down the stone flags. Indulf found his mouth was dry and his heart was pounding in his chest. He had never done anything more foolish or dangerous than enter the Temple of the Black Orb. Monstrous shadows flickered, silhouetting the demon-decorated braziers. The assassin, nonetheless, seemed quite relaxed. Revile might have been a better actor than his companion.

They followed the corridor as it wound down into the earth until it bent sharply left. There was a door in the corner of the bend and Indulf noticed it was slightly ajar. Without even consulting his companion, Revile pushed his way into the room – as if he had every right in the world to do so. Indulf paused for a moment, and then followed the assassin, almost immediately wishing he had stayed in the tunnel.

They had entered a large, imposing apartment carved out of the rock. It was well furnished with a dark-wood cabinet, chair and chest, a bed, and an ornately decorated table. The scribe hardly noticed even this. His mind was concentrating in the fact there was another person in the room. A dark-haired dusky man, dressed in a priestly robe, sat at the table studying some papers. His features were sharp and he had cruel eyes.

84

"Yes?" said the priest in a sharp tone. "What is it? Were you not taught to knock? What are you doing near the dungeons?"

"I am sorry, sir," Revile replied in badly-accented and broken Virini, the language of the Viri, "but I was instructed to find you with all haste and barring any manners. This brother here is a physician ..." Indulf nodded. "... and he is to examine The Chosen for it has come to our ears she may have caught the terrible Prassass's Plague which afflicts some of the barbarian tribes. I would be grateful if you could conduct me to The Chosen directly."

"What business is this of mine?" said the priest. "I am the Keeper of the Dungeons not a forest guide! How dare you enter my chamber uninvited! Who are you? I do not recognise your voice. You sound like a barbarian yourself. Why are you dressed in the robes of a novice? Who, by The Black Orb, are you?"

At this point, Indulf sincerely wished he did know who the assassin was and cursed the day he had first heard his voice.

Revile, however, eyed the priest coldly. "The business is yours because it was ordered so," he said angrily, "because it was ordered, by the Black Orb. I wear the robes of a novice and disguise my voice because this matter is to be kept secret – not even the garrison should guess, no one in the Temple should guess, of this possible catastrophe. You are the only man of sufficient rank free at this hour. Do you think we would disturb you without due cause? Now, by the Black Orb, take us to The Chosen or I will personally see you are severely punished!"

The Keeper of the Dungeons gazed at the two visitors, feigning normality but the tension in the room was palpable. "O yes," he said in agreement, "you must forgive my foolish and rash words. I had not realised the import of the situation. I will take you to The Chosen directly," he licked his lips, "but first I must ask who sent you?"

"You question my authority?" said Revile. "It is the will of the Black Orb!"

"Indeed?" said the priest. "That is most interesting, most interesting. But I must ask you again: who sent you? Perhaps this is some kind of stupid joke?"

"Aye," said the assassin, "that it is."

Revile smiled thinly but before the priest could do anything more, the assassin threw a dagger from a concealed wrist sheath, the dirk finding a home in the priest's chest. The Keeper of the Dungeons collapsed over the table, knocking the documents and an inkpot to the floor. A pool of red blood spread from his chest and dripped from the edge of the table.

"Nice going," said Indulf.

Revile lifted the priest over to the bed, covering the corpse with a thick blanket. He retrieved his dagger, wiping it on the blankets. He pulled a rug across to hide the blood on the floor. Then, after making a quick search of the place and finding nothing useful, the two companions listened at the door before leaving.

"What now?" asked the scribe nervously. "Shouldn't we try to escape?"

"No," replied Revile, "let's go on."

Indulf snorted.

They left the chamber, shutting the door, and then continued on down the corridor as it descended deeper into the earth.

They heard a sound they had been dreading: the many booted footsteps of warriors rapidly approaching them. There was nowhere to hide except in the room they had just left. While they hesitated, four warriors came into view round a bend in the corridor.

The leading warrior seemed surprised to see the two priests. There was an expression of anger on his swarthy features. He wore a captain's plumed helmet and the warriors were armed with scimitars and daggers.

"What are you doing here?" the captain demanded, "you know you're not allowed in this area. What, by The Black Orb, are you doing?"

"What did you say to me?" snarled the hooded Revile. "Is that impertinence I hear in your tone? Who are you to question my doings?"

The captain took a step back such was the venom in the assassin's tone. "I am sorry," he replied more politely, "but I have my orders. I mistook you for novices, it would seem I'm mistaken. But, nevertheless, no one is allowed into the dungeons until dawn. I am sorry but I have my orders!"

"Indeed!" said Revile. "Then I suppose when a prisoner is needed urgently for sacrifice – or all tomorrow's preparations will have been wasted – then the Black Orb must be kept waiting. You may tell my master but I certainly don't want to."

"I will gladly tell them," answered the captain with a slight frown, "although it was them who ordered it so. Indeed, perhaps you could take me to your master after I have taken you to the Lord of the Guard so I can tell him also. I'm sure we can sort out this sorry misunderstanding!"

Revile sighed. "Very well," he said, "but I assure you this will result in your severe discomfort – and maybe even a demotion. But take me to this Lord if you wish."

The captain seemed unperturbed by the assassin's warnings, telling the two priests to precede him up the corridor.

"What is that I hear?" Revile asked Indulf. "Could it be the running feet of an armed band of barbarian intruders? Could it?"

"Why yes," said Indulf, "I believe it is."

"What?" said the captain from behind the assassin.

But then the sound of running feet came echoing down the tunnel, many feet, quickly approaching them.

"But how?" murmured the captain.

"Quick!" commanded Revile. "This is what I feared: they've broken into the Temple. They approach even now – you must protect us!"

The warriors pushed past the two priests, looking quite doubtful, but taking up a defensive position across the corridor, side by side. Around a bend in the tunnel appeared a large, heavily-armed band of northern barbarians shouting heathen war cries and brandishing axes and two-handed swords.

The warriors of the Temple were even more surprised but they hurried forward to meet the intruders. But when they met weapons with the Northerners, they were shocked to find their scimitars passed clean through the yelling band without meeting anything more than the air. By

86

then it was too late. They were more vulnerable to attack from behind. Revile stabbed two in the back, Indulf a third.

The captain belatedly realised the band of barbarians was an illusion, that his real enemies lay behind him. He whirled around on his heel, mouthing obscenities as his men fell beside him.

He stopped in mid oath. There were now eight robed men arrayed across the tunnel, not the two he had been expecting to see. The nearest priest lunged for him, the captain instinctively raising his sword to meet the dagger. His sword hit nothing but the wall. Another of the robed figures plunged an all-too-solid dagger into his exposed side.

The captain fell to his knees and then slid to the floor, a stupid look of confusion on his face.

"Are we discovered?" asked Revile.

"How, by Thor's scrotum, would I know?" replied the scribe. "But I have a mind the one or two corpses you've littered about may betray us ere too long!"

"You have a point," conceded Revile. "I think we better hurry. Come!"

They fled from the carnage, down the tunnel.

"That was pretty neat work," the assassin went on as he ran. "I never guessed you had such powers. It could be a useful skill."

"It was nothing," replied Indulf modestly, "the simplest of illusions."

"O well," said Revile, "if you say so."

As they descended even further, the atmosphere became hot and fetid. The tunnel was more roughly hewn, cracks and fissures across the walls and ceiling. The two companions slowed their pace as the smell became steadily worse.

"The dungeons?" suggested the scribe, out of breath. "Nothing else smells quite like it."

"Aye, I'd guess so," replied the assassin, wiping a bead of sweat from his nose. "I think we've arrived."

The tunnel widened and they slowed to a walk, expecting to find further guards. They peered round the last bend in the tunnel but there was nobody about. Iron-shod doors with rusty grills ran the length of the walls beyond sight. Other corridors led away from the main tunnel. There were dungeons enough to house an army of captives.

"By the Cross of Callanish!" whispered Indulf. "It'll take us a month to find her!"

They went on a little further. There was a large mosaic decorating the floor. It was in the form of a huge eye, outlined in red, with a black pupil, and covered the floor between the walls of the tunnel.

"Don't you think we should be careful?" suggested Indulf, hesitating before entering the dungeons. "It could be a trap."

"Don't be silly!" said Revile. "Its just decoration: don't be an old woman, Indulf."

He marched boldly across the mosaic and peered into the first of the prison cells. Indulf followed him more reluctantly.

There was a strange slithering sound. The two intruders whirled round. An iron gate came tumbling down from the ceiling, barring the entrance to the dungeons. There was a mighty clang, which echoed through the passageways and tunnels. Indulf ran towards the gate and rattled the bars. It was of solid iron and too heavy to move.

"Damn!" said Indulf. "'*Don't be an old women, Indulf.*' Well, it looks like we're trapped, you brainless git! Why did I ever listen to you?"

There was a huge deep booming noise like the sounding of a massive gong.

"What was that?" muttered Indulf. "Do you think it was anything to do with us?"

"I don't know," said Revile. The assassin went to the first prison cell and peered in through the grating. It was gloomy in the dungeon but he could just make out the hunched shape of a man against the deeper blackness of the wall.

"Well, that's not her," said Indulf from behind the assassin. "Unless she's grown a beard, of course."

"Thanks," replied Revile feeling a little irritated. "I would never have guessed. What would I do without you!"

The great gong sounded again. Indulf shook his head as the reverberations slowly died away. "What is that?" he muttered. "Some kind of alarm?"

They looked into many of the other cells but none of them contained the Lady Ingioborg as far as they could see. One did contain a young woman but that girl had dark hair and was of the Viri. Revile decided to open the cell door anyway.

"So," said Indulf, "how, by the Seven Serpents of Set, do we open the door?" There were no keys.

"I've thought of this much at least," replied the assassin, digging into his robe and removing a large bunch of strangely-shaped keys. "Should be able to get into anything with these."

But he could not open the lock and the cell door remained tightly shut. Revile cursed for the first time since entering the Temple of the Black Orb.

"Have you ever done anything like this before?" asked the scribe acidly. "Or is making a fool of yourself your profession?"

Revile eyed his friend for a moment. Once more reaching inside his clothing, he took out a lock-pick set.

To his frustration, he had no more success with the lock-pick than he had with the skeleton keys.

The great gong rolled away again.

"What do we do now?" asked Indulf, starting to feel nervous again. "We should get moving."

"We'll wait until someone show up," replied the assassin with a frown. "Besides, we can't get out."

The silence lengthened.

"Great!" muttered Indulf to himself after a pause, hardly able to control himself. He shook his head. "We just wait here until someone turns up! Brilliant! Where do you get this amazing tactical sense from, I wonder!" He stomped off down a new corridor, fuming away to himself.

Revile stood motionless for a moment, leaning against one of the cell doors. He needed to do some serious thinking. The gong rolled again, then he heard shouts and cries as the bodies of the four warriors were discovered. Running after Indulf, he caught up with him near the end of one of the side tunnels.

"They've found the soldiers," he breathed, "they'll be down here any minute."

The scribe swore violently at the assassin.

"Hang on," interrupted Revile suddenly, "where do those stairs lead?"

"Why don't we find out?" suggested his companion. "They lead up."

Without hesitating, they climbed the stairs as fast as possible. They sprinted up the steps four at a time until they reached a door in the wall. Both were gasping for breath.

They crashed through the door without hesitating and broke into a small temple. A rite of some kind was being held. A naked infant was bound to a small altar and his pale body was red with blood. Several robed priests were chanting some evil spell. The priests stopped and stared at the appearance of the two intruders.

"Ah sorry," blurted out Indulf over his shoulder. "Our mistake. Must rush." They ran through an archway and into a dimly lit corridor, leaving the angry priests to their rite.

The sounds of pursuit were closer now. The assassin and the scribe tore round an intersection, Revile sprinting head first into a bewildered warrior, felling him.

"Quick!" the assassin cried. "Stop these men who're following us. They're impostors!"

Revile and Indulf ran off. The warrior stood at the intersection looking wildly about him.

They turned another corner and started to ascend a steep passageway – but they slithered to a halt as more warriors approached, running towards them with swords drawn.

"O shit!" cursed Indulf.

They burst through another door to their left. Their breath wheezed and their hearts laboured, but the thought of what would happen to them if they were caught spurred them on.

They had entered a richly-ornamented chamber and they rushed through it into another room with a large table and a silver candelabra. They came to a broad set of gently-rising stairs. They climbed the steps in threes and finally came to a landing. Here they stopped short. To their left were the huge steel and silver gates with freedom beyond. But Revile and Indulf were not overly hopeful of escape. A strong body of armour-clad warriors waited there, spears and javelins at the ready.

Revile and Indulf slipped from the top of the stair into another corridor. The assassin suddenly had an idea. "Indulf," he said, "use an illusion to make them think we've escaped."

"What good'll that do," wheezed the scribe. "We still be trapped inside the Temple."

"It'll get the pursuit off our backs," said Revile.

The scribe shrugged. From the head of the stair two robed and hooded men appeared and sprinted towards the opened gates as if the Hounds of Hell pursued them – which was not that far from the truth. Just as they left the top of the stair, a large group of warriors hurried after them. Warriors also ran forward to intercept them. With superhuman dexterity and fleetness of foot, the two priests avoided the thrusting spears, eluded the warriors after a series of feints and side-steps, and managed to gain the gates.

"Shut the gates!" bellowed a voice. "Shut the gates!"

It was too late. The two priests ripped through the entrance and out through the gates just as they clanged together.

"Open the gates!" bellowed the same voice, sounding even more agitated. "Open the gates!"

When the gates finally ground open, the two priests had disappeared into the blackness of the night.

"You idiots!" said the voice. "Do you know what will happen to us? You've let them escape! This could mean death for all of us! Quickly, out after them! Arrest anyone you meet! Bring them back here."

Many warriors hurried out and ran down the steps to the court before the Temple.

Revile and Indulf slipped away, climbing a flight of stairs to the upper levels. There was no indication they were still being pursued but they went on warily.

"I've got to rest," moaned Indulf the scribe and illusionist, sweating profusely. The two companions listened at the first door they came to, and, hearing nothing, they tried the latch and cautiously entered.

The chamber was unoccupied and a large, spacious apartment, furnished with a polished hardwood table and thirteen upholstered chairs. Tapestries lined the walls. If they could not be said to be in the best taste – being of a rather cruel and distasteful nature – then neither of the companions had any complaint. They both collapsed into chairs, trying to regain their breath. Revile mopped his perspiring brow with the sleeve of his robe, grinning at his friend.

"So far so good," he said.

Indulf the learned scribe to the Lady Theogigios of Heraglion, and a scholar and illusionist of some standing and note, exploded into language which would not have shamed a low-born dock worker in the port of Llaith.

They rested in the chamber for some little time. Their respective heart beats gradually returned to something like normal. Occasionally, footsteps could be heard, passing outside the door. The two intruders would brace themselves for discovery. But each time the footsteps would recede without entering the chamber. This was very wearing on Revile's and Indulf's nerves. Even the flickering candlelight started to play tricks with their eyes. The figures and demons on the tapestries appeared to have gained a life of their own, staring and gesticulating at the two companions. Fear stole into the chamber, as the time lengthened, like a pale maggot into the core of a sound apple. Indulf shivered with the clamminess of sweat and fear. By unworded agreement, the two men rose to leave. Steeling themselves, they opened the door and stepped out onto the stair.

"Which way?" asked Indulf softly, trying to hide the tremble in his voice. "By the Five Circles of Mar, it's quiet!"

"We should go up, I think," replied the assassin, sounding just as nervous. He shivered. "Come," he said, "we should keep moving."

The whole building seemed to have become more sinister and brooding since they had entered the chamber. Terror and evil radiated from the walls. By degrees, the emanations were becoming stronger. The atmosphere was dry and cold like the breath from a defiled tomb.

"What's happening?" muttered the illusionist in a whisper as if the very wall might betray him.

90

Revile shrugged. "Whatever it is," he said softly, "it's not good, that's for certain. It's like the feelings at Ragnir's haven only much worse, even more powerful and malign." The assassin had told his companion about the events at Ragnir Haroldson's longhall. "I don't like it!"

"At least on something we're agreed."

The two intruders stole furtively up the stairway. The feelings of evil receded somewhat.

"Whatever is happening," whispered Revile, "is below us."

The stair came out onto a small landing with corridors leading off to the left and right. There was no one about so they turned into the right-hand branch for no better reason than it was well lit. The whole building was horribly quiet. They thought they could hear their joints creaking in the tense silence.

Padding down the passageway, but still making a good deal more noise than they cared for, they stopped at a pair of ornately-carved double doors, embellished with hideous gargoyle and demonic pictures. This part of the corridor was gloomy, although it had looked bright from the stair. The torches appeared unnaturally dim.

The two companions examined the door, listening closely. They only vaguely noticed a curtained alcove. So it was they at least had some warning when someone emerged out of the semi-darkness of the recess. There was a tinkling of small bells.

They spun round to confront whoever it was.

Both of them relaxed slightly. A tall woman appeared before them, clothed in a tight-fitting gown of some clinging fabric which emphasised the fine contours of her body. Silver thread was woven through the bodice, and silver bells tinkled when she moved, laced around her ankles and wrists. A veil covered her face but could not hide the aristocratic cheekbones and sensuous mouth.

"Can you help me?" she asked. "I am lost and looking for a man!"

The two intruders retreated for no conscious reason.

"What is the matter?" she said, pouting slightly. "I need a man desperately. Will one of you not help me? Am I so unlovely?"

She undid the clasp of her shift and the garment tumbled to the floor with a silky slither. She presented herself at them, revealing the naked delights of her body. She ran her hands over her breasts.

Revile and Indulf looked even more alarmed – of all the things they imagined might have happened this was the least expected. Both were at a loss.

"Do you want me?" the woman asked in a husky voice. "I want you."

Revile motioned to the illusionist to follow him in retreat, but Indulf was entranced as she seductively bared herself. Indulf took a pace forward, and then another. The girl smiled at him, running her tongue around her red lips.

The assassin watched the scene in horror, unable to shout or warn his friend.

The girl opened her arms in welcome to Indulf. He eagerly accepted the embrace.

"No!" shouted Revile at last. "Indulf, no!" He leapt forward, brandishing a dagger.

But he was too late.

As Indulf touched lips with the girl, he gave out a gurgling noise, a gurgling choking scream. The girl clasped him tightly and kissed him. Smoke from charring flesh wisped from contact with the woman. Her veil was ripped away revealing eyes without colour, eyes which had been filled with black, cold as the abyss.

Revile struck the demon-woman's hand with the dirk. The blade melted away and he let go of the hilt with an agonised cry. The blow had some effect, however, for the girl let go of Indulf and advanced on the assassin. Indulf twitched on the ground, blackened weals across his belly and chest, his lips mangled and scorched. He lay still.

Revile turned from the demon-woman and crashed off the wall. He sprinted away as fast as his legs would carry him. The girl followed at a more leisurely pace, an evil but quite enchanting smile across her face.

The assassin launched himself back down the staircase – but his head was swimming from the pain of his scorched fingers. He stumbled against a door which yielded inwards, sprawling into the same chamber where they had rested only minutes before. Scrambling to his feet, he put the heavy table between him and the door.

In a few seconds the demon-woman appeared. She smiled slightly, gazing at him with sockets filled with Helgard. Revile could not help but stare at her nakedness. Her skin took on the colour of warm honey in the candlelight. She was the most desirable and beautiful woman on whom the assassin had ever set eyes.

He swallowed.

"Come to me," murmured the girl. "Do you find me so unattractive you must cower behind a table?" She snorted, her nostrils flaring. "Or do you find men more appealing?"

She fondled her flesh again, letting out a small moan as her long fingers explored the soft skin between her thighs and abdomen, into the wisp of golden hair which flared there. "Come to me," she whispered, her tone almost pleading. "I am lonely and need loving." Her caressing became more frantic and wanton. "I need loving."

Revile was torn between lust for the fair evil girl and self-preservation. Although his limbs trembled and his manhood throbbed, he managed to remain where he stood.

"O, I see," she said, nibbling on one thumb nail, "perhaps you are shy. But I can cure you, that I can. Shame this table is in the way."

She leaned gracefully over the table, her nipples pressed against the polished surface. Then she stood up and elegantly, but with superhuman strength, threw the table to one side, smashing it against the wall.

She took a step towards him, and then another. Revile retreated further back but there was no escape. His eyes glinted like a trapped beast's. The girl shimmered in the light from the candles above her. The assassin could not take his stare from her body.

His gaze rose from her hips, up over her belly and breasts, and up to her eyes. There he was caught. He felt his soul pierced, a scorching fire of lust flared in him. His desire consumed him, he felt a great compulsion to walk those few paces into the girl's fiery embrace. The assassin fought his lust for no other reason than it was in his stubborn nature. He had little power left to

92

deny the demon-woman. He took a half-stride forward before he could check himself.

There was a noise behind the demon-woman. Revile managed to break the stare to look for the cause. Indulf stood tottering in the doorway, his face pale, haggard and shiny with sweat, looking more dead than many a long-interred corpse.

The girl faced him, smiling warmly.

"Ah, my lover," she said, "I fear I did not satisfy you to the full. Yet how much more of a man you are than this pale cringing creature. He spurns my advances. Come, let us make love again!"

"Stop where you are, demon!" gasped the illusionist, his face strained from the effort of speaking. "You took me for a weak and foolish mortal. But I am the mighty sorcerer, Indulf the Golden, and I will rend you with Prassass's Fire if you dare to move, I will banish you back to the frost of the Pit." His bold speech took so much out of him he was hardly able to stand.

The girl smiled. "I am at your command, my lover," she said. "Come and penetrate me with this manly fire. I am trembling at your pleasure."

The illusionist clung to the wall, feeling his way along towards Revile. He stood up straighter, standing beside the cord of the candelabra, swaying slightly from side to side.

"As you wish, demon," he replied, and he started mumbling and waving his hands as if he was casting a spell.

Nothing happened.

The demon-woman appeared disappointed, and she sighed. "I had hoped for something rather more than that," she told him, but then her face brightened. "But I have thought of something even better. Come, both of you. I have never had two lovers at the same time. You have teased me long enough!"

"Most beautiful vision," said Indulf, "you but leave me one recourse!" He took a dagger from his belt.

"Come then," she murmured, "come then."

The illusionist stood up more strongly. "Your passion would be too much for me the twice," he said. "You are too hot to handle." He swept his arm back as he spoke and cut the cord beside him. The silver and iron candelabra was freed from its tether and fell onto the demon-woman with a large crash. It crushed her under the great weight of metal.

She howled as her flesh was pierced but could not free herself from the candelabra. Gradually her efforts diminished until she lay still and unmoving. Her eyes dimmed until the black wavered and coursed, disappearing as if it was being sucked into some void. Her eyes turned blue, the whites returned.

There was a great relief from tension as if the last echoes of a mighty storm had passed. The girl became human again, blood seeping from where the candelabra stabbed her and soaking the carpet crimson. And, despite everything, on the girl's face was an untroubled smile as if she recounted some pleasant memory.

The two men looked at each other without saying anything. Words seemed inadequate to express their thoughts. Indulf could hardly hold himself upright and he staggered back against the wall.

After a long moment, Revile broke out of the trance. "Are you all right?" he asked Indulf, although he could clearly see the illusionist was badly burnt.

The illusionist sank to his knees, then fell unconscious. Revile hurried over to him, ignoring his own pain and the receding fear. The assassin found a pulse. He hoisted his friend on his back, staggering under the weight. Revile made his way back up the stairs and then laid Indulf outside the double doors.

Checking there were no more demons lurking about, he tried the handles and was vaguely surprised to find the doors were unlocked. He hurried into the chamber, dragging Indulf behind him. The corridors and passageways remained empty and quiet.

Revile closed the doors and, finding nothing to bar them, put Indulf across the threshold.

The chamber was used as a prison. There was a stone plinth in the middle of the floor on which the Lady Ingioborg slept, lying on embroidered cushions. Revile hissed through his teeth at the sight of her. Wandering over to the young woman, he tried to wake her but she was unconscious, enchanted or drugged. She did not stir even when the assassin slapped her with some force.

When he tried to lift her from the plinth, he found she was manacled about the wrists and ankles. The chains were thin but made of some very strong metal and Revile could neither break the links nor pick the locks. Eventually, the assassin gave up and went to the window, feeling a little disheartened.

He pulled the curtain aside and gazed out over Lasithii in the first shimmering of the dawn. He was glad to find the window was unbarred for he would, at least, be able to escape. The climb down did not appear too difficult. He stood for a moment more, pondering the situation.

Then, coming to a decision, he hurriedly left the room and hurried back down the stairs to the chamber where the demon-woman had met her demise. He took the cord which had secured the candelabra, then returned to Indulf. The assassin tied one end of the cord to the illusionist's chest, securing the other to the plinth. It was not an easy task to lift Indulf out of the window and lower him to the ground below – the illusionist was heavier than his build belied and Revile's hands were scorched. But somehow Revile managed it and Indulf gently touched the flagstones of the courtyard surrounding the Temple of the Black Orb. Revile gave out a long sigh of relief and blew on his palms.

To Revile's surprise, Indulf stirred and staggered to his feet. The illusionist looked confused. Then he noticed the assassin gesticulating from a window of the Temple.

Revile cursed. Around one corner of the Temple approached a patrol of the town watch, yawning and marching in haste to get to their beds. Indulf saw them too for he untied the rope from around his chest. Revile released the cord and it slithered to the ground. Indulf coiled it up and then shambled off into the labyrinth of narrow streets. The patrol marched by without a glance.

When they had disappeared out of sight, Indulf returned and stood below the window, resembling more a wraith caught in the dawn light, wishing only to return to its grave. But Revile just managed to hear the illusionist's voice wafting up to him on the gentle morning breeze.

"Revile, you're an arsehole!"

The assassin grinned. Indulf turned from the Temple and staggered out of the courtyard. Revile left the window for he did not intend to escape just yet. He went back into the chamber, ignored the Lady Ingioborg, and listened intently at the double doors.

He still had work to do.

VI

The new day dawned bright and fair. The sun emerged out of the mountains to glint off the gold dome of the Temple of the Black Orb. It was a beautiful day, all silver and golden.

If Indulf failed to appreciate any of the morning's beauty, or in fact any of the morning at all, he could hardly be blamed. The illusionist was in pain and although his burns had been tended properly and with skill, his wounds still throbbed in an excruciating manner which only massive quantities of strong red wine could dull. Despite his agony, his thoughts once turned to Revile. His companion was, as far as he knew, still at large in the Temple of the Black Orb. Of course, and far more likely, he might have been caught by now and was suffering such tortures of body and mind that the imagination of Mortals could not comprehend or dimly appreciate.

Indulf smiled broadly.

The illusionist also knew this was the first Day of the Festival of the Viri. He could barely hazard a guess at the demonic rite which was to be performed, imagining it would at least be unpleasant for himself – and probably a good deal more so for the Lady Ingioborg. Not that he cared one way or another he admitted, but he supposed he could pity her, albeit from a safe distance. After all, he liked to think he was a kind compassionate character.

Indulf spent the rest of the morning moaning like a spoilt child with an upset stomach, no matter how gentle the ministrations of his tenders.

Eventually the illusionist rose from what many had believed would be his deathbed, and, dressing in a new robe, demanded food and more wine. He ate with difficulty for his lips were scorched, trying not to scratch at his burns.

Over his meal, his mind turned to the previous night. He wondered how Revile had been able to resist the demon-woman's charms better than Indulf had himself. The illusionist was far more familiar with the type of spell which had been placed on them, but that made no difference. It occurred to him if it was not for the assassin he would be dead, but then he would have never been in the Temple of the Black Orb if it had not been for Revile. Yet there was obviously more to the assassin than met the eye. Indulf thought for a minute more, wondering how Revile had managed to restrain himself from taking those few steps into the demon-woman's arms.

"Must prefer men," he concluded.

Yet he had the sneaking suspicion he had not seen nor heard the last of Revile.

His thoughts were interrupted by the arrival of the Lady Theogigios searching for Worm, her Master of Slaves. She wanted preparations made for leaving the tavern for the square surrounding the Temple. Indulf concocted a plausible-enough story of overindulgence in the whore houses of Lasithii. There had been an epic feat of drinking, not Revile's first by any means. It was some time in the earlier hours of the morning he had lost touch with Worm, and only a little later Indulf had been stupid enough to spill burning oil from a lamp all over his clothes. In truth, the Lady thought the tale likely and left, muttering about her Master of Slaves.

About midday, the Lady Theogigios and her people left the tavern for the Festival. The streets were filled with throngs of jostling humanity, streaming towards the Temple of the Black Orb. They reached the square and located a position where they might get a good view.

A small pyramidal structure jutted from the side of the Temple. It was crowned with a stone altar, carved with deep channels for the flow of the blood from sacrifices. Iron hoops were hammered into the altar to secure live victims. Steps led down from the pyramid to the square, and the crowd was most tightly wedged about its base. Although the altar was deserted, all eyes were turned in that direction.

Tension filled the assembled crowd but it was a kind of happy excitement. This was the highest day of the year, the beginning of the most important festival of the calendar, the Third Sabbat of the Viri. That in itself would be enough to attract a massive crowd. But this day the Inner Sanctum of The Black Orb were to attempt an ancient rite, dating all the way back to the era when they had been powerful and none dared oppose them. This rite would restore their vigour, restore their might and strength, make the Viri great again. What exactly was going to happen few but the Inner Sanctum could guess, but it was rumoured a mighty demon would be summoned and it would prey on the body and soul of The Chosen.

Time passed slowly and Indulf became light-headed and tired from his labours and hurts – and the flagon of wine he had drunk to fortify himself. His throat was parched and he found it difficult to focus his eyes. As the minutes dragged, the illusionist fidgeted and twiddled his thumbs in a nervous sort of way.

But gradually the seething crowd became quiet by degrees and a silence fell as day slipped into night.

Almost as if on cue, a postern gate onto the top of the pyramid opened and a long file of hooded men walked around the altar, surrounding it in a ring. The illusionist counted twenty seven of them and they were cloaked in black, their faces shrouded and hidden. The Lady Ingioborg shambled between them yet it appeared she was not led unwillingly. Revile had undoubtedly failed in his mission to save her, although Indulf's mood was not seriously darkened by this revelation.

The tallest of the priests, and by far the most sinister, took the Lady Ingioborg by the hand and had her manacled naked to the altar, spread-eagling her arms and legs. The high priest, the same individual Revile had seen at Ragnir's haven, turned to the crowd with his arms outstretched as if he wished to embrace the every member in their common purpose.

"Friends, Viri, countrymen and woman," he said in a booming, echoing voice, "we are gathered here to celebrate The Rite, the Sabbat of the Viri, an ancient ceremony we have not per-

96

formed in the long age since we fell from grace, since we surrendered our power to the barbarian hordes."

Indulf made a rude noise and the Lady Theogigios favoured him with a sour expression.

"But since that most accursed of days," continued the high priest, "when light entered Acheron, we have always remembered the glory of the past – and the mysteries of our old power. And now, and now, once again, we shall rise and regain our ancient empire. Today, on the Third Sabbat of the Black Orb, we will summon The Ancient. His seed will bear fruit, bringing into the flesh the spirit of our acclaimed god, bringing us a saviour, a king, an emperor who shall lead us to glory. The preparations have been long, many years have passed. But, at last, we are ready, by the will of the Black Orb!"

There was cheering around the courtyard. The faces turned to the altar were excited, expectant, hungry for empire and conquest. Not in a thousand years had they forgotten the humiliation of defeat at the hands of the barbarian hordes. And thus it was a barbarian princess lay atop the altar, awaiting her doom.

Indulf swallowed. Something gnawed at him, a feeling of growing evil. And he knew, despite his drinking, he was deeply disturbed.

The high priest turned from his congregation, raising his arms high to the heavens. He began to chant a spell in a loud harsh voice which echoed from the buildings round the Temple. The other priests took up the incantation. Indulf did not understand the words for they were in a lost and archaic language of sorcery. The illusionist recognised single words and phrases but he was wary of translating them. He had no wish to discover their secrets. But to his heightened perception, the feelings of power grew stronger as the chant continued.

The crowd in the square was silent now for they had begun to feel tense and fearful. The wind died, the sunshine grew hazy and thin, the whole world seemed hushed. For Indulf, time itself slowed and a great rush of terror filled him, consumed him, yawned before him like a bottomless abyss. He could discern the approach and then the solidification of a mighty presence, superhuman, malign, evil beyond measure. Many in the crowd cowered or cringed, only aware something troubled the very fabric of their being. Indulf's deeper perception made his skin crawl and left his heart thumping in his chest, thumping as if to deafen him. Looking about wildly, he searched for some escape.

The priests continued their invocation, heedless they conjured something which tore the fundamental laws governing their world. Such was not their concern. Out of the insubstantial air above the pyramid appeared a vague and shifting outline. It was a smoke at first which only had the tracings of humanoid form – but gradually it took a more rigid shape as the vapours consolidated and thickened. Indulf cowered with the Lady Theogigios. The malign presence grew. The illusionist could feel a fierce, untamed will which would break the barriers the spell set on it – if it could. Indulf muttered half-remembered charms under his breath,

But the demon could not be undone by the weak spells of Indulf, magician that he was. It did not even notice another will trying to hinder its coming, as a great armoured beast might take no account of a stinging fly buzzing round its flanks. The illusionist covered his eyes.

But then, at the top of a crescendo, the chanting stopped and there was a dark, pregnant pause.

Almost against his will, Indulf raised his stare to the altar.

Hovering just above the Lady Ingioborg, there was a demon. It was manlike in form for it had the number and shape of human limbs, but it was completely smooth like a sculpted statue from obsidian or jet. The perfection and proportion of form were beyond nature-born creatures. Its features were beautiful, wearing the face of a strong and worshipful king of legends. It was as if a hero of an earlier age had returned to the light of modern day. Only its eyes were of another texture or substance, for while its body was as solid as mountains, its eyes were a nothing, a window into the void.

The demon surveyed the courtyard with an intelligent gaze, measuring the crowd, and the Temple, and the black-robed priests and their offering.

Then it spoke. Its voice was musical but of a lower timbre than any mortal could achieve. "Why have you disturbed my long rest?" it boomed. "Why have you summoned me again?"

The high priest stirred. "So The Rite might be practised again," he said nervously. "So that the God of the Black Orb might once again have form in this world to lead loyal subjects to domination and conquest by the will of the Black Orb!"

The demon nodded as if dimly remembering.

"Where is The Bearer?" it asked. "Where is The Chosen of the Black Orb?"

"It is at your feet, lord," replied the high priest. "She is The Chosen as decreed by the Laws of The Ancient." He indicated the Lady Ingioborg lying manacled to the altar. She was very beautiful and she smiled in her dreams. The demon lowered itself towards her, drinking in her naked body. The priests scattered to give it room. The demon grinned and knelt just above her.

But then the demon's expression changed. It gave out a huge bellow of rage which shook the very ground and split the silence of the courtyard. It leapt from the altar in an easy bound, its eyes filled with wrath as it held the high priest in its stare. The man backed away towards the postern door of the Temple in terror.

"What is wrong?" stammered the high priest. "What is ..."

The demon gesticulated with one arm and the man screamed in fear and pain. His body bulged and bubbled and slowly expanded as if it was being filled with air. His eyes popped as his bloated torso grew, blood spewing from his mouth. There was a sickening, squelching noise. The high priest exploded, spraying the walls and altar, hosing the crowd with blood. Apart from a smear on the wall of the Temple of the Black Orb and few other smatters, nothing remained of the high priest.

But the demon was not satisfied with this one death. Its face took on a bestial visage as if its features were malleable to its changing moods. Once the demon had appeared handsome and worshipful, now it was full of hate and revenge, hardly resembling the beautiful image of moments before. With superhuman strength, it plucked priests from the pyramid and threw them against the altar; or dismembered them like a sadistic child pulling the legs off a spider, flinging their limbs into the swarming crowd.

The crowd swayed to and fro, trying to escape, only succeeding in thwarting its own course, forcing many of its number to the ground, trampling and crushing the weak and unfortunate. Indulf remained free of the crush, protecting himself and the Lady Theogigios by a spell. The illusionist stood motionless and waited – although for what he did not know.

Some of the priests had gained the postern door of the Temple, but most of their companions were dispatched speedily: whether they met the demon begging for life; or bravely, awaiting their doom. The pyramid was covered in dismembered torsos and severed limbs, the steps to the ground running with blood like a crimson waterfall. The demon was splattered with gore as it searched for more victims, stooping to grasp members of the crowd and crush them into ruin. The area around the pyramid was clearing and demon was quickly exhausting its supply of victims.

The slamming of the postern gate roused the demon further. It gave out a terrible cry, its eyes shining with blood-lust and unrestrained power. It stretched out its two perfectly-formed arms and its fingers fused into the wall of the Temple. The demon's muscles bunched as it exerted unearthly force on the masonry, cracks appearing in the edifice. As it did so it uttered a Word of Destruction.

Blocks of stone fell from the towers and battlements, thudding into the fleeing crowd below. The Temple wall began to buckle outwards, a whole section coming away in the demon's hands, leaving a huge gap in the wall. The demon strode into the Temple through the hole, searching for warriors and acolytes, swatting them against walls, or standing on them, or biting them in half with black, razor-sharp teeth. Indulf watched the events unfold as if he was in a nightmare, dodging bouncing stone blocks and other debris as it tumbled towards him. The Lady Theogigios was struck in the chest, her rib cage crushed by a stone. The illusionist regarded her blankly as she collapsed, wiping spots of blood from his face. She lay on the cobbles of the courtyard gasping for every breath.

By now the square was cleared of all those who could run or walk or drag themselves shrieking. The cobbles were swimming in blood and covered in mangled bodies, some of which still screamed and twitched. Indulf was still unable to move from where he stood, even though he registered everything clearly.

Then he felt a thump on his back and he whirled round to see a man talking to him. The voice was incomprehensible and meaningless, and although the illusionist knew he should listen, he could not be bothered.

The other shook him rudely and then slapped the illusionist hard across the cheek. Indulf's anger stirred and he swept the figure away from him.

The other man was insistent, however, and returned to aim a boot at Indulf's groin. His foot connected squarely and managed to wake Indulf from his daze.

The illusionist sank to his knees, nursing his throbbing manhood, trying not to vomit.

"Thank Thor's Holy Phallus something woke you," said a familiar voice through a haze of pain. "What's wrong with you?"

"Some stupid git," wheezed the illusionist, "just kicked me!"

"Ah, sorry," replied Revile, not sounding very apologetic, "but I didn't know what to do."

"Great!" managed Indulf.

Revile helped him to his feet, but Indulf remained bent-double. Then the assassin noticed the Lady Theogigios lying on the ground. He went to her and found she was still alive.

"Greetings, Worm," she whispered, a little blood running from the corner of her mouth. "I had not expected to see you again."

Revile examined her. She was badly injured.

"Lady," he said, taking her head in his lap. "How are you feeling?"

"Not good," she replied, coughing. She smiled slightly: "We made a good team, you and I."

He grinned. "That we did," he said.

She coughed again, and this time bright red blood frothed in her mouth. The Lady Theogigios of Heraglion went limp in the assassin's arms. She was dead. Revile sighed, placed her head gently on the ground, then got to his feet.

"How did you escape?" asked the illusionist, sincerely wishing Revile had been caught and put to death horribly.

Revile turned from the corpse of the Lady Theogigios. "Now is not the time for tales," he replied, sounding cheerful enough. He hurried towards the carnage at the foot of the pyramid, dragging Indulf along behind him. "Come on," he added, "we still have things to do!"

"What in Hell's Teeth are you doing?" cried the illusionist. "We should flee while we still can!"

"We've still to rescue the fair maid in distress, don't we?" said Revile. "How else can we profit from this venture?"

Indulf did not answer that.

Revile left the illusionist at the foot of the steps which led up to the top of the pyramid and the altar.

"Shout if you see the demon," cried the assassin, bellowing over his shoulder.

He struggled up the staircase over corpses and severed limbs, the steps slippy with blood, fallen masonry hampering his way. He gained the top of the pyramid without too much trouble and, clearing carnage from the naked Lady Ingioborg, took a hammer and a chisel from under his clothing. He checked to make sure the girl was still alive, and was relieved to discover she was. With a couple of heavy blows, he managed to free her from the chains which spread-eagled her across the altar. He hoisted her on to his shoulders and descended the steps with care. Above him, without warning, the great golden dome of the Temple of The Black Orb collapsed inwards. Chunks of stone bounced down the stairs from the pyramid, making the assassin trip and fall the last feet to the ground.

Revile picked himself up, wiping blood from a cut on his forehead, but was otherwise un-hurt. He took the Lady Ingioborg in his arms again. She murmured something, but did not stir. Taking her on his back, they fled from the courtyard and into the maze of narrow streets around the ruins of the Temple.

Another side of the Temple crashed to the ground only feet from where they had been, engulfing the pyramid. The demon became visible in the devastation, reaching for fresh victims like a bear searching for termites in their nest. The demon was greatly increased in size and the companions stopped their flight and stared back in consternation. The demon was perhaps fifty feet tall, towering over the courtyard and the streets. As it stepped out of the smoking ruin which had once been the Temple of the Black Orb, Revile and Indulf once more took to their heels, fresh fear adding strength to their legs.

"The assassin heaved the Lady Ingioborg a little further up his back.

"Where ... are ...we ... going?" wheezed the illusionist.

"To the harbour," answered Revile whose breathing was a little less laboured. "We've got to get off the island."

Behind them they could hear the renewed sounds of destruction as the demon vented its fury on the dwellings and inhabitants of Lasithii. A great crack suddenly appeared in the ground as if the very earth could not support the demon. Out of the crack belched sulphurous vapours which could choke and suffocate. Fires burned unchecked in the town, and dust and ash fell from the sky like rain. The sun became weak like a red impotent eye shining through the smokes.

Revile and Indulf continued their flight, coughing and wheezing. They ran through the outskirts of Lasithii, past the last houses, hardly daring to look back. It was certain that the demon would overtake them and would reach the sea first – if that was its purpose.

The waterfront and harbours were still a mile away at least.

A few horseman rode past, galloping wildly, as the last of the Temple militia fled. Revile threw a look at his companion. Indulf nodded back.

As further horsemen approached, their horses reared as a host of intertwined snakes thrashed at their hooves. The riders were thrown. Revile dropped the Lady Ingioborg on the road and dispatched the warriors as they lay stunned on the verge. The illusionist caught the reins of two horses, murmuring to them as Revile heaved himself and Ingioborg into the saddle. Indulf leapt onto the other horse.

They rode off as the sounds of devastation, the cracking of stone, neared. Revile took a glance over his shoulder and saw the demon towering over the remains of Lasithii. It looked in their direction. The assassin muttered, cursing the demon's ancestry, spurring his horse on.

The demon pointed. A massive rend was gouged from the earth just behind them. Smoking lava spewed from the chasm, igniting the dry grass in the fields, engulfing the lines of trees by the edge of the road. Explosions and concussions sent burning embers hundreds of feet into the air. The horses bolted and Revile and Indulf tried frantically to stay in the saddle.

"Odin's Teeth!" gasped Revile, rubbing soot from his eyes.

Luckily for the two friends, their horses rapidly outdistanced the destruction of the demon. They sped towards the port and its many harbours. The Gods were kind and no cracks or gorges rent the earth before them and they praised any suitable deity which came to mind.

They rode through the deserted streets of the port towards the waterfront. Many ships of all shapes and sizes had already set sail, but a few craft were still moored to the quays, including one large trireme with three tiers of oars. The two companions rode up the quay and dismounted by the side of the trireme, leaping onto the ship. Mariners approached with cudgels, but the assassin made short work of them, throwing them disdainfully into the sea. Indulf lowered the Lady Ingioborg to the deck, then looked apprehensively over his shoulder for the demon.

The captain of the trireme barked an order, and a large group of mariners advanced towards Revile. There were rows of chained slaves, manacled at their benches. Without any warning, the slaves attacked the mariners, bludgeoning them with their heavy manacles. Revile and Indulf flung themselves into the fray, fighting with desperation, back-stabbing and skewering in frenzy.

In a few moments, the crew were slain and cast overboard. Revile, who normally hated the sea and everything about it, was never so glad to be on a ship.

"Cast off!" he cried. "Cast off!"

The slaves were only too eager to obey: they were aware of the demon approaching the port. Smoke and embers wafted across from the land, the sounds of destruction were nearing rapidly. Rowing boats towed the trireme from the quay and out of the harbour. The ship slipped through the water slowly, even when the sails filled with wind. Only when the slaves dipped their oars into the sea did the ship gather speed, a wave washing over its iron-barbed prow.

But it was not enough to save the trireme and its crew.

The demon strode towards the harbour, crushing houses underfoot. It waded into the water, towering over the trireme like a colossus. The slaves covered their eyes and ears. The demon grinned down on them, its eyes filled with fury and wickedness. It opened its mouth, exposing black fangs, and raised its arm to smash the ship.

Despite all the efforts of the men aboard, they would have been destroyed by the demon had Revile not noticed a priest of the Black Orb cowering in one of the holds.

The assassin rushed to the weeping priest. Gathering the struggling man in his arms, Revile threw him bodily at the demon, desperation adding strength to his limbs.

The demon snapped the bundle of rags from the air with ease. It tore the priest apart, discarding the remnants disdainfully.

The trireme sped away from the legs of the demon.

Even this was not enough.

The demon pursued the ship into deeper water off the coast. It was massive now, perhaps a hundred feet tall or so, envigored by its orgy of killing and devastation. It waded after them, the sea rising above its knees, its legs like two mighty monoliths fashioned from obsidian.

Behind the demon, the Isle of Viriggia burned and steamed with sulphurous vapours, bitter with the taste of brimstone. Great rivers of lava flowed over the once fertile fields and woods, engulfing whole regions as the earth cracked, laying waste to Viriggia. Towns were destroyed, rivers and lakes boiled dry. One flood of molten lava consumed the port and its harbours. The remaining ships burst into flames. Cries of agony and death echoed over the sea – along with the groan of super-heated stone. The land tilted and steamed and began to slip into the ocean. Never would the Viri rise again to trouble the world.

The crew watched in horror as the demon neared. There was nothing they could do to hinder it. The wind died, the sails flapped, and current and tide seemed to draw the ship slowly towards the sinking shore. The demon strode to the trireme's side, again raising its arm to crush those who stood on the after-castle at the stern of the ship.

The crew awaited their doom in silence.

"Any bright ideas?" asked Revile.

The illusionist shook his head.

But the demon never completed its blow.

It gave out a huge bellow of despair and rage. The demon cried again, its breath filling the sails and nearly tearing them from the masts and spars. Massive waves struck the ship causing it to list and shudder.

The demon's body became hazy and transparent as the spell which bound its flesh to its will unravelled and broke. It evaporated, the fine limbs becoming imprecise and wavering, mere tracings in the air wafting from the shore. Yelling and weeping in frustration, the demon was no more than a smoke shadowing the trireme. The sounds of rage were weaker as if the demon called from a greater and greater distance.

Soon there was nothing left of the Great Demon but the black glazed eyes until even these faded. Eventually only a black vapour remained which the freshening breeze blew away in curls and tendrils.

There was a long pause, during which there was an absolute peace. Not one of the crew found anything to say.

Sulphurous fumes wafted across from the shattered shore. The rivers of lava stopped their flow, the earth remained constant and unmoving. The clouds of ash and smoke broke and fragmented, and the sun shone through hazily. The remains and ruins of Viriggia quietly slipped into the sea.

Almost as one man the crew gave out a huge sigh of relief.

The assassin mopped sweat from his forehead, grinning at his friend.

"I love it when a plan comes together," he said cheerfully, "everything has worked out for the best."

"But why did the demon disappear like that?" asked Indulf, feeling weary and in a little pain. "What happened?"

"Tut, tut!" said Revile in an annoying tone. "Don't you know anything about demons? I would have thought you, Indulf the Golden, wizard and illusionist, wielder of Prassass's fire, would know when all a demon's summoners are dead it must return whence it came."

"And who told you that?" said Indulf.

"It is common knowledge."

"O really?" replied the illusionist, finding the assassin even more stupid than usual. "Anyway, how did you know that priest was the last summoner. There might have been countless others who escaped!"

"Ah," said Revile smugly, "that was the really clever part."

"You didn't," said Indulf.

"Exactly!"

VII

Revile, Indulf and their crew-mates travelled north and west for several days. The winds seemed favourable, despite the fact it was winter, and the sea was not too rough for the time of year. The trireme kept up a good rate of knots until the assassin was sure they must be approaching the islands of Jarl Thorfinn the Ugly. Revile was truly grateful.

The first part of the journey passed without event. The assassin could not find anything to do but stare at the sea and throw things at the few gulls that followed the ship. At least he could relax in relative luxury for he shared a large cabin with Indulf. There were provisions in abundance. Nevertheless, Revile seemed determined to deplete the wine and ale stores, a task at which he had some success, helped by Indulf.

The two friends were lucky that several of the crew were experienced mariners and competent navigators. Many of them were, indeed, kin to Jarl Thorfinn, and had been taken at Ragnir's haven. They knew the waters through which they travelled, or so they claimed, and Revile was content to allow them to take decisions on the course – perhaps sensibly as he had no idea where they were. The crew treated the assassin with respect and regard, despite the fact they had been his masters only months before. This was a little strange in itself – but far more strange was the fact they were reluctant to return home to the Brough of Jarl Thorfinn. Not one of them showed the slightest interest in the Lady Ingioborg and some even blamed her for their period of captivity. Their behaviour was baffling.

The Lady Ingioborg had failed to recover from her sickness, she remained in an unwaking sleep. If she was fed she would eat, if she was given water she would drink, if she was propped up in a chair she would stay there – but other than that she did nothing. Revile was not alone in being relieved.

The assassin and the illusionist were firm friends which was sensible as they shared the same cabin. Indulf, however good naturedly, blamed Revile for all and sundry. The illusionist had recovered from most of the physical hurts inflicted by the demon-woman, but that encounter had affected him in other ways, ways he dared not admit. Revile noted the changes in his friend's mood but said nothing. Indulf was preoccupied, and moaned and sweated in nightmares each night.

So it was on the thirteenth day of the journey home, they chanced upon land off the port bow. By agreement of all those on board – the supplies of fresh food and especially water had run low – it was decided to make for the island. The navigators admitted they could be off course for they had not expected to reach land for some days. They swore the island was uncharted and unknown at the Brough. Revile was not worried by this admission and supposed they

104

could handle anything that came their way.

The assassin sent a small scouting party ashore to spy out the island. The party landed on the beach without incident. The sun shone down on the narrow bay and the quiet ocean was azure blue. Gulls and other seabirds wheeled overhead and cried mournfully.

The landing party returned shortly. The island, they reported, was small, only being some two or three miles long and half as wide. They had found a thatched cottage, surrounded by well-tended fields and orchards.

Revile decided to go shore himself and to take only Indulf and the Lady Ingioborg. He also ordered no crops or beasts were to be taken until he had found the occupant of the cottage. Revile rowed across the bay to the shore, and then the three companions set off into the interior of the island.

After walking about a hundred yards or so from the beach, they chanced upon a well-used path leading into a light and airy copse. They followed this new track into the trees. The wood was a pleasant place with a green breeze rustling through the overladen branches. The air was rich and wholesome and full of colour. Indulf breathed deeply and smiled, but Revile began to have doubts and he sighed. It was approaching midwinter and the trees should have been bare and without leaves – if any could have grown on such a small island in the middle of the sea in these northern waters.

The trees thinned and they came out of the copse and into a region of fields. All manner of grasses, herbs and vegetables grew there. Each field was fenced to keep the many well-fed beasts from the gardens. Fruit trees lined the path and were laden with apples and cherries and pears.

The roof of the cottage came into view through the grass. It was a small stone-built dwelling with thatched reeds for roofing and carved wooden shutters by open welcoming windows. It was a pleasant place with wild flowers and shrubs lining the walls and the front of the house.

Revile frowned inside, but he walked up to the door and knocked, not really expecting a reply. The door was opened by a young woman, a girl younger than the Lady Ingioborg although just as fair. The assassin jumped back in surprise, digging in his clerical robe for a dirk. But the girl was not threatening and she regarded her visitors with some interest.

"Hullo," she said in a strange but pleasant accent. "What can I do for you?"

Revile looked at her suspiciously for a moment, but then relaxed and withdrew his hand from the hilt. "We are from a ship," he replied, "we've just arrived."

"So I guessed," she replied, "it is not east to get here any other way."

"Of course, how silly of me," replied assassin with a thin smile. "We came to ask if we may have, or buy, some fresh stores. We're on a long journey and had run a little short of fresh produce."

"I see," she said, looking a little amused, "it is stores you have come for. Very well, come inside and make yourselves comfortable. We can discuss the price."

"Why not?" said Revile brightly enough, then followed her into the cottage with the reluctant Indulf following, leading the Lady Ingioborg.

The interior of the cottage was neat. The single chamber was furnished with a table, chairs and stools, cot and stove. Shelves ran the length of the walls, covered with phials, bottles, pouches, jars, boxes, casks, pots, chests, scrolls, and several volumes of a large leather-bound book with mystical devices on the spine.

Indulf was certain they had stumbled across a witch and tried to conceal his conclusion from his expression.

The girl peered at the illusionist.

"I reckon your friend does not like me much," she told Revile, but without much malice. "No, I reckon he does not."

"Think nothing of it," replied the assassin. "He's just a little wary." He sat down on a stool next to the fire. "He's recently had a bad experience with a girl and is shy."

"Indeed?" she said, and then returned to stir the cauldron which steamed over the hearth. She straightened up slowly, and then regarded her visitors. "But I am forgetting my manners," she continued, "I have not introduced myself. I am Albezzia Rassman, and this is my island of Avalosgog."

Revile got to his feet and introduced himself and his two companions. The girl smiled at him but there was something unfathomable in her eyes, and he did not think the warm expression too genuine. He grinned back, his own gaze equally as blank. For although Albezzia was quite beautiful, and moved with an elegance which might warm a man's blood, Revile did not trust her or anything about her. None of his thoughts showed in his manner and it was left only to Indulf to glower at this new turn of events. The illusionist was no more comfortable than if he had been in the den of a dragon.

Albezzia invited them to eat with her. Revile eagerly agreed. The girl spooned generous helpings of stew from the cauldron over the fire, and the sat down with her guests, tearing newly-baked bread. The assassin ate ravenously when he found out the meat was not pork, and drank freely from a large jug of ale. Indulf picked at his food as if her feared it might be poisoned. This displeased their host.

"That was great," said Revile, and Albezzia favoured him with another of her smiles.

"Forgive me for being blunt," said Indulf coldly, "but who exactly are you? What do you do here, miles away from anywhere?"

Albezzia looked at the illusionist distastefully as if he was something she might have trodden in. "I am Albezzia Rassman," she answered with a frown. "I do what I choose and that is no business of visitors or guests. Kindly remember you are in my house on my island of Avalosgog. I will not tolerate insolence from the likes of you: you who are here under sufferance."

"Indeed?" muttered Indulf, ignoring any threat in her voice. "What exactly do you do? Study botany? The rearing of pigs? That at least you seem successful at!"

"I do not like your questioning or your tone!" she replied angrily. "This is my home, you are my guests: I did not ask you here! I am not here to answer your suspicion, your suspicion angers me. I suggest that if you find my company so unappealing you return to your trireme. Or you might well regret it!"

"Will I, in sooth?" retorted the illusionist. "I think I should warn you I am far from powerless. I think that ..."

Revile interrupted his friend and apologised for him. The illusionist's mood did not improve. Evening was falling outside and Albezzia reminded Indulf he could return to the ship. The illusionist readily agreed this time and immediately prepared to depart. He frowned over the welfare of his friend. Nevertheless, he did not delay and he left, mumbling farewells. Revile was alone in the cottage with Albezzia and the gently snoring Ingioborg.

"Are you a witch?" asked Revile after the illusionist had gone. "I don't mean to be rude."

"Perhaps," she thoughtfully replied. "Witch is an ugly term and it is not a title I would use of myself. I have certain special skills and knowledge in the realms of what you would call magic. Why do you ask? Your friendly companion claimed to have powers of his own."

"Hmmm," said the assassin, "perhaps he was not lying. But I think he would see a difference between you."

Albezzia frowned at Revile.

"I don't care one way or the other," he went on easily, "but I was curious because I thought you might be able to help this Ingioborg. I would have her cured if its possible. I was wondering if you could help her."

"Perhaps I could, but tell me why I would want to? I do not usually grant favours to interlopers and trespassers on my island. To be sure, they serve me after a fashion. So tell me why I should not turn you and your crew into toads – or any other beast I fancy? That is what witches are supposed to do, is it not?"

"I know I'm trespassing," he replied, "but I do not come to steal or take that which is not freely given or sold. If you wish me gone I will go. But please withhold your magics. I have no taste for flies or warts – or to snuffle for truffles in the woods."

"What do you mean by that?" she demanded.

"I have noticed the large number of pigs which share your island." Revile smiled slightly. "I am swine enough without the addition of a curly tail and a ring through my nose."

She regarded him curiously. "Perhaps you are not as stupid as I first thought," she relaxed a little. "But this changes nothing."

"No?" said Revile. "Maybe not. But there is no reason why we should be enemies. I need your help, I need the Lady Ingioborg here restored to health, I need fresh food and water if you can spare it. I will pay if necessary. It is true I have no gold – I doubt it would interest you if I had – but I am in command of a large crew. You can have such members as you like, saving enough mariners to sail the ship, and barring myself, Indulf and the Lady Ingioborg."

"You would sell your own crew?" she exclaimed in surprise. "You must be the most mercenary fellow I have ever met!"

"Perhaps," he said, "but what is the crew to me? Most of them were my masters, my Jarls, when I was a slave. They had little regard for me then and I have no love for them now!"

"I see," she said, "but tell me why I should not have them all – and you? How could you stop me if that is what I wanted?"

"Ah," he said with a smile, "I think we would fight fire with fire. My friend, Indulf, is a master of magic and illusion. Are you sure you are powerful enough to defeat him?"

She shrugged.

"Besides," he added, "what is hard and pink?"

"I do not know," said Albezzia, grinning at her visitor, "but I am sure you will tell me."

"A pig with a dagger," he replied, "and so would I become if you used your witcheries: an assassin pig ever waiting the chance to hoof you to death!"

Albezzia laughed. "You are the most foolish fellow I have ever met," she said. "But I think I admire you a little. Never has any visitor walked more boldly through my door, or made himself so free with my home and self. Are you a brave rogue – or merely foolish? I wonder. Very well, I will help you on one condition – you tell no more jokes. Besides, the thought of an assassin pig terrifies me greatly: lurking in its sty with murderous intent or sneaking about the island on silent trotters. Very well. Tell me more about the Lady Ingioborg and what has befallen her."

Revile spent some time recounting his adventures on Viriggia from the destruction of the longships at Ragnir's haven to the final demise of the Great Demon. Albezzia was not surprised by anything she heard. She listened intently and quizzed the assassin on details. When he finally finished his tale, it had become dark in the cottage. Albezzia rose and lit some candles.

"Have you any wine?" asked Revile. "All this talking makes a man thirsty, don't you know?"

The girl produced a large skin and he helped himself to a large mug of wine. Albezzia looked at him for a moment and he grinned back. She examined the Lady Ingioborg carefully, searching her head and body for injury. But she found nothing which could explain Ingioborg's condition.

She sat down again at the hearth and thought for a while.

"I can find no indication of a blow or concussion," said Albezzia at last, "but then such outward injuries would have healed by now. I do not think she had been drugged, nor do I think an enchantment or spell has been cast upon her. I think her state is self-inflicted, a retreat from some terrible event with which she could not cope. Something of a particularly horrific or frightening nature. I guess it happened in the longhall of Ragnir Haroldson. She fled from reality."

"I can hardly believe that," said Revile, breaking into the girl's thoughts. "I've known the Lady Ingioborg for some little time now and I couldn't say she was a delicate or fragile creature. Even the crew, freemen who used to serve Thorfinn, do not care for her. She is needlessly cruel and brutal. She would have slaves, children, whipped to death for no better reason than an expression – she would take pleasure in watching them suffer. She even had a perfume merchant boiled in oil for charging her for his perfume."

"Really?" said Albezzia grimly. "She did all that? What a charming creature you have brought into my house. I begin to wonder why you risked so much in trying to save her. But I do not think what you have told me matters. The events at Ragnir's haven could have been of an especially horrific nature."

The assassin admitted that was true. "So can you help her?" he asked. "Can you cure her?"

"Perhaps," she replied, "but what I will attempt will be dangerous for her. I intend to erase the memory of these events – but I may only destroy her mind. And, in that case, she would revert to a childish state from which she would never progress. Are you sure it is worth the risk? She may recover without any help. What does this charming creature mean to you?"

108

"Gold," he replied slowly, "nothing more. I have no love for her. I think I'd be better rewarded if I returned her the way she was before."

"Hmmm," said Albezzia, "you hope to earn a reward from her father, I suppose. I warn you that your reward could be quite unpleasant. You have forgotten, I think, as far as Jarl Thorfinn the Ugly is concerned, you are still a slave and have no rights. He will hold you to that. It would be your duty to rescue the Lady Ingioborg if you could – or die in the attempt. You are branded so he may repay your daring and bravery with cold steel rather than gold."

"I suppose you are right," said Revile, sounding a little gloomy, "but I'm counting on the fact that Thorfinn loves his daughter."

"Then I hope he does, although I find it hard to believe anyone could love the Lady Ingioborg – apart from another maniac perhaps – not even her father. Very well." She sighed. "What I intend to do is to take her back to the events at Ragnir's haven those many months ago. With any luck that will wake her from the sleep."

Albezzia went to a shelf and removed a casket from its place. From the casket, she took a mortar and pestle and ground up some dried leaves with the contents from a small phial. She smeared the Lady Ingioborg's forehead with the paste, mumbling a few strange words as she worked. Then, taking a crystal ball from a leather pouch, she sat down at the table and peered into the globe.

Revile watched the girl with more than a touch of scepticism, but he grew thoughtful as the crystal ball suddenly went dark. Night had fallen in its depths. Small vague images appeared.

Albezzia trembled in exertion, a drop of sweat running unnoticed down her nose. Within the globe appeared a distorted vision of Ragnir's haven.

Revile peered into the ball and saw the longships dropping anchor in snatched pictures; and the beginning of a banquet which he somehow knew was boring. A man came into view, and the assassin guessed it must be Ragnir Haroldson, although the face was cruelly caricatured. Then the Jarl Ragnir rose to his feet and welcomed Ironhelm the steward into the longhall. Revile then knew what doom had befallen those at the feast, saw Ironhelm remove his helmet, saw the jet black eyes and the terrible wound on Ironhelm's head which parted his skull to the brain. The assassin witnessed the deaths of Bjorn and Ragnir, the slaughter committed by the demons.

Albezzia called out something and then collapsed across the table. Revile jumped from his stool and, in truth, his first instinct was to murder the girl while she was in this weakened state. Changing his mind reluctantly, partly because he feared he might not be able to kill her, he tried to wake her. Her face was shiny with sweat, her breathing harsh and irregular. The assassin took her head in his arms and removed the sodden tresses of hair from her face. Albezzia's eyes opened and her gaze was dull with fatigue.

"That was not easy," she said hoarsely. "How is the Lady Ingioborg? Did it work?"

Revile turned to the Lady and was surprised to see she had regained consciousness.

"You have done it," he told Albezzia, "she is cured."

"What is going on?" demanded the Lady Ingioborg. "What is happening, slave? Where am I?" she asked, looking around. "Where am I, by Thor! Who is this woman?"

"I will explain later," said Goat the ever obedient thrall. "If you will just give me a moment, my lady."

"I will certainly not!" she angrily replied. "You will do as I command now and without delay! Tell me what has happened! Where are my slaves, where are the crew, where are my clothes and jewels? Where, by Thor's Hammer, are we?"

"My lady, please," pleaded Goat. "I will explain everything presently. But first I must see to this woman here. She has undergone a sore test in curing you. My lady, you have been ill for months – that is why you don't remember what has happened. You should not become angry in case there is a more painful relapse. I will see to your needs and comfort presently."

The Lady Ingioborg started to speak, but then she found the paste smeared across her fore head. "What is this disgusting stuff?" she demanded.

"Please?" asked Revile.

"O very well!" she snorted. "But be quick!"

"Very good," he fawned. He helped Albezzia to stand and poured her a large mug of the wine. She drank deeply of the beverage and some colour returned to her cheeks.

"I do not wish to do that again," she said, holding his eye, "so be careful the Lady Ingioborg does not have one of your relapses!"

Revile nodded.

Albezzia smiled slightly at him, and then addressed the Lady Ingioborg "I am sorry," she said, "but I was weakened from helping you. You have been suffering from a strange illness these past months. But do not worry now. You are quite safe and are, in fact, on your way back to the Brough of you father. This slave rescued you from the Viri, a black and evil people, who had kidnapped you from Ragnir's haven and were to sacrifice you to a demon. He saved you. I know he is only a slave but nevertheless you should still be grateful."

"Where are my jewels, my dresses?" asked the Lady Ingioborg in confusion. "Where are my slaves? What has happened to them?"

"The dowry was stolen," replied Goat, "and I am afraid, despite our greatest efforts, we could not recover it. Most of your entourage are slain although I have a remnant with me. They await you at our ship."

"The longship?"

"No, my lady," he said, "your ship was sunk. It is ship we stole from the Island of Viriggia."

"This is preposterous!" exclaimed the Lady Ingioborg. "Surely you are lying? Who are these Viriggians? I have never heard of them or their stupid island. This is a most unlikely tale!"

"My lady," said Goat, "your men can confirm it – those who are still alive that is. I assure you we are telling the truth. I am returning you to your father so you may be reunited with your own folk."

"Anyway," said Albezzia, "I am, once again, forgetting my manners. I am Albezzia Rassman and this is my island of Avalosgog, four days journey south and west from the Brough of Jarl Thorfinn. How do you feel? Are you hungry or thirsty?"

"No I am all right," replied the Lady Ingioborg. "In all truth, I am a little tired, I suppose. I think I shall rest for a while."

110

"Then take my cot," said Albezzia. "I am sorry it is not as comfortable as that to which you are accustomed. Yet I hope the bed is suitable."

The Lady Ingioborg peered distastefully at the cot for a moment, opened her mouth to complain, thought better of it, and eventually laid herself disdainfully on the bed. "Slave," she ordered, "have water warmed so I may bathe tomorrow and have my breakfast prepared for when I awake."

"Very good, my lady," replied Goat.

Albezzia drank more of the wine, relaxing in front of the fire. Revile joined her, glumly staring into the heart of the flames.

"What is wrong?" asked Albezzia. "Have I not done what you wanted?"

"Indeed!" he said ruefully. "I think you've done too much! I'd forgotten how difficult it is to be a slave." He sighed. "Yet I suppose I must."

"I think that would be sensible," she told him, "you hope to secure some reward and your conduct towards the Lady Ingioborg is very important."

"I know," he said.

"Anyway," she went on, "I fear I may have to depress you further."

"Why?" asked the assassin wearily.

"I require payment for my labours and hospitality."

"You can have as many of the crew as you like," said Revile, and then lowered his voice, "and twice as many if you change her back."

She smiled slightly. "I did not mean that," she said, "I want to show you something."

Revile raised his eyebrows.

She rose from her stool and, taking a shawl, opened the front door. It was dark outside although it was cloudless and stars speckled the heavens.

"Come," she said.

Revile grabbed the skin of wine and followed Albezzia out of the house, shutting the door behind him on the sleeping Ingioborg. They went along a wide path, barely visible in the gloom. The air was cool but not cold, and it was fresh as if it was new and wholesome. It was the sweetest air Revile had ever tasted. He took a drink of wine.

Albezzia led him into a wood, the path sloping gently upwards. They came out on the lip of a dell. Below them there was a clearing in the trees with a glittering pool of water in the centre. Albezzia climbed down into the clearing and went to the edge of the pool.

"This is what I wanted to show you," she said. "This is my place."

"It's very nice," he replied, not sure what was special about it. "Very, ah, dark."

Albezzia laughed. "I suppose it is," she said, "put your hand in the water."

He touched the pool. The water was warm but he shrugged slightly.

"Have you guessed my secret?" she said. She slipped her dress over her head and then waded into the pool, the stars glittering from her naked body. "Come," she said, "join me."

111

VIII

Revile stayed on the island of Avalosgog for a further two days.

He treated the Lady Ingioborg very well on the whole, and never once lost his temper, although she tried to provoke and irritate him in every way possible. After only two days he was already becoming a little tired of her and with meeting every whim and desire. However, it would hardly pay to anger her. So he withheld his tongue and hand, and thought instead of the riches he would earn from her father.

Indulf visited the cottage several times and was friendlier with Albezzia. He never stayed too long. But the island of Avalosgog seemed to have worked a change in Indulf. He was more relaxed and was his old self, the Indulf Revile had known before the demon-woman. The illusionist still felt it necessary to bandy words with Revile and make jokes on his account. If Revile minded the cruel taunts, he kept his feelings well hidden. Indulf spent the tedious hours inventing new jests and baiting his friend with them when they next met. In truth, it afforded little amusement to either of them but it was something to do.

Finally, it became clear Revile would have to leave Avalosgog for the mariners were becoming disgruntled and restless – as was the Lady Ingioborg. On the evening of the third day, as he and Albezzia sat at the fire in the cottage, he broke the news, wondering what sort of reaction it might prompt. Albezzia looked at him sadly but made no protest.

"Why don't you come with us?" he asked. "You must get pretty fed up here all the time."

"I cannot," replied Albezzia with a faint smile. "My life is here and I must stay – just as your life lies over the ocean, and you must go on to whatever end. I do not think you would be content to spend the rest of your days here. Besides, I would be far from happy following at your heels as you wandered hither and thither across the world." She looked into his eyes and he was pierced by the clarity in her gaze. "Anyway, one day your luck will desert you, and you will die. It is always the same with men like you: you can never settle down, there must always be one more reckless adventure, one more dangerous robbery, one more perilous murder. Do you not see it?"

Revile thought for a moment, and then said softly, talking as much to himself as to his companion. "I suppose you are right," he told her, "but then all people die, even me. All people die, some in infancy, some are slain in battle, some starve, some die of disease, others perish in the dotage of old age. All men die. While you live, however brief it may be, you have to make the most of that life and enjoy it while you can. Come with me and we could enjoy life together."

"No," she said, "I cannot leave my island. If you cannot guess the reason then I am not going to tell you. But I could equally say to you: give up your life of thievery, murder and adventure, and spend the rest of your days in peace on Avalosgog. But you would not give up your life for me and I will not give up my life for you – even if I could. Tomorrow you will sail away to wherever your fate lies, yet you will have a place here in my heart."

"Very well," he said, "I should have realised you could not leave your pool."

She smiled. "As I said before," she replied, "you are not entirely stupid."

"Perhaps, then," he said, "I will visit you again."

"That would be pleasant."

"I guess you'll still be here?"

"I guess I will."

He nodded.

Revile rose early the next morning and stood alone at the door of the cottage. His expression was blank but his eyes were merry as he peered at the fields and woods, alive and healthy in the bright sunshine. In truth, he was a little glad to be leaving the island. He had no wish to stay any longer, although he would miss Albezzia and her pool in the dell.

Yet, Albezzia troubled him for he could not help thinking the many pigs on the island were once luckless mariners. He had no desire to share their fate. Revile had considered trying to murder, or at least incapacitate, Albezzia so he could leave in peace – but had nagging doubts which prevented him doing anything. He had witnessed only a fraction of her power in healing the Lady Ingioborg and supposed Albezzia had many more potent spells.

Besides, he was quite fond of her.

Albezzia broke into his thoughts and she grinned at him as if she could read his mind. "Ah," she said, "you weigh up possibilities?"

"Indeed," he replied, sounding quite untroubled but his eyes were guarded, "for I was wondering what would happen if I tried to force you to come with us."

"Then," she replied, "but reluctantly, I really would turn you into a pig!"

"That's what I'd imagined." He sighed. "Ah well, such is life."

"Look cheerful," she added, "you friend approaches."

Indulf came striding through the grasses.

"Greetings," said the illusionist, "are you ready to depart?"

"More or less," said Revile, "although the Lady Ingioborg is still in bed." The assassin looked gloomy. "I will wake her shortly. Then we'll go, although having you for a cabin mate even for four days makes me wish I was staying here."

"Aye that," grinned Indulf, looking at Albezzia, "and one or two other things I shouldn't wonder!"

"This island has worked wonders for you," said the assassin, yawning. "Perhaps we could find you a permanent place here. How do you fancy a curly tail and a ring through your nose?"

Indulf snorted. "More than likely," he retorted, "that's what's happened to you already, porky."

"I'll meet you at the ship," said Revile shortly, turning away from the illusionist.

"All right then," said Indulf, and then walked back towards the ship.

Revile went back into the cottage and gently woke the Lady Ingioborg. Her eyes blazed with fury for a moment until Goat the slave explained they must leave to catch the tide. He debased himself and then returned outside, joining Albezzia at the door.

"Well, I guess it's goodbye then," he said. "I'll miss you."

"Perhaps," she replied, "and I will miss you. But enough of this for I shall think of you as you wander about getting yourself into trouble. And my heart tells me you will need all your wit and strength and cunning if you are to survive. The clouds will gather but will you survive the storm? Who knows?"

"Are you a fortune teller, then?" asked Revile in alarm. "Am I going to my death?"

"I do not know," she said, "and I could not claim to be a fortune teller, I only read you, not the future, to a degree. You thrive on risk and peril and these may, in the end, be the death of you. That is all." She squeezed his arm. "Farewell."

The Lady Ingioborg emerged from the cottage and threw her slave a sour expression. "Come!" she commanded. "I will not be kept waiting! If you do not obey immediately I will have you punished!"

"Yes, of course, my lady," cringed Goat. "I will take you to the ship speedily – if that is your will, my lady. I beg your pardon if you feel I have been neglecting my duty but I have been undertaking many difficult tasks on your behalf."

"O very well!" she conceded. "Lead me to my ship, slave!"

"She will be the death of you," whispered Albezzia into Revile's ear.

"Hmmm," muttered Revile, "I hope you are wrong."

"What was that?" demanded the Lady Ingioborg sharply. "How dare you whisper. What did you say?"

"I am so sorry," apologised Goat. "I said: I hope the wind's not strong. I am a poor sailor. Forgive me, my lady."

"Hurry up," she swore, "we have to catch the tide."

"Take care," cried Albezzia as they finally parted. Revile nodded slightly and then became Goat the thrall, leading his mistress towards the trireme.

The Lady Ingioborg and her faithful slave reached the shore a little later. Goat helped her into a rowing boat and they were quickly ferried out to the ship. With no further delay, the trireme slipped out of the quiet bay and into the deeper waters of the sea. Avalosgog disappeared into the a golden mist behind them as they sped north. Revile sighed.

When the Lady Ingioborg had gone below, Revile joined Indulf on the forecastle and the two friends grinned at each other.

"Did you get the supplies?" asked the assassin.

"Aye," replied his companion, "the holds are full to bulging – but I took your advice and brought vegetables. I find I had little taste for pork on Avalosgog."

"That I can understand," replied Revile, "and I think we have been lucky. Don't let me persuade you to land on a strange island again although I'll miss Albezzia."

"Hmmm," said Indulf, "I'll do my best although I don't reckon I'd have much success."

"Did you manage to arm the ship?"

"To a degree," said the illusionist. "There was some store of arms aboard: bows, arrows, spears and the like. We collected stones as you suggested and have filled containers with oil."

"Good. I know this is a warship and has its iron prow." He sighed. "Yet I don't know how much use it will be against the longships of Thorfinn."

"I wouldn't worry too much," said Indulf, "I think we can survive an attack, even in great numbers."

"I hope you're right."

"Then you fear the worst?"

"I am afraid so," said Revile glumly, "but we have come this far and I suppose we must take the gamble even if the odds are stacked against us."

Indulf grinned slightly. "The Lady Ingioborg could have a sad accident," he said. "She might easily slip overboard."

"Don't think I've not considered it!"

IX

So they undertook another sea voyage. This one passed all the too quickly, and they soon approached the waters surrounding Jarl Thorfinn the Ugly's domain. Revile spent as much of the voyage as possible away from the Lady Ingioborg. He had come to loathe both her and her continual moaning and complaining about everything, from the freshness of the food to the colour of the sea. If the voyage had lasted much longer, Ingioborg would have ended her days in the ocean with an anchor tied to her ankles.

Revile and Indulf were positively restrained and they spent much time together in their cabin plotting and scheming and planning for any eventuality. It was agreed that only Revile should go ashore with the Lady Ingioborg and the trireme was to make for the open sea – and only return that evening when they knew how events unfolded. Other than this, they could be sure of nothing and even the assassin was depressed about the whole affair.

Eventually, one afternoon, the Brough was sighted and the stumpy ship pulled in towards the island. Not one of the crew was happy about their return and only the Lady Ingioborg was pleased. There were many shouts of alarm from the Brough, many of the warriors and other inhabitants thought the strange ship was on a raiding mission. When it was discovered the Lady Ingioborg was aboard, there was much amazement, confusion and consternation, especially amongst the slaves and perfume merchants. Revile even thought he heard a cheer.

The assassin ordered that the trireme was to hold its position and suffer no strangers to board, but his orders were mostly for the Lady Ingioborg's ears. Revile left Indulf in charge. The illusionist, however, threw his friend a sly, calculating look – a look which was noted by the girl.

Goat the thrall climbed down the side of the ship, preceded by the Lady Ingioborg, and into a small rowing boat. The boat slipped across to the causeway which connected the island fortress of the Brough to the mainland. Ingioborg had an expression of triumph on her fair features, and that one brief expression was nearly the death of her. Revile had to take several deep breaths before he could take his hand from the hilt of a dagger.

The rowing boat reached the shore, and the girl and her slave stepped onto the solid rock of the Brough. Jarl Thorfinn the Ugly was there to greet them. He quickly embraced his daughter, then eyed Goat with even less enthusiasm.

"Well, thrall," he rumbled, "we meet again but under even stranger circumstances."

"Yes, my Jarl," replied Goat, "and I have many strange tales to tell."

Thorfinn considered for a moment, gazing at the trireme thoughtfully. "I see," he said at last, "I admit I had not expected to see either of you so soon. Where does this ship come from? I have not seen its like before. What happened to the longships?"

"We were attacked at Ragnir's haven, my Jarl," said Goat, "the longships were destroyed there. But the tale is very long and I would guess it would be better told indoors for your comfort, my Jarl."

A flash of anger lit Thorfinn's eyes, but his voice remained calm. "Very well," he said, "but I hope the tale is worth the telling – for your sake!"

Goat the thrall bowed slightly, then followed Thorfinn and his daughter up the rocky rise to the gates of the fortress. He was taken to a chamber by four warriors and there given fresh clothing and food. Revile retained his priestly robe and ate nothing, being content to drain a jug of ale to bolster his flagging spirits.

The wait was long and Revile wondered why there was a delay. He now wished he had told Thorfinn the essence of his tale before the Lady Ingioborg could have talked to her father. The assassin had treated her well, but he knew she was a poisonous creature and had no love for Goat the thrall. That could yet prove fatal.

At last, several warriors arrived to conduct Goat to the longhall, making escape impossible. Not that the assassin had anywhere to escape to. Revile steeled himself, checked his concealed weaponry, let himself be taken to the hall.

The long chamber was full of men as Goat entered from the far end. The expressions on the faces of those assembled were far from encouraging and men muttered at the thrall's appearance. Yet Goat seemed oblivious of their anger, approaching the high table without a sideways glance. Thorfinn's face, alone, was nothing if not cordial.

The Lady Ingioborg sat to the right of her father, grinning as maliciously as was possible for one of her beauty. Goat remained untroubled, his face as calm as a becalmed ocean. He stood before his masters, quite the picture of tranquillity and assurance. Only his eyes betrayed his true feelings and they glinted in the torchlight.

"Greetings, Goat," said Thorfinn in a loud voice. "Welcome back to the Brough! We have missed you. I suppose I must also thank you for rescuing my daughter – if that is the way to put it. You are a worthy fellow and have done no less than I would have expected from one who is so obedient and faithful. Perhaps there is some favour you would ask of me?"

Goat stirred. "Perhaps indeed, my Jarl," he replied slowly but distinctly, "yet I would have humbly thought a father best able to judge the value of his only daughter's rescue from a very demon."

"Most truly said," replied Thorfinn. "You are most correct. The Lady Ingioborg has spent some little time recounting your deeds both to me and my men. I was most enlightened by her account – and you shall be rewarded to the full!" The Jarl could not longer maintain his pretence, his act of gratitude became too much for him, and he exploded in temper. "How dare you beat and threaten one of my family! How dare you abuse her! How dare you lay one slimy

116

hand on her!"

"My Jarl," replied Goat nervously, "I don't understand. I treated your daughter with courtesy and respect as my lowly station warrants. My Jarl, I don't know what she could have possibly told you to the contrary."

"So, my daughter is lying?" Thorfinn rumbled on. "You did not savagely beat her for no reason than your own pleasure? You did not threaten to kill her if she did lie with you? She has told us it was only the intervention of the crew which prevented you violating her. You are telling me that my daughter invented all this?"

"No, my Jarl," trembled Goat. "No, my Jarl. Of course, the Lady Ingioborg could not be knowingly lying. But she has been ill, my Jarl. Perhaps in the heat of fever she dreamed these fantasies. I assure you, my Jarl, they are not true. I acted properly at all times. I would hardly have returned here had it been otherwise."

The Lady Ingioborg shrieked in false fury. "My father," she cried, "I cannot listen to his voice a moment longer. I grow weak at the sight of him and the terror churns in my stomach. But I tell you: he beat me often and insulted me, he would have used me if he had been allowed. Please?"

Thorfinn's face became cruel and was even less pleasant than normal to look upon. He snarled at Goat, like a cat toying with a mouse and trying to decide the cruellest time to kill it.

"Thrall," he said, "your denials are worth nothing. All you succeed in doing is compounding your crimes with your lies. Your death will be even more painful than I had first intended. You shall be flayed alive until all the skin is peeled from your body. Then you shall be boiled in salted water, slowly, relentlessly, until you scream for the release of death – but your prayers shall not be answered. My daughter has told us of this girl, this Albezzia, who you stayed with. I shall have her brought here and my men shall reap such pleasure from her as their vivid imaginations can invent. You asked, in your insolence, what my daughter was worth to me? Her value is the destruction of everything you hold as valuable: your life, the life of this girl, and the lives of the men who crew your ship. That is your reward!"

Goat the thrall started to weep, burying his head in his hands.

"What say you, you stinking coward?" Thorfinn thundered on. "What do you say to that? Will it please you to see the woman you lay with torn apart by the attention of my men – real men, not half-men or cowards like you? Perhaps she would enjoy it after your puny efforts!"

"Perhaps she would in truth," said Revile, uncovering his face. His eyes glinted and his guards took a step back, "although I guess your men would not – whatever the truth in their reported manliness."

Jarl Thorfinn choked back a cry of surprise and the Lady Ingioborg went suddenly pale with fear.

"Be assured," the assassin went on, "Albezzia can look after herself. You asked me what I'd say to all this? I suppose, as your loyal slave, I should try and answer you truthfully. Well, I reckon you missed your true vocation in life, Thorfinn. You should have found employment as a theatrical villain in a second-rate company of actors for you've no talent for anything else. Did you honestly think I'd weep at the sound of your voice? Did you? Why did you arrange this farce?

He sneered. "And do you really think I would want to violate you daughter? I would rather take a vow of life-long chastity than lie with Ingioborg. She is a sow, a sow on heat, more at home amongst pigs than men – but then I expect that's the company she keeps in this sty of a hall. What do you say to that, Thorfinn, lord of the pigpen? Truly is she your daughter."

"I say, enough!" said Thorfinn and when he spoke again he had transcended his wrath and his tone was cold and perilous. Revile kept his peace, fidgeting with the sleeves of his robe.

"So you feel ill-done do you, thrall?" said Thorfinn with a thin smile. "Well, that is no concern to me. For see you, Goat, I do not care whether or not my daughter is lying." The Lady Ingioborg started to protest but her father stopped her with a look. "I do not truly care whether you rescued her from all manner of perils – even from the very gates of Helgard. Such was your duty as a thrall. It was your misfortune to take passage on a ship which my men decided to plunder. You allowed yourself to be captured for good or ill, rather than fighting and dying with your freedom and honour intact. Clearly you are no merchant as you have claimed. Your demeanour and character and looks betray you for one of the warrior class. But you chose the lowest role and must accept the consequences. Your fate is in my hands and I never make idle threats, of that you can be certain. When you surrendered your liberty to me, you surrendered you honour, future – and life. And your doom is sealed."

Revile shrugged. "Thorfinn," he replied, "I have no honour – and never have – so how could I surrender it, or anything else, by being enslaved? I am not a fool to throw my life away over such stupid ideas as honour. For gold and silver I risk my hide as I've done today. But you think, Thorfinn, this talk of honour is all very well for one born to a full ..."

Without warning, the assassin's hand came free of his robe and he clutched a dagger. In the same action, the threw the weapon, sent it whirling towards Thorfinn's heart. The Jarl's eyes were transfixed by the shining blade.

There was a clang of metal against metal. The dagger rebounded off Thorfinn's chest, embedding itself quivering in the table before him.

Revile muttered something, as warriors ran forward and pinned his arms.

Thorfinn peered down at the assassin. "I will take heed of your words concerning honour in the future," he said, "and I will remember not to listen out a rogue. Take him away – and search him this time you idiots!"

Warriors took Revile towards the back of the Hall.

"One moment," commanded Thorfinn, and the men stopped, turning to face their lord. "Goat, there is one last question I would ask you."

"What?" said Revile shortly.

"Why did you throw the dagger at me," asked Thorfinn, "and not the Lady Ingioborg. After all, it is she who has condemned you."

"Don't you know?" replied Revile. "I would not have done either you, or your people, the service."

Thorfinn the Ugly nodded. "You are right, of course," he said, "and I should have known."

The assassin was led from the chamber.

"Father?" cried the Lady Ingioborg. "Are you hurt?"

"No," replied Thorfinn, "my breast plate turned his dagger although it could not wholly protect me from his words. Have I been unjust? Perhaps, but that does not matter. Are you pleased, my daughter? You have been instrumental in this man's death."

"That thrall is a rogue!" she cried. "He beat and insulted me! He would have ravished me if he could. He would ..."

"Peace!" commanded Thorfinn. "I have heard what he is supposed to have done and do not believe it! No one would be stupid enough to treat you so and then return you back here to secure a reward – however much they deserved it! I believe, in truth, he did rescue you. So be it. He remains my slave to do with as I choose. But I will think on his words awhile, my daughter, I think that is what I will do. I almost regret he aimed his dagger at me and not you, Ingioborg. You are poisonous, my daughter, truly poisonous. I have sired a snake!"

The Lady Ingioborg flounced from the chamber, a door slammed as she left.

Jarl Thorfinn the Ugly sighed.

X

The sea was a flat calm, and in the evening light the surface took on the colour of burnished pewter. The stumpy ship sped towards the south and east, the three banks of oars dipping and then rising out of the water with a quick and precise regularity. The sails, too, were raised, but they collapsed and folded against the mast for there was too little wind to fill them. Yet the trireme still managed a fair rate of knots as the oarsmen laboured manfully at their benches.

Two men stood at the iron shod prow of the ship, leaning over a low railing. There was a deep-cut wash, and apart from the sound of rushing water, the creak of oars, the grunt of mariners, and the thumping of a drum, the two companions found the world a peaceful, quiet place.

The taller of the two men turned from the racing water and peered at his friend. The tall man was a rangy sort of character, dressed in a dark and worn clerical robe. His face was sharply featured and lined about the eyes with a trident of a beard covering his chin. He regarded his companion with an intelligent gaze.

His friend was similarly dressed, but he was less tall and much broader. He was a pallid, dark-haired man, but was otherwise nondescript apart from an old scar running from eye to mouth. At that moment, it seemed he was well content with the burnished ocean and the descending sun.

"Well?" said the taller man, now lounging with his back to the prow. "It seems that you are – once again – in my debt. How do you intend to repay me?"

The other eyed him. "I don't intend to," he replied, "or have you so quickly forgotten the hot embrace of the demon-woman?"

Indulf snorted. "You got me into that particular little escapade!" he said. "Or had you forgotten that?"

"No, I had not," said Revile. "To tell the honest truth, I am indebted to you. I wasn't certain you would return for me. I didn't relish being flayed alive and then boiled in brine. It lacks a certain style, don't you think?"

"There is that," said Indulf more lightly, "and the fact it is a truly appalling way to die had nothing to do with it, I suppose?"

"Indeed not," replied the assassin, and the added more seriously: "I do thank you, but there is little I can do to repay you except to say that at least you now have your freedom. If it had not been for me, you would still be balancing figures and determining accounts in Viriggia."

"That is true, I suppose," admitted Indulf. "At least I can return home to my wife and sons."

"You don't sound too keen!" said Revile with a grin. "Anyway, your wife has probably run off with some other man. It has been five years."

"It is so good of you to remind me!"

"Sorry," said Revile absently. "Anyway, what happened last night?"

"We were attacked by the Jarl's men," replied Indulf, "just after you left us. But the sides of this ship are high and they had great difficulty trying to board us. We even managed to run down one of their longships and we did terrible damage with the oil, pitch and stone. Eventually they gave up, thinking we were retreating, fleeing from the Brough. Anyway, we returned in the wee hours of the morning and, with my help, we managed to land unnoticed on the Brough. Finding you was the biggest problem, that and getting the loot back aboard. You know the rest."

"There's still one thing I don't understand," said Revile. "Why did those of Thorfinn's folk help you free me? After all, I was a slave and they were my masters."

"A little matter of honour," replied the illusionist. "These men had been enslaved and therefore lost all honour and standing amongst their people. If they returned to the Brough they would have been treated as thralls – no matter how rich or important they had been formerly. Unfortunately for them, the Viri branded them, or they might have got away with it. So they needed no persuasion to help you, robbery was a good enough reason in itself. One or two of the crew even had a little regard for yourself although the Gods alone know why. I guess they reckon you saved them from the Great Demon." Indulf shivered. "Which I suppose you did in a way."

"I see," said Revile, "I should have guessed as much from what Thorfinn told me in the longhall."

"Why didn't you kill him?" asked Indulf. "Or at least take your revenge of the Lady Ingioborg?"

"I couldn't be bothered. I think living with old Ingioborg must be a greater punishment than Helgard – or whatever he believes in. I thought – stupidly for Albezzia warned me – he loved his daughter, but I think he really despises her."

"That I can understand," said Indulf. "I've never met a more infuriating, destructive person than the Lady Ingioborg. But there are one or two things that have been puzzling me: we have not talked of this before. It was too close for me." He shuddered. "Anyway, how did you escape from the Temple of the Black Orb? And why did the Great Demon start pulling the place apart in the first place?"

120

"It's quite simple," replied Revile, "and I don't doubt you've guessed at least part already. Nevertheless, I will tell you, for I like the sound of my own voice, especially when it's telling how clever I've been! I escaped from the Temple by hiding in a storeroom until the Great Demon started to tear the place apart. As you can imagine, there was chaos inside and nobody questioned or even noticed me. I fled out the main doors of the place as soon as I got the chance.

"As for the Great Demon? It was greatly angered by The Chosen. That would be no surprise in itself had it met her, but let's say it found her unsuitable. The Chosen needed to have several requirements: she had to be born on a certain day when the stars were just right, she had to be of "high birth", a barbarian, and many other things. But, most importantly, she had to be a virgin. I could do little about the other things but I found it in my power to undo her chastity." He shuddered slightly. "One of the most unpleasant parts of the whole adventure."

"That is what I'd guessed," said Indulf thoughtfully. "It makes sense, I suppose."

"And there is yet more."

"Hmmm," said Indulf, "she's pregnant?"

"Yes, Albezzia confirmed it. She reckoned the Viri must have given her some drug to make her especially fertile. In truth, I wouldn't have thought a Great Demon would have needed such help – but then I don't know that much about the breeding habits of demons."

Indulf nodded.

"Anyway," added Revile, "it looks as if I will be a father."

"I now appreciate all the more our need for haste," the illusionist went on. "I wouldn't worry too much about pursuit. We burned every longship we could find."

"And I am glad of it," said Revile. "Let's just hope the weather holds."

"So where are you headed?" asked Indulf.

"Llaith," replied the assassin. "I think I'll have a short holiday with my share of the loot. I've had rather too much danger and adventure lately."

"As have I," said Indulf, and he laughed. "I must admit to having enjoyed myself a little. And think: we saved the world from the evil and despicable Viri."

"I know it," said Revile, "but don't tell anyone. My reputation would be quite ruined!"

Indulf grinned back. "We must do this again some time," he said, "but not too soon."

Both the companions burst into merry laughter – they had survived again. One or two of the crew found their good spirits very irritating as they strained at their benches. They did not understand the urgency which prompted their leaders, but if they had, they might have laughed themselves, and redoubled their efforts.

***

T
here!" said Revile, his mouth dry from talking. "I hope that was suitably entertaining and sweetened your ill-humour."

Alwyn could not contain herself and she started to laugh. "Yes, I believe it was," she said brightly. "I am truly astonished by your cunning, determination and courage. Truly – although I reckon a less-gullible person wouldn't believe your story. Nevertheless, I do. I have heard of both the Lady Ingioborg and Thorfinn the Ugly. They talk about them at court. This Ingioborg has a child despite the fact she's not married."

"Really?" said Fergus in surprise. "You mean that stupid story was not a lot of shit?"

"How do I know?" replied Alwyn. "I only know that Thorfinn and Ingioborg exist and that she has a daughter – but Revile too could know all this and more. So how do I know? Yet I hope it is true: the men of Jarl Thorfinn are ever the scourge of the North."

"I know," said Fergus, "I went to war against them."

"Whereabouts?" asked Revile.

"O, in Cymbria," said the farmer, "to the west."

"I know where Cymbria is," said the assassin.

"I supposed you would," replied Fergus. "Anyway, then we were allied with the men of Cymbria – the only time I can ever remember our two nations being in league."

"Aye," said Revile, "it shows the power of these men, these Norsemen, these Vikings. They terrorise lands far from their own shores."

The farmer nodded. "We fought them just along the coast from Caerisle," he said. "We had the victory that day! It was glorious! We drove them from the beach into the sea until the very water was red with their blood. Aye, it was a good day, all right! It still makes my heart pound to think about it." But then he added with a laugh. "Mind you, the Norse returned the next year and burnt all Cymbria to the capital. And they came to stay, forming settlements all along the coast of the Firth of Solloway. But that does not make our victory any the less. I remember when we got back to Caerisle, I remember after the battle. The women of the town sang our praises and showered us with flower petals from the walls where the Norse heads were spiked." Fergus laughed again – but this time sadly. "Then we returned to Bamburg and nobody cared about the battle or its outcome. It was just a little skirmish in a foreign land. Nobody cared how brave we'd been in defeating the Norse – an all the too rare occurrence." He grinned. "Even my wife forbad me to talk about it in the house."

"O yes," said Margaret, "I remember. You all came back full of tales of slaughter and death – the innards of men splattered across your stories. Do you find it surprising no one wanted to listen? What concern was it of ours? Who'd been looking after your homes when you'd been away enjoying yourselves?"

"There's gratitude for you!" said the farmer. "You can't honestly believe Bamburg is preserved by the work of women alone? The incursions of the Norse, these Vikings, these pirates, affect us all – from the highest to the lowest. Already they settle all along the coast of Cymbria and the Gallianmerse, threatening the White House and its pilgrims. They are heathens, ever willing to kill good honest religious folk. And if Cymbria should fall under their weight then we may have an army of Norse knocking at the gates of Bamburg before long!"

"And do you think that would make any difference to me?" said Margaret with a touch of anger. "Vikings are men, the same as any other men. I would continue to pursue my occupation as before, only the clients would be different."

"I guess you're right," said the farmer. "I suppose you are right. It would just mean a change in masters, a change in who you pay homage to. Vikings still have need of farmers, serving wenches, prostitutes and assassins. Yes, you're right, Margaret. It's folk like Prince Bregorin who'd really suffer. I don't suppose it made any difference who I'd been fighting, it was the victory itself which was glorious. At other times I have fought raiders from Dalria, Pentland, Mannan and even Cymbria. Even men from the Merse and Lothland which are parts of our own realm. I don't suppose it did make any difference."

"I think you're both wrong," muttered Revile. "The Norse are different. Maybe they do need farmers and whores the same as other folk but you are talking as if they would come as peace-loving invaders. In my experience, they loot and murder first – and come to stay later. It would not just be a cosy change in masters. The Norse make slaves of the folk they conquer. Perhaps the battle you fought will not stop the Norse tide sweep all before it, but it has, at least, checked it to the shore."

"Have you fought in many battles yourself?" asked Fergus.

"In enough," replied the assassin, "but only for money, only as a mercenary, never for loyalty or a cause or because it was expected of me. They are too chancy: survival is just down to luck."

"I know what you mean," said the farmer, "but although Cymbria was my only large battle, I will remember it until I die."

"Why do men revel in slaying?" asked Margaret coldly. "Why do you enjoy tales of death and slaughter?"

Fergus paused for a moment, and then replied. "I don't really know," he told her, "it wasn't something I understood myself until that day on the beach. I don't think it's the slaying; and the battle itself was frightening, too much down to luck as Revile says. I think it's the camaraderie, the knowledge that the grip on your spear is sure, that you won't flee. And it's the winning, the winning and surviving to tell the tale – if you can find anyone to listen. I don't suppose that is much of an answer." He tried again. "When I stood there," he went on, "as the Vikings charged out of the waves towards us, some of my companions, even veterans from Cymbria, broke and fled. But I didn't." And then he added with some little wonder. "I didn't care, I didn't care if I never returned to Bamburg. Yes, that's it. I awaited the Vikings calmly, I wanted to kill them. It made me feel brave and earned me the praise of our captain and a bag of silver."

"I'll take your word for it," said Margaret, sounding a little bored with Fergus. "Well, we've found this Revile has at least one friend," she continued, changing the subject. "Have you seen this Indulf again, my trusty adventurer?"

"Yes and fairly recently," replied the trusty adventurer, "and it was as I had prophesied: his wife had run off with another man. She was, I guess, my trusty slattern, not content to keep home and wait for the return of her man."

"Sensible woman!" replied Margaret. "Yet you yourself have no wife, sir assassin. How do you find your pleasure? It makes me laugh to think that you, with all your grand stories and pretensions, sleep with the likes of me!"

"Only when I'm down on my luck," said Revile. "I pay for women as I pay for food or lodgings or wine. When my luck is good, I have the best – albeit of what Llaith has to offer. When I have no gold or silver, I needs have sour wine, poor food and old hags like you. Such is the fate of the adventurer!"

Margaret laughed, ignoring the obvious insults. "I see," she said, "don't you ever want to settle down."

"No, I get bored too easily," said Revile tiredly.

The assassin fell silent.

"And I thought you'd never grow weary of your own voice!" said Fergus.

His words prompted no reaction.

The silence had lengthened.

"This night seems endless," said Margaret at last. "A trial from which there is no hope of any redemption. Yet it is all the too short. It must be only about the third hour of the new day. Seven hours! By the Rood, I'm not ready to die!" She hung her head. "What else can we do?"

"Wait and hope," said Alwyn, who had been quiet, alone with her thoughts in the dark. "As you say: what else can we do?"

"Nothing," said Fergus, "except listen to stories – but we must find courage."

"Yes," said Margaret more strongly, "we must endure, an opportunity may yet present itself: we may yet escape."

The farmer laughed. "That would be a fine thing," he said, "we four will escape the noose and thwart the designs of Prince Bregorin. See if we don't! But what should we do to escape?"

Revile yawned.

"First," said Margaret, "we must lure the guards into the cell. But how could we do that? They're bound to be wary."

"I know," said Alwyn eagerly, "I could claim I wished to see Bregorin, that I had changed my mind and now wished to be his mistress. That might work. The guards would at least have to go and ask him."

"We would need to overpower them," said Fergus, "they wouldn't expect that from the likes of us. We would take them by surprise."

"They might expect such a move from the likes of Revile," mentioned Margaret.

"No, but ..." Alwyn paused. "Damn!" she said. "I should've known there would be some flaw."

"What?" demanded Fergus. "What flaw?"

"Our manacles," said Alwyn. "The guards don't carry the keys. There would be no point overpowering them unless we can escape from our manacles. The jailer has the keys."

"Yes," replied the farmer, "but if the Prince was to see you, the jailer would have to free you from your chains. That is when we would need to strike." Fergus punched the air. "It's our only hope. But that we had weapons!"

124

"Our chains!" said Alwyn. "We could use them against the guards and the jailer. We would need to be quick."

"What have we got to lose?" added Margaret. "Even if they killed us we would still escape the gallows. The only thing is: what would we do after we escaped from the Pit? I don't know the Tower at all."

"I can lead you," said Alwyn. "We could slip out of Bamburg. The Tower is quiet at this time of night and there is a postern gate which is hardly watched. I know how to get there."

"Hell!" muttered Revile. "Hell's Teeth!"

"What is it now?" demanded Fergus.

"If only things were that easy!" said the assassin. "Do you really think your idiotic plan would work? Do you? I can't believe your stupidity. It is well said that peasants are simple!"

"What is there to lose?" said Alwyn. "Why won't you help us?"

"To do what, child?" replied Revile. "To get yourselves – and more importantly me – killed, or worse? The guards may be in the pay of a depraved prince but that doesn't make them incompetent or stupid. Don't you think scores, maybe hundreds, of people have sat here as we've sat, trying to think up some plan to escape? Did they succeed? We're just four no-account folk waiting to be hanged. Four less tomorrow will cause little grief to the hangman. Put all thoughts of escape from your mind. Only if we were aided from the outside might we live – and that's scarcely likely. No, better to give up hope than hope in vain."

"Why didn't you say this before?" cried Alwyn.

"I couldn't be bothered," said the assassin. "You peasants can dream all you like about escaping and thwarting Prince Bregorin's noose. It's only when you start putting your absurd plan into action that I get worried!"

"If we won't escape anyway," said Alwyn, "why won't you give our plan a go? Or are you angry because we three dull, stupid peasants thought of it for ourselves?"

"I can't disagree with your description of yourselves," sighed Revile. "But we won't survive your plan."

The assassin fell silent again.

"So we do nothing?" said Fergus despondently. "We just sit here and meekly await our deaths?"

"I suppose so," said Alwyn sadly.

"I don't see why we shouldn't give our plan a chance," said Margaret. "We've got nothing to lose."

"No," replied Alwyn, "I reckon Revile wants to live as much as the rest of us. I think that if he saw any hope we would escape he would help us. We should do nothing."

"All right!" said Margaret angrily. "All right. But this waiting is difficult. I try not to get myself into a panic but I feel so helpless."

"Do you indeed?" muttered Alwyn. "Do you feel helpless, Margaret? Well you're lucky you don't feel that way all the time – I know I do."

"Why, child?" asked Margaret softly. "Why do you feel so helpless?"

"I doesn't matter," she replied. "It doesn't matter any more. But I very much want to live so

I might have a chance to do all the things I wish. I don't want to die tomorrow morning, but I want to die now even less!"

"Alwyn," Margaret told her, "to you, I am maybe an old woman. But to me, I am still young and I want to die as little as you."

"Would you go back to your old life if we escaped?" said Alwyn slowly.

"I suppose," replied the older woman. "What else could I do? I still have to eat."

"Well," said Alwyn more brightly, "I have grown tired with Bamburg. There is nothing here for either of us. Why not come with me, Margaret? We could travel together and see some of the world. Anyway, if your occupation is so appealing you could still follow it away from here, couldn't you?"

"I suppose so," said Margaret uncertainly.

"I'll come too," said Fergus, "there's nothing left for me here either."

"But what about your wife, Fergus?" said Margaret. "Would you just go and leave her with your children?"

"What about her?" said the farmer. "I'm sick of her and her brats. Our marriage was arranged by our parents and she has ever thought herself above me. I have lost my land. The only time in the last few years I have felt at peace was on the battlefield. To be honest," he added with wonder in his voice, "I don't care if I never see my family again."

"Why did you make all that fuss before, then?" said Margaret. "God above, Fergus, you went on and on. What has suddenly changed your mind?"

"I don't really know," said the farmer thoughtfully. "I suppose over the last hours I've had more time to think than I've had for years. When I look back, I see only the fighting with my wife, the bitterness, the hatred. This Revile has shown us more of the World with his stories, he has shown us our lives don't need to be the way they are. Pity it came now. I have spent my whole life doing nothing more than survive and support an ungrateful family. Do you know that my wife didn't even bother to come to my trial? Now I wonder why I bothered all those years. I say: damn them! I'll come with you."

"Good," laughed Alwyn. "All we need to do now is to escape. Would you come with us too, Revile?"

"What?" said the assassin. "Sorry, I was thinking. What did you say?"

"I said: would you come with us?"

"No," said Revile, "I have other things to do. Anyway, we aren't going to escape, although I suppose you can dream." He laughed, scratching at his head. "Aye, how jolly it would be with the three of you. Could you rob and steal and murder and cheat? Or if that doesn't make your fortune, will Margaret, and Alwyn too if we can loosen her chastity, support us on their backs? Will Fergus learn what it is to be on the losing side, will this farmer know what it is like to be hunted like a wolf? Aye, then you'll learn, then you'll flee back to Bamburg and try to find your old dull, boring lives. Better to die on the gallows, noble peasants, much better, much safer for you."

Margaret grinned. "I would take your wise speeches more seriously if you weren't to share our deaths."

126

The assassin shrugged.

"So what do we do?" asked Alwyn. "There's still several hours before they hang us."

"How about another story?" said Margaret.

"All right," said Revile. "Have you heard of Pergol's Seven Precepts?"

"Are you joking?" muttered Fergus.

"Well," said the assassin, "they are written down in a book."

"Can you read?" Alwyn asked him in surprise.

"O yes," said Revile. "Anyway, the Seven Precepts are ways, methods and strategies, of fighting and winning wars. Eochaid's Paradox is one of the chapters. It is an idea, a description of a hidden snare which cannot be avoided whatever the snared attempts to do. But there is no snare in reality – the victim creates the trap himself, and by trying to escape, traps himself further. It is like a spider spinning a web which entangles itself. I'm not sure if that made things very clear, but here is the story..."

A True Son

We are gathered here to investigate the death of Edwin, son of Athelstane, heir to the lands of Colde'head. He died of stab wounds three nights ago in his chamber in this castle – and without doubt he was murdered. The purpose of this trial is to find this murderer and punish him for his foul offence. We have a suspect and there is weighty evidence which points to his guilt. What say you, Snake, son of Serpents? Do you wish to confess to this crime or must we prove it to your shame?"

Revile smiled. "My lord Hengist," he replied. "You must prove my guilt, which may be easy. If I am to hang, I would hear this weighty evidence."

"Then you plead innocence?" said Hengist. "You claim you did not murder Edwin?"

"Is that not what I have just said?" muttered the assassin. "I am innocent of this crime."

"Very well," said Hengist scornfully. "If you must waste our time! Very well, so be it, we will let the King's Justice take its course. My lord Athelstane, father of the murdered Edwin, if you would proceed?"

Revile stood, bound and hobbled, in front of a large group of seated nobles and lords. The men were Bernecians, dressed in colourful tunics and trousers, their long hair braided or flowing about their shoulders. Their beards were full and they had down-turning moustaches. They wore torcs and amulets made of gold and encrusted with precious stones.

Revile was drearily dressed in comparison. His woollen shirt was dirty and his boots were scuffed. He was dishevelled and looked tired, blue smudges shadowing his eyes. The leather thongs binding his hands cut cruelly into his wrists and his fingers had gone numb. Yet despite his unhappy predicament, he yawned hugely for he had had little sleep for several nights. The chamber was packed with almost every inhabitant of the castle. The atmosphere was hot and stifling – and more than a little stuffy.

"I'm glad to see you take this trial so seriously," Mordris told the assassin. He was Edwin's brother and was seated amongst the other lords.

"I'm weary," said Revile. "Hengist's interrogations have allowed no sleep for three nights. Perhaps if could be permitted to sit?"

Mordris glanced at Hengist. "Yes," he said, "our faithful steward is a thorough man."

Mordris picked up a stool and placed it behind that assassin, helping him to sit. He then retook his place amongst the other lords.

"Thank you," said Revile.

Athelstane took this kindness hard. "I am glad to see you so kind even with your brother's murderer," he told his son.

Mordris shrugged. "That has yet to be proved," he replied. "By The Grail, how do you know this man is the murderer? A man is surely innocent until proven otherwise."

"Do you defend this dog?" said Athelstane angrily. "Do you defend and help all who wound me?"

"If that becomes necessary then yes," said Mordris with an untroubled smile. He ran his hands through his long braided hair. "As this Snake has pointed out, we have yet to prove his guilt under the King's Justice."

"You heap scorn on my House!" cried Athelstane, glowering at his son. "Devil's bile! You heap scorn on the memory of your beloved brother! As you have ever done! You have no respect or sense of duty! You always mock me and the beloved Edwin even although he is dead! By God, he was the true son, you wastrel!"

"I do but return everything back in its exact measure," said the younger man sadly, but then he grinned. "Perhaps if you were a true father I would be a true son. Why should I regret Edwin's death? He ever despised and disliked me. He was you favourite." But then his tone changed again, and he appeared sorrowful. "Well, by The Grail, I do regret he is dead. I did love him after a fashion although I had no reason to – that is certain. As I said, he was ever your favourite and both of you scorned me. If our positions had been reversed, Edwin would not sit here and grieve."

"No, you craven," cried Athelstane bitterly, "he would not, and neither would I. I have only one son and he is dead. You, Mordris, I cast out and shun! You are no longer my son!"

"So be it!" said Mordris, unconcerned by Athelstane's wrath. "So be it, my father."

"Enough!" declared Hengist loudly. "I am in charge here. I am steward of this castle for the King. Enough, I say. Let this trial commence under the King's Justice. Keep these family disputes for your own chambers!"

"Very well," said Athelstane, attempting to control his temper. "Very well." He swallowed. "As Hengist has said, we are here to find the truth and prove the guilt of this villain, this ill-named Snake, son of Serpents."

"You all know," he went on, "that this Snake arrived here four days ago past Thorsday. He told us he was an adventurer, a wanderer going south to seek his fortune. He asked for lodgings and provisions. In our famed generosity, we took him under our roof and gave him food and drink enough for ten travellers. We asked no payment for our kindness. So how does he repay our hospitality?

"By that very night brutally murdering my beloved son!

"But as the thrice-accursed Mordris has said: we must prove this evil villain's guilt under the King's Justice before we hang him.

Athelstane paused. "Firstly," he said, "my son was loved by all men who knew him – of that there can be no doubt. This Snake is the only stranger in our castle: he is the only one we do not know and cannot trust. He has an evil look, the look of a murderer. By elimination, he is the only one capable of doing this foul deed.

"But that would not be enough to convict him, to be sure. It is well known that this Snake carries an assortment of daggers. All have marked them! When we discovered the body of my dear son, we hurried to Snake's apartment in the hold. We searched his room thoroughly and found one of his daggers hidden in a pile of rags. It was his dagger, he does not deny that! The dagger was covered in blood, fresh blood, from the blade to the hilts. The blood was congealing, evidence positive that the dagger had just been used and was the murder weapon.

"This I say is damning proof under the King's Justice!

"Thirdly, this Snake does not deny that he had newly returned to his chamber when we arrived there. He cannot account for his whereabouts but claims he was out taking the night air! He claims he was walking the battlements because he had a headache. A headache? I ask you! This was in the small hours of the morning yet no sentry saw him.

"Lastly, Hengist saw this Snake leaving my son's chamber just before he discovered the murder. This Snake, this evil murdering villain, had both the opportunity and the means and I say the evidence against him is damning! There is no doubt in my mind he should be executed and there should be no doubt in yours. This Snake is guilty under the King's Justice!"

"Very well," said Hengist, "short but to the point. I must admit, Snake, this evidence does seem damning. Do you wish to change your mind? Or can you challenge this evidence and refute it? Do you have anything to say? This is your opportunity."

"I have much to say," replied Revile, "but I do not deny anything that Athelstane has told you."

"Then you admit your guilt?" said Hengist. "By The Grail, you did murder Edwin?"

"No, I did not," said the assassin. "These accusations, this weighty evidence, can be explained away – although I doubt you'll enjoy the explanation. But first let me ask you this: what was my motive in brutally murdering this much-loved Edwin? Why, by Thor's Hammer, would I want to kill him?"

"That is one of our reasons for holding this trial," Hengist told the assassin, "to discover your motive."

"Then all you will discover is that I had none," said Revile. "Quite the opposite in fact – I wanted Edwin to live. The whole idea is plainly absurd. And all the more stupid for the idiotic way I am supposed to have committed this murder. Do you honestly think me – or any man – is that stupid?

"Well, you don't need to answer that," went on the assassin, "but let me answer this evidence.

"You say I am a stranger in this castle and that, therefore, makes me the only possible suspect? I would say that is not so. For I hardly know – or knew, that is – Edwin so what possible motive could I have? I've nothing to gain, nothing in the least. Now a brother, if you forgive me Mordris, who might have inherited his lands? Or a jilted lover?" And the assassin threw a look at Hengist. "They might have. But surely me being the stranger makes me the most unlikely culprit. Any of your friends and family might have a hidden motive.

"And this dagger was discovered in my room? I ask you! Being well pleased with my butchery, I neither clean my dagger nor dispose of it. No, that would be much too intelligent. Instead, I hide it in a pile of rags in my room where it is certain to be found. As I have said: the whole idea is absurd!

"I don't deny I wasn't in my room that night. I had no headache. But I will explain my whereabouts presently.

"But first, Hengist, you say you saw me leaving Edwin's room. Tell me, what was I wearing?"

"What were you wearing?" repeated Hengist. "What difference does that make?"

"Please," said Revile, "just answer the question!"

"Very well," replied Hengist a little angrily. "You were wearing what you are now."

"Thank you," said the assassin, "then I was not wearing my tunic?"

"No," said Hengist, appearing puzzled. "No, you were dressed as you are now."

Revile nodded and smiled. "All of you have marked my daggers," he told those assembled. "Did you also mark they are strapped to the front of my tunic? And therefore in my room when I was supposed to be murdering Edwin. Any might have slipped into my chamber when I was out and stolen a dirk. Anyone might have stabbed Edwin and then hidden the dagger in the pile of rags. Is that not so, Athelstane?"

But it was Hengist who answered. "Perhaps," said the steward, "but you could have had a dagger concealed. It might have been hidden under your shirt, in your boot, anywhere!"

"Hengist," grinned Revile, "Athelstane, any of you, how was Edwin slain, how did he die?"

"He was stabbed," said Hengist curtly, "stabbed to death."

"Yes, I know," said the assassin, "you have already said. But where was he stabbed? How many times?"

"Twenty or more," said Hengist, "it is not easy to be certain. The body was mutilated. There was blood everywhere."

"Indeed," said Revile, "and when you saw me, was I covered in some of this blood?"

"No," said Hengist, "not as far as I could see. But what does that prove?"

"Hengist," said Revile wearily, "was the dagger not found in my room covered in blood? Wasn't there blood everywhere? How could I have killed Edwin in this manner without covering myself in blood? Could I have even carried this dagger back to my room? Did you find one spot of blood anywhere on me?"

"No, by The Grail," said Athelstane softly, "but you might have washed yourself."

"And left the dagger begored and badly concealed? Is that likely? And where did I wash? Where could I have washed and left no trace? When did I have time? Is it not obvious I have been wrongly accused of this murder?

"But lastly, I must return to the motive." He paused, shrugged slightly and then went on. "I had good reason not to kill Edwin. You see, I was invited to this castle. I am an adventurer but I am also an assassin, a killer for hire. Edwin wanted to give me work and offered me a small fortune for my services. That is why I visited him that night, to discuss terms and the price. We agreed on a fee and he hired me. And if I killed him I would not be paid!"

The chamber fell deathly silent.

The audience was mostly stunned by Revile's admission. Few could think of any reason why Edwin would want to employ an assassin; yet fewer could think of any reason why Revile would lie. For his admission would hang him as surely as if he had murdered Edwin.

It was Hengist who recovered first.

"But surely that does not prove you did not kill Edwin," he said. "You might have argued over the fee or the terms or over anything. Who knows? Devil's Bile! I say you still brutally murdered Edwin!"

"Why?" asked Revile. "Why did I murder him? He offered me two hundred pieces of gold. He showed me the money, it was in a chest in his room. If you don't believe me then check. It should still be there. I could have murdered him but would I not have taken his gold? The murderer is not shy of a little thievery. Why did I not leave the castle immediately, why did I hang about until you caught me? After all, I like to think I am a skilful and experienced assassin."

"We have only your word for that," replied Athelstane, "and if you are an assassin as you claim, would not lying be the least of your crimes? But this is truly ridiculous! Who could Edwin want murdered? Answer me that, you dog!"

"Must I?" asked Revile. "I would rather not – for your sake, old man."

"Hell's Teeth! You must!" said Athelstane. "You must tell us!"

Revile hesitated, smiled thinly, and then said, far from reluctantly: "There were to be three deaths in the coming weeks – trouble always comes in threes. I'm not sure I should tell you: the truth will do you injury, old man. Are you sure you want to know?"

"Tell me!" cried Athelstane. "Devil's bile! Tell me, you spineless dog!"

"Be it on your own head then," muttered Revile, "but don't forget I warned you. There were to be three deaths as I have said. For see you, old man, this Edwin was not as loyal and true a son as you might have imagined, far from it indeed. There were to be three sad accidents, three sad deaths. Mordris was to be the first; then Hengist's daughter, Catharine; then you yourself Athelstane!"

There was an instant of silence, then the chamber burst into uproar. Men shouted, some argued angrily with their neighbours, others looked shocked. Only Revile was content to grin at their discomfort.

Hengist appeared appalled, the colour draining from his face. Athelstane's features went totally blank as if he did not have the strength for the shock and instead chose to disbelieve his ears.

"By The Grail, this is impossible," Athelstane whispered, then slumped back in his chair.

Mordris, too, shook his head, made sure his father was all right, and angrily addressed the assassin.

"No," said Mordris, "by my sword, I cannot believe this of my brother, Edwin could not have done this under any circumstances. I could understand if it was just me he wanted to murder for he never liked me. But my father? No. Catharine? No. It is impossible. I know he loved Catharine."

"Yet," said Revile slowly, "nevertheless, what I have told you is true. I told you you wouldn't like it."

"But why?" rasped Athelstane, looking pale and fragile as if with one weak blow he might shatter into pieces. "Why?"

Revile sighed. "He wanted his lands," he said, "and yours too, Athelstane. I'm sorry if you are hurt. It must be a cruel thing when a son turns against his father and family. Edwin wanted his inheritance but was not prepared to wait. He knew no suspicion would ever fall on him, he knew he was the much-loved first-born."

"I cannot believe it," said Athelstane, his eyes full of tears. "I cannot believe it. Why did he want Mordris dead?"

"I don't know for sure," answered Revile, "but I know he hated Mordris. I guess he was jealous. He thought Mordris was showing, ah, too much undue attention to Catharine."

"By God, but Edwin loved her!" cried Mordris. "Surely you are lying? They were betrothed and to be married. All men know this! Why would my brother be jealous of me?"

"I'm sorry," apologised the assassin, not sounding too sincere. "Edwin told me that Catharine carries a child. He believed the child is yours. I don't know what you did to give him cause." Revile smiled, and then added: "Or perhaps I do!"

"Withdraw that allegation!" shouted Mordris. "Withdraw that allegation now, you filthy dog, or by my sword you won't live long enough to hang! I promise you, you low-born swine, I will have your tongue! I have never acted in any way but honourably with Catharine. This is a complete lie!"

Revile laughed. "Please, Mordris," he said with a grin, "don't be angry with me, I do but repeat what your brother told me. How could I, a stranger, know the truth of the matter?"

"Hengist," asked Athelstane suddenly, "is your daughter carrying a child? We need to know!"

"Yes, she is," snorted Hengist at the bluntness of the tone, "but that is hardly unusual in this land. They were to be married, so what did it matter? And Catharine has assured me the child she carries is Edwin's. Without doubt. I know for certain she has never lain with any other man. I know Mordris and Catharine have been friends but nothing more. I do not know why Edwin should have thought otherwise."

"I wish Edwin had confronted me with this foolishness," said Mordris. "I could have laid his fears and jealousy to rest. Did Catharine know he was suspicious of her? Did she know he thought the child was mine?"

"My daughter did not know," replied Hengist. "Of that, at least, I am certain. But she did say he had changed towards her but she only believed it was the thought of settling down and marriage. He had become cold and uninterested in her. Catharine thought he might have blamed her for getting pregnant and thereby trapping him into marriage. To be honest, my daughter believed he no longer wished to marry her."

"I see," said Mordris, "but I still do not think that would justify her murder and mine. By The Grail, my brother was far too honourable a man to ever think ill of the Lady Catharine – let alone employ an assassin to kill her. Are you sure of this?" he asked Revile. "Or are you only telling us this to cause trouble?"

"It is what he said," replied Revile, sounding bored, "but then he had been drinking." He raised his hands in frustration. "How would I know when you don't? Why do you ask me who knows the least, when you are his brother?"

"Had Edwin changed towards you?" Hengist asked Athelstane. "Had he become cold?"

"I suppose so," replied Athelstane, looking ten years older than at the beginning of the trial. "He had become reserved and cold towards me, and others it seems. I thought it was merely because of his extra duties and responsibilities – and forth-coming marriage. He could no longer be carefree. But I cannot believe this of him. I was about to give him his lands and titles anyway."

Athelstane's voice cracked and he buried his head in his hands and wept.

"This alters nothing," said Hengist at last. "These revelations are lamentable but they do change anything. However treacherous and dastardly Edwin was – and we only have this assassin's word for that – this Snake still most likely murdered him. That is for sure under the King's Justice. Perhaps they argued and in the heat of anger this assassin slew him. We have heard nothing which persuades us to the contrary."

Revile sighed. "Have you heard anything I have said?" he muttered. "I don't doubt you will hang me now from what I've already told you. But I still have my professional pride. I am an assassin. Many men and women, aye and even children, have died at my hands. By dagger and sword, garrotte and poison, trap and snare. I am an experienced assassin and it grieves me you think I am so incompetent. No one has ever caught Snake with blooded dagger or hands. If I had killed this Edwin then no suspicion would have ever fallen on me, of that you can be sure. The very fact I was caught with such damning evidence only proves, paradoxically, I could not have done it. He would have paid me two hundred pieces of gold. It was not in my interest to murder him.

"I promise you, by what little honour I have, I did not murder Lord Edwin, son of Athelstane.

"And since I did not murder him," he went on, "it follows that one of you must have. That means that one of you is the cold-hearted fellow who brutally murdered this beloved Edwin."

And Revile grinned, peering about the chamber as if he was sizing up and contemplating each person for the deed.

"Maybe it was Mordris," he said, "wishing his brother's inheritance; maybe Hengist, avenging his abandoned daughter; maybe it was Catharine herself, fearing he might betray her; maybe it was Athelstane, guessing his son was plotting his own father's murder. Who knows but the murderer his or herself?

"For see you, the man or woman who did murder Edwin was not as callous as my good self. I might have neatly sliced his throat or skewered his heart. But I would not waste my effort and time stabbing a man twenty times or mutilating his body. No, Edwin was slain by somebody who not only wanted him dead but hated him also. Of that, at least, there can be no doubt!"

"Mordris!" cried Athelstane. "Devil's bile! Was it you? It would not surprise me for you had much to gain by his death. I know you always hated him. Was it you, you wastrel?"

"Me?" replied the young man coldly. "You would accuse me? And what have I to gain? You disowned me, remember. And do you honestly think I am either that cruel or dishonest?"

"Where were you when Edwin was murdered?" said Athelstane. "Defend yourself if you can!"

"So you accuse me," said Mordris, and this time he sounded hurt, "your only surviving son. You have ever loved Edwin the more – and for the less reason if what this assassin has told us is
134

the truth. He would have murdered you, me and the Lady Catharine. So much for your love, my father, so much for your true son and the affection you showed him. But I did not murder him and can give proof should that be necessary."

"I think you will have to," said Hengist stiffly.

"By The Grail, my good steward," Mordris went on with a smile, "I was with Catharine, your daughter. And may I add," he went on hastily, "we did nothing more than talk. She was unhappy about my brother's attitude – with some reason it appears. We arranged to meet in secret for this reason, so no one would guess we were seeing each other. But I repeat we are just friends – although I have a high regard for the Lady."

"Then it could not have been Catharine either," muttered Athelstane, "for you were with her. You both clear each other of any involvement, unless you were both in league and I do not believe that of Catharine. As for myself, I spent the night in my chamber. One of the wenches can vouch for me."

"So that just leaves you, Hengist," grinned Revile. "What were you doing lurking outside Edwin's room when you just happened to see me leaving?"

"What were you doing, Hengist?" exclaimed Athelstane, suddenly suspicious. "What were you doing there? I wondered about that. Devil's bile! Is it you?"

"No, of course not ..." started Hengist.

"But you had a motive, did you not?" said Athelstane coldly. "Were you not angry with Edwin for deflowering your daughter and then abandoning her? Tell me! Would a loving father not take revenge in such circumstances, would he not be entitled to? Tell me! Tell me, damn you to Hell!"

"By The Rood! I did no such thing," cried Hengist. "Of course I was angry when I found out. Who would not have been? But that does not mean I would slay him. Indeed, Edwin asked me to visit him in his chamber for he wished to explain the situation and an unhappy misunderstanding between him and my daughter. I never found out what that was about. He was dead when I got there!"

"Perhaps he really told you he no longer intended to marry Catharine?" suggested Revile. "He had abandoned her?"

"Silence, you craven dog!" yelled Hengist in unrestrained fury. "Silence!"

"My name is Snake," said Revile. "But I tell you Edwin was very much alive when I left his chamber. How long was it after that that you visited him, Hengist?"

"Minutes barely," replied Hengist angrily.

"Ah," said the assassin, "so you were lurking outside!"

"I was not!" cried Hengist.

"Tut, tut," went on Revile, "how very naughty of you, Hengist. Very naughty!"

"Very clever, you dog!" shouted Hengist. "But how did I have time to return the dagger to your chamber before you arrived there yourself."

"I think you already know the answer to that one," replied the assassin. "I did not return directly to my room from Edwin's chamber. I wandered about the castle for a while." And he added with a grimace: "I went via the window of Athelstane's bedroom."

"So that was you!" muttered Athelstane.

"Ah, yes," said Revile. "Forgive me." He smiled. "But that gave you plenty of time, Hengist. I guess you thought you were being clever, putting the dagger back in my room, I guess you did."

"So," cried Mordris, "it was you Hengist!"

"What?" said Hengist. "What do you mean?"

"You took the dagger!" said Mordris. "You had time to return it!"

"No," said Hengist, becoming heated in his turn. "How dare you accuse me!"

"Devil's blood and bile! Hengist," said Athelstane coldly, "did you murder Edwin my beloved son? Did you? For you had motive enough, and you had both the opportunity and the means. Something this Snake said comes to mind. Who ever killed my son would be covered in blood – and you were!"

"But that was from examining the body," Hengist protested. "This is ridiculous! You can't really believe ..."

"Of course," interrupted Athelstane, "of course! You have been so very very clever, have you not? But not clever enough, I reckon. You put yourself in charge of this trial because you said you were unbiased! How could you be when you discovered the body, with your daughter carrying the child of my son. How could you be? I say that you murdered Edwin, that you took a dagger from Snake's room, killed my son, and then returned the weapon before raising the alarm. You have been cunning, Hengist, but not cunning enough!"

"This is pre ..." began Hengist.

"By God, be silent!" demanded Athelstane. "Silence!"

"Let me speak!" cried Hengist.

"No!" said Athelstane. "You have already said quite enough." He addressed those assembled. "What say you, lords ?" he asked them. "What say you? We gathered here to try Snake for the murder of my son but I say it is Hengist who is guilty under the King's Justice! Do you agree?"

"Guilty!" they replied as if one voice. "Guilty!"

They hanged Hengist the next morning. He no longer protested his innocence and he repented for his brutal murder of the much-beloved Edwin.

Athelstane handed over his lands and titles to Mordris, and then entered the abbey on the Holy Isle to live out the rest of his days. Mordris married Catharine after some months, and, despite the fact her child was not his, he loved both of them deeply. He also inherited Hengist's property, there being no other heir.

Revile was not hanged. He escaped the following evening when his cell door was left carelessly unlocked.

Anyway, all things considered, Lord Mordris did very well from his beloved brother's death. But then he was a true son.

***

I think I understand," said Margaret. "This Mordris wanted to marry Catharine and at the same time steal his brother's inheritance. That was the purpose in the whole affair. It was Mordris who employed you?"

"Yes," said Revile, "we planned the whole thing."

"And Hengist did murder Edwin," went on Margaret thoughtfully. "But why? Did he believe Edwin would abandon his daughter? Or was there more to it than that?"

"There was," replied the assassin. "Hengist was given reason to believe I was hired by Edwin to murder Catharine – which, of course, I wasn't. Hengist sought out Edwin in his chambers, I watched him going in and heard them. They argued violently and then Hengist stabbed poor Edwin in a fit of a rage – although he had planned it sufficiently to have already taken a dagger from my room. Poor Hengist. He thought he was being so clever! He only entangled himself further."

Fergus sneered. "And I suppose you think you're so clever too!" he told Revile. "But how did you know that Hengist would kill Edwin? How did you know they would argue at all? They might have resolved their differences peaceably."

"That was scarcely likely," replied Revile. "We couldn't be certain what they would do, there was always some risk they would have done differently. Yet it was almost certain that it would end in violence. Edwin had made Catharine pregnant but he didn't want to marry her. Hengist knew this and was angry. And Edwin, too, was angry: angry that his father was forcing him into a loveless marriage with the promise of his inheritance. In all truth, Edwin might have employed me if he could; or he might have killed Catharine, Hengist, and even his own father. Hengist and Edwin were snared by their anger, distrust and dislike of the other. Although Mordris devised the final outcome, perhaps it would have ended the same without me – I just brought about the same conclusion more quickly. In the end it doesn't matter – except that Mordris got what he wanted: Catharine and his brother's titles and lands." The assassin shrugged. "And that's all that mattered to Mordris."

"But then surely there wasn't any trap," said Fergus wearily. "Surely all you did was use an already existing situation?"

"That is Eochaid's Paradox," replied Revile. "You see, I guess it doesn't matter if there's any trap or not. All that matters is that the victims are destroyed and the creator of the trap gets what he wants. Simple really, even for you Fergus."

"So who was this Eochaid?" asked Margaret unwisely.

"He was a King of Mannan – eventually," said Revile. "Have you heard of the land of Mannan?"

"It's to the north, isn't it?" replied Margaret, thinking she was going to get more of an explanation than she needed. "Beyond the border of Bernecia."

"Yes," said the assassin. "Mannan is the land between Pentland, Bernecia, Dalria and Strathclwyd. It neighbours Calatria and is where most battles are fought in the north. The folk there are a mixture of races and peoples although lately Bernecia has dominated Calatria and its influence now stretches to Mannan also. Anyway, the folk of Mannan have a rough time of it, what with invasions and the like.

"During a period of relative peace, Mannan prospered and was left more or less alone by its

137

more powerful neighbours. Eochaid had a claim to the throne although he never pressed it. For the King of Mannan at that time had two sons and there was also nephew. All three had equal claims to the throne as men of the royal house, but the succession had already been decided by the then king.

"Anyway, the younger of the King's sons, Constantine, was elected to rule when his father was dead. Of course the older son, Duncan Dubh, a rash and hot-headed character, and the nephew, Earl Kull, were none too pleased by the decision. Earl Kull especially felt he should have been chosen. They did all in their power to discredit Duncan Dubh – and each other – but the old king was not swayed by their whispers and would not contest the decision made by his nobles.

"Into this fracas comes Eochaid, a cousin to the old king. He seemed a gentle, unwarlike man who, because he had nothing to gain, was trusted by all sides. Eochaid mediated in arguments between the four players, and his council and advice was generally heeded.

"Then the old king died, and in suspicious circumstances that many called murder. Constantine quickly proclaimed himself king – although neither Duncan Dubh nor Earl Kull would accept it. Indeed, they formed an uneasy alliance, raised an army from amongst their supporters, and marched on the capital of Mannan. They were met by the loyalist forces of King Constantine and there was a savage battle. King Constantine's army was routed and he was killed, surrounded by enemies, although rumours abounded that the short-lived king had actually been captured and then slain.

"Now both Duncan Dubh and Earl Kull claimed they were now king. An assembly of nobles was called to choose between them. On the eve of the assembly, Earl Kull said he had discovered a plot to assassinate him. He had Duncan Dubh arrested and executed that very night.

"Only Kull was left to contest the throne.

"But the assembly of nobles decided that Kull was unfit to rule. They had the Earl imprisoned for there was sufficient evidence to suggest he had poisoned the old King; and no evidence of an assassination plot by the dead Duncan Dubh. Kull had Duncan put to death on the basis of a groundless accusation.

"After a trial, Kull was executed for treachery.

"And there being no man of the royal family left, Eochaid was made king. His rule was long, and while he reigned, Mannan did well under him. His reign lasted over twenty years until Eochaid died peacefully in his bed. But it became clear after he was dead that he had planned the deaths of the old king, Constantine, Duncan Dubh, and Earl Kull. And the trap which he devised was later given his name: Eochaid's Paradox."

"So how did this Eochaid do it?" asked Margaret, trying to sound interested.

"Firstly," said the assassin, not unaware of her tone, "he was a good judge of character. He knew that the three competitors to the throne were ruthless, ambitious men; and that given a chance, they would seize the crown by any means. Eochaid needed to do very little to realise his own ambition.

"Secondly, he told Constantine that the old King had changed his mind and was going to recommend that Duncan Dubh be made his heir despite what the king and an assembly of nobles had decided. Constantine had his father poisoned before word could be spread. He, of course, tried to make it look as if one of the other competitors had done the wicked deed. The only thing was that neither Duncan Dubh nor Earl Kull had anything to gain by killing the old king. Few of the people believed they had done it. Consequently, when Duncan Dubh and Kull marched on the capital, King Constantine could only raise a small army from his own supporters. He was soundly defeated and actually killed in battle.

"This left Duncan Dubh and Earl Kull in control – although they didn't like or trust each other. Both claimed that the other had had poor Constantine murdered. It was inevitable they would destroy one another such were the plots hatched.

"And so Duncan Dubh died, accused of trying to assassinate his competitor. But when Earl Kull attended the assembly of nobles he was denounced by the supporters of Duncan Dubh and Constantine. They feared that if the Earl was made king they would be persecuted. There was some evidence to suggest Earl Kull had poisoned the old King, left by Constantine, and none that Duncan Dubh had plotted to murder him, for that had been caused by rumours spread by Eochaid.

"You see from the death of the old King, it was inevitable Eochaid would become King of Mannan. It did not matter which one of the competitors won at any point. They all discredited each other and the one who proclaimed himself king was the one most suspected of treachery. The only way they could secure their position was by removing their opponents, making them more vulnerable to removal themselves. They snared themselves with their own ambition and plotting.

"And that is Eochaid's Paradox: a trap which would not have existed and could not have been sprung, but for those it was designed to catch."

"I see," said Margaret, and then despite everything, she yawned.

"I am boring you, I think," said Revile.

"No, not at all," she replied. "I think it is quite an interesting idea. But surely it can't arise that often? If Edwin and Hengist were not the kind of folk to quarrel and fight then your plan would never have worked, the situation would never have arisen. Isn't that right?"

"Aye," said the assassin with a grin, "it would not have worked. And it was not my plan. But then there would never have been a trap to begin with. Then I would have needed to murder Edwin and make it look like Hengist had done the wicked deed! It would have been more risky – obviously – but the end result would have been the same."

"You talk about these things so coldly," said Alwyn. "Have you no feelings of remorse when you murder folk? Have you no regard for another's life?"

"No, not really," said Revile lightly. "But I don't kill for pleasure or even usually for malice: I kill for money, money to survive."

"Hmmm," said Margaret thoughtfully. "You still surprise us with your lack of emotion. Maybe we don't help people when we should, but none of us have murdered and the like, even to survive. Yet somehow I thought you would be different. I had imagined that a man like you would instinctively feel guilty, that folk would somehow know and shun you. I wish I could see how you look, I wish I had seen you properly, before evening fell. Is your appearance frightening? Do men step out of your way for your aura is tinged with blood?"

"My appearance is unremarkable," replied the assassin. "It would have to be. I must remain anonymous. If I looked terrifying – and my aura was tinged with blood – I could not be an assassin. No one would trust me or come near me."

"I see," said Margaret, "yet you must look the part."

"I honestly don't think so," said Revile. "True, I have a rascally look, but then there are thousands of robbers, brigands, mercenaries, warriors, thieves, bandits and rascals all over the place. And in that way, I am unremarkable."

"I suppose," said Alwyn thoughtfully, "we do not understand you. You are outwith our ken."

Revile the assassin laughed. "What is there to understand?" he said. "Have you not listened to my tales? An assassin – or a successful one anyway – must have many things: patience, determination, courage, cunning, and other things besides. And above all else, he must have self-control. All emotion and sentiment must be suppressed. And in that, at least, I am the assassin. But really underneath it all, an assassin is just a man, the same as any other. He needs to eat and sleep, friendship and company – especially female company – the same as the farmer, whore or wench."

"Would you murder me?" asked Alwyn in a soft voice. "Would you kill me now if someone paid you? After all we've been through together?"

"More than likely," said the assassin. "If I was paid enough I would not give it a second thought. But you would die cleanly and without pain."

"That would be a great comfort," said Margaret sourly.

"Would you rather I lied to you?" asked Revile, feeling a little tired with their innocent indignation at a little murder. "You are not so quick to condemn Fergus who went to war, who went to kill people because his lord ordered it – and was rewarded for his bravery and murder with a bag of silver. Does a soldier question himself and the morality of what he is doing? No, he just murders whoever his lord commands and, at least in Bernecia, takes his pay. Have you ever seen a war, ever witnessed an invasion?"

"No," said Margaret shortly.

"You would not find it nice," said Revile. "Innocent folk, people like you three, are brutally tortured and slaughtered in their hundreds. Defeated armies are hunted down to a man and slain. Whole lands and regions are devastated, monasteries burned, priests and monks murdered, holy relics stolen or destroyed. Yet if I was a soldier you would not so harshly judge me. But because I kill who I choose, or who I am paid to, then I am evil."

The others said nothing for a moment.

"To be honest," said Margaret at last, "if you were a loyal soldier of the Tower I don't think we would treat you any differently, just as you would still despise us for being peasants. It is not because you are an assassin we do not understand you, it is because you are an adventurer, warrior and assassin; and we are whores, farmers and wenches."

"Aye," admitted Revile, "maybe you're right at that."

"Anyway," said Margaret, "we've talked that one to death. How about another story? Something notable and heroic?"

The assassin laughed. "Very well," he said.

Fool's Gold

D arkness descended in the hall. The many guests, lords and nobles were struck silent. For a moment nothing happened.

There was a flash of lightning and a deep roll of thunder. The darkness was thrown back to reveal details of the hall – but was as quickly replaced by an even deeper gloom.

A woman laughed, joyfully, in triumph.

Light grew, a sick pale light, illuminating the middle of the chamber. The radiance came from a strange crown, a circlet of black iron. It lit the face of the woman who carried it, turning her face a deathly hue.

"I have done it!" she cried. "I have finally got the Crown, the Crown of the Black Templars. Fools! Fools all! What a gift you brought me! What a dowry for my cursed stepdaughter! Its value is a thousand times her worth, ten thousand, maybe! And more! I have done it at last!"

The radiance steadily grew.

The woman laughed again.

"Please, Angelica Amhach," said another voice, that of a girl. "Please give up the Crown. It will destroy you, destroy you and consume you with its power."

"Give it up?" scorned Angelica. "Give it up? You are mad, girl, truly mad. With it I will rule all the north! No one will be able to stand against me! My armies will be invincible! I shall be an empress, a queen of a mighty kingdom! And you tell me to give it up?"

"You are a queen already," replied the girl. "Your kingdom is powerful enough. Take off the Crown! You will age a day for every hour. Please?"

Angelica Amhach sneered, studying the girl. "No, Mira," she said. "I think not. Not after all the trouble I have gone to get it. I think not. But you, you do not learn. I have already defeated you the once. Foolishly I was merciful and let you live. I will not be so foolish again!"

"Yes, you should have killed me when you had the chance," said Mira. She was a small blonde-haired girl with a round face. Her eyes were red for she had been weeping. Her simple robe was torn; her arm and face were bruised. In her right hand she carried a staff, a staff made of wood and carved with many animals and birds. "I won't give you the chance again," she went on. "Angelica, I beg you, take off the Crown and discard it. If you use it, it will destroy you as it has destroyed all others before. The Crown is too potent a talisman. It will destroy you!"

"O no," said Angelica. "Never! Fool! It is you who will be destroyed!"

The evil light continued to grow.

Mira shook her head. "I cannot let you do this," she told Angelica. "You will destroy more than yourself." She took her staff in both hands. "By Saint Aiden, I command thee! *Kru Yagg nan Bas an Krachog!*"

Angelica Amhach's eyes burned, her shoulders hunched, her hands twisted like an eagle's talons. A ball of light grew between her fingers; she weaved and conjured the ball into a pulsating sphere of dark fire.

Mira hammered her staff on the floor. A ripple of energy radiated out from the tip towards

142

Angelica. A light grew between Angelica's feet, a white light which brightened and strengthened. The ground became transparent, vague, shifting and without substance.

Angelica's jaw dropped. "No," she cried, "no, not that, I ..."

The ground at her feet became a Nothing. She was sucked into the shining hole, there was no substance to support her. The hole dropped away down beyond sight. Angelica Amhach tumbled head over heals, down and down, taking the Crown of the Black Templars with her.

Mira struck the floor again. The white light glazed over, sealing the hole down into the Nothing. The glaze thickened, the radiance dimmed until the ground of earth and charred rushes returned.

The fire and torches burst back into life.

Mira collapsed to her knees, weeping anew with misery, as life returned to the hall.

It was almost as if nothing had happened.

But Angelica Amhach was gone and with her the Crown of the Black Templars.

I

Late one afternoon two men rode through a long glen which led south and west out of the hills of Lothland. The riders were unkempt, rascally looking fellows and as they clopped along they scowled at anyone they met on the road or in the fields nearby.

The larger of the riders was an aged fellow although he looked all the more formidable for that. His beard and hair were grey, yet his grizzled face was grim with an icy stare as cold as a northern waste.

The old warrior was heavily armed. A notched, two-handed axe was strapped to his saddle; daggers were belted around his mighty frame. He was dressed in a long coat of stiffened leather, over a woollen shirt, with studded armlets and grieves, and worn boots. A dinted helm and battered shield were amongst his other belongings.

His poor pony strained under the massive weight of flesh and iron, looking as if it might collapse at any moment.

The old warrior's companion was slight and unassuming in comparison – although he was a considerable number of years younger. He was merely of average height and build: although his pony looked the happier. The smaller man had close-cropped black hair, and an old scar ran from the corner of his eye to his mouth.

The smaller fellow wore a leather tunic, studded with plates of rusty iron. Across the front of his tunic was strapped an assortment of daggers, each of a different size, each with a curved hilt shaped like a striking serpent. The hilt of his sword was similarly decorated; the blade of the weapon shone through the cracks in the old battered scabbard. The fellow also carried a bow and quiver of arrows, a helmet, and a shield.

The two riders continued to scowl at all and sundry as they plodded along on their ponies.

In truth, they were both in fine spirits – it was just that their sort of behaviour was expected of them and they had reputations to maintain.

The two riders travelled south through the lower marches of Lothland towards the Merse. The land about them swelled and dipped, from high hills and passes to deep valleys and glens where the road was muddy. Sheep and cattle grazed the steep pastures above the dense thickets of trees and gorse. A few peasants toiled in the wet fields by the fertile banks of the wide river Twyd. It was a pleasant enough day and the sun warmed the chill of the breeze, although clouds were rolling over from the west.

"How much further are we travelling today?" asked the old warrior.

The two riders had entered a wood and there was no one about to frown at or frighten.

"O stop moaning!" replied the smaller fellow. "We've hardly come ten miles since we stopped for lunch!"

"Well, I'm tired," said the old warrior. "I'm fed up trudging south. I'd forgotten how many miles it is to Caerisle. I wish I'd never bothered now for I'm sure we'll miss the muster."

"Don't forget this is your idea, lardbelly. I was quite content in Llaith, whoring and drinking. Besides, it is your pony that has been doing the trudging, not you. I pity the poor beast!"

"Pity this misbegotten beast?" said the old warrior. "Do not waste your effort! It is the most ill-tempered and lazy garron I have ever had the misfortune to ride!"

"Pshush. It is fitter than many and stronger than most. It's not you who should be tired for you've done nothing but complain. But your poor pony? Now, it must be truly exhausted!"

"Perhaps. But only from over exposure to your feeble humour, laddie!"

"Never mind, lardbelly. I'm sure we'll find an inn and some food and drink soon."

"And I will be glad of it," said the old warrior.

"As will I, Douglas," said the smaller fellow quite seriously. "I've heard rumours about these lands and I've no wish to test their truth by spending a night in the open. But, if I remember rightly, there is a small town not far from here. With a bit of luck we'll reach it before dusk."

Douglas laughed merrily. "I'd not thought you so easily frightened, my brave friend. Next you'll be telling me you're afraid of goblins and ghosties and things that go bump in the night!"

"Don't be stupid, Douglas. I'm not worried about goblins or ghosties. These, in case you had forgotten in your advanced dotage, are the lands of Earl Eadolfa, Lord of the Merse and Terror of the North. People have disappeared from these parts although I don't think you need to look far for the cause. You must have heard the stories in Llaith?"

"I did, laddie, and I don't understand your concern. They are just stories to frighten old women or make peasants gape – they are not for folk like us. I didn't think you of all people would have fallen for such fantasies." He clicked his fingers. "Gold mines, pah! Sorcery, pah! Rat, son of Rodents, the brave adventurer, pah!"

"I wouldn't be so quick to scorn, blubberguts. There may be more to these fantasies than you imagine. Travellers have disappeared, that's no idle tale: well-protected troops and merchant companies – as well as folk like us. You may have no other plans but I don't wish to spend the rest of my life breaking rocks in the Leadhills."

"And I tell you there is no truth in these stupid, stupid stories! Hell's Teeth, Rat, how can you believe such pig shit?"

"Listen to me, Douglas," replied Rat, "even if it is only to pander to my cowardice. I ask you:

be cautious in your dealings with folk of the Merse. Control your temper and we may well live to spin a yarn or two about the place ourselves."

"O very well! Although I don't see the need!"

"Perhaps you don't and perhaps there isn't any, but I still think it's better to approach such things with caution, whatever the truth in tavern tales. Much better – and possibly much healthier for both of us."

Douglas grinned and his face cracked into a smile. "But that is not in my nature," he told his friend. "I believe it is usual with men to become more cautious with the toll of years. They lose the recklessness and adventure of youth. It has been different with me. When I was young there was so many things I wanted to do, so many things I wanted to see, so many places I wanted to explore. I've done them all now, there's nothing left. Yet I still crave this kind of life, wandering hither and thither as the whim takes me, doing what I please. I still love the excitement, aye, the excitement and the fear in my guts ..."

"It must be a mighty fear to fill your guts!" muttered Rat.

"... I would have no other life, that is for sure. For one thing: I can still take offence at the most innocent of remarks – never mind obvious insults!"

"Yup," said his friend, "you are a fat grumpy old bastard!"

"Aye, I am that, you whore's son," growled Douglas, his eyes blazing. "You would do well to remember it! For I'm neither too fat nor too old to split you head like a rotten turnip. So please, please, have a care with your jests – for your sake! That would be so much healthier for you!"

Rat laughed easily. "I will have a care," he said, "I will. So withhold your hand. I still value my hide even if you don't yours. I will be cautious enough for both of us. Anyway, your thirst for action and splitting heads will be quenched all the soon enough when we reach Caerisle. I am not so sure: I make a poor soldier."

"You'll be all right," said the old warrior, quickly regaining his good humour. "We're joining the mercenaries, not the loyal soldiers of Cymbria. Discipline is slack. Besides, we've more than a few advantages over the other soldiers."

"Such as?" asked Rat.

"Ah, laddie," said Douglas, "how do you think I've survived to acquire this noble girth? For I have fought in more battles than you've been with whores."

"Gad," said Rat, "that must be a lot."

"Indeed, laddie," said the old warrior, "and many better men have died than Douglas MacGalbrain. For see, mercenaries fight on both sides and, if wise, they don't wear livery or carry standards. It is so easy to become confused as to which side you joined – especially in the

'ur property which is plundered. There is usually plenty of

'and if the worst does come to the worst, I always make

'nd."

jobs to do," said Rat. "All the dirty and dangerous

'ley are often the most profitable."

'ot appear convinced by Douglas's reasoning.

145

The weather was steadily worsening, even as they spoke. The wind had veered and strength-ened: there was a heavy feeling of moisture in the air. Clouds were rolling in from the west.

The two travellers prodded their ponies into a faster trot.

The sun was suddenly eaten by a dark mass of clouds. The hills about Rat and Douglas frowned over the valley, and the copses and woods became shadowed and secretive. A silence fell which was only broken by the clop of the pony's hooves and the 'craw' of a single crow.

Despite his ridicule earlier, Douglas peered anxiously over his shoulder.

"Not so quick to scoff now, greybeard," grinned Rat.

They were now over the border and into the Merse. They rode on for some time in silence.

"Well," continued Rat eventually, "this soldiering business does not sound as bad as I'd remembered. I thought that buying our swords bought our loyalty as well."

"Some mercenaries might see it that way, I concede, but they don't tend to live very long. To be sure, it's a chancy way of life and I won't try to deceive you about the danger. But the rewards can be worth it. I've earned, or acquired, a fortune in my time. I've had gold and jewels and the best of what there is to have." He sighed, shaking his head.

"What became of it?" asked Rat.

"I spent the lot," replied the old warrior with a rueful smile. "On women and wine." He thought for a minute. "I don't really know. You, more than most, must know how it is. Anyway, have you fought in many battles yourself?"

"Aye, one or two," said Rat, "but nothing on this scale. And I have been on the losing side too often for my comfort. But as you say: the pickings can be rich, and that's what concerns me. Do you know what this battle is about? Why are the Cymbrians fighting each other?"

"I've no idea," replied Douglas. "I never bother to find out – it makes things so much clearer. I fight because I am paid seems the best cause to me. You know," he went on, peering over his shoulder, "if I didn't know better I would say that rook is following us."

"It is said that Earl Eadolfa is notably fond of rooks and ravens." Rat threw a glance at the old warrior.

Douglas sneered at him but set a brisk pace on his garron. "I thought that I could see smoke ahead," he said, trying to peer through the deepening gloom. "I reckon it's from this town you mentioned? Clovenfords was it?"

"Aye, how far away is it, do you reckon?"

"A mile maybe, or a couple of miles at the most. Perhaps we'll escape the coming rain and whatever else besides."

But almost as if to prove him wrong a large raindrop landed on his hand.

The two companions cursed.

Digging their boots into the bellies of their ponies, they encouraged the beasts into a slow gallop – about as much as the garrons could manage. Douglas's stout pony thundered down the road but was quickly overtaken by the lighter Rat. With a shout, Rat sped towards a narrow log bridge which spanned a gurgling stream deep in the vale.

The rain began to pour from the inky sky.

But Rat pulled up his pony short of the bridge and came to a halt in a slither of mud. Four horsemen were crossing the stream from the far bank. Douglas would have ridden on but Rat stopped him with a shout of warning.

"Remember the Pits!" hissed the pale fellow. "These are soldiery of Earl Eadolfa of the Merse!"

"How do you know?" demanded the old warrior.

"Fool!" said Rat in a low voice. "Old fool! I know their standard: a golden unicorn on a black field!"

Douglas nodded but his quick temper was not eased. The rain pattered on the crown of his head and ran down his face. He could feel water trickling down his back under his shirt. And the four Mersian horsemen seemed to take an age to cross the bridge.

The old warrior's eyes flashed, but he swallowed back his anger with some effort, uncurling his hand from the haft of his axe.

The soldiery of Earl Eadolfa cantered to the bank, then rode up to the two adventurers, stopping in front of them, barring their way. The tallest of the Mersians – his men beside him in a line – sat up in his saddle, eyeing Douglas and Rat.

"Who are you?" he demanded. "And what business have you in the Merse of my lord Earl Eadolfa?"

Rat bowed his head. "I am Rat, son of Rodents, good captain," he replied in a friendly tone, ignoring the menace in the Mersian's tone. "My friend and travelling companion is Douglas MacGalbrain. We are journeying to Caerisle and are looking for an inn where we can spend the night and escape this rain. Is there an inn at Clovenfords?"

"Perhaps," muttered the Mersian captain, "but we do not want ruffians or brigands in the Merse. I must ask you again: what is your business here – and have you any gold?"

"No, we've no gold, to be sure," said Rat easily. "But we have a little money – sufficient for our journey. We're neither ruffians nor brigands. We're warriors on the way to Caerisle. But our business here is simply as travellers."

"There is a toll to cross the bridge," said the captain. His men grinned at each other.

"O aye?" said Rat.

"Yes," muttered the Mersian, "and if you not pay you must come with us. We do not want beggars in this land. We will take you back to the border with Lothland – if we get that far."

"How much is this toll, good captain? For we are in a hurry and cannot afford to miss the muster."

"Ten silver merks!" replied the proud Mersian. "I hope you have that much!"

Douglas snorted in indignation. They had asked for a fortune.

"I am not sure," said Rat. "I would need to check. But perhaps there is some other way to the south which avoids this bridge and its toll?"

"No, there is no other way!"

"I'll see if I have enough money," said Rat and produced a thin purse. He peered into it and started to count out several silver-coloured and few gold-coloured pieces.

"Give me that!" ordered the Mersian captain, his hand straying to the hilt of his sword. The Mersians bunched around their leader.

Douglas stirred but said nothing.

Rat, son of Rodents, hesitated for a moment, then reached forward, handing the Mersian his money pouch.

"Good," said the captain and relaxed slightly. "You may pass. But your companion must also pay. Give me your purse, old man!"

"Now, you're being greedy!" Douglas forced out through clenched teeth. "Very greedy!"

"Better do as he asks," said Rat in an easy tone.

"Yes, you had better!" said the Mersian. "We have places for people like you, old man, places where you would spend the rest of your dotage in torment, places where you would work all day and suffer all night. We will take you to these places if you want. Give me your purse, old man!"

"Very well," started the old warrior, "I'll just look ..."

As he spoke, and without any warning, Douglas grabbed the handle of his axe and it sang through the air. The old warrior spurred his pony forward, cannoning into the nearest horse and unseating the rider. Douglas's axe sought the captain. Although the Mersian swept out his own sword, the axe broke the blade and sliced into the captain's neck, lodging in his breast bone with a spray of bright-red blood.

Ripping the axe free, Douglas met the sword of the horseman to his left. The two men struggled against each other, but the old warrior had the greater strength. He twisted the sword from his opponent's grip. Douglas cried savagely and brought his axe down on the warrior's head, splitting helmet and skull with no more effort than a rotten turnip.

Rat had no more difficulty dispatching the last Mersian. He feinted for his opponent's head, but his sword went low, biting into the horseman's thigh with a splash of blood. The Mersian gave out a thin scream of pain but Rat ended the cry with another flash of his sword. The Mersian fell headless from his horse.

Then Rat felt a biting blow in his back as if he had been punched in the kidneys. He twisted in the saddle and struck out desperately at the back-stabber, the rider who Douglas had unhorsed at the outset. Luck was with Rat for his wild sweep severed the man's dagger arm. Leaping from his pony, Rat hewed the maimed warrior as he shrieked and pleaded for mercy.

Rat grunted with pain. When he examined his back, his hand came away sticky with blood. He knew that the wound should not prove fatal provided he could stop the bleeding. He had been saved from more serious injury by his studded tunic.

"You stupid, fat fool!" he swore at Douglas. "You nearly got me killed! And what for? Your stupid pride and a few copper pieces!"

The old warrior dismounted, quickly checked the Mersians were dead, then examined his companions' wound.

"It's not too deep," he said, trying to sound reassuring. "Just another to add to your collection. Should I seal it?"

"I suppose you'd better," replied Rat. "But before doing that we'd better hide these bodies." And he grinned slightly through the pain. "And search them."

They dragged the corpses of the Mersians into trees by the roadside.

"Ye Gods, I hate this weather," muttered Rat despondently.

They hid the bodies in the undergrowth of the wood and covered them with fallen branches and leaves. Rat retrieved his purse and added such other pieces and trinkets as he found. The two adventurers rummaged through the Mersian's saddlebags, then chased the horses away across country. Both knew the horses would most likely return to where they were stabled. They also knew the bodies of the Mersians would not remain undiscovered for long – anyone with a nose would see to that – but there was nothing else they could do. Anyway, they did not intend to stay in the Merse for any longer than was strictly necessary.

"We'd better get this over with," muttered Rat, peeling off his tunic. The old warrior found a sheltered spot and built a small blaze with some dry kindling and half a flask of oil. Heating a dagger in the flames, until rain hissed and steamed off the blade, Douglas pressed it firmly against Rat's wound.

Rat clenched his teeth so that he could not cry out in agony.

The old warrior handed him a skin of wine.

"You fight well," said Douglas. "I don't think I'd like to stand against you. But sorry for getting you into this mess. As you said: you might have been killed – and then I would have had no one to insult and abuse me until I reached Caerisle."

"True, you fat old blubberguts!" managed Rat, spilling some of the wine down his chin. "But we were lucky. I think these Mersians were more used to bullying peasants and frightening merchants than dealing with the likes of us. And so much the better!" He stood up with some difficulty. "But come. Let us go to this inn."

Rat redressed, and then heaved himself onto his pony, grunting with pain. Prompting the beast into a trot, he crossed the bridge and climbed up the far bank, followed by the singing Douglas. The old warrior was celebrating the victory of the battle at the bridge.

They rejoined the road and headed for the town of Clovenfords and its tavern.

They arrived at the town of Clovenfords a short time later.

The downpour had not relented and both the adventurers were soaked through to the skin. The wind now came from the north-west, and Rat shivered as the garrons plodded through the mud and refuse of the main street. He bleakly gazed through the rain at the shabby dwellings, then forward to the town square where a market was being held despite the weather. The two companions hurried towards the people and were directed to the large tavern across the square from the prison.

Rat and Douglas dismounted and led their ponies through a gateway into the courtyard of the inn, calling for the taverner. A large, bustling man appeared and, after a brief haggle over the price, they secured rooms for themselves and stabling for their bedraggled ponies. Rat immediately went inside while the old warrior took care of the garrons.

When Douglas was finished, he joined his companion for a drink in the large common room. A bright fire burnt in the grate and the chamber was warm after the chill of the wind. They sat down on a bench with their pots of ale.

"Are you in pain, laddie?" asked the old warrior, doing his best to sound concerned. "You don't look very happy."

"Aye, a little to be sure," reluctantly admitted Rat. He shook his head but he could not clear the dark mood. "I'll be all right in a moment."

"It's my fault, I suppose. I should have been more careful. My quick temper is ever my downfall."

"Don't worry about it," said Rat, after draining his pot. "They got no more than they deserved – and we are the richer for it."

Douglas refilled Rat's mug from a large jug. "You're too generous," he said. "I know I was foolish, but I will try to be more careful in future."

"As I have said," replied Rat in irritation, "don't worry about it!"

"I don't think you're very well," said Douglas. "You seem even paler than usual. You should go straight to bed and rest."

"I think I may," said his companion. "But what are you going to do?"

"I reckon I'll go out for a while and take a wander around Clovenfords. The slave pen looked interesting and I have a few purchases to make."

Rat, son of Rodents, sighed. "Well, be careful. For Hell's sake, don't get into any more trouble. All right?"

"I can't promise anything," replied Douglas with a grin.

"Gad! You are as bad as a naughty child, always up to some new mischief! How, by the Seven Serpents of Set, have you managed to survive this long without a wet nurse?"

"Ah laddie!" said the old warrior with a glint in his eye, "one day I may have to teach you my secret!" And he patted the haft of his axe. "One day!"

"I can't wait!" said the younger man darkly. "Then I'll see you later." Rat lowered his voice. "Don't imagine I'll rescue you from the slave pen – or the Slave Pits – if you're caught!"

"I'll bear that in mind," replied Douglas, getting to his feet. He put down his beer pot and wiped his lips. "And you look after the gold and silver. I couldn't believe you handed over your purse like that with all that money!"

"Douglas," said Rat with a scornful grin, "I wouldn't be travelling to Caerisle with you if I had that amount of money – not even for your sparkling conversation. The gold pieces you saw are copper in a wash of gold."

The old warrior laughed. Rat got up and went to find the innkeeper so he could buy some wine, good strong southern wine if he could get it.

Douglas MacGalbrain waved as he passed the window of the common room.

Rat climbed the wooden stairs to his bedroom. He entered the chamber, closing and bolting the door behind him. A fire was already burning in the hearth and it was quite warm and welcoming. His room was furnished with a cot, stool, chest, bench and table with a bowl and jug.

Adding a few more logs to the fire, he then stripped off his wet clothing. He found dry garments in his pack and dressed in a woollen shirt and leggings, hanging his wet tunic in front of the fire. It began to steam, and filled the room with a pungent reek. Sitting down cross-legged, Rat unstoppered his bottle and took a deep drink of wine. He sighed and stared into the fire. And although the wine eased the pain in his back, and relaxed the hunch of his shoulders, Revile the assassin could not escape from his gloomy mood.

Part of his depression was caused by the wound in his back – and how close to a useless, profitless death he had come. Just a little deeper, just a little further to the left, and Revile might have been dead now, having breathed out his last in the rain. What would it have been for? A few copper pieces and the quick temper of a hot-headed old man.

But it was not just that.

Although Revile was not tired of adventure and peril, he had not found his life over the past months exciting or challenging. It was not enough to murder merchants or nobles, or to ride in the armies of petty wars, or sell his cunning and dagger to rich princelings.

It had been different in the past. His adventures on the island of Viriggia with his friend Indulf had been interesting. He smiled when he remembered the witch, Albezzia, and her pool in the dell. There had been the time spent at Dundonald with the Lady Shona of the Feni. There had been a mad chase and adventure through Deira, following the woman Lathspell who had slept with him and then robbed him of everything except his revenge.

What had happened since then? Not much really. He had drunk a lot, he supposed, drinking his way through the loot from his last murder. It was not enough. Why was he riding south with Douglas MacGalbrain to join an army in Caerisle? He did not even know what the fight was about. Yet he was in the Merse, the domain of Earl Eadolfa-nan-Bas, Eadolfa the Immortal, Terror of the North, and the Earl intrigued the assassin.

Revile wanted a change: some adventure that would push his resources of courage and cunning and strength to the limit; something notable and memorable to shake the thrones of kings. Otherwise, Revile might end his days like Douglas MacGalbrain – if he was lucky enough to live that long.

Gradually his mind wandered, and he began to doze in front of the fire. But his choice was made: he was not going to Caerisle. Revile would tarry for a while in the Merse and try to discover Earl Eadolfa's secrets: the truth of the gold mines and slave pits rumoured to be in the Leadhills. Which, he reckoned, would prove dangerous, interesting and maybe even profitable, the latter being by no means the lesser consideration.

He rose yawning from the floor, drained the last of the wine, and lay down on his cot, pulling the furs up to his neck.

Before too long, he fell into a deep untroubled sleep.

II

He woke an uncertain amount of time later.

It was dark in the room for it was now full night and the fire had burned low. He propped himself up on one elbow and groaned, for his back was tender and stiff – and the wine sat uneasily in his stomach.

There was another knock on his door.

Revile considered ignoring it, but curiosity got the better of him, and he rose and padded across to admit the visitor. It occurred to him that it might be Earl Eadolfa and his warriors, come to exact a terrible revenge, but the assassin was too tired and his digestion too troubled to care. Withdrawing the bolts awkwardly in the cold, he opened the door and was more than a little surprised to see a beautiful young woman standing there.

Revile relaxed. "Who are you?" he yawned.

The girl did not reply for a moment, but stared at him, weighing him up. Revile scrutinised her back.

She was tall and slender. Her hair was long and as black as a rook's wing, and tumbled about her shoulders; her skin had the colour and sheen of copper. She had dark smoky eyes and high aristocratic cheek bones. The girl was dressed in a rough tunic, belted at the waist by a length of frayed rope. Her feet were bare and dirty. All in all, she was as lovely a vision as Revile had ever seen late at night in a tavern.

It could only mean trouble.

"I am Aliannia, master," she said at last. Her accent was strange, broken and harsh – although pleasing to the ear. She added the 'master' reluctantly, almost as an afterthought.

"What do you want?" asked the assassin wearily. "I'm trying to get some sleep."

Her gaze dropped to the floor between her feet. "I was sent, master, by Douglas MacGalbrain. He ordered me to tell you that he is sorry for what happened at the bridge today. He hopes that this present will lessen the debt between you."

Revile shook his head. "I suppose you are a slave, then?" he said. "That he purchased you from the market, from the slave pen?"

"Yes, master," she replied, and then added slowly: "I was purchased to give you pleasure."

"Hmmm. A more than reluctant present, perhaps? But tell Douglas MacGalbrain I am grateful he took the trouble but there is no debt between us. Tell him I can't accept his present – no matter how well it is packaged."

Aliannia hesitated.

"What is wrong?" said Revile impatiently. "Why do you wait?"

"Master, I do not wish to return to the slave pens," she said and then whispered: "And Douglas MacGalbrain said he would have me beaten if I did not please you."

"I see." Revile sighed. "I suppose you can come in – but just for this night."

The slave girl entered his chamber, and Revile closed and bolted the door behind her. He lit a lamp and built up the fire.

"Look," he told her, "it's nothing personal but I have no need of you or any other slave. It was kind of Douglas to take the trouble. But don't worry, you don't need to go back to the pen. I'll free you instead and then you can go wherever you will."

"No, master," she cried, "you must not do that!"

"Bugger me," moaned Revile.

"What would I do?" she went on. "My home is uncounted leagues from here and I have no friends or money. To free me would be to condemn me to a terrible death. That would be even worse than the pens."

The assassin made a strange exasperated sound, like he might be choking. "Like I've said: you can stay for tonight. You can make up your own mind about what you want to do. I can't be bothered thinking about it. But whatever, I'm going back to bed."

"I will stay," replied the girl.

Revile grunted and lay down on the bed.

"Blow out the lantern, will you?"

"Yes, master," she replied. The light was extinguished.

The assassin pulled the blankets up to his neck and settled down to sleep. Aliannia curled up by the fire, but she was restless and fidgeted. The floor was uncomfortable and Revile, who was feeling as uncharitable as ever, had not given her any blankets.

The dawn, such as it was, lightened the impenetrable murk, and the deeper darkness was slowly replaced by a vague grey twilight. Everywhere was the sound of water: dripping from the trees and the eaves of the shabby buildings; splashing and overflowing from guttering and sewers; cascading in waterfalls over the rocky slopes; or just falling persistently from the inky sky.

Revile stood at the window of his tavern room, staring dismally at the rain. Aliannia was still asleep by the cold hearth and the assassin left her to her dreams.

Revile shivered, muttered something, then went to the fireplace with kindling and fuel. Aliannia was maybe tired but Revile the assassin was cold – and tired waiting for her to wake.

"What is it?" said the slave girl in fear, startled out of her slumber. She shrank away from Revile. Then she recognised him and she relaxed. "O, it is you."

Revile looked at her thoughtfully. "Aye, it's just me," he said, "I was going to light the fire."

She stared back at him, and he frowned in response, rather more darkly than he intended.

"You do not like me," the slave girl said sadly.

"I have to admit to being quite indifferent to you one way or the other."

"Is there anything I can do for you, master?" she asked.

"Yup, you can shut up. I'm hungry. I'm going down for some breakfast. You can come, if you like, then I'll return you to the pens."

Aliannia looked miserable, and there was never a more heart-rending picture of beauty and despair.

"Master," she pleaded, "please do not send me back. I will do anything, anything." She even looked as if she might mean it. Despite himself, Revile was slightly intrigued but remained far more irritated.

"I'm sorry," muttered Revile, "I hadn't realised this was open for question. I had thought you were a slave and would do what you're damn well told!"

"They will kill me, they may take me back!"

"That's a shame, to be sure, but no concern of mine."

"Could you at least take me from the Merse before you sell me?"

"Sell you?" said the assassin. "Who said anything about selling you? I'll be quite happy just to give you away. I have sufficient a burden with Douglas MacGalbrain, without you as well. Anyway, I'm not sure I'm leaving the Merse."

Something inside her seemed to break. "Very well," she said and there was a catch in her voice, "but you will have my blood on your hands. If you return me to the pen then I will be caught and you will condemn me to a terrible death. Will that please you?"

"I really don't give a damn," sighed Revile, sounding bored. "I already have plenty of blood on my hands so I guess a little more will not make any difference."

"You are a cold-hearted bastard!"

Revile grinned like a tiger. "Strangely enough," he told her, "you are not the first person to reach that conclusion. Now, do you want some breakfast before your terrible death?"

When they reached the common room, Douglas MacGalbrain was already seated at one of the tables. A large ham, a loaf of bread, a pat of butter and a round of cheese were in front of the old warrior – and were rapidly disappearing into his mouth, washed down with a jug of ale.

"Greetings," hailed Douglas with his cheeks bulging. "How are you this glorious morning?"

"Better," replied the assassin, "although the back is still a little tender. I'm hungry. Have you emptied the larder or is there anything left to eat in the whole of Clovenfords?"

"I dare say there are a few crumbs," replied the old warrior, "and a small lump of mouldy cheese the mice are finished with. Shall I order them for you?"

"Yes," said Revile, "and quickly."

Douglas stood up and called for the innkeeper, ordering them a large breakfast.

"Did you like you present?" asked Douglas when he had finished bellowing at the innkeeper.

"Yes," said Revile, "it was much appreciated. But would you be offended if I returned her to the pen?"

"Why?" said Douglas. "Didn't she please you? I promised her a beating."

"No, it's not that," said Revile. "It's just that she'll get in the way as we go on."

"Aye, I suppose you are right. Do what you will. You can do what you like with her – she didn't cost very much."

Revile nodded, smiling.

Then Douglas lowered his voice. "Listen, friend Rat," he whispered, "some soldiers arrived here with the dawn. We could be in trouble because we're the only strangers in Clovenfords. I think these Mersians are searching for the four men we met by the bridge – I believe they've found their horses. They've been asking the innkeeper questions."

"Where's my food?" said Revile loudly, and his breakfast was brought at last. He devoured the food eagerly. "I guess we should leave this morning, right after breakfast," he said to Douglas, spraying him with crumbs, "or we may miss the muster for ever."

Revile finished his meal. "Come, girl," he said, getting to his feet, "you can help me pack."

"Yes, master," said Aliannia uncertainly.

Douglas laughed. "Aye, we've delayed long enough," he said, "I guess we must leave Clovenfords to face the rain."

But when they reached the door out of the common room, their way was blocked by six

Mersian warriors. The leader of the troop stepped forward and said, courteously enough: "I am Patrick, Lord Rothstor, Warden of the North March of the Merse. We are seeking four of our soldiers who disappeared north and east of here yesterday."

Revile introduced his companions. "I am Rat, son of Rodents," he said. "This is my friend, Douglas MacGalbrain, and this girl is my slave, Isobeau, who is from a land far to the south."

Patrick, Lord Rothstor, pulled at his beard for a moment, the unicorn of the Merse proudly emblazoned across his broad chest. He was a sturdy-looking fellow, even dressed in all his finery, but he had risen to the Warden of the North March more by strength in arms than keen wit. He shook his head and said softly: "I believe you travelled from the north yesterday?"

"In a manner of speaking," replied Rat with a warm smile, "for we lost our way in the rain and forded the river east of here, nearly drowning our horses and ourselves. We'd meant to take a short-cut but we managed to get hopelessly lost. Such is life, I guess. The weather was quite awful and we were soaked through to ..."

"Yes, yes," interrupted Patrick, "but did you meet anyone on the road?"

"What is this?" demanded Douglas MacGalbrain. "What are you saying? Are you accusing us of waylaying your companions?"

"Peace, Douglas," said Revile. "I know we're in a hurry but we can spare a little time."

"Sorry, Rat," muttered the old warrior. "I suppose it's just the thought of travelling all the way to Caerisle in this rain. Forgive my outburst, Lord Rothstor. The rain and me make poor travelling companions."

Patrick waved the apology away.

"We met a few folk," said Revile, "but mostly before the border and scarcely anyone after the rain started. True, there were some shepherds and peasants, aye, and a merchant and his entourage. But that is all. What did your friends look like?"

"They were soldiers of the Merse, under my leadership," said the Warden of the North March, "their horses returned but they did not."

"We saw no soldiers," said Douglas. "Now we really should be going. I want to reach Caerisle tomorrow if possible."

"Are you sure of this?" asked Patrick.

"Aye," said Revile, "we saw some merchants but no one else of any important. Anyway, the rain was so heavy we could hardly see each other. We had terrible trouble crossing the river for it was swollen with flood water and for a moment I thought I'd be washed away. Our minds were occupied with finding warmth, shelter and a hot meal. I'm sorry but there's nothing else I can say to help you."

Patrick, Lord Rothstor, Warden of the North March of the Merse, looked thoughtful for a second, and considered Rat, Douglas and especially Aliannia. "Very well," he said at last. He turned from them and Revile took this as a sign they had been dismissed. Douglas grunted and pushed past the Mersians. Revile and Aliannia followed the old warrior, and they hurried up the stairs to their rooms.

"I think we've been lucky," said Douglas. "But we should leave with all haste. This town could become a little unhealthy before too long."

"Indeed," said the assassin briefly, thinking that outside would hardly be safer. He left Douglas at the landing and hurried to his chamber.

"I think I'll take you along after all," the assassin told Aliannia as he opened his door. "You might prove useful."

"Thank you, master," she replied, "but where are we going?"

"I think I'll have a look at the Merse," replied Revile with a grin and a cunning look, "maybe even at old Eadolfa in his hall. And there's these famous slave pits in the Leadhills to find."

"Do not be a fool," cried the slave girl. "The miles to the Wells of Snar are many and the road will be very dangerous for all of us. Could you not take some other route, back north perhaps? Would that not be more wise, master?"

"You're not too good at this slave business, are you girl?" said Revile, eyeing her. He began to gather his belongings together. "Anyway, they know we came from the north and might guess we'll return the same way. We shall travel west for that is the unexpected direction."

"Please, master!"

"Hold your tongue, girl! Ye Gods, Aliannia, I didn't mean it literally! Just be quiet! Or would you prefer to be returned to the pen after all?"

Aliannia said nothing.

"Why don't you say something?" demanded Revile.

"You told me to be quiet, master, and I am just doing as you ordered."

The assassin frowned at her again, a dark expression even for him.

"I will come with you, master," she went on quickly, "although travelling towards the west fills me with a great fear. I am not sure I understand your reasons for staying in the Merse, but if you meddle in the affairs of Eadolfa-nan-Bas, Eadolfa the Immortal, you will be the worse for it."

"What do you know of the Earl?" asked Revile, hoisting his heavy pack onto his shoulders and then strapping on his sword.

"Too much, master," she said mysteriously. "If you seek gold in the Merse you will find only death!"

Revile made a rude noise but could not be bothered pursuing the subject, at least not there and then.

They left the room and met Douglas climbing the stairs to find them. "God," he said, "where have you been?"

"We've been talking," said Revile.

The old warrior nodded. "Anyway," he went on, "I've paid the innkeeper for the rooms and the meals. We can get off now."

"Good," said Revile, "and I've decided to bring the slave girl along."

"O aye?" grinned Douglas.

The three companions left the tavern and went to the stables in the courtyard near the rear of the building. They peered in through the common room windows to see Patrick talking to the innkeeper.

"The sooner we're away from here," said Douglas softly, "the better."

They led their ponies into the dreary town square, loading on their packs and other gear.

"I can't say I'm sorry we're leaving," said the assassin as he climbed onto his garron's back. The ground was muddy and Clovenfords looked even more dingy than the evening before.

And it was still raining.

Revile helped Aliannia onto the pony, placed his sword across its shoulders, and wiped the water from his eyes. The slave girl shivered. "There's a spare cloak in my pack," he told her.

"Thank you, master," she replied, rummaging through his belongings.

The assassin took one last look at the inn, then rode out of the square down a street leading to the south. His pony strained under the combined weight of him and the girl yet still looked the happier of the two beasts. It said much for Douglas MacGalbrain and his girth.

Just as they reached the outskirts of town, Aliannia gazed back and nudged Revile in the ribs.

"What is it?" he asked.

A group of men had ridden into the town square and had stopped at the front of the tavern.

Revile pulled his pony to a halt, turned the beast around, and sat there peering back through the shifting sheets of blinding rain.

The party of horsemen dismounted and some of them disappeared into the inn. The men were Mersian warriors and a banner, with the golden unicorn of the Merse, fluttered in the wind. The assassin could not help noticing a large, bearded individual who was obviously in command. He moved with a sort of youthful ease although he must have been a man in his fifties or older. There was something odd about him, something different, something dangerous and frankly unpleasant. A rook fluttered down out of the sky and landed on the bearded-man's shoulder.

Four spare horses were tethered to a rail. Each of the horses had some burden slumped across their backs. Revile could not be certain but the burdens appeared to be men: dead men.

"Damn!" said Revile, dragging the head of his pony around to the south.

"Master," breathed Aliannia, "we must flee!"

The assassin's pony splashed in the mud as it gathered speed.

"Why?" said Revile, guessing her fear.

"I think that I saw Earl Eadolfa amongst the others," she whispered. Revile heard a tremble in her voice.

"That's nice," muttered Douglas as they overtook him.

III

The three companions spent a cold uncomfortable night in a patch of woodland some ten or so miles west of Clovenfords. The journey had been difficult and they had made very poor time, partly because their ponies were so overburdened, partly because of the rough pathless terrain – they dared not take the road – and foul weather. They had neither seen nor heard any pursuit. It was unlikely they would be followed. Visibility had been poor and the heavy rain washed away all sign of their tracks almost as soon as they made them.

All three seemed relieved.

Revile and Aliannia huddled together under their furs and blankets, but Douglas had to be content with his axe to keep him warm. They had tried to light a fire but had given up for there was little dry fuel and they could not be bothered searching for more.

Douglas muttered about the stiffness of his joints for some time before finally falling asleep. By then, Aliannia was already lost in her dreams, and only Revile remained awake. The assassin was well content in his own perverse way, his mind alive with plots and schemes.

Revile woke the next morning to find it had stopped raining. He smiled even more broadly. It was still overcast but the clouds were breaking into a few patches of blue sky. Stretching, the assassin gently removed the slave girl's head from his shoulder, then stood up, breathing deeply of the cool woodland air. His spirits were fully revived, the depression all but forgotten in his quest for adventure. Revile grinned and made himself a light meal, draining a flask of the last of his wine.

Aliannia joined him. "Good morning, master," she said.

Revile peered at her. Her hair hung in damp sticky tresses about her shoulders and her face was streaked with mud, yet he found little fault with her appearance. She smiled at him a little shyly. Revile looked away and the expression died on her face.

"Do you know where we are?" he asked her. "I guess we must be south-east of Clovenfords."

"I am not sure," she replied coldly.

"Come then," he said with a thin smile, pointing to the west. "There is a hill. Perhaps from there we can see over this forest."

"Yes, master."

Revile walked to the edge of the clearing and into the trees. He soon found a path which lead off towards the hill. The ground beneath his feet was soaking and his boots squelched in the mire. Disturbed branches dripped on his head, making him curse.

Aliannia followed in his wake, gazing anxiously into the woods. There were no animals to be seen, but the calls of birds and other beasts were loud in the trees. There were more noises in the undergrowth, inexplicable noises which seemed too loud for any creature smaller than a man. But although Aliannia was unfamiliar with northern forests, and perhaps Revile could have told her the sounds were made by rabbits or deer or other harmless creatures, she did not ask him. She could not be bothered with any more of his sour temper so early in the morning.

They came to the edge of the hill. Revile emerged out of the trees and climbed up the rocky rise towards the summit. The ridge was bare except for rough grass and a few gorse bushes.

"Tell me what I can see," he said, pointing to the east, when they finally reached the top.

"That is Earl Eadolfa's palace," she replied, a little out of breath.

The palace was situated some distance away on a steep rock which rose out of the bend of a wide river where it met a strong tributary. The palace had many towers and turrets and spires

158

pointing skywards like broken teeth and old fangs.

Revile turned to the west. Just on the edge of sight and many miles distant, there was a line of dark hills on the horizon, as grey as slate in the morning light. From where they stood it appeared that nothing grew on these hills, and huge fissures and ravines cut into the naked rock of the shouldered slopes.

"And those," continued the girl softly, "are the Leadhills – and the mines, the Slavepits of Louther, that men once called the Wells of Snar."

"Then you've been there?" asked Revile as he shielded his eyes from the sun, looking from east to west. "You seem to be very well informed for a slave girl."

"No, indeed not," she replied, "but I know they lie there. Few return of those who see the Pits." She shivered. "Very few."

"So I'd heard," said Revile. "There are tales in Llaith yet I didn't know whether to believe them. They say that gold is found there, in the Leadhills. Is that right?"

"So it is said, master," she replied, looking at him, "yet I do not know the truth of it. But whatever is found there will do you no good, master. You will gain nothing by going there. They are tightly guarded – and not only to stop the slaves escaping."

Revile nodded slightly, peering for a moment longer. "Good," he said with a smile, "very good. We'll take a look at these mines, I think, but not just yet. I quite fancy visiting old Eadolfa in his palace." He grinned broadly, and turned to leave the top of the ridge.

Aliannia hesitated. "I thought you were travelling to Caerisle with Douglas MacGalbrain," she breathed. "You have not told him of this change of plan."

"We've spoken of this before," said Revile, starting the climb down from the ridge. The girl followed him reluctantly. "Aliannia," he went on," you are my slave. You're in no position to question me; in fact, you're supposed to obey my every command without question. Douglas may still want to go to Caerisle, but I do not. His soldiering is not for me. But I will choose the time to tell him."

"Then I beg you not to go to Rooksburg."

"Rooksburg?"

"Earl Eadolfa's palace, master."

"Why?" said Revile. "Tell me why I shouldn't. You've already said something much to the same effect. What's wrong with this Rooksburg?"

"It is dangerous, master."

"Aye, and maybe it is at that," said the assassin, "yet it's the dangerous jobs which pay the most."

"Master," said Aliannia earnestly, "it is very dangerous. Earl Eadolfa," and she spoke the name softly as if she feared something evil might hear and betray her, "is a terrible man and holds all the Merse, and beyond, in great fear. Some say he is a demon, that he drinks the blood of children and feasts on human flesh. The stories are dark but the reality is worse."

"And I guess I've heard all these dark rumours before." He climbed down one last slope, but stopped before entering the trees. The assassin peered back over his shoulder with a frown.

"What is it?" asked Aliannia, following his gaze.

"Nothing," he replied and strode into the forest. "Do you know Eadolfa?" he went on. "You talk as if he inspires much fear in you."

"I was his slave," she said, walking just behind him. "I was his slave and know much about him."

She peered anxiously over her shoulder again. But the forest, and the surrounding countryside, remained quiet and peaceful, and there was no alarm from bird or beast. Yet she could not help feeling they were being watched.

"I escaped," she went on, "I ran away from Rooksburg two nights gone." She hung her head. "I was recaptured and put into the slave pen at Clovenfords. Yet, still, I have been lucky, master, for I was not recognised as Earl Eadolfa's property."

"You have no brand," mentioned Revile.

"Earl Eadolfa does not brand his slaves, master."

"Then you were lucky," said the assassin. "Old Eadolfa is kinder than the Men of Thule. What did you do for the Earl?"

"I did the same as any other slave: serving at table, washing, scrubbing."

"I see. Is Aliannia your true name?"

"Yes, master, it is my true name. Earl Eadolfa gave me another which I will not repeat."

"Yet you have lied to me," he said, "or not told the whole truth, anyway."

"Yes, master, will you punish me?"

"Perhaps I should," said Revile and he sighed, "but I'm as poor a master as you are a slave. Besides, I couldn't be bothered. In my turn, I have lied to you, to Douglas, to countless other people. It is of no matter."

They approached the camp and the loudly snoring Douglas.

"It could be important, master," she whispered, "I do not think you understand."

Revile went over to Douglas MacGalbrain and prodded him with his toe. The old warrior stirred.

"Come, master greybeard," said Revile, "it is well past your breakfast and I fear you may fade away if you don't eat soon."

Douglas yawned and sat up, scratching at himself.

"What did you mean there, girl?" said the assassin. "Why is it important?"

"I may have placed you in trouble, master," said the slave girl, "for if Earl Eadolfa asked questions at the inn he is sure to have discovered I am travelling with you and Douglas. He will have reason to find you and kill you."

"I wouldn't worry about that," said Revile. "We've already given him plenty of reason. But we are safe for now. No man could have followed us in the rain last night. For all they know, we're already miles from here and have escaped from the Merse completely."

"I think not, master," said the girl.

"Why, by Odin's dick!"

She reluctantly told him. "There is the Twyd river to cross only a little further south of where we turned into the forest. With the rain, the fording places would have been impassable, and there are no bridges south of Rooksburg."

160

"Great," said Revile. "I reckon it's time we were moving. The morning is already growing old. Come on, lardbelly."

"Very well," grumbled the old warrior, still munching at his breakfast. "Very well, I will be finished soon."

Revile quickly packed his gear and belongings.

"I think we should keep to the forest," mentioned the assassin.

"Why?" asked Douglas, stuffing his mouth.

"My over-zealous caution again, Douglas," replied Revile. "We can't go south. The fords are impassable but will be watched anyway – you kindly told Eadolfa's minions we were going that way. We can't go north, not without returning through Clovenfords. No, we should go east. They won't guess we'll go that way." He hesitated. "Besides," he added, "there was a raven over that hill a short while ago. Perhaps it was searching for snails amongst the gorse, perhaps it was searching for us. Remember that rook we met before our meeting at the bridge – and it is said that Eadolfa is fond of rooks. Is that true, Aliannia?"

"Yes, master," she said, "and I noticed the bird too."

"I think we should keep to the trees," said the assassin, "to hide us from unfriendly eyes." Revile paused and went to his pony. "And we should also find some disguise," he added as an afterthought.

"Really?" laughed the old warrior. "Are you being serious? You have cracked, laddie, if you think rooks have started spying on us! Should we be wary of other birds too? Look! There is a blackbird, aye and two sparrows. Should we hide from them? Perhaps even my fleas are in the pay of the Earl. Is there no escape?"

"Perhaps your fleas are," replied Revile, climbing into the saddle and helping the girl join him. "Yet I doubt even Eadolfa could support so great an army, even one so well fed. I still think we should keep to the forest."

"Pah!" spat the old warrior, heaving himself onto the back of his own depressed-looking pony. "Which direction should we go in? Or are all paths watched by killer blue tits?"

"We should go east," said the assassin, ignoring Douglas. "But we're in no hurry – we must find our disguises."

"And what do you think we should disguise ourselves as, o brilliant one?" snorted Douglas. "Perhaps we could stick a few feathers on and run about squawking and flapping our arms. You at least are able at the part for you've a bird brain if nothing else!"

"Ho ho ho," muttered Revile. "I thought, rather, you might undress and lie belly up for then you would easily be mistaken for a mountain, albeit of lard. But if that should fail, I thought we might wait and see what other travellers we chanced upon. A few extra pieces would not hurt my purse."

"What is the point?" said Douglas. "Why do you want these disguises, you cretin?"

"I haven't decided, yet, lardbelly."

Douglas threw Revile a dangerous look, but the assassin grinned, spurring his pony into a trot.

"You would do well to treat Douglas with more respect, master," whispered Aliannia into his ear. "He is a mighty warrior, yet you treat him like a stupid child."

"Don't lecture me, Aliannia!" said Revile angrily.

He rode along the forest path, followed by the now happily whistling Douglas, and headed to the west towards Rooksburg and the frowning Leadhills.

IV

"Hail, good priests," cried Revile from the trees by the side of the road.

The two hooded men turned to look at him, then peered at each other.

"Hullo," said the taller priest but his tone was wary, his knuckles whitening about his staff. His companion swallowed.

"Can I talk to you?" asked the assassin, approaching them with his arms outstretched to show he carried no weapons.

"Yes," said the taller priest carefully. "Be at peace with us!"

"Thank you, good sir," said Revile. "Where are you headed?"

"Rooksburg," replied the priest. "We are on a mission from Abbot Athelwoodis of Saint Aiden's Abbey on the Holy Isle of Bernecia. I am Brother Wilmund, and this is Brother Horsla, a novice under my charge. Who are you, my son, and what business have you with us? Are you a servant of Earl Eadolfa?"

"Indeed, I am not, good sir," said Revile, and then he paused. "Brother Wilmund?" he went on, sounding surprised. "Brother Wilmund. I know you, I think. We met in Dundonald in the lands of the Feni on the eve of the last battle feast. This is a strange and unlikely meeting!"

Wilmund smiled. "It's Maggot, isn't it?" he said. "I remember you. We talked at the feast. Aye, you arrived under strange circumstances, then as now. And stranger things happened later, what with the deaths of Lord Malcolm, King of Lornland, and King Eocha ap Gawain, King of Strathclwyd. It must be three years now – or is it four?"

"Four, I reckon," replied the assassin. "You were on your way to the monastery on I. I see you escaped from the frugal life of that holy little place. But come, come to our camp. It is close. Night is near and I would be glad of your company – especially in this Merse of Earl Eadolfa. And," he added in a whisper, "I am Maggot no longer. Now I am called Rat."

"Very well, friend Rat, we will come," said Brother Wilmund. "I am gladdened – I had not expected to meet friends, here, near Rooksburg. Yet, when you first approached and said who you were, I couldn't help thinking you had some other reason for greeting us. I thought, only for a moment of course, that perhaps the Earl paid you?"

"You've naught to fear from me," sighed Revile, "and be assured: I'm not in the pay of any earl, lord or king. I don't know what made you think I would be."

"No reason," said Wilmund. "Anyway, take us to your camp."

Revile grunted.

They left the road and joined a forest track until they saw the glimmering of a fire through the gloom between the tree trunks. Revile made a strange whistling sound like an owl. They

162

heard the snap of a twig and Douglas emerged out of the trees before them, an arrow loosely fitted to his bow. The old warrior was grinning. Aliannia appeared with a soft rustle and joined them. The assassin looked at her thoughtfully for she had made no more noise than a ghost. It seemed a strange talent for one doomed to be a slave and so unused to the open.

Aliannia looked to him for approval. The assassin nodded his head slightly.

They reached the camp and were soon seated around the fire. Revile introduced his two companions and then asked Wilmund for the reason behind his visit to Earl Eadolfa.

"I should not really say," replied the priest, "for I was sworn to secrecy. I was to tell nobody of what I was up to. Yet I know you are a man of discretion and I judge that you and your friends have no love for Eadolfa. Anyway, my master, the abbot, sent me to Rooksburg after I had brought him disturbing tales about the Merse. At first he was loath to listen but in time I persuaded him of the evil which was going on here and at the Leadhills. I was sent, with three novices, to discover the truth and report back to Abbot Athelwoodis. It is a mission on which I would rather not have been sent for I fear its end may be black."

"That I can understand," said Revile. "For our part, we are fleeing the soldiery of the Earl. We had a fight, we killed four of his men. And then there's Aliannia here. Anyway, I believe we're being pursued – although hopefully they've lost us for now."

"I see," said Wilmund and he licked his lips. "Then you had better leave, you had better flee with all haste; and hope, beyond hope, he does not catch you. One part of Eadolfa's evil we have already witnessed. The Slavepits of Louther, the mines in the Leadhills, are truly terrible!"

"You've seen them?" said Douglas in surprise.

The priest hesitated, and then said: "Yes, I have seen them. They are more horrific than words can adequately describe. We are newly returned from the Pits, from the mines and the stench and the squalor. You would need to see that place for yourself. But suffice it to say: we have seen the Slavepits of Louther and have lived to tell the tale. Now I travel on to Rooksburg to confront Earl Eadolfa with what we know."

"Is that wise?" asked Revile. "Surely Eadolfa will not take kindly to you meddling in his affairs. He will have you both silenced."

"Possibly," said Wilmund. "Probably, even. I have made contingencies for such an occurrence but I'll say no more about that except that I sent others of my party back to the abbey. Yet it is my duty and we must go on." And he sighed, staring into the fire. "It is a pointless mission, perhaps, yet, in truth, we should be safe enough. We are from the Holy Isle and the Earl dare not harm us."

"Yet," said Revile, "I can't help thinking that anyone who is capable of creating the Slavepits of Louther won't stop at a little murder – even stooping to kill the priests of the Holy Isle."

"We'll see," said Wilmund gloomily.

"Don't worry," said the assassin grinning from ear to ear. "We'll come with you."

"Are you sure?" asked the priest. "Of course I'll be glad of your company but it will be dangerous. I doubt you fully appreciate your peril – or perhaps indeed you do. But yes, come with us if you will."

"Do you have any spare robes?" asked Revile

Wilmund smiled. "Yes, friend Rat," he said, "and you may borrow them if you wish."

"Thank you," said the assassin, feeling pleased with himself. "Then we'll leave with the dawn."

"Master?" said Aliannia softly.

"Yes, girl," said Revile, "what is it?"

"I do not wish to enter Rooksburg again."

Revile patted her arm. "You won't have to. I want you to take care of our belongings and ponies. We can't take them with us."

"Thank you, master."

Douglas stirred. "I don't want to enter Rooksburg even the once," he muttered.

Four robed and hooded men approached the gatehouse of Rooksburg. Three of the men were of average height and build, but the fourth was a man of truly notable girth, and despite his similar dress, would have stood out in any company. They were dressed in similar dark grey habits, and two of their number carried plain, unadorned staffs. They appeared otherwise unarmed. Stopping at the edge of the ditch before the gates, the leading monk raised his arm and called to the sentries on watch.

For a moment there was no reply.

It was mid-morning of a clear and bright day. The granite and timber walls of the palace, built on a steep rugged rock, loomed over the river valley and cast a huge shadow over the four companions. The river Twyd and its tributary Tyvot surrounded the palace on three sides and on the fourth there was a huddled town of huts and hovels. The inhabitants were an incurious, ugly lot and never gave the priestly party a second glance. The streets of the town were filled with mangy chickens, dog, pigs, and crows – but mainly crows.

There were crows and corbies, rooks and ravens, sitting on the roofs of houses, hunting in the fields and woods, wheeling about an immense rookery in the dead trees of a forest to the north, soaring and circling the many towers, spires and battlements of the palace. The smell was quite overpowering – not the rank odour of people and their muck – but the disgusting and suffocating smell of birds. Everywhere was bird's filth, colouring the walls of the palace and town a speckled white.

"Hail," shouted Brother Wilmund again. "Hail. I am Brother Wilmund, servant of Abbot Athelwoodis of the Abbey of Saint Aiden on the Holy Isle of Bernecia, Protector of the Sacred Faith in all the north. I have business with Earl Eadolfa, Lord of The Merse, vassal of King Sivard of Bernecia."

His proud speech got an answer this time.

"Wait, sir priest," replied a voice. "I will inform my lord, Earl Eadolfa, of your arrival, then await his answer."

They did not have a long wait.

Almost immediately there was a terrible creaking noise as the two mighty gates swung apart. The captain of the guard emerged from between them and walked across the bridge which spanned the ditch.

"I hate to mention this," whispered Revile, "but you were expected."

"Yes," muttered Wilmund, "this does not bode well. But I cannot turn back, not now."

The assassin nodded.

The captain of the guard approach them. There was a smile playing about his lips and, although his sword remained in his scabbard, there was something offensive and mocking about his manner.

"Welcome, sir priest," he said, addressing Wilmund. He bowed his head slightly. "Welcome to Rooksburg and the palace of my lord, Earl Eadolfa. I hope that your visit here is pleasant. My lord, Earl Eadolfa, will see you presently. Follow me – if you will."

The captain led them back over the bridge and through the gates into a long gloomy tunnel which sloped sharply upwards. The air was dank and water dripped from the ceiling.

They came out into a central courtyard. The area was cobbled and timber buildings had been constructed against the stone curtain wall to the west and east. In the middle of the yard were three dead trees, their branches bare and leafless. On every branch and limb sat rooks, silent and motionless, each regarding the company with cold, beady, unblinking eyes.

The four men felt uncomfortable under the inspection. Brother Horsla swallowed several times, his youthful features holding an expression of gnawing fear.

They were taken into the great keep of Rooksburg, a massive, intimidating donjon which stood many storeys high facing the gatehouse. Climbing a flight of stairs, they were led into a torch-lit corridor without windows. They stopped outside a door.

"My lord, Earl Eadolfa," the captain told them with a smirk, "has given you these apartments so that you may eat and rest awhile after your difficult and perilous journey. I will return when my lord, Earl Eadolfa, is disposed to see you."

The captain of the guard opened the door and ushered his guests into the apartments. The four visitors went reluctantly inside.

"Farewell for now," said the captain, closing the door behind them. There was a loud click as the door was locked.

Revile removed his hood and surveyed the rooms.

They were small chambers but were well and comfortably furnished with beds, stools, a table, and a jug and basin for washing. There was a narrow window in the wall opposite the door and another in the adjoining chamber.

The assassin frowned. Comfortable it might be – but it was a prison all the same.

Revile went to the window and peered out, his frown deepening. Hurrying over to the door, he checked the lock – then the assassin grinned.

It was a lot later before the priestly party were disturbed. It had become cold and gloomy in the apartments as the sun sank towards the hills. Revile and Douglas were lying on the beds, seemingly asleep.

Their door was suddenly unlocked and opened. The captain of the guard stepped across the threshold. "My lord," he told them, "Earl Eadolfa, will see you now."

"Thank you, good captain," replied Wilmund. "I will accompany you with Brother Horsla, here. My other companions stood watch last night and will remain here to rest. What needs to be said can be done so without their presence."

"My lord, Earl Eadolfa, will be greatly displeased if he does not meet all his guests."

"That I think, good captain, is inevitable."

The captain looked grim for a moment, but then his expression lightened. "Very well," he said with a smile, "very well. Come then, sir priest, and bring whoever you want as witness."

Wilmund nodded, and then, followed by Brother Horsla, left the apartments. The door was closed and locked behind them. The two blanketed figures continued to snore loudly.

Wilmund's reception was far from what he expected.

A side door to the great hall was opened and the two guests were admitted into the castle chamber. Torches flickered and hissed, and although they burnt with full vigour, the hall was strangely dimly lit. Shadows hid in the corners and amongst the beams of the ceiling.

Almost directly in front of Wilmund and Horsla sat Earl Eadolfa-nan-Bas, Eadolfa the Immortal, Lord of The Merse and Terror of the North. He smiled warmly as his guests approached, quickly rising to his feet.

"Hullo," said the Earl, striding eagerly forward to greet them. "Hullo, my friends. Welcome to Rooksburg. I hope that you journey here was not too taxing or difficult?"

Wilmund hesitated. His flesh suddenly crawled for no earthly reason he could think of, and his tongue stuck to the top of his mouth. He took the outstretched hand of the Earl. "It was not ..." Wilmund faltered, his heart labouring in his chest. "It was not worse than expected," he managed a second time.

"Good," said the Earl. "Very good. But come and be seated at my table."

Eadolfa directed them. The table was covered in a dazzling assortment of gold and silver plates and platters, each filled with some delicacy, if the aroma was anything to go by. The two guests seated themselves opposite the Earl.

"Please help yourself," said Eadolfa with a kind of boyish enthusiasm. "You must be hungry after your long journey."

"Will you be joining us, lord," asked Wilmund, suspiciously eyeing the food.

"Actually, I have eaten already," laughed the Earl, his body shaking with mirth, but he then helped himself to a portion from each of the platters and plates. "But I think I shall," he went on, "I believe that gluttony is one of your sins, my good priest, but a man must have the odd failing, don't you know? Come. I shall be most angry with you if you refuse to eat after all the trouble I have gone to in preparing this feast. Most angry!" He seemed serious for a moment, but then he burst into renewed laughter and clapped his hands together. The two priests quailed.

Wilmund sighed, composing himself. "My lord," he said, a little breathlessly, "we have much to talk about. I have already been delayed by the weather and I must make haste or Abbot Athelwoodis will become concerned for my safety."

Eadolfa grinned again, exposing his teeth. Each tooth was notably white and clean, and they seemed filed to a point. Wilmund looked into the Earl's mouth and he shuddered.

"You have sufficient time," said the Earl.

Earl Eadolfa had an ageless face, unlined and unshadowed by the toll of years. His hair was black, as black as a raven's wing, and his eyebrows and beard bristled with vigour. Only Eadolfa's stare was aged but that rather with experience and knowledge.

Wilmund looked at Eadolfa and was caught by the power of the stare. It was as if he was peering into a great bottomless well which drew the thirsty to drink – to drink of some terrible and deadly poison. He shuddered. To his sight and hearing and senses, Wilmund knew the Earl as a healthy, burly, ruddy-faced man. But he felt as if he sat opposite an animated corpse. His skin crawled.

Wilmund, almost against his will, took a plate and helped himself to a spoonful from each of the glittering platters. He took a hesitating mouthful of food. It was the most delicious thing he had ever tasted, rich and intoxicating, but it made him want to vomit and caught in his throat.

"Good!" exclaimed Earl Eadolfa. "Good!" He filled his mouth with food, some of the sauce dribbling from his lips and spilling on his beard and tunic. Brother Horsla joined him in devouring the food.

"We must talk," said Wilmund in a dead voice, his heart pounding in his chest.

The Earl frowned like a peeved child and put down his knife and spoon. "Very well," he said, "if we must!"

"I was sent by Abbot Athelwoodis," said Wilmund, "for he has heard disturbing rumours about the Merse. He was greatly worried that you might have a hand in these crimes. I came to Rooksburg to find the truth."

"Did you indeed!" scoffed the Earl. "Would you know the truth if you heard it?"

"Perhaps," said the priest, recovering a little from his fright, "yes perhaps I would. Yet that does not concern me. It has been said that people disappear from your realm. Is that true?"

"O yes!" hissed Eadolfa.

"And there are rumours of terrible slave mines where you force men and women and children to slave and dig for gold. Do you deny that?"

"Why would I bother?"

"Then you do not deny it," said Wilmund in an empty voice, more to himself than to Eadolfa.

"Indeed not," said the Earl. "Yet I wonder why you must ask these questions for you already knew all of this before you arrived here. For you have visited my mines, you have visited the Wells of Snar."

Wilmund found nothing to say in reply.

"Have you lost your tongue, good priest?" said the Earl, taking his cutlery and spooning some of the gravy from a plate into his mouth. "Or is honesty that one virtue you cannot tolerate in others? There! You have heard the truth as you dimly perceive it!"

Wilmund shrugged slightly.

"Ah," said the Earl, "I see. You think that the two novices who accompanied you to the mines will inform the old abbot of my adventures here in the Merse. You left them two days ago to the south and east of here. You are a sensible, some might say, cautious man. If these novices had travelled all night they would have reached the Holy Isle by now, wouldn't they? But that will be of little consequence to you, my friend. You were clever, Wilmund, but not clever enough.

Tell me: did Athelwoodis raise this matter with you?"

"Of course," said Wilmund.

"But tell me," replied the Earl, "was it not you who broached the subject? Wasn't it you who wanted to find out the truth about evil old Eadolfa and his wicked ways?"

"Yes, it was me," replied the priest, "but the abbot sanctioned my mission!"

"As well he might!" said Eadolfa, leaning back in his chair, clearly enjoying himself. "As well he might! It was a good plan. You left cursèd Aiden's abbey at night, telling no one of your mission but the three novices who were to accompany you. If you were challenged, you were to say you were on a pilgrimage to the White House in the Gallianmerse. You travelled first to the Leadhills and spied on my operations and then sent back two of the novices to the abbey to report on what you had found. It was a good plan and might have succeeded. What do you think, my friend?"

"I think," muttered Wilmund, "you love the sound of your own voice!"

"And why shouldn't I?" The Earl roared anew with laughter. "I have a fine voice, to be sure," he went on, "and perhaps you should listen to it!"

Wilmund looked at Brother Horsla. The young novice was pale and fearful. An empty plate stood on the table before Horsla but his eyes were transfixed on two huge platters which had remained covered. Wilmund himself was frightened but anger stirred in him.

"Firstly," continued the Earl, but Wilmund hardly heard him, "I think you should know that Athelwoodis is an old friend of mine. He had been in my pay for some years and told me all about you and your mission – hence my generous reception. Nothing else would suffice for servants and friends of the abbot."

Horsla continued to stare at the two covered platters.

Eadolfa grinned, his eyes burning fiercely. "I think your friend has guessed some of the rest."

Eadolfa lifted the covers from the two dishes, revealing the severed heads of Wilmund's two companions. The two young novices had died in great terror and Eadolfa had had their eyes taken out to leave blackened sockets.

"I think," said the Earl, "these are the remains of the two novices who you left to travel back to the Holy Isle. You wonder what happened to the rest of them? Well, fear not! I am afraid they were little use as messengers so I put them to some better use – for filling your stomachs and mine!"

Brother Horsla rose unsteadily to his feet and was sick across the table.

"Why, why, sir priest," laughed Earl Eadolfa, his eyes dancing with pleasure, "I fear that your companion's manners are quite shocking, quite quite shocking. But never mind. Where you are going, it will not matter. You shall both end you days in the Slavepits of Louther unless I can devise a more miserable death. I will give it some thought." He hesitated but then added thoughtfully: "Or perhaps I might spare you, Brother Wilmund, perhaps I might. This novice I do not need but you might be useful. We could learn 'truth' together. You could become my friend and servant – and would benefit from it."

Wilmund found nothing to say. He was not sure this offer from Eadolfa was not some fur-

168

ther attempt to torment him. Eadolfa smirked at his discomfort.

"What should I do with the other two men?" asked the captain of the guard who had been quietly watching the proceedings. "They are sleeping in the apartments you gave them."

"What other two men?" asked Eadolfa sharply, drawing his stare away from Wilmund. "There should only have been two in the party!"

"The two other priests in the rest chambers, the two who accompanied these here." The captain faltered, then lamely said: "Did you not know?"

"No," cried Eadolfa his voice full of sudden wrath, "I did not know. Why didn't you tell me sooner? Why didn't you?"

"I thought you already knew," replied the captain backing away in fear, cowering. "But I followed your orders to the word. Have I done wrong?"

"Perhaps," said Eadolfa, cold now. "We shall see."

The captain of the guard swallowed.

"Go," continued the Earl, "go and fetch them here."

The captain of the guard bowed low and ran from the hall.

"Who are these men?" Eadolfa asked Wilmund. "Who are they? The abbot said there was only to be four in your party."

Wilmund shrugged slightly and Brother Horsla stared vacantly back at the Earl.

"If you want to live," said Eadolfa, "you'd better tell me. Who are these men? Remember, sir priest, two novices have already died because of your foolishness. Shame if it should be a third! Who are these men?"

Brother Horsla tried to speak but nothing of sense issued from his mouth.

"So," continued the Earl, lounging back in his chair, "you will be stubborn. You leave me no option but to loosen your virtuous tongues by torture. I cannot pretend that it will not give me great pleasure to make you suffer."

Wilmund hesitated, glanced at his companion and then at the two severed heads of the other novices. Nodding slightly, he turned to the Earl. "That will not be necessary," he said, "for I will serve you if I can. My two other companions are assassins in the service of King Sivard of Bernecia, your overlord. He feared Abbot Athelwoodis's treachery and sent them secretly with me in case we failed in our mission. And my lord, Earl Eadolfa of the Merse, I do not think we shall fail. You are unarmed and alone. I, on the other hand, am armed for your foolish captain forgot to search us before admitting us into Rooksburg. A costly oversight, I should imagine!"

Wilmund reached into his robes and produced a dagger.

Earl Eadolfa threw back his head and roared with mirth.
"O you men of God, you make me laugh!"

Wilmund took the opportunity, leaping to his feet and plunging his dagger into the Earl's shaking chest. But no blood coursed from the wound, and Eadolfa laughed all the more loudly, making the walls of the great hall shudder. The shadows thickened and crept along the walls. Wilmund tore the blade out and stabbed the Earl again and again and again.

But the blows had no effect. When removed, the weapon left no mark in Eadolfa's chest.

"By all the Saints in Heaven!" cried Wilmund, jumping back from the Earl. He licked his lips.

169

"All the Saints in Heaven, protect me!"

"Indeed," grinned Eadolfa, rubbing at his chest, "but not even with their help will you escape or could your weapon harm me; nor with the help of these stupid assassins you have talked about! I am Eadolfa-nan-Bas, Eadolfa the Immortal, Eadolfa the undying terror of the Merse! I cannot be killed, no disease can harm me, age will not wither my body or malice! Think on it, sir priest, and tremble: no matter what you did I would not die for I no longer have a soul!"

Eadolfa began to laugh again and the torches flickered and spluttered in the terrible sound.

"What do you reckon, Rat?" whispered Douglas.

"Well," said Revile in a hushed voice, "it depends on which way you look at it."

Both men were crouched in a gallery overlooking the great hall. They had just witnessed the uncovering of the severed heads and then Wilmund's unsuccessful attempts to murder the Earl.

"We could be brave," went on the assassin, "and attempt to rescue our friends."

"Hmmm," thought the old warrior, "and the alternative?"

"Well, we could be cowards and flee Rooksburg."

"I see," said Douglas. "Not much of a choice really, is it?"

"No," agreed Revile.

They both rose to their feet without a sound and left the gallery to the reverberating bellows of manic laughter from the hall below.

There was a commotion outside the door of the hall. The captain of the guard suddenly burst into the chamber.

"My lord, Eadolfa," he cried, "they have escaped! When I reached their apartments they had already gone. And I fear they may have fled from Rooksburg."

Eadolfa turned towards the captain, his eyes filled with a deep fire. For a moment he did not seem to recognise his servant. Stretched out the table below him was the body of Horsla. The young novice was dead, his eyes plucked from his sockets, his chest and abdomen opened with a carving knife. Gore covered the Earl. Wilmund was slumped across one of the chairs, blood running down his face.

The captain looked at Eadolfa, and, despite the fact it was not the first time he had witnessed such a grisly scene, he faltered.

On the table there were several silver dishes. In each was some organ: liver, kidneys, heart, lungs, spleen in its own plate. On one plate were four eyeballs.

Sense seemed to return to Eadolfa's gaze as if he was pulling himself back from some deep place. "Find them," he said softly. "Find these men and bring them back to Rooksburg."

The captain turned from his master.

"And, captain," added Eadolfa, "do not fail me again."

The captain nodded, swallowed, and fled from the hall.

Eadolfa returned to his butchery, his fingers smeared with blood. He took one of the eye-

170

balls from the plate and placed it in his mouth. He bit into it, jelly running from his lips.

Earl Eadolfa threw back his head and roared with laughter.

V

"It's a shame about Wilmund and Horsla," mentioned Douglas MacGalbrain as they rode north.

"Aye, it's terrible," replied Revile from beside him. "And yet, such is life: a bitter painful experience from the cradle to the grave." He sighed. "O well, never mind. How far do you think we've come?"

"Twenty miles or so," said Douglas, "but not far enough." The old warrior frowned. "Do you think we'll be followed?"

"Aye, I do," said the assassin. "With luck they won't find us. Ye gods, I could hardly find myself in this fog!"

"Are you sure we're still going north?" asked the old warrior, turning his head from side to side.

"I've no idea," said Revile, "but I feel we're going in the right direction, back towards Llaith. What do you think Aliannia?"

"I think we are going north, master," she answered, "and yet I am troubled. I do not like this fog: it does not feel right."

Revile pulled his pony to a halt and then listened, looking to the north. The fog closed in about them and curled across the ground to the pony's hooves. The air was moist and heavy, and caught in the chest as if it might choke the inhaler. The assassin could see barely yards ahead or behind him, and he heard nothing. The road was silent except for the drip of water, the skittish neighs of the ponies, and Revile's own breathing and movements.

More fog billowed towards them in silent clouds.

The assassin stared, feeling the cold, clammy touch against his face.

"I don't like this much," grumbled the old warrior with a shiver.

Revile shrugged. "We're agreed on that much," he said softly.

"Master," whispered Aliannia, "we must keep moving." There was something like panic in her voice. "Any delay here hasten our capture. We must flee from the Merse with all speed."

"I agree with the girl," muttered Douglas. "I still don't know if all this about mines and gold and Eadolfa is true, but there's something odd about this fog, something, well, creepy. What are you waiting for, laddie? Let's go!"

"I'm not waiting for anything," answered Revile. "Nothing at all. But I'm thinking we won't escape from the Merse this night. It will be dark soon and we can't go on because of this fog. We should get off the road. The road will be watched. Come, into this forest. Let us find a camp as far away from the road as possible."

The assassin dismounted and Douglas joined him.

"Are you sure this is a good idea?" asked the old warrior, wiping moisture from his beard. "If we start off across country we stand a good choice of getting lost."

171

"No, I'm sure we should leave the road," replied Revile. He shook his head and smiled grimly. "Our garrons don't want to go on. Mine has been pulling at the bit for some miles. These beasts are wiser than us in many things. They don't run heedless into danger, they follow their instincts."

"What sort of danger?" asked Douglas, looking puzzled. "What sort of danger could a pony possibly know about?"

"Goblins and bogles and things which go bump in the night," said the assassin. "That sort of danger. Come. These trees may hide us from unfriendly eyes, be they man or evil bogle. Come – and be silent!"

Revile led his pony into the trees, first drawing his sword. The ground was broken and trunks loomed up at them out of the fog. Travelling did not prove to be too difficult and the assassin found a path through the undergrowth.

Revile led the way, a grey shadow which flitted through the trees, followed by the soft clop of his sure-footed pony. Aliannia was altogether silent but she gazed nervously around her. Only Douglas saw no need for stealth. He muttered as he walked, disturbing branches overhead and tripping over roots underfoot.

The three companions continued into the forest but the fog grew thicker.

"How much further have we got to go?" complained Douglas.

"Hush," said Revile softly.

The fog billowed about them. The three companions stood in a clearing, several miles from the road, huddled together with their ponies. The fog had become so dense they could not see more than a few feet in any direction. The silence was deafening. Around the clearing huddled the trees, and the fog was even more dense and dank.

"I knew I'd seen something," said the assassin, almost sounding relieved. Walking forwards with his hands outstretched, he came to a tall finger of stone which stood in the middle of the clearing. Many nails were hammered into the standing stone, and offerings of broken brooches and pins has been left in any crevice or crack. A small rivulet of water issued from the foot of the stone and fell into a carved basin. It gurgled over the lip of the well and flowed away into the mist.

Revile found the trees and bushes around the edge of the clearing were adorned with rags and pieces of cloth. The fog was a little thinner and less impenetrable; and the stone was pleasantly warm.

"What is this place?" asked Aliannia.

"A clootie well," said Revile. "Folk use it for healing and good luck."

"We need some good luck," muttered Douglas. "What do we do now?"

"I think we should make camp," replied Revile. "This seems as good a place to stop as any. The fog certainly seems thinner in the clearing. You get some rest if you want, Douglas, I'll take first watch."

"And what are you supposed to be watching for?" asked Douglas.

"I don't know," said the assassin. He placed his sword on the ground beside him and sat down against the stone. The rock was reassuringly solid against his back, and the water trickled from the basin. Taking a torch from his backpack, the assassin busied himself with tinder and flint, and soon had the torch burning merrily. He planted the torch in the turf and took hold of his sword, testing the edge with his finger.

Douglas MacGalbrain laughed. "What would they say in Llaith if they could see you now?" The old warrior shook his head sadly. "What would they say?"

"They would say," muttered the assassin, "that you are a fat, foolish old man without the sense to ask yourself why two normally placid, even docile, ponies have started sweating and trembling. Me, I take heed of such things."

"Why don't the ponies run away?" said Douglas.

"The fog is all about us," replied Revile, "maybe there is nowhere to run to. Maybe this is the best place to be."

Douglas cursed, unrolled his blanket and stretched himself out on the ground.

The assassin smiled grimly. "Douglas," he said, "haven't you forgotten something?"

"What?" said the old warrior.

"Well," said Revile, "this is the first time since I've known you that you've forgotten a meal. Dinner is long past."

"I'm not hungry," snorted Douglas.

Revile grunted, and looked at Aliannia. "What do you think this is?" he asked her. "You knew Eadolfa, you were his slave."

Aliannia was plainly as nervous as the ponies. "I do not know and I would rather not guess." She hesitated, turning to him. "I want to run, to run and hide, but I do not know where."

"I see," said the assassin. "Before I might have thought Douglas was right in ignoring this fog, but not since I saw Eadolfa stabbed to no effect."

"He must have been wearing a breastplate," said Douglas.

"Must he?" replied Revile. "I'm afraid I'm not so sure. But, Aliannia, you've got to help us. What should we do? Should we flee?"

"I do not know," she answered, "yet I fear Earl Eadolfa will not let us escape from the Merse."

"Perhaps this clootie well has some power," said Douglas hopefully.

Aliannia threw him a look which suggested she thought otherwise.

Revile lit another torch. Night had fallen, a night without the light of stars or moon, a night as black as pitch. Still the fog gathered around the standing stone and billowed around the edge of the clearing, but within the clearing it had cleared a little. Or so Revile hoped. The assassin could smell the fog and feel it, and it had deepened beyond the bounds of the healing well. The silence was unbearable. Revile could hear his own short breaths and the loud crackling of the torch.

Yet time dragged.

But the silence grew. Even Douglas dared not make a sound.

"What should we do?" Revile asked Aliannia again. He was trying to speak quietly but his voice seemed harsh and loud, croaking like an old raven.

"I do not know." Aliannia raised her hands to the heaven. "I still do not know – but it will not be long now, it is nearly ready."

"And what is 'it'?"

"Something ..." started Aliannia. "Well, something ..."

"... evil?" finished Revile. "Great!"

"We should get moving," said Douglas.

"Where?" said Revile quietly. "Where should we go?"

They said nothing for a moment.

"This is stupid," said the old warrior loudly, "very stupid. Now you've got me believing in the gods alone know what. I tell you there's nothing out there."

The torches flared, casting dim pools of light about the standing stone and onto the water of the clootie well.

"And I tell you there is!" muttered Revile.

Revile sat with his back against the stone, clasping his sword. His hands were moist and he rubbed them against his tunic. Aliannia sat beside him on one side; and Douglas was sitting by himself on the other side of the stone.

The assassin sighed.

There was a groan, very close, so close that Revile was not certain it had not been made by Aliannia or Douglas.

"What, on earth, was that?" whispered the old warrior.

"It has begun," said Aliannia, her voice trembling. She started to mumble in a strange tongue but Revile did not understand what she said.

There was a long pause. Revile could feel his heart pounding in his chest.

This time there was a blood-curdling scream that sent a chill down the assassin's back. Revile could have sworn that the cry had come from beside him or behind him. One of the ponies whinnied in fear. But when Revile looked behind them there was nothing but torchlight flickering off the surface of the standing stone. Revile peered at Aliannia; the girl stared back, her eyes wide in fear, still mumbling words under her breath.

Another scream, and then another.

A cold groan.

A cackle of terrible laughter.

Each followed the other, some far away, others so close that Revile thought he could feel cold breath in his ear. But gradually the frequency of the calls lessened and their power diminished.

And, then, almost as soon as it had begun, the attack ceased. The fog started to break and shift in the now strengthening breeze. Relief washed over Douglas as if he had been redeemed from some terrible peril. He smiled to himself. But Revile's knuckles whitened about the hilt of his sword.

Yet, nothing had happened as time lengthened.

The fog curled away into the woods and a few stars twinkled in the heavens above them.

174

There was a rumble of thunder in the distance, and then the double flash of lightning. From the south approached a great storm, eating up the stars before it.

A raindrop fell on Revile's head, and then another. Before long, water was pouring from the sky. Thunder rolled again and again and again, rumbling away like a mighty drum. Flashes of lightning lit up the clearing. And the rain came lashing down, driven by a freezing gale.

"What the ..." said Revile.

The assassin and his companions sat there, battered by the elements. A trickle of water ran through the clearing. The assassin looked at it stupidly. The trickle slowly grew until a stream flowed past the standing stone. The rain poured down.

"A flash flood!" cried Douglas. "We'd better move, we've been idiots! This must be a dried-up river bed. We'll drown if we don't move!"

"Stay where you are!" commanded Revile. "The storm will pass!"

But the stream of water grew into a river, washing about the assassin's legs with the coldest water he had ever felt. The river lapped about the standing stone and the well – but did not touch it. The water was icy cold and the wind was freezing. Revile felt pierced, shivering and trembling.

Lightning flashed, thunder rolled.

There was a rumble on the woods, like an earthquake.

Revile's eyes opened in disbelief. A wall of water swept towards them, a torrent which would wash them away. He braced himself against the stone just before the water hit. The assassin had never felt anything so frigid and bitter. He thought he was drowning. But he held on, and soon he found he was able to breathe.

"Gad!" he spluttered. "Thor's Hammer! And the Seven Serpents of Set!"

But he held on and gradually the waters subsided. The storm rolled away towards the north, and almost suddenly, the rain stopped. Revile sat with his back against the stone feeling like a drowned rat.

"What is this?" demanded Douglas MacGalbrain, coughing and rubbing his eyes.

"Gad!" replied Revile.

The storm passed and stars reappeared in the sky.

It was then that Revile realised Aliannia was not by his side.

"Aliannia?" he cried.

Just then they heard the harsh laughing of men. Torches appeared through the trees and approached the edge of the clearing. Then, on the border of the forest, Revile saw Patrick, Lord Rothstor, with several Mersian warriors. They had captured Aliannia and her hands were bound behind her back.

Patrick smiled and had Aliannia tied to a tree. He unsheathed a dagger and cut her clothing from her, throwing the rags away disdainfully.

Revile did nothing but watch, fascinated by what he saw, his back resting firmly against the standing stone. Douglas MacGalbrain called out in anger: "Rat, we must do something, we can't just leave her!"

The assassin made no reply, his eyes transfixed on the edge of the clearing. The rags and pieces of cloth around the clearing flapped in the breeze.

Aliannia cried out in fear: "Revile, help me. Help me." Her eyes were filled with tears of terror.

The assassin shook his head in answer, but he could not tear his stare from hers.

Patrick, Lord Rothstor, drew the dagger across the girl's breast, down over her belly, and down towards her abdomen. Aliannia struggled and screamed in vain. Blood ran down between her breasts.

Revile continued to shake his head.

Patrick sneered and drew his sword.

"By Helgard!" swore Douglas. "We can't just leave her!"

Lord Rothstor viciously cut Aliannia again and again. She screamed. Blood gushed out.

Douglas sprang to his feet, swinging his axe about his head.

"No," said Revile. "No, Douglas, we can't do anything!"

But the old warrior did not hear him and he bounded towards the woods.

"Thor's Hammer!" cursed the assassin and dived after his friend.

"By all the Saints in Heaven!" cried the voice of Douglas MacGalbrain in absolute and complete terror. "Aieee!"

Revile shut his eyes, closing them tight, and threw himself at the old warrior's feet. Clasping both Douglas's ankles, the assassin brought Douglas tumbling to the ground. Revile scrambled backwards until one of his feet touched the standing stone.

"Aieeeee!" shrieked the old warrior. "Aieeeee!"

Revile tried to drag the old warrior back towards the standing stone. But something prevented him, something picked up Douglas MacGalbrain and tried to pull him from the assassin's grip. For a moment Revile thought his arms had been torn from his shoulders so powerful was the pull. Douglas was weeping like a child.

Revile could feel his grip weakening. His foot seemed solidly fastened to the standing stone but his fingers were being prised from Douglas's ankles. The assassin's arms trembled with the strain and he could not hold on.

Douglas howled.

"That is it!" cried a woman's voice. She uttered a sentence in a language Revile did not understand. Revile felt water being thrown over him: not the chill blast of the storm but water from the well.

The pressure was immediately released and Douglas sagged to the ground. Revile relaxed his grip from round Douglas's ankles although he did not yet dare open his eyes.

"Are you all right, master?" asked Aliannia, her voice unsteady.

Revile took the plunge and opened his eyes, peering about him. He was lying in a clearing in the forest. Above him stars twinkled and beside him a torch burned. One foot was pressed against the standing stone, and water still gushed from the well. Revile sat up and rubbed his arms.

"What happened?" he asked.

"I am not sure, master," replied the girl softly, "I am not certain. All I know is that something

176

had gotten a hold of Douglas. A shadow. A demon. I could not see clearly although I sat here all the time. Shadows, master." She shook her head. "I do not want to know. I threw water from the well over it."

Revile shivered. He got up and went over to Douglas. The old warrior lay face down in the turf, and for a moment Revile thought he was dead. But the old warrior did not stir when the assassin shook him.

Aliannia took some of the water from the well and dribbled it over Douglas's lips. This seemed to revive him, and he dragged himself to a sitting position.

"What is it, Rat?" muttered Douglas. "Did I fall asleep?" He rose to his feet, his eyes bleary, his legs unsteady. "I was dreaming," he went on, "well, a nightmare, I guess. What was it about? You know, Rat, I can't remember. Ye gods," he cried, "how did I do that?"

Revile peered at the old man's thick wrists. They were blackened as if burnt by some intense heat. There were marks, like long fingers, scorched into the skin.

The girl washed his wrists, and the marks became less angry.

"The torch," said the assassin, "it fell over and burned you."

"O," said Douglas. "Strange. My memory is blank. What happened? I don't remember anything. O yes, it was raining, wasn't it? But the ground isn't wet. Isn't that odd?"

"You must have been dreaming," Revile told him.

"Yes, I must have been," agreed Douglas.

"Anyway, I think we should move again," said the assassin. "This is not a good campsite."

"At least the fog has gone," said the old warrior cheerfully.

"Aye," replied Revile, "at least that is something."

Douglas quickly gathered together his belongings.

Revile turned to Aliannia. He smiled and took a tress of hair from her eyes. "We have been lucky," he said, "very lucky."

She nodded.

"Did you see what I saw?" he asked.

"No, master, but I can guess," she replied. "We were saved by the stone and the water of the well. They hold some power."

"Aye," said Revile, "that and your charm. I heard your voice but I didn't understand the words."

"It is a charm in my own tongue, master. It took me a little time to remember it."

"Then it was lucky it came to mind when it did." Revile smiled again, patting the standing stone. "Aye, we've been lucky." His fear quickly faded.

"How did you know about the stone, master?"

The assassin looked at her. "I followed the ponies," he said. "They led me here, but we'd better go. I think we should put more miles between us and the road. We may have more than goblins to deal with should we stay. Eadolfa is bound to send out men. They may already be on their way here."

The girl nodded.

"This will do," said Revile

"Very well," yawned Douglas.

They stopped on the top of a mound by the banks of a swift-flowing river. A few patches of black sky appeared through the canopy of the forest. Stars glimmered in the mirrored pools of the river and danced away across the surface. A refreshing breeze had risen from the north.

"No fire," said the assassin as Douglas began gathering fuel.

The old warrior swore. The marks on his wrists had faded but the pain had not gone. Moaning again about the stiffness of his joints, he settled down to sleep, clutching the haft of his axe for comfort.

"They make good bed fellows," said Revile softly.

"Yes, master," replied Aliannia from by his side.

The assassin turned and gazed at her. "Come," he said, "I wish to talk to you – but where we will not disturb Douglas."

"Master," she replied, "you must be tired. We could sleep here."

Revile thought for a moment. "I don't intend to sleep tonight," he said finally, "even if I could. One of us should keep watch. Eadolfa may have more tricks up his sleeve. Anyway, as I have said, come."

They climbed down from the mound, forded the river, and walked a way down the further bank. Revile found a dry spot under an old oak tree and seated himself cross-legged on the ground. Aliannia sat beside him.

For a while Revile said nothing as he gathered his thought and doubts together.

"Aliannia," he said at last, "I want to thank you for what you did earlier tonight. You saved Douglas – I couldn't have held on for much longer – from a fate, well, most likely worse than death. But I have been thinking about all I know about you, about all the things which have happened since we met. You know more than you are telling. You are not just some pretty slave girl Eadolfa picked up on a whim."

"I have answered your questions honestly," replied Aliannia. "There is nothing more to tell."

"I wonder," said Revile. "I don't know. But I think you know more. You are a slave, yet I know once you were much more than that. Are you of noble birth, a princess perhaps? I wonder where you fit into Eadolfa's schemes."

Aliannia shrugged slightly. Revile could not read her expression in the gloom.

"I was a princess, once," she said sadly, "yes, once. It seems a thousand years ago now. My home is far to the south and east, beyond many rivers and seas and mountains, where the sun shines all day and the grass is scorched in the heat." She paused, and then continued: "I was taken by pirates while travelling between Antioch and Kriti, stolen from my lands and titles. I was brought north. The journey took most of a year for my captors were in no hurry and they travelled in secret. I was sold to Earl Eadolfa, I, of nobler lineage than any of your kings and lords, was sold into bondage. Is that enough of an answer to your question? Or," she went on, and pride stirred in her, "do you delight in making me miserable? I am your slave but I little like the part!"

178

Revile shook his head. "It still doesn't make sense," he said. "What does Eadolfa want with you? Why did your captors take you across all these mountains and seas and plains of scorched grass? I have heard of both Antioch and Kriti and know you would have fetched a huge price in their slave markets or a ransom from your people. Why were you brought to the Merse to be sold?"

"I do not know," she said, holding his stare.

"Aliannia, Eadolfa must have had some reason in buying you. What was your father's name and kingdom? I have travelled widely. Perhaps I have heard of your realm."

"You would not have, master."

Revile frowned slightly.

"I have a mind," he said, "to visit the Slavepits of Louther. It is said that gold and silver are mined there."

"I would advise you not to go there," replied Aliannia, "but I am your slave and must do as you wish."

"Is gold found in the Leadhills?" asked Revile in irritation. "It is strange that I had never heard such a tale until a few months ago. And if there was much gold to be found I would have heard. You have been Eadolfa's slave and have lived at Rooksburg. You must know. Is gold found in the Slavepits of Louther?"

"So it is said, master."

"But is it true, damn you!"

"How would I know?" cried Aliannia in sudden anger. "How would I know?"

"Please?" said Revile, softening his tone. "Please, Aliannia? I sense fear in you and would learn the reason. I know you are not afraid of me or Douglas nor even necessarily for your own safety. But you are terrified of Eadolfa, understandably perhaps, and what he might do. I have seen Earl Eadolfa survive wounds which should have killed him and now I reckon he has some other reason for levelling the hills. I want to know why!"

"I do not know," repeated the girl.

The assassin paused, and then said: "You must tell me – or I will give you back to Eadolfa."

"What would you have me say?" she asked him, staring at the ground between her bare feet.

"I would have you tell me the truth. I think I know something of Eadolfa know. He says he's immortal; I've seen and heard things I wouldn't have believed. What is Eadolfa searching for in the Leadhills? What would interest Eadolfa-nan-Bas, Eadolfa the Immortal? Not gold, not women – however pretty – and not wine. Power, perhaps? Yes, power. But why in the Leadhills? What is, or are, the Wells of Snar. You have used the name, so has Eadolfa. What are these Wells?"

Aliannia's shoulders slumped, and when she spoke again it was sadly and softly. "Earl Eadolfa-nan-Bas," she told him, "Lord of the Merse and Terror of the North, searches for the Crown of the Black Templars. I was taken from my home so that I could help instruct him when he finds it for its uses are cunning and deadly. And before too long he will find the mighty talisman and a new age of darkness shall descend on the world. For see you, my master, the Crown was perilous to the wielder: it was too potent for mortals. It sucked out the life of the keeper so that they aged years in days. But Earl Eadolfa is immortal: he has lost his soul and he cannot die. On him the Templar's wizardry would have no effect but to make him ever the more wicked. A new and deadly terror will be unleashed. That is why I fled from Rooksburg although I have imperilled myself by doing so. I know the uses of the Crown and he needs me."

The assassin looked puzzled. "That is not possible," he said softly. "The Crown of the Black Templars fell into the Darkness with Angelica Amhach, the witch queen of Dalria. Several years ago, now. Angelica was banished from this world with the Crown at the Fortress of the Staff. I know the story. Why would Eadolfa search for it in the Leadhills?"

Aliannia swallowed and her voice shook as if she uttered words of doom. "In the Leadhills," she said, "are the Wells of Snar, a gate into the Darkness. There might the banished be summoned, there might Angelica Amhach be raised from the Nothing, bringing with her the Crown of the Black Templars – for it fell with her but was not destroyed. There will Earl Eadolfa gain that fearful talisman and all will be doomed!"

"But will Eadolfa find these Wells of Snar?"

"Indeed," she replied. "He believes he is close to discovery. But he will flatten the very mountains to get what he desires. All it will take is time – and Eadolfa has the rest of time."

"I see," said Revile, and sighed. "Well, this doesn't sound too good. I can't see any profit in it for me. I wish you had told me all this when we first met and we could have fled the Merse. I just hope we'll still be able to. But you should have told me."

"Would you have believed me, master? While you believed there was hoards of gold there nothing would have dissuaded you."

"No, maybe not. Anyway, leaving the Merse seems all the more attractive. Come, let us return to the camp." He got to his feet, rubbing his bottom. "With luck, tomorrow will see us miles from good old Earl Eadolfa, the Slavepits of Louther – and the Crown of the Black Templars. But there is still one thing which I don't understand. Why were you of all people brought here?"

"My father was the lord of the Black Templars," she replied, biting at one her fingers. "He perished when the Crown was seized by Ailred, Lord of Pentland, and taken to the Fortress of the Staff. All the Templars perished in that final disaster. So it was that I who knew the most – and wished none of it – was brought halfway across the world. So it is that I, of noble lineage and high birth, am the slave to you, Rat the adventurer and villain." She hastily added: "Sorry, master, I forgot myself for a moment."

"Or remembered it?" laughed the assassin. "Yet all the too true, I'm afraid. It's a strange old world – and very very bad! At least for you."

Revile's teeth glinted in the starlight as he grinned.

"So this is the end of your adventure into the Merse?" said Aliannia sounding relieved.

"Aye, girl," replied Revile, laughing at his own foolishness.

This time he had had rather more adventure than he wished.

They returned to the mound and the gently snoring Douglas MacGalbrain.

Revile sniffed the air. "Will the fog return tonight?" asked the assassin.

"No, master," said the girl. "My charm and the water dispelled it."

180

"Good. One last thing," he said, "were you Eadolfa's mistress?"

"No!" she said angrily. "I was not his mistress. And I wanted no part of his wickedness. Anyway, he is not interested in such things."

Aliannia had a strange look in her eyes.

The assassin nodded. "Get some sleep," he said.

She turned away for a moment, and when she looked back the assassin had disappeared without a sound.

The morning dawned lazily. It slowly grew light with the watery sun shining on the trees and dancing about the forest floor. Aliannia woke out of some pleasant dream and smiled slightly. Then she heard the snoring of Douglas and felt the coarseness of her tunic and the dampness of the ground. Her smiled faded. She rubbed at herself for a moment but the dream and its feelings were gone. The bed was cold. She sighed and got up, going to the river to bathe.

She waded into the water, shivering a little. A shadow fell across her. She started and whirled round only to find Revile grinning down at her. Turning from him, she washed under her tunic. "You frightened me, master," she said. "You have no need to come sneaking up on me."

"My apology, my lady," replied the assassin with a smile. "Strange than you should call me 'master' with your noble birth and all."

"You own me, master," she told him.

"So I do," said Revile, "but if you get tired of my wretched company then return to Rooksburg. Your noble friend awaits you there, no doubt. He will be glad of your company even if I am not. Now fetch water and make me some breakfast."

"Yes, master," she replied and started to wade towards the bank

.   Revile smiled at her. "Aye," he said, "It's all right. I was only being nasty to you." He walked back towards the camp.

Aliannia stood still for a moment. She was thoughtful as she watched him go.

The assassin went to where Douglas MacGalbrain was sleeping and woke the old warrior gently.

"O hullo," yawned Douglas, "what is it?"

"Nothing," said Revile, "it's just time we were leaving again. We should be out of the Merse by nightfall. How are your wrists?"

"All right," said Douglas, "I've had worse. Listen, Rat, what did happen last night. I've been thinking about it and it doesn't make sense."

"I've told you already," replied his friend, and then paused. "Douglas," he went on at last, "I'm not going to Caerisle. I'm returning to Llaith."

Douglas said nothing for a moment. "Then all this has been wasted," he muttered, "I'm not even to have company on the road to Caerisle. Anyway, I guessed you were wanting to take a look at the Merse, and especially the Slavepits. They say that hills of gold are found there. What has changed your mind?"

"It's too dangerous," replied the assassin. "And I'm sorry, my friend, but soldiering is not for me. The more I think about it the less I like it. I've had enough of Earl Eadolfa and adventure to last some time."

"So. You will skulk in Llaith without profit from our journey. Why, laddie? What is there in Llaith which is so exciting?"

"Lardbelly," said Revile calmly, "we can talk about this later. First let us leave the Merse and find safety."

"I will be no better pleased then, laddie," scowled the old warrior.

Revile looked at Douglas MacGalbrain's two-handed axe.

"The gods protect me!" he thought.

A little while later, the three companions set out, heading to the north through the forest. They had decided not to return to the road because it would be watched, but consequently they did not make good time. As they travelled on, the land became hilly and was cut with deep valleys and ravines across their path. It was difficult to find a route their ponies could manage. They met no other people in the forest – folk did not live in that part of the Merse. Even beasts and birds were few and wary.

They stopped briefly at midday for lunch, but they had only gone about ten miles and they had done more walking than riding. After a cold meal, they went on again but their path was blocked by a ridge which ran from east to west.

"This is going to take longer than I'd hoped," said Revile, and he sighed, nudging his pony forward. "Maybe we should risk the road, after all?"

Douglas peered about him. "I don't think that would help," he said. "It would take as long to find a path back. No, we should go on."

The assassin nodded. "Besides," he added, "it's unlikely anyone could find us in this wilderness. We should be safe."

"As long as the fog does not find us again, master," whispered Aliannia.

"What a cheery thought," muttered the assassin. "Is that likely?"

"Who knows?" replied the girl.

"What do you think we should do?"

"Go on, master," she replied. "We can not turn back."

Revile sighed again.

The trees thinned as they climbed the side of the ridge. The undergrowth became sparser, and nothing moved on the slopes. Revile dismounted and led his pony towards the top, followed by his companions. Behind and below him stretched the Merse as far as the eye could see. It had become warm in the afternoon sun and vapours and mists were gathering in the river valleys and gorges.

When the assassin reached the top, he turned and gazed back. The tree-covered hills fell away. In the distance he could just make out Rooksburg on its rock between the rivers. Revile peered for a moment more and then started to descend down the other side of the ridge.

It was getting dark when they finally had to stop. They had found an old track which led in their general direction and they were glad to follow it after the pathless wilderness. But they were still in the Merse and they could go on no further.

They had been searching for a suitable campsite when they saw buildings ahead of them.

"I don't remember there being a village round here," said Douglas.

"There's no smoke," Revile pointed out, "perhaps it's been abandoned."

They rode on and approached the ruins of an old town. The houses had been deserted for some years and roofs had fallen in. The fields and paths were overgrown and rank.

"Strange," said Revile, and he drew his sword and jumped from his pony. The assassin padded across to one of the houses, followed more loudly by the old warrior. For once Revile was glad of his company. Pushing the door back slowly, the two companions peered into the house. The floor was covered in debris and old broken furniture – but there was no sign of the occupants. They searched the other houses without discovering anyone, alive or dead.

At last they came to a large building which stood a little apart from the others. It looked as if it might have been a chapel or small church. The door collapsed as they went in. In the middle of the floor was the remains of a large fire, charred wood strewn about the aisles. Amongst the ashes they found bones, human bones, bones of adults and children alike.

"Why would anyone do such a thing?" asked Douglas, shaking his head.

"The gods alone know," replied the assassin, "but you can be pretty sure this is Eadolfa's handiwork. The Earl is certainly mad enough. But why put a whole village to death?"

"We shall never know," said Douglas, and he shuddered. "Let's leave this place. It gives me the creeps."

They rejoined Aliannia and the ponies.

"I would rather go on," admitted Revile, "but I don't think we'll find anywhere better, or safer, to stop. Some of these houses still offer some shelter. What do you think, lardbelly?"

"If you think it's a good idea, laddie," said Douglas wearily.

The assassin shrugged.

They went to the house furthest from the chapel. They lit no fire and after eating, Revile and Aliannia settled down to sleep – Douglas was to keep watch. The slave girl was restless, fidgeting and wriggling under her blanket.

"What is it?" said Revile. "Have you caught some of Douglas's fleas?"

"It does not matter, master," she replied and then hesitated. "I am ..." she started, but then obviously changed her mind, "... a little uncomfortable, master. It is nothing."

"Good," said the assassin and lay down to sleep. And soon he was lost in his dreams.

There was a crow, a carrion crow, as large as an eagle, with a yellow beak and beady black eyes alive with evil intelligence, a crow that soared and wheeled high above the earth, its eyes staring downwards, nothing passing unnoticed under its gaze, now flying over a towered palace that Revile recognised as Rooksburg, now giving out a huge and terrible cry which was answered from below by a thousand harsh voices, now wheeling over the battlements, setting off to the west for a line of grey hills which shimmered slightly in the sun, and as the crow approached the hills it grew in size and power until it cast a shadow which darkened the world before it, travelling onwards, travelling on until the carrion crow reached the Leadhills where it spread its great wings to their full span, looking below, looking below to where an army of ants worked, only they were not ants, Revile realised, they were people, people covered in filth and dirt and their own blood, people with blackened sockets where their eyes had once been, and then, without warning, a landslide engulfed the army of ants, a crack appearing in the side of the hills, and the great crow circled lower and lower, down and down, and entered the crack, entered a cavern which led into the bowels of the earth, lower and lower, down and down into darkness, down and down beyond the memory of light and sunshine, down and down until the earth groaned and all light was extinguished – and yet there was a light, a light glimmering in the pitch black, a radiance that came from a crown, a crown of fabulous workmanship, fashioned from jet and gold, a crown that glittered, glittered in the dark where the deep-throated bay of horns echoed in the cavern, horns raised to greet the great carrion crow, the mighty crow, the evil crow that settled on the crown and took it in its talon, and then soared ever the upwards towards the day and the light and the sun but with the crown drawing the dark and the horns with it from the cavern, and then into the world, there to soar over the land, extinguishing the sun, a chill wind rising from the cavern and hissing over the moor where Revile ran heedless through the heather, running from some unknown terror, throwing away his weapons as he fled, above him the stars flickering and going out, and ever the wind rushing in his ears as if with great wings, wings which beat to the sound of deep-throated horns, wings which chased him over the moor, and with eyes that could pierce all darkness for they were darkness incarnate, hunting him, hunting him the assassin who hunted others, hunting for him: Revile the assassin.

But then Revile turned. He was grinning.

The great carrion crow hurtled towards him, a deeper black against the black, its eyes burning with desire.

Revile woke and sat up with a start. Aliannia moaned slightly in her sleep and rolled over, and Douglas was seated by one of the shattered windows, singing some ballad softly to himself. The assassin peered about him, quietly taking his bow in his hands and fitting an arrow to the string. Revile aimed and loosed the arrow.

"What the Hell?" swore Douglas.

By the door there was a cry of pain, a squawk like the call of a bird. Revile ran over to the door, his arrow still quivering, embedded in the door. But there was no sign of the watcher apart from a few black feathers and spots of blood.

VI

They reached Edwinsburg the next afternoon.

The morning had passed without event. The three companions followed a track from the abandoned village and it took them by an easy route through the forest and to the edge of a wide moor. Here it rejoined the road from Rooksburg to the south, and they decided to risk the road in the hope it would prove quicker than fighting their way through bog and heather. Luckily, they met no soldiery of the Merse.

Edwinsburg appeared from behind a ridge. It was a large settlement, surrounded by a wooden palisade with an unusual round donjon guarding the approaches. The donjon was very old, and was a huge stone enclosure with very thick walls and a battlement around the top. For all that, it was built in a weak position on the side of a hill and overlooked by higher ridges. The many streets were busy with people, inhabitants and travellers.

The road began to descend from the moor, and grass replaced heather as they clopped along. The three companions passed farms and houses, and soon arrived at one of the gates into the town. They were admitted without comment.

Revile heaved a deep sigh of relief. They had escaped from the Earl Eadolfa – although they had not left the Merse.

Edwinsburg was in fact an independent town, governed by a provost elected by the inhabitants. It was nominally in the Merse but had been given its freedom by King Sivard of Bernecia some years before. It had withstood a long siege by the men of Strathclwyd and had been rewarded for its people's bravery. Edwinsburg had its own militia and the Earl of the Merse had no jurisdiction there or in the surrounding countryside.

"This looks like a good place," said Revile brightly.

Douglas's spirits revived and a smile lightened his scowling features. The three companions stood outside the doors of a dingy building. Laughter and music came from the open windows, and, while Aliannia appeared a little alarmed by the raucous noise, Revile and Douglas eagerly pushed the doors open and entered the drinking den. They went first to the bar to buy large pots of frothing beer. They took the drinks to a table where they sat down, lounging on their stools and supping their ale with relish.

There was a silence while the two companions made short work of the contents of their pots.

Douglas grinned. "Ah, that tasted good," he said, "and all the better for we've escaped."

"Aye," said Revile, "it was a bit of luck finding ourselves back on the road to Edwinsburg. I didn't want to spend another night in the open in the Merse. Mind you," he added, "Aliannia was taken from her home thousands of miles away. I guess we're not safe, even yet. I'll be happier when we reach Llaith."

"Well, I won't!" Douglas told him.

"I'll get us another drink," replied Revile, "and see if they have any rooms." The assassin scurried off.

When the assassin returned to the table, Douglas grinned at him. "Easiest drink I've ever had bought for me," he said.

"Good," said Revile, putting the drinks down. "Anyway, I've got us two rooms."

Douglas nodded. "So," he said, "you are returning to Llaith. I have trailed at your heels round the Merse. I entered Rooksburg against my own wishes because you wanted to, I risked life and limb and the gods alone know what else. And what do I get as a reward, laddie? You won't even accompany me to Caerisle – even though that is where we set out to go! I think you should reconsider, laddie, I think that it would be good for your health."

"Douglas," replied Revile, "I am not going to Caerisle. All the south will remain unhealthy for us."

"We can avoid the Merse, laddie, if that is what concerns you. There are many ways south. We can go over the border into Strathclwyd or take passage by sea."

Revile sighed. "We could," he said slowly, "but, Douglas, what would be the point? It is too dangerous. We've only just escaped from the Merse and even Edwinsburg may not be safe. All routes to the south will be watched, and you can be sure that Eadolfa will search high and low for us. I don't think you appreciate the peril!"

The old warrior spat. "You overrate your own importance, laddie. Eadolfa's got better things to do than chase after the likes of us."

"We know too much, lardbelly, and, besides, ..."

"I cannot believe my ears, Rat," interrupted the old warrior, "for you have become a whimpering coward!"

"And, besides," continued Revile, "if you'll let me finish, we have something Eadolfa needs."

"O aye, laddie, and what would that be? A dose of your sparkling wit, perhaps?"

"He wants Aliannia, you old fool!"

"Then why don't you just give her to him, laddie!"

Revile was surprised because he had not even considered that option. "No, I won't do that," he said, "I have become fond of her."

They fell silent.

"Besides," said Revile, sometime later. Douglas was in better spirits. A hour or two had passed. The tavern was now packed and the drinkers were in boisterous mood, and their singing and jesting shook the walls of the building. The tavern was a rough establishment, frequented by the town militia and other such brigands as had time and money on their hands. Douglas and Revile felt quite at home – although Aliannia was not enjoying herself.

"Besides," shouted Revile again, over the noise, "I have been talking to some of the garrison. They say that there is to be no war and that the men of Cymbria and Strathclwyd have resolved their differences. It is rumoured that the armies are to be disbanded. Yet there is also talk that the two armies may unite and attack Lornland and Fenis of Dalria – indeed that may have been the point in the whole affair. I don't know. Nothing is certain but there is to be no war in Cymbria. Come. Drink up and I'll fetch us another. And a more perilous quest may it yet prove than our party through the Merse."

The assassin struggled to his feet and disappeared into the mass of drinkers. Fighting his way through the people, Revile forced a passage to the bar and stood there, holding a silver piece before him. He shouted his order but was ignored and he had to content himself with finding someone to talk to. Seeing a pretty face which he recognised a little way down the bar,

Revile went over to speak to her.

"Hullo," he said, "what's a nice wench like you doing in a place like this?"

"Very witty," she replied sourly. "I've been looking for you. I have news which concerns you."

"O aye," said the assassin with a frown, "it wouldn't be anything to do with Earl Eadolfa?"

"Good god no!" she said. "What do I know about Earl Eadolfa? I suppose you've been down in the Merse getting yourself into trouble again. Anyway, my news is quite different. What name do you go by now?"

"Rat, son of Rodents," he said, bowing slightly. He peered at her. "You're no uglier than I remember."

She was a tall woman with long brown hair, tied in a pony tail; she was dressed in a scored leather tunic, belted at the waist. Two crossed swords were strapped to her back, and the hilt of a dagger protruded from the top of her right boot. A brooch was pinned to the front of her tunic. It was of fabulous workmanship, fashioned in the likeness of rearing horse. And although his companion was a woman of some beauty, she was left alone by the other revellers. It was something about the way she moved, something cat-like and supremely violent.

"I am fine," she replied. "You, I think, are getting old."

"Old?" laughed Revile. "Old! Pah! I am in my prime." The assassin pulled a face, but then grinned again. "You said you had news for me?"

"Indeed," said the woman. "I was sent from Llaith to look for you – they said you were on your way to Caerisle – although I thought I'd find you too late if at all. Anyway, my friend has a job for you. It's not exactly your usual work, but it's in the same line. Our mutual friend in Dundonald requested you – I don't know why! She could not come herself, of course." The woman lowered her voice to a whisper. "The men of Cymbria and Strathclwyd march north to attack Fenis. Ere long Dundonald will be under siege, for Dalria in not prepared for war. I was told to find you and tell you to come to Dundonald with all haste."

"Then I will come," said Revile, "but not tonight. I've just got back."

"I know," she said, "but spare me the details."

"As you wish. How much will I be paid?"

"Two-hundred merks of gold," she said, peering into his face.

"Good," he smiled, staring back "Very good. Although I'm not sure how I'll be able to help."

"I'm sure you wouldn't have been asked if there was anyone else."

"I dare say," said Revile. "Anyway, you have brought me luck."

"Then I've brought you more than you deserve," she said, but then her face lightened into a thin smile. "Who is the girl, and the old man?"

"The old man is a friend of mine. The girl is my slave."

The woman laughed. "It's a long time since the inn room in Sveinhold," she said. "A long time."

The assassin grunted. "Aye," he said, "that proved an expensive night for both of us."

"Indeed," she replied. They clasped hand to wrist.

"I'll see you tomorrow," said Revile, finally managing to get served. "In the town square, about midday. Unless you'd like to join us?"

"No thanks," she muttered. "I will suffer enough of your company on the road to Dundonald."

The assassin nodded. "Farewell, then," he said to her, scooping the tray of drinks from the counter and then ploughing back into the mass of revellers.

By the time Revile reached Aliannia and Douglas he had spilt most of the drink and the tray was awash with ale and spirits.

"You took your time, laddie," scowled Douglas, peering at his beer pot. Finally, deciding the tray held more drink than his mug, he put the mug on the table and the tray to his lips.

"Sorry, blubberguts," apologised Revile, "but then I have found us a job in the north – and well paid at that. It should be far enough away from Eadolfa to suit us both. And it pays ten gold pieces!"

"Good," said Douglas, "what will we be doing?"

"Does it matter?" asked the assassin.

The old warrior thought for a moment. "No, I don't suppose it does," he said. "Will it be dangerous?"

"I'm not sure," said Revile, "although I expect so."

"Excellent!" said Douglas MacGalbrain and drained the tray.

"We leave tomorrow," said the assassin, and he yawned. "Anyway, I'm tired. I'm going to have a bath and then go to bed. I haven't slept much over the last few nights." He got to his feet. "I'll see you tomorrow. Don't drink too much, we've got a long ride ahead."

The old warrior muttered something.

"Come, Aliannia."

The assassin and slave girl left the drinking den for their room.

Revile sat by the fire in his chamber. Beside him stood a large iron bath, steam rising from the water.

"It is not quite hot enough, master," said Aliannia with a shy smile. "Shall I get you more water?"

The assassin turned to look at her. Her wet hair hung about her shoulders like polished jet and her tunic clung to her for it was damp from the bath water. Revile grinned back.

"Whatever you think," he told her.

She nodded and left the chamber. The assassin watched her go.

Revile suddenly felt uneasy. Aliannia had been gone a long time and he could no longer hear singing and laughing coming from the tavern. Something prompted him to stand up.

There was a rap on the door and a note was pushed under it.

Revile hurried across to answer the knock. But when he opened the door, the passage outside was empty and quiet. Picking up the note, the assassin opened and read the small roll of parchment.

It said, quite simply, 'Flee!'"

Without seeming in any haste, Revile closed and bolted the door. He quickly packed his belongings. Walking over to the window, he opened the casement and peered down into the courtyard two storeys below. There was a group of horsemen leading their horses through the gate.

Revile went to the fire and pulled some of the embers onto the floor with his sword, and, standing well back, he cracked a flask of oil into the coals.

There was a commotion outside his door: the sound of many running booted feet.

The assassin returned to the window and shouted: "Fire! Fire! Fire!" Flames flared from behind him. "Fire! Fire! Fire!" Taking a blanket from the bed, he dipped it in the oil and then threw it from the window. The horsemen in the courtyard watched as the tumbling brand fell amongst them. Their horses neighed in fear at the fire and fought against the reins.

The door of Revile's chamber crashed inwards and soldiers jumped across the debris, their swords drawn and ready. They shielded their eyes and faces from the spreading flames.

But the window was open and the room was empty.

Patrick, Lord Rothstor, Warden of the North March of the Merse, swore repeatedly while two of his men braved the flames and hurried over to the window. There was no sign of Revile.

The fire crackled greedily.

It took until morning to put out the fire that Revile had started in his inn room, and by then the flames had consumed the tavern and the two adjoining buildings. There was only a smouldering pile of ashes where the inn had stood.

In the chaos of the fire Revile had escaped, and although a watch had been set on the walls which encircled Edwinsburg, the assassin had not been seen leaving the town. In truth, the inhabitants of Edwinsburg were more than a little alarmed by the arrival of a large company of Mersian soldiery, led by the Warden of the North March. Not that the Mersians were made unwelcome by the local militia – bribes must have changed hands.

In the raid on the tavern, both Douglas MacGalbrain and Aliannia had been captured.

Douglas cursed and swore. He had been taken almost unawares as he sat in the tavern. It hurt his pride to think that he had been captured so easily when Revile had escaped using such a simple trick. The old warrior had not even been given a chance to struggle. Aliannia had fared little better. She seemed frightened although, despite everything which had happened, she still entertained some hope of redemption while Revile remained at large.

And the assassin was not found. Yet no one could have remained undetected within the town walls. The Mersians made an exhaustive search of every house, stable, storeroom, barn, chapel, and courtyard. All the inhabitants and travellers were checked; every basement and cellar, attic and loft, well and chimney, sewer and drain, box and barrel, dungeon and pit were thoroughly explored.

Eventually the Mersians gave up the search. Patrick, Lord Rothstor, contented himself with much angry shouting. He marshalled his forces in the town square and prepared to leave for the south.

Douglas and Aliannia had been taken and manacled in an iron cage which had been slung

189

on top of a horse-drawn cart. The old warrior greeted his imprisonment with more curses; but Aliannia was quiet and withdrawn, perhaps more fully appreciating the import of this new turn of events.

Patrick, Lord Rothstor, rode up to the cage.

"Greetings," he said to the prisoners, and introduced himself again. "I am Warden of The North March of The Merse. We have met before, I think, at the inn at Clovenfords on the road to Caerisle. Where is your other companion? My lord, Earl Eadolfa, requests his presence also. Indeed, he greatly wished to see and talk to all of you. In that you were lucky. For if I had my desire, you would die here. So tell me! Where is your other companion?"

"I don't know," muttered Douglas, "and I wouldn't tell you if I did!"

Patrick sighed. "Very well," he said, "very well, we can delay no longer. Normally I would extract the information from you, old man, but there is no time. My lord, Earl Eadolfa, said you were to be brought back unharmed. Yet there is a debt between us, old man. Four of my men died by your hand. Later, maybe, we shall have an opportunity to talk properly – when my master has finished with you. Very well," he said, and then lowered his voice to a whisper, addressing Aliannia: "My lord, Earl Eadolfa, bade me say this to you, Templar's child: the entrance to the Wells of Snar has been discovered!"

Aliannia went pale.

"Ah, you understand," said the Warden of the North March. "You the most perhaps."

Patrick pulled his horse round to the south under the shadow of the round tower of Edwinsburg. There was a smell of burning on the morning air. He shook his head, raised his hand in signal, and led his men through the gate of the town. The iron cage, atop its cart, jerked into motion and the column set out for the Merse, the Leadhills, and the Wells of Snar.

The woman Revile had spoken with the previous night stood in the town square, watching the Mersians as they filed out of the town. She sighed, and considered returning to Llaith.

VII

"What are the Wells of Snar?" asked Douglas. Aliannia shrugged.

The journey south had been unpleasant for all those in the party but all the more so for Douglas MacGalbrain and Aliannia. The rain had returned to torment them and fell from the sky without relent. The two captives were cold, wet and ravenously hungry – at least in Douglas's case. They had travelled back over the moor where a freezing gale had risen to hiss through the heather; then back into the forest where mud sprayed from the wheels and splattered the old warrior with mire. The Mersians did not stop for food or the coming of night – on they went through the north of the Merse, west towards the Leadhills.

Douglas muttered again as they were thrown about in the cage. Every jolt of the wheels was transmitted through the cart and the road was rough with many potholes, loose stones, and freezing puddles.

The grey days had dwindled into greyer nights until they were unsure how many days they had spent in the cage.

But what could they do?

Douglas had no idea. "What are the Wells of Snar?" he asked again. "I've heard old legends. Are these the same? Tell me, girl!"

Aliannia looked at him for a moment, wondering whether she should say. She sighed, and repeated what she had told Revile on the bank of the river some nights before.

"So that is it," said Douglas MacGalbrain when she had finished the tale. He shook his head as if he did believe his ears. "I don't believe it. It sounds like another of Rat's stupid stories."

"Nevertheless," said Aliannia, "it is true."

Finally, the journey neared its end. The Leadhills approached and the deeper grey of the slopes loomed out of the rain ahead.

And the Mersians increased their speed all the more.

A high stone wall came into view through the drizzle. Every hundred paces or so there was a embattled tower upon which Mersian guards spied upon the surrounding countryside. The road led up to a gatehouse in the wall. It had many storeys and battlements, and was built of some dark stone, presenting a grim edifice to Douglas MacGalbrain. From the highest turret flew a huge banner, Earl Eadolfa's standard of a gold unicorn on a black background. Rooks and ravens wheeled about the towers.

The two mighty gates remained tightly shut as the party approached. The gates were made of wood and shod with iron bars and long iron spikes on which the rotting bodies of men were impaled. Crows screeched, and the clop of the horses hooves and chink of harness sounded deadly as if muffled by the brooding gatehouse.

There they paused briefly, under the walls, while Patrick, Lord Rothstor, talked with the captain of the guard.

The huge gates ground open to the rumbling of a drum.

The horsemen edged forward again, under the arch of the gatehouse, passed the iron-shod gates, and into the Slavepits of Louther.

As they came through the gatehouse, it was as if they had travelled from one world into another, from the real, normal world into one of mad nightmare and darkness. And not even in their wildest and most-fevered dream could they have created a place of greater despair, evil or corruption.

Nothing grew there, no tree of flower or strangled weed. All was grey, grey with bare, broken rock hewn from the grey slopes, stripped of all life-giving soil, grey with a liquid ooze which seeped from every fissure and hole. There were untidy piles of rock and foul-smelling, stagnant pools of slime. A gravel road wound through the mounds and ponds towards the edge of a huge pit dug deep into the earth.

The cart shuddered as it rolled along the road, heading for the pit. People lined the way, grey people, people so emaciated and filthy that they were as dark and noisome as the hills they mined, people of every height and age but all dirty and vacant eyed.

Douglas and Aliannia stared at the long silent rows of slaves. They had never imagined that Eadolfa could have taken so many. The old warrior shook his head from side to side as if he could not quite believe his senses.

"Yes, old man," said Aliannia, "it was all true, everything they said about Earl Eadolfa and the Slavepits of Louther."

Douglas looked at her. "We must try to escape," he replied, "we must try to get away from here. We musn't become like these others."

"Where would we escape to?" she asked him. "It is said that no one has ever escaped from the Pits. Besides, I do not think Earl Eadolfa has brought us all this way just to dig. So, fear not. Whatever our doom, it is not to break rock in the Leadhills."

"That is not much of a comfort."

"No," she agreed, "it is not. But I would rather not think what he might do to us. Anyway, Eadolfa will make the whole world like this if he can, we will all be his slaves. What use is there in running away? There will be nowhere to hide if he has found the Crown of the Black Templars. Yet we must endure."

"Why?" said Douglas. "What is the point?"

"Perhaps there is no point," she said quietly, "but I think we should submit to Earl Eadolfa, that we should submit and beg his forgiveness." She paused for a moment, then smiled thinly. "Not that I think it will do you any good," she went on, "but it might just save me. Yes, master, and if that is the case I will make you suffer."

"Why?" asked Douglas.

"I was a fool!" she cried. "I should have stayed with my lord, Earl Eadolfa, from the beginning. Why did I run away?"

"Probably because he's an insane maniac with some pretty nasty habits," replied Douglas, "just to mention one thing."

Aliannia sneered at him.

"Lass," said Douglas, "you'd better act more convincingly when we get dragged before Eadolfa."

She smiled slightly.

The column of horsemen and the cart made its way into the Leadhills, through valleys and plains of grey desolation. There seemed no end to it all. Ahead they thought they could see the trunks of old trees but as they neared the stumps turned out to be gallows lining both sides of the road for over a mile. Corpses creaked on the ropes. Other victims had been strung up by their wrists with their stomachs opened for the sport of carrion crow. When they had passed the last gallows, they came to a huge mound of emaciated corpses standing scores of feet high. The smell of rotting flesh was overpowering, and Aliannia and Douglas covered their noses.

Earl Eadolfa, Lord of the Merse, was truly named Terror of the North.

The column slowed as the road steepened. They had ridden along the edge of the great pit, but now they followed a new track which led upwards, towards the highest summit of the Leadhills. Even the Mersian soldiery were quiet now, perhaps dismayed by what their master had achieved in the Slavepits of Louther. Yet, in truth, they were all cruel men, renowned for their delight in torture and murder, and perhaps they were just overawed and inspired by the show of Earl Eadolfa's wickedness.

But on they went, climbing the road.

"Why?" asked Douglas. "Why would anyone be mad enough to do all this?"

"Who knows?" replied the girl. "For the answer lies in the nightmare of a deranged mind. But part of it is the desire for power, power and immortality. Do you not feel that yourself, Douglas MacGalbrain? Do you not revel in slaughter and slaying? Would you want to live for ever? Douglas MacGalbrain the immortal, Douglas-nan-Bas, Terror of the North?"

"Not particularly," muttered Douglas.

"Maybe," she said, "but to me Eadolfa is no different from any other man – it is only that the means has been placed into his hands."

Douglas shrugged. There was really no answer to that so he said nothing.

The cart and its contents rolled to a halt and the Mersians dismounted. They had stopped on a narrow ridge high above the valleys below, high above the massive pit which was sunk far into the earth. Steep slopes soared away to the pinnacles of the Leadhills, a thousand or so feet above them. Rooks and ravens wheeled and circled the fingers of grey rock amid the desolation.

The track led no further. There was an entrance in the cliff ahead, a high-arched door that led into a tunnel which sloped downwards into gloom. Strange symbols were carved into the lintel above the arch, and there were two statues in recesses on either side of the door. The statues were of two warriors carved in stone. Both had one arm raised, the palm outward, in a gesture of warning.

"The door to the Wells of Snar," breathed Aliannia.

"That's nice," said Douglas.

The iron cage was opened and the prisoners were released. Douglas and Aliannia struggled down from the cart and were quickly surrounded by a strong guard.

Earl Eadolfa stepped out of the tunnel. A grin played about his lips. The Earl was clad in a magnificent black silk robe adorned with the golden unicorn of the Merse. His glittering belt was encrusted with diamonds and jet; about his shoulders was a thick cloak lined with black fur. He wore leather boots and silk trousers – the same colour as congealing blood.

Around his neck was an amulet with the largest ruby Douglas had ever set eyes on.

"Welcome," said Earl Eadolfa with a warm smile, his expression one of delight at seeing Aliannia. "Welcome indeed, my guests." Then he tugged thoughtfully at his beard. "It was most rude of you to refuse my invitation. Most rude." He frowned and there was something very dark and unpleasant in his eyes. "I shall have you both punished, I think, but we can talk about all that later."

"I am sorry, lord," cried Aliannia, and threw herself at Eadolfa's feet. "A madness took me. I am truly sorry and I have regretted my foolish decision to leave you almost as soon as I had made it. Please forgive me, lord, and accept me back into your affection and service. I will not betray you or your trust again. Let it be as it was before, lord. Please forgive me."

Earl Eadolfa peered at the girl for a moment, his frown darkening as he eyed her. But then his mood quickly changed and he smiled like a child, his eyes dancing with pleasure. "Very well, Templar's child," he said brightly, "you are wise. Very wise, indeed. Stand," he ordered, and Aliannia got to her feet. "Very well," he said again, "I forgive you and I will accept your service for it is valuable to me. But do not betray me again, I beg, or I will not be so merciful."

"Yes, lord," she replied shyly, then smiled.

"Yes, very good," said the Earl. "When I have the Crown of the Black Templars you shall instruct me in its uses. I will build the greatest empire the world has ever seen and you shall accompany me into glory. Come, girl, our destiny awaits."

Earl Eadolfa took Aliannia by the arm, then turned to the door to the Wells of Snar.

"You bitch!" spat Douglas MacGalbrain. "You treacherous bitch! I should've known you would prove faithless in the end. The gods damn your soul to the blackest pit!"

Aliannia approached the old warrior and her eyes were cruel. "You I have not forgotten," she said coldly, through clenched teeth. "You and your companion I have suffered in silence these last few days. But I have not forgotten. You promised me a beating if I did not please your vile friend. I hope I get the chance to repay you for your kindness!"

She turned half away from Douglas but then whirled back, striking the old warrior on the chest with the heel of her hand. And although she appeared a slight figure compared to the old warrior, she sent him tripping backwards. Douglas picked himself up from the ground, his eyes blazing.

"We shall talk later," she told him lightly, then rejoined the Earl.

Douglas MacGalbrain took a stride towards her, but soldiers hurried forward and caught the old warrior, binding him at the wrists.

A crow, with feathers as black as Helgard, fluttered down from the sky and landed on Earl Eadolfa's shoulder. The bird's beady eyes shone with an evil intelligence.

"Hullo, Regnir," crooned Eadolfa over the raven, tickling under its beak. The bird nibbled his ear.

"Excellent!" said the Earl with boyish enthusiasm. "Excellent! Now we are all assembled and everything is at last ready. Come, my friends, my destiny awaits and you shall all be part of it. Yes, come now."

Brother Wilmund was brought out from the entrance to the tunnel leading to the Wells of Snar. His eyes had been taken out to leave gaping sockets, and he staggered as he was pushed. Wilmund's hands were twisted like talons, broken and mangled, the nails ripped from the fingers.

"You have all met, I think," went on Eadolfa.

Wilmund was prodded forward. Standing proudly and without apparent fear, he nodded at where Douglas stood.

Earl Eadolfa, Lord of The Merse, threw him a scornful expression.

Wilmund smiled back at the Earl. Douglas shuddered. All Wilmund's teeth had been drawn or broken and his gums were bleeding.

The Earl, with Aliannia by his side, plunged into the relative gloom of the tunnel, striding towards his destiny. Douglas and Wilmund were dragged along behind, both of them watched by a strong guard led by the Warden of the North March.

The tunnel descended sharply, and Wilmund stumbled. The tunnel walls, ceiling and floor were smooth without crack or crevice. Douglas had never seen such fine workmanship and had no idea what craft or sorcery could have smoothed the passageway. Every ten or so paces there was a brazier but the torches burned without smell or smoke. The air was crisp but not cold, and even as they descended further, it stayed pure.

"We found this tunnel only last week," said Eadolfa from the front. He smiled slightly. "Even as it is now. There is no dust or dirt and the torches never need replaced – such is the magic of the Wells."

"Yes, my lord," said Aliannia with a shy smile.

Douglas peered about him. Many other tunnels and corridors led away from the main passageway but there was no sign of where they might lead or why they had been dug. Only one thing did the old warrior notice – here and there, lying in a tunnel or corridor, were bones, human bones. Douglas MacGalbrain sighed: this had not been one of his more sensible adventures. Rat was right: they should have stayed in Llaith, drinking and whoring.

"This was a temple," continued the Earl, "for acolytes who came to the Wells of Snar. An age ago, thousands of years, relatives and families of The Dead could come here and gain council or advice – or just hear or see a loved one again. So the legends say. But as time went on, the keepers of the Wells became afraid. A necromancer, called Ulcedor, had discovered a spell which could raise The Dead – not just conjure a voice or vision – from the void. When the keepers of the Wells found this out, they hid the gates, they blocked the entrance, they buried themselves alive under the Leadhills. Such was their skill, no man could find the doors again. They were hidden by magic deep within in the hills. So Ulcedor died. But his invocation remained. I, Earl Eadolfa of the Merse, am Ulcedor's heir – I have the spell!"

At last the party came out into a larger chamber. It was a huge cavern, deep in the ground, and the roof was lost high above them in the gloom. The floor and walls of the cavern were rough and unshaped, and shot through with quartz and coloured rock. The cavern was lit by a wicked red radiance which came from a chasm which split the chamber in two. The light flickered and pulsed, the red deepening then receding.

Earl Eadolfa walked to the edge of the chasm. It fell away down, beyond sight.

"What Ulcedor started," he said, "I shall complete."

Eadolfa clapped his hands together and laughed, the sound reverberating round the cavern.

"Take the prisoners over there," Eadolfa ordered, indicating a position at the edge of the chasm. "And guard them well. If they try to resist or fight, kill them. I must not be distracted!"

195

Douglas and Wilmund were taken to the side.

"I shall deal with you two later," the Earl went on, "but for now I want you to witness my triumph."

"For see you," Eadolfa cried in a mighty voice. "For see you, Douglas MacGalbrain and Brother Wilmund. See you, Patrick, Lord Rothstor, and my warriors. See you, Aliannia, child of the Templars, my partner, my empress to be. I, Earl Eadolfa, Lord of the Merse, Eadolfa-nan-Bas, Terror of the North, say to you all: this marks the beginning, this fateful day marks the beginning of the greatest and richest empire the world has ever seen. It is a famous day for all of us, both friends and enemies. When I have the Crown of the Black Templars, I shall have the power to take what I wish and I will have fulfilled my destiny! I shall summon Angelica Amhach from the abyss and she shall bring with her the Crown and place it in my hands. That is our common destiny!"

The Earl paused for a moment and then went on in a softer voice: "But I will need word spread of my triumph, I will need ambassadors to go from Rooksburg into all the kingdoms of the North and West – to tell them that resistance is useless and pointless. Two of my ambassadors will be Wilmund and Douglas MacGalbrain. You shall be my voice, you shall be my witnesses. I have chosen you to take word to all the other kings, lords and earls throughout. A fitting punishment it will be for you, Brother Wilmund."

"I will never serve you!" swore Wilmund, the words difficulty said through mangled teeth. "I will never help you willingly in your mad designs. Eadolfa, you are an insane, power-crazed maniac. Nothing will ever make me serve you, nothing I tell you!"

"Very well, Wilmund," grinned the Earl, "very well, you poor, blind fool. If you will not serve me, you will be thrown into the chasm, you will be cast into the abyss. Take him guards. What do you say now, Wilmund?"

"Go to Hell!"

"No," said Eadolfa, "I do not think so, not in my case. I have asked you this last time and you have refused me. So be it! You will have a host of sinners to convert in the abyss. A host, no less. Your vocation awaits you, Wilmund. Guards!"

Wilmund was taken to the very edge of the chasm. The Mersians held him there, tottering on the brink.

"God damn you!" cried Wilmund.

"Save your empty curses," laughed the Earl. "They are worthless! Your god cannot help you here. I am immortal and will outlast this world. When your god is dead, I shall still be here alive. It is you who are damned, Wilmund! Damned to the abyss for eternity."

Eadolfa nodded to his men.

Brother Wilmund was cast into the chasm. Yet as he tumbled head over heels he crossed himself and prayed. A flame, blinding in its intensity and purity, flared up from the Wells of Snar and gathered Wilmund in its radiance. And, as suddenly, the light died – Brother Wilmund had disappeared.

Earl Eadolfa smiled slightly. He turned to Douglas MacGalbrain. "Will you be my servant?" he asked the old warrior. "Or would you rather follow your friend into the abyss?"

Douglas thought about it for a moment, peering into the chasm. "I'll do whatever you wish, my lord," he said after a very brief pause. "I will gladly be your servant, my lord, Earl Eadolfa."

"You at least show some sense," replied the Earl. "Good! Then we may begin. Aliannia you may have to help me with this." He smiled slightly. "It is the first time it has ever been attempted."

"Of course, my lord," she said and smiled warmly.

Douglas looked at her.

Earl Eadolfa, Lord of the Merse, stepped forward and stood on the edge of the chasm, his arms outstretched. A smile played about his lips.

In a terrible voice, he began an incantation in some ancient tongue, all but forgotten in the modern world. The words were harsh and guttural but contained power untold. While he spoke, flames licked up the Wells of Snar, higher and higher, towards the Earl. First the fire burned red but then it deepened through crimson and violet and purple to black, a pure, unadulterated black as deep as the darkness of Helgard.

The incantation continued and the flames licked at Eadolfa, caressing his arms and legs, fingering through his beard with fiery hands.

The Mersians gasped and took a step back.

Then the flames died and it went completely black.

An evil pause followed.

At the bottom of the Wells of Snar, or at least at some great depth, the black grew and deepened until it seemed a thing in itself, a hole into the void through which all light was sucked from the material world and extinguished in the dense cold of the abyss. There was a mighty click, as if the lock of a great door was released, and voices, despairing voices, were raised in chorus to Eadolfa's incantation. Many of the soldiers covered their ears so loud and alarming were the voices.

"Angelica Amhach, come to me," said Eadolfa's voice out of the black. "I summon thee from thy rest. Come to me Angelica Amhach. I summon thee from thy rest!"

There was a last cry, like the braying of a goat, and the chorus of despairing voices fell silent.

A reek of charnel issued from the Wells on a sudden vapour. Men coughed and muttered. Some fled.

"I hear," answered a woman, but the tone was as dead and sharp as slate. "I obey. I have been summoned."

A light grew in the chasm, a point which slowly grew in intensity and size. Within the radiance a woman stood, holding a black crown before her. The spectre grew and the smell of carrion and rottenness filled the cavern. It was too much for more of the Mersians and they ran shrieking from the chamber.

Angelica Amhach glowed red, a tracing of form in the black. Slowly she rose up the Wells of Snar, the Crown of the Black Templars glistening and glimmering before her.

And the sickly red light grew to the braying of harsh horns.

The Crown glowed.

197

Up and up the Wells came Angelica Amhach.

"Come to me," purred Eadolfa. "Come to me."

But the spectre slowed its ascent and the Crown glowed more fiercely.

"I cannot," answered Angelica in her monotone. "I cannot."

The spectre began to fade and evaporate.

"Why not?" demanded the Earl in sudden anger.

"I cannot," whispered the spectre of Angelica Amhach for the last time as it slowly disappeared.

The wailing and braying of horns reverberated around the cavern, then fell silent. Torches burst back into life.

Earl Eadolfa frowned. "But I repeated Ulcedor's spell down to the last word," he muttered. "Perhaps there is something I have forgotten." But then realisation dawned on him. "Templar's child!" he cried. "Aliannia. I should have known, I should have guessed. You used the Crown to prevent me getting it! How dare you! You have tried to thwart me this one last time! Soon you shall die, but not here, I do not have the time or equipment. You shall die in such torment." He went on, his voice cold with frustrated rage. "Yes, you shall die. But I will have your eyes. Now!"

"What?" stammered Aliannia in obvious alarm, backing away from the Earl. "I have done nothing, my lord, nothing I tell you." She retreated further under his ire-filled glare. "I have done nothing," she pleaded. "Nothing. I beseech you to believe me."

"You used the Crown of the Black Templars to stop Angelica Amhach from placing the talisman into my hands," said the Earl in anger, hissing through his teeth. "And you shall pay. I will have your eyes!"

Aliannia looked terrified. "Douglas, please," she begged, "do something."

"Me?" said the old warrior. "What should I do? My lord, Earl Eadolfa had not bade me do anything. I need his order."

"Please?" she cried.

Douglas shrugged.

Earl Eadolfa grinned an awful grin and, waving his hands, he mumbled some strange words. Aliannia was suddenly struck motionless.

"Fool!" grated Eadolfa. "You fool, Aliannia. I offered you life and power beyond your comprehension. You have scorned both good sense and all wisdom to try to thwart me. Guards, bring her to me."

Aliannia was dragged before him.

"Why?" asked Eadolfa, and his voice sounded sad, like an aggrieved child. "Why, Aliannia? I offered you status and power beyond your dreams, beyond the dreams of any mortal. I will yet rule the greatest empire the world has ever seen – without your help – it will but take longer. Why did you forsake me? Why have you chosen to throw your life away?"

Aliannia spat. "Earl Eadolfa," she said with a curl of the lip, "I would rather spend my life as the slave of a low-born vile adventurer than rule an empire with you!"

Earl Eadolfa snorted. "It seems you will do neither," he told her. "I will deal with you properly later. But for now? Guards, hold her still. I will have your eyes!"

One Mersian soldier stepped forward, unsheathing a dagger. The hilt was shaped like a striking serpent. Another two pinned her arms. Aliannia closed her eyes and tried to cower away.

The Earl smiled. He reached forward with both arms towards her face. His hands were contorted almost, the fingers twisted like talons, the nails long and cruelly sharp. Aliannia struggled uselessly against the soldiers. Eadolfa's fingers caressed her cheeks, edging towards her eyes. She gave out a little whimper of terror.

"Keep her still!" commanded Eadolfa, licking his lips. All his attention was given to the Aliannia.

The soldier holding the dagger to her throat grinned, whirled round, and struck Eadolfa on the forehead with the heel of his hand. The Earl staggered back towards the edge of the chasm. The soldier caught hold of the front of the Earl's silken robe. Eadolfa gaped in absolute horror.

"Aye," said the cold voice of the soldier, "you know! Nothing will save you now – not spells, not men, not anything. This is the one place in the whole world where you can be destroyed. You sought the Crown of the Black Templars but you have found only destruction!"

The raven on the Earl's shoulder launched itself at the soldier, pecking at his eyes. But the bird was skewered through the heart with a flash of the dagger. The raven tumbled away down into the Wells of Snar.

"I can offer you riches and power beyond your dreams," Eadolfa pleaded as his robe tore.

Revile the assassin grinned.

The Earl screamed as he fell into the chasm. A lick of black flame leapt up from the Wells to greet him. The Earl screamed again. An opening appeared and engulfed Eadolfa in black fire. Eadolfa-nan-Bas, Terror of the North, was welcomed into the dark by a thousand despairing voices.

There was one, last cry of fear and dismay before it fell silent. The black flames flickered and went out.

There was an eerie silence.

Then the ground shook and there was a noise, like a great belch, which issued from the chasm.

Revile the assassin peered into the Wells of Snar and hoped that was the last he would ever see of Earl Eadolfa, Lord of the Merse, Terror of the North.

But Patrick, Lord Rothstor still stood there with ten or so Mersian soldiers. The men were frightened and looked nervously at each other. Douglas stood beside the assassin. His hands were freed and he held his axe – having recovered the weapon from one of the Mersians.

"About time you turned up, laddie," he told Rat. "What took you so long?"

"I had wine to drink," replied Revile. "How did you get your hands free?"

The old warrior smiled. "It's an old trick," he said, "but it worked."

"Good," said the assassin. "Aliannia, you can open your eyes now."

The slave girl staggered forward.

But Patrick, Lord Rothstor, turned towards the assassin. "What have you done?" he whispered. "What have you done?"

Flames licked up the Wells and the ground trembled.

Revile shrugged. "It is ended," he said simply.

"Is our lord dead?" asked one of the Mersian soldiers. "Is Earl Eadolfa gone?"

"Yes," breathed another, "you saw him fall."

"But he was immortal," said the first man. "Immortal," he repeated, "yet he is no more."

"What have you done?" said Lord Rothstor more strongly.

A rock fell from the ceiling, landing with a plume of dust.

"We must go," said Douglas peering about. "I think the whole place is about to come down around us."

"I know," said Revile, never taking his eyes from the Mersians. "I know, Douglas. We should all go," he said loudly. "You have lost you master but you still have your lives. To stay here may mean death for us all. Let us go. Now."

"What have you done?" cried the Warden of the North March and his hand strayed to the hilt of his sword.

The assassin opened his mouth to reply – but no words came. Revile's sword was whipped from its scabbard. Revile cut down Patrick without warning like a striking cobra. Lord Rothstor collapsed backwards, his sword clattering to the ground. He lay by the edge of the Wells of Snar, blood gushing from the wound in his side.

The remaining Mersians still hesitated.

"If we fight it out here," the assassin told them, "we will all die!"

One of the soldiers broke and fled, then another. The ceiling cracked and stones rained down on them. The stink of sulphur grew. In a moment, Revile and his friends were left alone in the cavern.

Douglas gave out a huge sigh of relief.

"Come," said Revile, taking Aliannia by the arm, "we'd best hurry."

The three companions fled, leaving the cavern, and ran into a steeply-ascending tunnel. Behind them, the walls of the tunnel buckled and rock snapped and cracked like dry tree branches.

"I hope you can remember the way out," muttered Douglas.

"So do I," agreed the assassin, dragging Aliannia along. "Look, girl," he said to her, "snap out of it. Eadolfa's gone. You're safe now."

She nodded and managed to run without help.

They came to a junction in the tunnel. Douglas did not remember the place but, without hesitation, the assassin chose the right-hand branch.

"Are you sure that's right?" the old warrior called after him as he hesitated at the junction. "Damn!" he swore and followed Revile and Aliannia. It said a lot that he managed to keep up with them.

A fissure appeared in the floor and Douglas had to leap to avoid falling to his death. Stones fell crashing to the floor behind him.

Revile sprinted on ahead, followed by Aliannia, then the struggling Douglas.

"Come on, blubberguts," shouted the assassin over the sound of ruin.

Ahead the assassin could see daylight. He hurried towards the end of the tunnel eagerly, not waiting for Douglas to catch up.

The old warrior could hardly breathe and his face was red and covered in sweat.

The tunnel collapsed behind them.

They emerged coughing and spluttering out into the sun, a huge plume of dust issuing from the mouth of the tunnel.

The Mersian soldiers had fled. Two horses still stood there, tethered to the cart which carried the iron cage. The beasts were terrified as the ground shook, and stones and boulders tumbled down from the slopes above them. The three companions freed the horses from the cart and then set off at a mad gallop down the road.

Revile only dared to look back the once. The ridge and the road to the Wells had disappeared in a landslide, engulfed under half the hill. The assassin grinned, spurring his horse towards the gatehouse of the Slavepits of Louther.

Douglas laughed. "We made it just in time." He mopped his brow.

Revile nodded.

"Thank you, master," whispered Aliannia softly. "I did not think I would be saved." She shuddered. "Thank you, Rat."

The assassin rode on. They arrived at the grim building of the gatehouse. The gates were open and the soldiers had fled. Slaves were streaming out of the Leadhills – so great a number Revile could hardly believe his eyes.

"Where are we going now?" asked Douglas.

"Rooksburg," replied the assassin.

"Why?" said the old warrior. "I would have thought you would have had enough of the place."

"I fancy going on a spot of looting," admitted Revile.

"Master, it's not over ...' Aliannia hesitated.

Revile looked at her, then followed her gaze back the way they had come. True the entrance to the Wells had gone, a huge plume of dust and smoke billowing up into the sky was all that told of its existence. But something was not right. Revile squinted. Although it was full day, there was a darkness about the hills, which perceptibly was growing even as the assassin watched.

"It's not over," repeated the girl with a troubled look. "Something is wrong."

"Why is nothing ever simple," sighed Douglas.

VIII

"What should we do?" asked Revile, shaking his head.

It was now evening and the three companions rode through the gloom back towards Rooksburg in the east, riding hard without rest. Behind them the sky was darkening, a blackness like a great cloud of fear followed them from the Wells of Snar. It was growing and deepening with each passing hour, and it seemed to Revile that another cloud was coming to meet it from the east, from Rooksburg glowering somewhere ahead. It was probably his fear, but the darkness looked like a giant crow's wing. The sky was shot through with red as the sun set, but its rays were eaten up by the black.

"I do not know," she said. "Eadolfa should not be able to escape from the Wells. Yet my heart tells me that that is to happen. But it is not from behind us that the danger comes. It is from Rooksburg."

"Perhaps we should go the other way, then," suggested Douglas.

"If Eadolfa escapes there will be nowhere to hide," replied the girl with a catch in her voice. "He will have the Crown, and we will have no place to hide and no hope."

"Then it is on to Rooksburg," sighed Revile.

They only rested when their ponies became too exhausted to continue, and by then it was too dark to continue anyway. They spent an uncomfortable night in the open. It was as black as pitch: there was no moon or stars. As soon as it grew light they set off again, but as the day dawned weakly their fear grew.

Above their heads was a broiling cloud of darkness, twisting and spiralling across the sky from the Wells of Snar to the west, to the approaching fortress of Rooksburg. It still grew and deepened with every passing moment. The whole world was hushed.

"This is not good," said Douglas.

On they travelled until their ponies were sweating and stumbling, and they were weary in the saddle.

Finally around the middle of the day they could see the towers of Rooksburg, and soon they were riding up to the gatehouse. The light was dim and shifting, and the day was darkening even with the sun high in the sky. The three companions jumped from their horses.

Rooksburg was deserted, both the palace and village: all had fled, soldiery and slaves. The whole place was eerily quiet and still, but a huge funnel of cloud seemed to rise from the very fortress itself and join the vapours from the west.

Revile ran through the entrance to the passageway and into the gatehouse of the palace, followed by Aliannia and Douglas.

But even as they came out into the wan light of the courtyard, they found that Rooksburg had not been deserted by all. The courtyard was filled with flocks of crows and corbies, rooks and ravens: crowding on the branches of the dead trees and anywhere else they could find a perch.

The three companions had no time to stop and they sped across the courtyard. But even as they emerged from the passageway the birds attacked, flying recklessly into Revile, Douglas and Aliannia: pecking and clawing with their beaks and talons. Aliannia screamed – Douglas and Revile at least had armour to protect them. Douglas took his axe and swung it about his head, but this did little to discourage the flocking birds.

Aliannia stumbled under the attack, but Revile dragged her across the cobbles and into the

202

donjon, Douglas on his heels. They dragged the door shut behind them, but still the birds came, pecking anything that moved in a whirl of black feathers.

The door slammed shut with a huge clang. A few birds had entered the donjon, but Revile and Douglas quickly killed them all, wringing their necks.

Aliannia lay on the floor panting, and Revile wiped blood from his face. Douglas stood, bent double, his breathing laboured. Outside the attack continued: the birds were apparently flying heedlessly into the door. The timbers shuddered but held for now, yet the concussions were growing and the door groaned under the assault.

It was virtually dark in the donjon, and Revile took out and lit a torch. It crackled but seemed to give little illumination.

"Quick, master," breathed Aliannia. "We do not have much time."

"What should we do?" said Revile.

"I know not," said the girl wearily. "But I know where our peril lies." She pointed upwards towards the upper floors of the donjon. "That is where it comes from."

"Come then," said Revile.

The three companions hurried down the corridor. They came to a flight of stairs, and Aliannia led them up into darkness. The whole building was silent and still, unless it was that the ground shuddered slightly.

They leapt up the stairs, and reached the top of a winding spiral stair into another passage. If it had not been for the torch they would have been blinded so complete was the darkness. Aliannia led them without hesitation through a maze of stairs and corridors until they came to a large iron door.

The ground moved beneath their feet: this time there could be no mistake.

Aliannia stopped at the door. "This is it," she breathed. "This is Eadolfa's chamber – he never let any enter it." They stood scores of feet above the courtyard. Although there were windows in the passageway and stair, there was no light except for the failing torch.

Revile tried the handle, and to his surprise the door opened. They entered a large chamber, empty except for a pillar of light, a shifting illuminance, in the middle of the floor and a wall of shelving. The light ebbed and flowed, shedding a ghastly light on the room. The shelves were bare but for several leather-bound books and one large elaborate jar which was decorated with various magical symbols. The spluttering torch flickered.

Douglas gasped and Revile hesitated in the doorway.

In the column of light was a man, or at least his skeleton. They could only assume it was Eadolfa for his form was not complete. Imperceptibly he was solidifying, the bones were forming, and muscle and organs and sinew were growing on the bones.

The torch went out, and the assassin desperately relit it.

"What should we do?" asked Revile.

But Aliannia was at loss: she opened her mouth to speak but no words came. Douglas was muttering inanely.

The assassin steeled himself and entered the chamber. It was unpleasantly stuffy and warm. Revile drew a dagger and attempted to stab the Earl but the blow had no effect: every time he penetrated Eadolfa's forming flesh the wound sealed up as soon as the blade was removed.

Revile gave up and hurried from the column of light, going to the shelves of tomes and the jar. He opened the books but they were all written in some tongue of which he had no knowledge. Aliannia recovered and joined him, poring over the pages. But they held nothing to help them and there was no time to waste.

Douglas stood aghast as Eadolfa's body continued to solidify, layer by layer it was becoming whole. The heart and lungs and liver and intestines were being created as he stared. The old warrior shuddered. Eadolfa's eyes appeared in the sockets, his perfect white teeth gritted in a grin.

Aliannia grabbed the large jar, dragged it from the shelf and placed it on the floor. It was stoppered and sealed.

"What is this?" asked Revile, one eye on Eadolfa.

Time was running out.

Aliannia was trying to decipher the symbols on the jar.

The floor beneath their feet trembled and the ceiling seemed to wheel.

Revile went back to the books, leafing through the pages in desperation. But still he found nothing.

Time was running out.

Eadolfa stood in the column of light. Skin was appearing all over his body. Lips and eyelids. Fingernails and hair. He was nearly complete. Douglas thought that one of his limbs twitched and the old warrior's heart nearly gave out. He gasped.

Revile whirled around.

Time had run out.

Eadolfa's eyes flicked open; he had a terrible smile on his lips.

Douglas collapsed and fell to the ground.

Aliannia and Revile huddled together under the Earl's terrible gaze.

Eadolfa laughed. "Well met at last," he grinned. "Fools! Did you think you could so easily be rid of me!" He threw his head back and laughed long and bellowing, a foul and evil noise that reverberated around the empty passageways, stairs and chambers, louder and louder, until Revile thought that his ears would burst. Aliannia shrank by the assassin's side.

The Earl leapt stepped out of the light.

"So," he grinned. "So, Templar's child you could not leave me in the end." He took another pace forward.

Revile swept out his sword, barring his way, although his hands shook.

"Ah, we meet again," said Eadolfa. "You have caused me much trouble. I am looking forward to rewarding you by tearing out your eyes and feeding them to you, followed by your own sweet meats. Only, of course, after you have dined on this girl: devouring her raw flesh until you are fat and bloated on her meat, drinking her hot and treacherous blood until you burst."

"Thank you, but I have eaten," managed Revile, but his words were barely audible through his fear.

The Earl edged forward, his attention bent on the pair of them.

Aliannia whimpered, and staggered. The large jar at her feet tottered on its base, but did not fall over.

Eadolfa hesitated, just for an instant, and just for an instant Revile sensed his fear.

"Smash the jar!" he cried.

"Of course!" said Aliannia.

"Noooo," cried Eadolfa.

Gathering all her strength, the slave girl raised the jar above her head and brought it crashing down on the ground. It smashed into several pieces and sherds, but appeared to be empty.

Eadolfa gave out a long and angry howl.

Revile grinned, but the expression died on his lips.

Nothing happened.

Eadolfa still stood before them, but now his features were consumed by a mad fury. For a moment nothing of sense issued from his lips, just twisted snarling noises.

"Now you will die!" he finally managed, staring intensely at Aliannia. "Now you will die. Did you think you could destroy me this way?"

"No," said the girl, "I think I have made you alive."

Earl Eadolfa, Earl of the Merse and Terror of the North, leapt forward, arms outstretched, dark power rippling in his hands and fingers.

It was the last thing he did.

Behind him Douglas had silently risen to his feet and with a swing of his axe he cleanly decapitated the Earl, Eadolfa's head bouncing across the floor. The rest of the Earl's shuddering corpse collapsed to the floor and blood coursed out of his neck into a large pool. He was dead, finally. Or so they hoped. Douglas decided to make sure by dismembering the corpse and leaving the Earl's body a ruin of flesh and bone.

Revile sighed, breathed again, and found Aliannia had taken his hand.

"Douglas," he said, "I thought you were dead."

The old warrior smiled crookedly, and patted his axe. "Not bad for a fat old blubberguts, laddie," he said. "Now let's get the hell out of here."

IX

There were three people riding shaggy ponies.

Two were unkempt, rascally-looking characters, while the third was a dusky girl of some beauty. Their saddle bags were bulging with loot plundered from Rooksburg. Behind them, and now some distance away, there was a large plume of black smoke rising into the sunny day: Rooksburg was burning.

"I said it was the dangerous jobs which paid the best," said Douglas.

Revile laughed. "Aye," he said, "that you did, although we've got a lot richer by not going to Caerisle. Anyway, we can't complain after the way things have turned out."

"And now you have me, master," said Aliannia. Gone was her rough woollen tunic. Now she wore a rich dress of deep-blue silk and about her shoulders was wrapped a cloak lined with soft fur. "We should not have met if you had gone straight to Caerisle."

"Aye," agreed Revile.

"You were lucky, anyway," said Douglas, "and all the more for that I slew Eadolfa. Or think I did."

"I know," said the assassin.

"Did he die there?" asked Douglas softly. "And what were the Wells of Snar? A gate into the underworld or otherworld, heaven or hell? I don't think I really understand."

Revile said nothing.

"Well?" said the old warrior.

Aliannia shrugged. "The Earl is not dead," she whispered, "not dead in the true sense – or so I believe. But he is imprisoned, caught in the Nothing: his immortal being or spirit or soul is trapped. Angelica Amhach was similarly caught. The Wells of Snar was the only place where Earl Eadolfa could be destroyed – or imprisoned anyway. It was his last hope that he could return to Rooksburg by finding his soul, using it as a way of returning to this world and rebuilding his form. When I broke the jar he was mortal in that body, and that mortal body you slew. His immortal body is still in the Nothing. But we are free of him forever."

"And do we all end up there?" said Douglas who was clearly confused. "Do we go into the Nothing when we die?"

"I do not know," replied the slave girl.

"So that jar contained his soul?" asked the old warrior.

Aliannia nodded.

Douglas MacGalbrain paused, smiled ruefully, and tugged at his chin. He shook his head, gave up trying to understand, then said: "Are we travelling far today?"

"O don't start moaning again!" muttered Revile. "We've hardly come ten miles since lunch."

"Well, I'm tired," said Douglas. "I'm fed up trudging north, Rat. I'd forgotten how many miles it was to Llaith."

"Never mind, lardbelly, I'm sure we'll find an inn and some victuals soon!"

"And I will be glad of it," said the old warrior more cheerfully. "And I'm glad we're out of the Merse."

"As I am, Douglas," said Revile quite seriously. "We should find an inn."

"Don't tell me, Rat," said Douglas. "You have heard rumours about these lands and you have no wish to test their truth by spending another night in the open."

Revile laughed, but his eyes were on the slave girl.

***

The others were silent and for a moment Revile thought they had all fallen asleep. There was little sorrow in that, perhaps, and the assassin leaned back against the wall, staring into the darkness. His eyes were empty of emotion and he felt tired. He might have sighed.

"I liked that one," said Margaret softly. "I enjoy epic tales even when you are the hero – although not much of a hero, to be sure. At least you saved your friends – and, if you are to be believed, the world as well – from the evil Earl Eadolfa and his minions. Do you like being a hero, friend Revile?"

"I wouldn't know," replied the assassin, "I don't ever remember being one. Yet it doesn't sound that much fun. How many of the heroes in the old sagas and tales ever enjoyed themselves? Or never did their duty? Or lived to a ripe and happy old age? Not one as far as I remember. No. They were poisoned, or murdered, or fell in battle defending their honour, or got torched by a dragon. If it was me, I would take as much gold as I could carry and make for the hills. No cause or kingdom is worth it. All heroes are stupid fools!"

Margaret laughed, running her long fingers through her hair. "How like you to say such a thing!" she told him. "Anyway, you are hardly doing any better: you are to be hanged! Perhaps heroes are fools, and perhaps all their deeds are stupid, but at least it makes a good story. If they all ran away, there wouldn't be any sagas, would there now?"

"No, I guess not," said the assassin. "Tales about whoring and brawling and noble deeds of drinking would get a bit boring."

"Especially for me," said Margaret with a half smile.

"Ah, yes. I'd forgotten for a moment: the whore with a heart of gold." Revile grinned. "What heroic deeds have you performed under the sheets?"

"You're making fun of me again," said the woman.

"Perhaps I am," admitted Revile, "but then I know so little about heroic deeds. I've never done anything unless there was a good chance I'd survive or there was a lot of gold at stake or I fell into it by mistake – with hindsight maybe too many of the latter. I have run away lots of times – and, you are right, it does not make such a good story. Anyway, I might be interested to hear what you have done: the noble deeds of a whore."

"Do you really think I could be heroic?" asked the woman, not certain he was still joking with her. "What about Fergus? Was he heroic in not running away in the face of the Viking onslaught? Or Alwyn because she refused to sleep with the prince?"

The others did not say anything.

"I think they're asleep," said Revile softly.

Margaret nodded. "Do you think we are heroic?" she asked again.

"As far as I knew," answered the assassin, "being heroic is not what you do but why you do it. I am sure Alwyn's reasons for not sleeping with the prince are not very virtuous, more that she wanted to be queen, and that Fergus only fought because he didn't really care if he was killed or not." Revile laughed softly. "So are you a heroic bunch? No, not really. I think it is usual in tales for the villain or the warrior or the down-on-his-luck prince to break down and admit the farmer is brave in tilling his fields against ravages of fortune and weather. Or the wife is brave for keeping house when the men are away at war. *'Aye,'* they say, with a tear in their eye, *'how noble you are, brave farmer, for caring for your beasts, for battling against weather and soil and ill chance. How brave you are, dear farmer, for bringing in the crops so the people can eat. Now I will away off back to my grand palace and sod the lot of you!'*

"But I don't think that. No, I reckon farmers, serving wenches and whores are a stupid cravenly lot without an intelligent thought between them. But you know my mind on this matter, by now. I've said all this before. Besides, you, yourself, do not think you are brave. Do you now?"

"No, I suppose not," replied the woman. "But like you I have only survived long enough to go to the gallows. Perhaps there have been no heroic deeds along the way – but still you, the bold assassin, are to share my fate."

"I cannot challenge that," laughed the assassin. "You are right, I suppose. If I am such a clever cunning fellow how come I am to die with the likes of you three? Anyway, who knows? It is not us who can judge whether our lives have been brave or not."

"I know mine hasn't," said Margaret quietly. "Don't you of all people try to persuade me otherwise."

"Perish the thought."

"I wish my life had been," she went on, "or at least I wish I had done things which mattered like you have. But I haven't. What have I to show for the past years? Nothing! No one will mourn my passing, Revile, no one will remember me. My death will not make any difference."

"Perhaps it won't – but what makes you think I'll be remembered any more than you? I have few friends. No, at least some men may remember you for the pleasure you've given them."

"Exactly. They will remember that I was a whore!"

Revile shrugged. "Well, that's better than what folk will remember me for," he said. "You must have given some men a good time. But whichever way you look at it, hanging's a better way to die than the pox or starvation or gangrene or a sword in your guts. What would you have done when you were old? How would you have supported yourself? Who would have cared for you then?"

"Like you," she said, "I have no one."

"So you have said – and very depressing it must be."

"Anyway," she said, "I am not old – not too old – nor do I have the pox or gangrene, nor am I starving. I had a very comfortable life so going to the gallows is not much of a comfort, I'm afraid. I can't believe you think otherwise!"

"I don't," said the assassin. "I didn't know what else to say. I was trying to comfort you but I have had too little practice to be any good at it. Who cares in the end, Margaret? We've perhaps four hours to live, maybe a bit more, maybe a bit less. Yet I'm cold, very cold. I am damp. I am numb. Not to mention being tired and depressed and hungry. I don't give a damn. Not now. Even Fergus and Alwyn sleep, sleep away their last hours and minutes on this earth."

"It is a tribute to your storytelling."

"You're too kind."

"Anyway, you are still awake," said Margaret.

208

"I'll have a sleep later when it's light."

"Why?" asked the woman.

"It's too quiet and dark just now," he lowered his voice to a whisper. His expression was both amused and grim at the same time – if she could have seen it. "I can never sleep when it's as dark as this. I always have a fire or torch lit. I guess I'm just not used to it."

"God above!" cried Margaret in surprise. "You mean you are scared of the dark?"

"Hush," said Revile. "Not so loud. You'll wake the others. But it happened some years ago. I've never been able to sleep in total dark since then. Foolish really!"

"What happened some years ago?"

"I'll tell you later," said the assassin. "It still frightens me now when I think about it – still, even though I am to be hanged in a few hours."

"Am I to believe you are scared?" asked the woman. "You, the noble and brave assassin, who has overcome all manner of terror and evil, are afraid of nothing more than the dark?"

"I have good reason," said Revile, sounding aggrieved. "But I'll say no more for just now." The assassin shivered. "No, the mood will pass. Anyway, I have said enough about me and my noble, brave and heroic deeds. What about you? How did you end up in this dungeon sharing the doom of a hero like me?"

"I told you," muttered Margaret. "Didn't you listen? I stole a piece of jewellery from one of my customers. He found out, had me imprisoned, tried and executed. That is all there is."

"Perhaps," said the assassin with a grin, "but I was more interested in what happened before that: I wanted to find out more about your past. How is it that you found an occupation on your back? What reduced you to steal from your customers? These things interest me, albeit only very slightly."

"Why?" said Margaret. "What business is it of yours?"

"It isn't," said Revile, "but if I only minded my own business I would have had a very dull life. Perhaps you have something to hide?"

"Perhaps it just isn't interesting."

"Maybe, but tell me anyway. Let me be the judge."

"O very well," said the woman reluctantly. "I was born in Bamburg some thirty or so years ago." Although she had seemed unhappy to start, once she got going her story was confidently told. "My father was a merchant and travelled about buying and selling. We were quite well off and my father had a house in the town square near the Gallowsgate. We used to watch the executions from the balcony.

"I was about twelve years old when he went away that last time. That is when all the trouble started for me. My mother said his ship had been sunk with no survivors off the coast of Pentland. My father never came back. We still had some money and there was the house. My mother was distraught but we managed.

"But then my mother took a lover. She was still quite young and you can't blame her. They married after about a year. My stepfather took no interest in me – not as a child anyway. When my mother was pregnant, she refused him and he slept with me. That was not a happy time." The woman faltered but forced herself to go on. "In seven or eight months it started to show, I could no longer conceal my shame. I must have been about thirteen or fourteen. What could I do? I felt so guilty yet I had done nothing wrong."

Margaret sighed. "My mother threw me out when I could hide the truth no longer, my own mother threw me out onto the streets. I wandered about that day, weeping in sorrow, wandering about aimlessly. I returned home but my mother chased me away and cursed me. It was getting dark. I had nowhere to go. I tried to sleep in a doorway.

"I'd never known hunger or real fear before. I was cold and lonely. How would I live?

"Well, I reckon there are parts of you that will do anything to survive. My mind was dead but these other parts took over. And I got enough to eat. My time came and my baby was born dead. I nearly died myself. I never knew a body had so much blood. But I survived although I'm not even sure I wanted to.

"And that is more or less it. As you have so kindly pointed out: I make my money on my back – or whichever other position suits. I had some success, enough to see me comfortable."

"Then why did you steal?"

"Why do you think?" asked Margaret. "Sure, I could make a good enough living just now, sure enough. But it didn't earn me gold or silver; nor, as you said, do most men want to sleep with an old crone or hag. I am not as young as I used to be. I thought thieving would supplement my income. As it did. I would have been able to retire soon. Unfortunately I was caught. You see, I never thought any of my customers – being married men – would ever admit to losing anything in my house. I was wrong."

"You were unlucky," said Revile lightly.

"As were you," said Margaret.

"Perhaps I was, although Bregorin trapped me. It saved him my fee. It's that simple. Not that it makes much difference. My luck was bound to run out. I should never have survived so long considering all the dangerous and stupid things I have done. I've had a fortune, Margaret, I have had a fortune in silver and gold and gemstones, earned from ludicrously perilous murders and adventures, the next one more risky and reckless than the last. And I spent the lot on drink and women. I am a bigger fool than you.

"This was bound to happen," he went on softly, "it was just a matter of time. And, Margaret, you own more than I do. All I have is an old sword in a tattered scabbard, a set of daggers, a stupid pony, and these clothes I'm wearing."

"You don't even have most of those now," mentioned the woman.

"Strangely enough," he replied, "they are actually safe. I was disguised as a beggar, with an eye patch and all, when they caught me. My valuables are somewhere safe. It's a shame I won't live to retrieve them."

Margaret laughed softly.

"You see," said the assassin, "we're alike in some ways, you and I. I, too, am a whore. I sell myself for silver and gold and to counter the boredom; and, if I am starving, for food and water. And we're to share the death of villains."

"What do you mean?" asked the woman.

"We are to be hanged," said Revile. "That is a villain's death. I would rather die with a sword

210

in my hand on some last great adventure. I suppose your equivalent would be to die on your back with half a ton of blubber between your legs. At least being hanged is less messy than being beheaded."

Margaret snorted. "Well," she told him, "if you have no notion of honour what difference does it make which way you die?"

"I don't know," said the assassin. "It just sounds better."

"Does it?" asked the woman.

"Probably not," muttered Revile. "Perhaps, rather too late in life, I am becoming the heroic sort after all. These kind of gestures can be very important to us heroes, especially when you are standing on the scaffold. Very important."

"Why?"

"Gad!" said the assassin. "Why ask me? Do you women never grow weary of asking more questions?"

"How would I know?" replied Margaret. "I know so little about women. Men, on the other hand, I know a lot about. Do you want me to tell you about your frail little egos? I am an acute observer!"

"No, it's all right," said the assassin quickly. "Anyway, I think very highly of myself."

"That I can believe! Then you should tell me why you are afraid of the dark!"

Revile paused for a moment. "All right," he said, "but only on the condition you tell me the real story of your past. I, too, am an acute observer. This won't sound that frightening in the retelling – you would have had to have been there."

The assassin began his tale although he was unusually subdued. Margaret thought she could hear a slight tremble in his voice.

It might have been the cold.

The Barrow

evile the assassin was not happy.

A freezing wind from the north howled through the steep-sided glen, making the assassin wrap his cloak more tightly about his shivering body. Revile's feet were frozen, for there were large holes in the soles of his boots. The track was muddy with a soft oozing mud which seeped through his toes.

Revile glowered. His purse was empty and he had finished the last of his wine two nights before – enough to make any bold adventurer glower.

"Odin's dick!" cursed Revile as he trudged along. "Thor's scrotum!"

The assassin stopped in the middle of the track, peering about. It was getting late and he searched for some place to spend the night. He sniffed the breeze. Despite the chill, the air was heavy with the promise of thunder. The assassin thought he could hear the echoes of a storm rumbling away in the darkening hills.

"Bastard!" he muttered.

A few trees grew in the gorges of the glen but he could not spy anywhere that would give him shelter.

"Bastard!" he repeated several more times.

Walking along the track a little further, he forded a shallow burn and headed for a small domed hillock. The hillock was covered in turf and crowned by a ring of old dead trees. The assassin gathered wood and climbed to the top of the hillock, surveying the area for a better campsite.

He sighed and took off his pack, sitting down against one of the tree stumps. He made a poor meal from his small store of dried and tasteless provisions, and when he had finished eating, rose and gathered more fuel. The fire he built was a weak affair and did little more than choke him with clouds of damp smoke.

Revile the assassin took off his boots and tried to warm his feet.

"Bastard!" he repeated several more times.

The wind died and the light failed. Huge black clouds, towering away into the heavens, rolled down the glen, eating the black sky up before them. The air was dank, heavy and close, and the whole world seemed hushed as if waiting for the next peel of thunder.

Revile stirred from under his blanket. The fire was almost out except for the glow of a few embers. He built it up until it cast flickering shadows across the hillock, silhouetting the crooked trunks of the trees.

Rain started to fall. Lightning seared across the heavens – to be followed an instant later by a crashing of thunder like mighty war drums beating away in the hills.

The assassin squatted down as raindrops ran down the back of his tunic. He was too depressed even to curse and stared into the heart of the fire.

His thoughts trailed away into nothing.

There was a loud slithering noise and the ground trembled.

Revile started, getting slowly to his feet and drawing his sword. He was unsure how much time had passed but the great storm clouds were slipping out of the glen. The downpour was relenting. A few stars twinkled in the deep-blue sky above the darker form of the hills. It was middle night but Revile could not remember having fallen asleep.

Then there was the sound again, very close, a slithering, slipping noise from the other side of the hillock. But it was made by no man or beast – of that Revile was sure – or none he knew about. He guessed the ground itself was slipping for he could still feel the turf shaking under his feet and there was a strong smell of wet earth. Revile relaxed slightly and went to investigate, taking a brand from the fire and using it as a torch.

He scrambled down the side of the hillock and walked round to the west. This side of the hillock had subsided and there were torn-up tree stumps and roots piled into a muddy mess. Poking in amongst them, he could find nothing untoward. He was just going to return to his cheerless camp when he noticed stonework almost hidden in the wet mud. The masonry was regular and well laid: Revile could not have slipped a dagger between the courses of stone. Wiping mud from the stonework with his hands, he wondered what he could have found. And the assassin smiled slightly. It could only be a barrow or cairn, a tomb of the long-forgotten people who once lived all over the north. Revile had seen their tombs while a slave in Thule, and heard many tales elsewhere.

Revile the assassin grinned to himself.

He cleared more mud from the masonry, removing a few rocks and broken tree branches. He impaled the brand in the mud to free his hands. In the flickering light, he could just discern an opening cut into the stonework. It was blocked by a stone door.

The assassin smiled even more broadly. The tomb had not been broken into – at least, not yet.

Scrabbling at the edge of the stone door, Revile managed to move it a fraction, breaking his fingernails on the rock. It was difficult to find purchase in the slimy mud; but he was determined – little could stand between an eager Revile and the promise of loot. Soon he had withdrawn the stone door to what he reckoned was about halfway out of the opening. He was sweating and stopped to wipe his brow, covering his forehead in mud.

Once more, he gripped the edge of the door and heaved. Finally, with a tremendous effort, it came free and he wrestled the stone away. An exhalation issued from within, as if a seal had been broken, dry enough to etch old bones. Revile's teeth glinted.

The passageway into the tomb had a low ceiling, and was barely high enough for a man to crouch. He got down on his hands and knees, sinking into the mud, and thrust his torch into the opening. It continued for some little way into the barrow before opening into a larger chamber. Without hesitation, he crawled into the passageway, his hands and knees cold against the stone flags. He held the brand before him and trailed his pack. The air was still and dry with a dull, dead flavour.

Revile reached the end of the low passageway and scrambled out into the larger chamber. It was bigger than he had expected. The roof was high above him, shrouded in shadows; the floor

213

was dusty and unmarked apart from his damp footprints. His movements sounded strange in the tomb, dampened but very loud. The light from the brand was wavering and imprecise, although there was no movement of air.

The assassin stood in the middle of the rectangular chamber, surveying the scene. The passageway back out was behind him. In the centre of each of the other walls, there was an opening, blocked by a stone door, its lower edge at thigh height. The chamber was otherwise empty but the assassin knew that beyond the stone doors would be cells, burial places of the old people. Sometimes there was gold and silver and jewels, or so he had been told in many a tavern story.

He took a large empty sack from his pack and placed it on the ground. Standing for a moment in thought, he tried to decide which cell to open first. He reckoned that the one opposite the passageway would prove the richest so he left it until last. It never occurred to the assassin – then – that he was the first person to stand in that place for hundreds of years. He knew next to nothing about cairns, barrows or their builders – or who lay buried, undisturbed, for half an age. Nor did he care particularly. His purse was empty and all other considerations were forgotten. It was not even certain there would be any treasure.

He went to the cell in the wall to the left of the passageway. Gripping the stone door, he dragged it from its place. The stone fell with a dead thump and a plume of dry dust. Inside the cell was gloomy – but the assassin could make out the form of a skeleton, that of a woman. The corpse was buried as if in a mother's womb. He peered into the cell, leaning in over the ledge, and to his delight actually found some treasure. He found a beautifully-carved jet brooch and some amber beads. Taking the treasure, he placed it in his sack.

He went to the cell in the opposite wall, to the right of the passageway. Another stone door fell to the floor, more dust rained down from the ceiling. A skeleton lay there, but, to Revile's disappointment, there was nothing of value interred with it. He poked around, despoiling the bones, but finally gave up and turned his back on that cell, ignoring the empty stare from the displaced skull.

Revile, assassin, despoiler and grave robber, went to the last cell.

The stone door was tightly wedged and seemed reluctant to move from the ledge. He gripped the stone again and this time it moved slightly. Its movement gave him more leverage and he finally managed to draw the stone out. His arms trembled and his face was red with effort. The stone was larger than the others and it tumbled to the floor with a huge crash, leaving the assassin's ears ringing with the impact. Wiping more sweat from his forehead, he waited until the dust had settled then peered into the last cell.

The corpse of a man was laid out there. While the other bodies had been fleshless and bony, this one was mummified, the limbs and torso wizened but covered in skin like leather. Clumps of wispy hair still clung to the head. The eye sockets were empty and the lips had disintegrated into a toothy snarl. The cell, itself, was larger than the others and the walls were carved with beasts and devices the assassin had never seen before nor could understand.

He hoped it was not a curse.

The assassin leaned into the cell and was pleased by what he saw. The long-dead king or priest was adorned with much jewellery and gemstones. Revile pulled the pieces away eagerly, a little surprised to find such valuable items. When he had completed his looting, the sack contained a gold belt, clasp, buckle, amulet, a dozen or so bangles, a circlet, two brooches, and a dagger in a bejewelled scabbard. The cell was covered in the disintegrated remains of the corpse. Bones, dried skin and flesh, and crispy fragments of clothing littered the floor. Revile's sack was heavy with gold.

He turned from the cell, well pleased. Walking over to the passageway, he stopped and looked back, checking that he had not missed anything of value.

He noticed a glint of metal in the red glow of the brand.

Going back to the cell, he searched through the remains again. He saw a ring on one of the wizened fingers. He hesitated, feeling vaguely uneasy. But greed got the better of him. He tried to pull the ring from the curled finger. The knuckles and digits were held tightly shut by mummified ligaments as strong as iron. Finally, Revile shattered the grip with the hilt of a dagger and took the ring in his hand. It was very beautiful, made of gold in the likeness of a writhing snake. The eyes of the snake were red with jewels – and a fire burned within, perhaps reflecting the torchlight. The assassin weighed the ring in his palm. Some instinct prompted him to throw it away. But Revile was not a man to trust to instinct when there was unguarded treasure about. Sighing, he put the ring into his sack with the other pieces he had looted.

He walked towards the passageway, thanking his luck.

Suddenly it was dark. The brand died. There was no light, not even a slight glow.

He threw down the brand and spun round, withdrawing a dagger. Why he turned that way he never knew. Certainly there was nothing there – nothing he could see anyway.

He could have been blinded. It was pitch black in the tomb. He was disorientated. He felt vulnerable in the middle of the floor so he made for the passageway wall. Hitting his head off some projection, he stunned himself and staggered about. Clinging to a wall, he tried to shake the stars from his eyes.

There was a long pause.

Despite the fact that nothing happened as the time lengthened, the assassin's muscles tightened around his chest. He found it increasingly difficult to breathe. He was trying not to make any sound. He did not want to betray his position. It was so dark he could not see his hand in front of his face. And it was quiet, quiet and watchful.

He recovered a little. Feeling along the wall, he searched for the passageway with his hands. He came to an opening about thigh height. His hand strayed to something cold on the ledge. It was with some fear that he let the skull fall to the floor with a clatter.

His heart thumped in his chest. The dry air rasped in his throat. He reasoned that there was nothing to be afraid of, that the brand had simply gone out on its own. Yet it was cold, and getting colder – or so he reckoned. Sense told him his fears were groundless. Fear told him his sense was wrong.

It was the denseness of the dark. It was the silence. It was the waiting. He felt that if something did not happen he would go mad or that his heart would burst in his chest.

But nothing did happen. The tomb remained still and silent. Perhaps the brand had gone out itself, after all, he reasoned. With a huge effort of will, he retraced his way back to where he thought the way out must lie.

His limbs trembled. It was so cold. His calf muscles were leaden as if they feared to go that way. Shuffling along the wall, he came to a corner and then proceeded along this new wall with hope in his heart. Still nothing had happened. He groped in the darkness with one hand; the other was firmly clamped to his sack.

He came to an opening.

It was too high for the passageway. It was the entrance to the largest of the cells. He could feel the bones and fragments of skin on the ledge. He nearly cried out in terror.

Standing as if he had been sculpted from stone, his ears strained for any sound.

And then, from a very short distance away, there was a scrabbling sound.

Revile's eyes opened wider.

There was another scrabbling sound again, very close.

Under any other circumstances he would have assumed it was a rat or mouse, but not there, not there in the barrow. It sounded as if fingernails were being drawn down over stone. The atmosphere seemed even more dank and cold. Yet a bead of sweat trickled down his nose.

The assassin could not move.

He thought he could hear a noise as if somebody else was breathing.

Seconds seemed like hours but the sounds did not stop.

Perhaps it was his imagination. Suddenly he acted. He leapt towards the opposite wall. He thought he could feel fetid breath on the back of his neck. Down on his hands and knees, he flung himself heedless into the passageway. Crawling along as fast as he was able, he fled out of the barrow and into the night. He had escaped.

The relief consumed him. On leaving the tomb, sense seemed to return. Walking back to the entrance, he peered down the passageway. All was dark within. Hastily he lit a torch. But there was nothing there. Sitting down in the mud, he began to laugh, quietly at first but then with more vigour.

Quickly he rose and pushed the stone door back to the entrance. With a mighty shove, he pushed the stone door back into the passageway until not even an edge showed against the surrounding masonry.

Revile sat down with his back against the stone and sighed. Searching in his sack, he took out the treasure and did some mental arithmetic to ascertain its value.

The terror he had experienced in the barrow quickly faded. Revile grinned. It had not been a bad night's work, all considered.

He stretched out his legs, oblivious to the mud which seeped through his clothing. He would have laughed if he could have seen himself. He was covered in mire from head to foot.

The first light of dawn was peering over the hills when the assassin was ready to set out. Hoisting his pack onto his back, he turned to say his farewells to the barrow. Something caught his attention.

He walked back to the entrance and felt along the edge of the door. There was definitely an edge showing around the stone, and it stood out against the surrounding masonry. Revile thought for a moment, then decided it was better to ignore it. He walked hurriedly away from the barrow.

But he had only gone a few paces when there was a loud grating noise. He stopped in his tracks, turning round slowly. The stone door had been forced outwards. Running back to the entrance to the cairn, he pushed the door with all his might. No matter how he tried, the stone would not move back. And then, even as he strained, the stone door pushed him back as it forced its way out of the passageway. Revile slipped and lay panting in the mud.

There was another grating sound and the door was nearly all the way out of the passageway. Revile could not breathe. Watching the door as if transfixed, he slowly got to his feet. He could either confront his fear, confront the thing in the tomb – or he could run away.

He fled, of course, running heedless from the barrow. Joining the track, he raced away to the west, not daring to look back.

In the end, Revile never found what had pushed the stone door out of the passageway to the tomb, although his mind was filled with goblins. The assassin never went near the barrow again; and he sold the jewellery, hoping any curse would transfer itself to the purchaser. So he was never certain. Maybe, just maybe, the thing in the barrow still sought him, stalking the assassin by night.

***

ow I know why you are frightened of the dark," said Margaret. "I would be too if I'd been in that tomb with you. Do you really believe some monster is pursuing you?"

"In the daylight, then no I don't," he replied. "But it was something about the completeness of the dark. Being locked in this cell reminds me very much of the barrow – too much maybe. Anyway, I expect I'm just being silly."

The woman shivered. "It is not a pleasant thought," she said. "It might be here with us now. What do you think it was? Have you any idea?"

"No," said Revile, "and that's what frightens me. Some goblin or hogboy, I warrant: there are many stories in Thule. Maybe if I'd seen it. Mind you, if I'd waited to find out what it was I'd probably be dead now so I shouldn't complain. Aye, it could be here with us," he went on softly, "we wouldn't see it, that's for sure. All you'd feel is one bony finger, and then another, and then another."

"Not there you wouldn't," said Margaret. "Not unless it was a very depraved spook."

"I'm not doing a thing," whispered Revile nervously. "It must be the hogboy from the barrow!" He grinned.

"In that case, Revile, please ask the spook to remove its bony fingers before I break them off one by one."

"Your wish would be my command," replied the assassin, "but I assure you it's not me. Besides, my arms aren't that long. Maybe it's Fergus."

"It is," said Margaret, sounding relieved. "I wonder what he's dreaming about." She gently removed his hand and Fergus did not wake.

"Sheep, probably," said Revile. "He most likely mistook you for one in the dark."

"Don't be nasty! What's he ever done to you?"

"He doesn't need to have done anything," said the assassin. "I like being nasty."

"I should tell this cowardly stupid farmer that the brave Revile is terrified of the dark. I'm sure that would make Fergus laugh!"

"I would deny it," said Revile, "and Fergus would not believe you. He would reckon I was joking and that you had fallen for my joke hook, line and sinker."

"So you are joking?"

"What do you think?"

"I'm not sure," said the woman. "But you are awake and that would show you are afraid of the dark."

"Or I'm not tired."

"Or you're not tired," repeated Margaret.

"Anyway," said Revile, "you are awake. Perhaps it is you who is scared of the dark."

Margaret laughed. "I'm genuinely not tired," she told him. "I never sleep until well after daylight."

"Ah, but how do I know that?"

"You'll just have to take my word for it."

"Not even a little frightened?" asked the assassin.

"No," said the woman, "not even a little."

"How about spiders?"

"No, not them either."

"Good," said Revile, "I'm glad. Because there is a huge one crawling towards you even now. It is has the hairiest legs I have ever felt."

"You're wasting your time, you know."

The assassin grunted.

"Anyway," the woman went on, "I've told you my story, the exciting tale of my life. Now you tell me yours – and not some epic tale – just the truth of how and why you became an assassin."

"Hmmm, maybe I will, maybe I won't," said Revile. "The only thing is I'm not as trusting as your customers. I know a pack of lies when I hear it. You told me something about yourself, maybe, but your story itself was most definitely untrue."

"What do you mean by that?" said Margaret angrily. "I was not lying! It is what happened! It hurts me that you think I would invent such a tale."

"I lie enough myself to know when others are. And your story was no more than that."

"How did you know?" asked Margaret.

"I just did," said Revile, and he shrugged. "It takes a liar to catch one."

"You're the first man to ever guess."

"I have many unique talents," said the assassin smugly.

"Anyway, you are right. It is the story I tell my customers – sometimes they give me more money."

"They must be a dull lot," said Revile, rubbing his bottom.

"Yes," said the woman, "they were. I certainly won't miss any of them. And it's not just the sex – although that's pretty boring even at the best of times. No, what I will be glad to miss is trying to flatter them, trying to boost their egos by admiring their sexual prowess. *'Yes, loverboy, your fat belly gets my juices running.'* You know the sort of thing."

"No, not really," said Revile, "although I can see it would be quite exhausting."

"I think you're making fun of me again," said Margaret. "I thought you visited whores often. Do your girls not use the subtle art of flattery on you, Revile?"

"I wouldn't know," he said. "I've never had to pay yet."

Margaret snorted.

"Think what you like," said Revile, "but it's true. Sort of. Anyway, what is your story? I'm dying of boredom here. How does a girl become a liar working from home on her back and well versed in the subtle art of flattery?"

Margaret laughed again. "Very well, since you grow impatient," she said. "My father was a merchant but he wasn't killed by pirates. When I was growing up I guess I was wild. I met this man – he was a business acquaintance of my father – and I found him very dashing. He swept me off my feet. I wanted to marry him but my parents forbad me. I didn't listen and married him anyway.

"Well, I guess it's an old story but it doesn't make me feel any the less stupid. A few months later I thought I was expecting a baby – one week later and my husband disappeared with everything of value from our house. The stupid thing is I wasn't even pregnant. My parents –

despite everything – tried to help. But I would have none of it, except their money.

"Eventually I got over my husband leaving. I didn't know what to do. I was very lonely. One night I met this man in a tavern and invited him back to my house. When I woke up in the morning he had left some money by the side of the bed. It went on from there and I became a whore.

"My parents were terribly upset, as you might imagine. They tried to persuade me to stop, to come back and live with them. But I was flattered by the attention men paid me and the fact I got money for just sleeping with them. So my parents moved away: they couldn't stand the shame. A couple of years ago they both caught a fever and, before I even had a chance to visit them, they were dead." She sighed. "At least I gave them a proper burial. That's more than I will get."

Margaret bit one of her fingers. "Anyway," she went on, "that is my tale. It all seems a bit of a waste now. I wish I'd listened to my parents for I've been so stupid." She shook her head sadly. "It all seems a bit of a waste."

Revile sighed. "Ah, Margaret," he said softly, "I wonder how many people have said that down the years. Yet would your life have been any better as the wife of Fergus the farmer, say? Or as a serving wench such as Alwyn? Or even as Revile the assassin? I doubt it. You sit here thinking you have nothing. But what has anyone got in the end except a short lonely walk into the black? I reckon folk will always rue all the things they had or hadn't done. Me, I wanted to die with a sword in my hand during some great adventure; but if it had happened that way I would feel as I do now – this is not the right time. There is no good time to die."

"Do you regret some things?" asked the woman. "You have some conscience?"

"No, not really," said the assassin softly. "Well, a little. I admit I've never given it much thought until now. I regret that some people died. Some, I guess. But it is the good times that make dying all the harder."

"I will be terrified when I go out there on the gallows," said Margaret and she shivered.

Revile nodded. "I guess you will," he said, "and I'll probably be nasty to you – making it even worse."

"Will you be frightened?"

"No. I am not looking forward to being hanged but I do have a reputation to maintain and my pride. And I've been in many tight corners where death seemed the most likely outcome. Illness, starvation, wounds, imprisonment, and the gods alone know what else. I survived all them. But then I'm not standing on the gallows. When I am I don't know how I'll feel."

"You'll be your cold and nasty self," said Margaret. "As you say, you have your pride. But I don't know how I'll manage."

"It won't matter," replied Revile, "they'll take you out and hang you whatever you do. Weeping and wailing won't save you."

"Is there any chance we'll escape?"

"Nope," he replied, "I'm afraid not. Unfortunately this is not one of my tales so I can't see the end. But I reckon this is the one where the hero doesn't escape and gets hanged with the peasants. A bit of a tragedy really – at least for you and Alwyn and Fergus. I, of course, get to make my final speech. I'm rather looking forward to that bit." Revile shrugged. "Anyway, who cares? None of us can live forever."

"I do," said the woman. "I don't want to die and it seems a shame you have to. Perhaps we could have been in one of your tales and then you could have engineered our escape."

"Hmmm," said Revile, "I wish I could. But we won't escape." He smiled slightly. "Anyway, there's no point worrying about it. The end is sure to be miserable."

"I suppose so," she said, "but we're talking about the end, not the beginning, and the end seems certain. So. Tell me the beginning, tell me how you ended up as an assassin. Were you a cruel child? Did you like pulling the legs off spiders?"

"I don't remember anything about spiders," said Revile. "But the rest is clear enough. I'll tell you if you want."

"I'm slightly interested."

"Very well, then, ..."

In the Hall of Dunslottir

L ord Edward of Elvingston grinned at his betrothed.

"Right," he said, keeping his eyes on the young woman beside him. "Right, sir priest. Begin the ceremony. And don't take too long."

The frankness of the young woman's expression made the priest even more embarrassed.

Lord Edward and the Lady Sarah, accompanied by the priest, made their way up the middle of the hall of Dunslottir Castle, in the north of Lothland, towards the dais. The many guests and visitors greeted them, slapping Lord Edward on the back, laughing amongst themselves. After all, he was a man in later years, while she was young and fair. It was a happy occasion.

The priest climbed onto the dais, then turned to the body of the hall, arranging the couple before him. He opened a book, and when silence had fallen over the chamber, he turned the pages, saying a prayer.

There was some mumbling in the audience.

"We are gathered here," said the priest after a pause, "to witness the marriage of Lord Edward of Elvingston and the Lady Sarah, daughter of David of Eldbotle, this summer's eve. It is a joyous occasion and all should be glad and give praise to our Lord God in Heaven. It is from Him that all happiness and fortune are bestowed – it is through His teachings that Mortal Men find love, mercy and compassion – and Eternal Life. And before I begin the ceremony, I would like to say a few words ..."

There was a loud groan from the audience.

"Get on with the ceremony, damn you!" cursed Lord Edward.

The priest swallowed. "It is usual," he said, "that the priest says a few words." There was a catch in his voice. "It is not a long tale and such things are customary."

"O very well!" muttered Lord Edward. The Lady Sarah smiled.

And the priest, falteringly at first, began his story.

"There was a lad," he said. "Many years ago. He was a wicked child, always up to some kind of trick or naughtiness. You see he had no parents. His mother was a whore in some port of Mannan; his father could have been one of the scores of her customers. So as soon as the lad was old enough, he took to the streets and stole to survive.

"An old priest found him there, for the lad had taken to begging by the roadside. Because the old priest was kind, he gave the lad food and took him to the monastery of Abercorn. In truth, the lad seemed ungrateful for the kindness but he followed the old priest as he was hungry.

"And there at the monastery the lad stayed. The monks and priests were gentle and indulgent. Often the lad would wander away and only return when he was cold or needing food; he would never work, nor did he readily attend the teachings or services. Yet, despite all this, the old priest loved the lad – and in time, the lad came to have a great respect for the old priest.

"The lad was taught his letters; he was taught to read and write.

"That lad was me."

The priest hesitated.

Lord Edward laughed. "Well," he said, "that's a lesson to us all! And a short lesson as you promised."

"My lord," replied the priest, "I have not finished."

"Perhaps in truth the lad would have given up his wicked ways," the priest went on, "perhaps he would never have. In the end, it doesn't matter. One day men came to the monastery of Abercorn, warriors and bandits of a local lord. The abbot of the monastery had argued with this lordling over some land. These warriors came to settle the dispute, and settle it they did. They called all the monks and priests to the church. The lad asked the old priest not to go, but the old priest would have none of it. So he went and the lad stayed.

"And when the warriors had gathered all the folk of the monastery together they laughed and drew their swords. The abbot begged them to spare his church but the warriors did not listen. No. They slew the monks and the priests, they slew everybody they could find; and when they had finished, they burned down the church and every building in the abbey.

"As they were leaving, laughing about their handiwork, they came across the lad at the gate. He waited for them there. He no longer cared. The captain of the warriors dismounted, unsheathing his sword. Raising the weapon high into the air, this man brought his sword whistling down to a hair's breadth above the lad's head.

"The lad didn't flinch.

"The man repeated the blow, then smiled for the lad did not move. Laughing, he took a money pouch from his belt. 'We were told to give the monastery this,' he said, stuffing the pouch into the lad's mouth. 'Since there is no one left, you take it.' And, still hollering with laughter, the man leapt onto his horse and, followed by his warriors, rode away.

"The lad took the pouch, opened it, and counted out fifty pieces of silver. The lad had lost his home but had gained a fortune, gained a wergeld. And with the money the lad would not need to steal and cheat and murder just to survive. So the lad left ..."

"I do not see the point of this story!" said Lord Edward with a dark frown. "Who told you this? And be careful, sir priest," he went on, lowering his voice to a whisper, "be very careful what you say now. It would be a shame if you survived that day only to end your life now!"

The priest swallowed again, and wiped one arm across his brow. "I'm sorry if my story has offended you, Lord Edward," he said nervously. "But there is a point to it. I have not finished. Please hear me out, I beg. You will understand."

Lord Edward said nothing more, so the priest continued, never taking his eyes off the couple before him.

"The old priest was a very good man," he said. "A very good man. He gave and took nothing in return. The lad himself was not worthy, and took the fifty pieces of silver and cherished them. He returned to the sewers, and there survived with the other vermin by thievery and murder.

"Eventually he left. The lad was older and more cunning by then: he was as cold as a snake, as honourable as a rat, as cunning as a fox. So he left for the wilderness, and joined a band of brigands. He easily adopted their brutal ways and hunted travellers and burned lonely settlements. And soon he became their leader."

"This has gone on long enough!" interrupted Lord Edward. "Quite long enough. What is the point of this stupid story?"

The Lady Sarah looked quite alarmed.

"I will have you punished for this outrage," the lord went on. "This is my wedding and not an occasion for mockery. Start the marriage ceremony or I will have your tongue served at the banquet!"

The priest appeared stricken. "Please, Lord Edward," he whispered. "Much good came. Please hear me out."

"Let him speak," said the Lady Sarah.

Lord Edward peered at her for a moment. "Go on," he told the priest, staring at him all the time.

The priest smiled slightly. "You are so kind, so very kind," he said. "Once this lad had cause to be travelling in a part of Lothland near to Elvingston. He chanced upon a fortress on a hill, and there, from the highest turret, he saw a flag like the one carried by the men who burned down the abbey. The lad grinned and gathered together his band of brigands. They waited together looking for some opportunity to seize the castle. Luck was kind, very kind. They chanced upon a priest looking for the castle, the same priest who was to marry the lord in his halls.

"So the lad made a simple plan. He stripped the real priest and dressed himself in his robes. Then he entered the castle and introduced himself to the Lord Edward, the very same man he had met all those years ago at the gates of the monastery at Abercorn.

"And just before the marriage ceremony the priest could not be found. Why? Because he is murdering the guards and opening the gates to his band of brigands."

There was a violent noise as the doors of the hall were thrown open and then the sounds and cries of fighting.

"You see, my Lord Edward," said the priest with a smile – albeit notably without warmth. "The lad had always felt guilty, terribly, terribly guilty. It was the fifty pieces of silver, of course. He cherished it but knew he would have to return it. And now I near the end of my tale."

Lord Edward had gone pale.

"For see you," said the priest, "the lad remained evil to the end. But he was honest after a fashion." Taking a pouch of silver from his clothing, he stuffed the pieces into Lord Edward's gaping mouth. "Here is my wergeld in advance, here is my wergeld for burning down your fortress, killing your servants and friends, and slaying your betrothed. Aye, Lord Edward of Elvingston, here is my wergeld although I fear you won't have long to enjoy it!"

***

S o you got your revenge," said Margaret thoughtfully. "I suppose it must have made you feel good."

"I got a certain amount of grim satisfaction," replied Revile. "It served Lord Edward right. He thought he could do whatever he liked and get away with it. Occasionally debts do get paid to the full."

"And what of the Lady Sarah? What had she done to you?"

Revile shrugged. "We didn't kill her as it happened. She was eventually ransomed."

"Was she harmed?"

"I never touched her," replied Revile honestly, but decided to add no more.

"You questioned the truth of my story," said the woman. "How am I supposed to know if your tale is true?"

"You have only my word – and that is worth nothing. But I have no reason for inventing the story. I could have thought up something much more heroic if I'd wanted to."

"Were you a happy child doing all this thieving and murder – and no doubt rape?"

"I never thought about it."

The woman nodded, then sighed. "I'm getting tired," she said, feeling both angry and exhausted. "It's funny – before if I'd thought about being in this kind of situation I would never have guessed I'd feel like sleeping. But now I do. It has been a long night."

"It will be getting light soon," said Revile. "The long night is nearly over."

Margaret swallowed despite herself.

"We still have hours," said the assassin, "so there's no need to worry about it just yet."

"I'll try not to."

"Put it out of your mind."

Fergus began to snore and Revile laughed softly.

"How long have we got?" asked Margaret.

"Three hours perhaps," replied Revile. "I reckon it must be about seven o'clock. Outside the first glimmering of the dawn is already old. And here the darkness is not as complete as it was." He waved his hand in front of his face with a clank of chains. "Before I could see nothing, now I can see my arm."

"God above!" she cried. "You are right! When did that happen?"

The assassin grinned. "Not to worry, we're no nearer death than a minute ago. The sun was due to rise much about this time today. It's not some trick to hasten you to the gallows."

"I'm frightened," said the woman.

"I would say something to comfort you," said Revile, "but I don't think anything would help. Try not to worry. There is still time and there is always hope while we're still alive. What else can I say?"

"We should try to escape," Margaret told him. "We suggested it before but you would not help us. What have we to lose? Please, Revile, with your help we might escape."

"No, Margaret, we must wait. There's nothing to gain. Don't you think I'd help you if there was any chance at all we would succeed? I don't want to die."

"I don't know why you're so sure we wouldn't make it."

"Margaret, you have lived in Bamburg all your life. Has anyone ever escaped the gallows in all that time? Hundreds have gone to the scaffold before us. Do you think they were any happier about it? They sat here, too, alone with their fear in the dark, trying to find some way to thwart the noose. They didn't succeed and neither would we."

"They did not have you with them! You are the brave adventurer who has escaped from all manner of tight corners. Unless your tales were all lies you should help us. Why don't you do something?"

"Because I'm just a man like any other and I am manacled to the wall in a dungeon with an iron door in a tower filled with suspicious armed soldiers. If I have any special skills or talents, they can't help me here. The jailer and his folk know their business. And," he added, "they will be even more careful because I am Revile the assassin. You would have been better served by a man with a lesser reputation."

"I still don't see what we have to lose," said Margaret.

"Then I will tell you: our lives. And even if they do not kill us they might do worse. I have no wish to be dragged onto the scaffold because my guards have beaten me to a pulp. And Alwyn has carefully preserved her chastity. Shame if she lost it to a gorilla of a jailer. We are nothing to them, Margaret, nothing at all. They can do whatever they like with us and there is nothing we could do to prevent it. Provoking them is pointless."

"Douglas MacGalbrain was right: you are a whimpering coward!"

"Perhaps I am," said Revile, "but I have survived this long. I have led a violent and dangerous life. This is my last adventure, maybe, but there is no point throwing away my life. No, the odds are against us but we must play out the hand."

"I wish I could share your certainty," said Margaret. "To do anything – whether or not it is dangerous – is better than to do nothing."

"Not if it leads to a worse end."

"I just wish I could believe you!"

"You're frightened," said the assassin, "angry and desperate. But you must listen to me – we will not escape. Better to accept that than hope in vain. But be sure, if an opportunity does arise then I will take it."

"But would you help Alwyn or Fergus or me?"

"Aye, if it did not endanger my own escape."

"Do we still mean nothing to you?" asked Margaret bitterly. "I know you are an assassin, that you despise us because we're slow and stupid and unadventurous. But surely this long night has brought us together."

"What do you want me to say?" Revile asked her. "I would rather see you live than die, but that's about as far as it goes."

"Have you no feelings at all?"

"Some," said the assassin, "but what have any of you done to gain my respect or affection? If things had been different all three of you would have come to see me hang – you would have been part of the audience and not the spectacle. And you wouldn't have cared a turd that it was Revile the assassin who was to die on the rope, or what kind of person I was, or even what I had done. I do despise you, but you despise me all the more. We are enemies out there in the real world. I am your worst dream, I am the kind who breaks your rules, I am the black and evil villain you love to come and see executed. Yet villains are all the same whether they are assassins or thieves or virgins who do not want deflowered. You are now of my class, those despised and feared by the good honest citizens of Bamburg and Bernecia. If we did escape tomorrow, you could not return to your house. You have lost everything. You would become an outlaw, shunned by all honest, god-fearing folk. That is you doom if you were to escape."

She nodded, and a sob caught in her throat. "What can I do?" she whispered, her eyes suddenly moist with tears. "I don't want to die."

"Who does?"

She managed to compose herself but the terror still lurked there, waiting to get a hold of her. She could still thrust it aside for just now. Turning her mind to other things, she wiped the tears from her eyes. "I'll be all right," she said softly.

"Good," replied the assassin, almost tenderly.

She hesitated, trying to find something to say. "One thing I do wonder," she asked him at last, "is why you told everyone your real name and town. In all your tales you were careful to preserve your real identity – even to your friends. Why did you tell them you were called Revile?"

"There was no reason not to tell," he replied, "and if I am to be hanged then I want to die as Revile the assassin – not Rat or Worm or Snake or any of the other names I've gone by."

She laughed. "And why is that important?" she asked him.

"It wouldn't be normally ..." he started.

Fergus suddenly awoke with a start. He struggled in his chains for a moment before realising where he was.

"God above!" he cried. "What has happened?"

"Relax, Fergus," said the assassin calmly, "you were asleep. That is all."

"What is the time?" demanded the farmer, waking Alwyn too. "How long have I been asleep? God in Heaven! It is getting light!"

"Peace, Fergus," said Margaret, "we've still got hours."

The farmer slumped against the wall, rubbing at his eyes. "What time is it?" he asked again. "It is light!"

"About seven," said Revile, "but not to worry. You weren't asleep very long."

Alwyn yawned. "Has anything happened?" she asked.

"Not a lot," replied the assassin. "Margaret and I have been talking. You both found my tale so interesting you fell asleep." He laughed. "I don't know that I can blame you."

Fergus sighed.

"Why don't you tell us another?" said Alwyn and she smiled. "I could do with more sleep."

"I'm glad to see you at least are a bit more cheerful," replied Revile, "but if you're all willing I've got one more."

"Make it a good one," said Margaret. "It's likely to be your last."

"I'll do my best," said the assassin.

Cursed!

Five horsemen travelled north and west from Llaith. They hurried into the lands of Dalria, journeying through Cowlsmark and Lornland and Fenis, riding to save the Lady Shona of the Feni from King Ku of Strathclwyd. Dundonald was already under siege and Shona's people were sorely beset on all sides. There was no army to save Dundonald. The rest of Dalria skulked in its own strongholds. Only five horsemen, five heroes perhaps, came to the Lady Shona's aid – and they were all that would come.

The leader of the little company of horsemen was a merry fellow. Revile the assassin was eager to press forward, the promise of two hundred gold pieces next to his heart. His sword had not tasted blood for over a month, his daggers had been forlornly strapped to the front of his tunic, his bow had not been given a chance to sing. He had grown bored in the taverns of Llaith, waiting for Indulf to arrive from the north, with nothing to look forward to but a violent hangover. His pale features were jolly as they trotted along, the old scar standing out against his skin. Scratching at his dark hair – and dislodging various bits and pieces – Revile turned to Douglas MacGalbrain and made a cruel joke at his expense.

Douglas MacGalbrain did not laugh. He pulled at his grey beard for a moment, his grizzled features thoughtful. Before the old warrior, across his saddle, was a large axe. Its twin blades were polished and the notched edges were as keen as a cat's claws. Douglas pondered a new home for the weapon, lodged somewhere between his friend's shoulder blades. He said as much to Revile, and the assassin laughed. Douglas smiled slightly to himself and took a drink from his canteen.

Beside the old warrior rode a tall gaunt man with a strong nose and a dark moustache. Indulf the illusionist peered forward, his dark eyes alive with knowledge and power. He frowned slightly. Indulf was not enjoying the journey and his bottom was numb from the long horse ride. Sighing, he touched his plain wooden staff. There was a little crackle of energy between his finger and the wood.

Behind the others rode two women.

The first was a girl of some beauty. Aliannia had features the colour of burnished copper and hair as dark as jet. Although she was nominally Revile's slave girl, she was well dressed in a fine clinging blue robe and a fur-lined cloak. On a silver belt was strapped a dagger, its hilt fashioned like a striking serpent, the companion to the daggers strapped across Revile's chest. Aliannia was a fine-looking woman but she was no soft creature: she was a tough as her companions.

At Aliannia's side, but riding a little apart from the rest of the company, was Lathspell, a tall slender woman, deadly as a rapier. Dressed in a studded leather tunic, trousers and boots, two crossing swords were tied to her back, the hilts at shoulder level to the left and right. Her face was cold as the others laughed and her eyes burned as she stared at the slave girl beside her. Lathspell, too, was a fine-looking woman – but there was a frost about her, a frost and an elegance and a violence as swift as a panther. Only a fool or a brave man would anger her intentionally.

And on these five rode to save Dundonald, five horsemen, five heroes coming to the Lady Shona's aid. They were all that would come.

And heroes they might have been. Yet to most folk they looked nothing more than a ragged band of cut-throats.

II

The evening sun dipped into the ocean and waves glittered gold in its falling rays. Revile stood on the beach, gazing out over the long loch to the sea, one hand raised to shield his eyes, searching along the horizon between the dark and shadowed islands.

"They are not coming," said the assassin. "We've waited long enough." He turned his back on the ocean and climbed up the beach to where his friends waited. "Are you sure you got the message right?" he asked Lathspell. "There's not much we can do without help."

"I got the message right," said the woman coldly. "Lord Duff was supposed to send us some men. They should have arrived by now."

"So what do we do?" asked Indulf. "We've trailed half away across the country."

Revile raised his hands in exasperation.

"Surely this Duff will come – or at least send men," said Douglas MacGalbrain. "He wouldn't just leave Fenis and Lornland and Cowlsmark to fall to Strathclwyd without any fight. They must have been delayed."

"I think not," said the assassin, "and soon it won't matter anyway. Shona has displeased the High King in the past. Duff's not coming. And only Mithra's shining arse knows what we're going to do. We can't even let Shona know we've arrived." He shook his head. "And what would be the point if we could?"

The others said nothing and the sun slowly disappeared, dark shadows creeping up the beach.

"Well, what do you all think?" asked Revile. "I gathered you and brought you here. What should we do? Return to Llaith?"

"I say no," said Lathspell. "We're here so we might as well try something."

"I agree," said Indulf, not looking forward to the ride back. "Are you sure we can't get into Dundonald?"

"I don't see how," replied Revile slowly. "The Cymbrians surround the town and besiege the fortress. Entry is impossible. Besides, the Feni might think we were the enemy if we climbed the walls or whatever. It would be sad if we were killed by the folk we've come to help. Anyway, that's my say. What do you think, Douglas?"

"I'm for staying, laddie."

"Aliannia?"

"I think we should at least have a look at Dundonald," she replied. "After all, you and Douglas entered Rooksburg easily enough – and escaped."

Revile nodded. "Only just," he said, "and that was different. That wasn't during a siege with a huge army marauding through the Merse."

"I think she means we could disguise ourselves," said Indulf. "How did you get into Rooksburg?"

"We were dressed as priests," said Douglas with a grin.

"Very well, then," said Revile. "Are we all agreed then? Back to Dundonald – but just for a look."

"I think so," said Indulf, tugging at his trident of a beard. "And a disguise might come in handy if we are to travel freely through Dalria. Ku's warriors are everywhere. Perhaps we should join his army for now?"

"Good idea," said Douglas eagerly. "I never was very fond of these upstart southerners. Let the Cymbrians beware!"

"Indeed, lardbelly," laughed Revile. "Come then, let's get going. I am sure old King Ku of Strathclwyd and his mighty army would be terrified if they knew we five stood against them."

The five climbed the rocks from the beach and returned to their ponies. They set out east along a path which rose and dipped by the shore of the sea.

"How far is Dundonald?" asked Douglas.

"About thirty miles or so," replied Revile. "But it will soon be too dark to go on." He looked about him. "We should start to think about finding somewhere to spend the night."

Away to the north there was a flicker of fire as some manor or other building went up in flames. Ku's army was abroad that night.

Revile thought for a moment, then turned his pony to the north.

Owen was pleased with the night's work. He had left the main force of Ku's army at Dundonald and moved north to forage. His saddle bags, and those of his small band of men, were heavy with plundered gold and silver from the nunnery. The smell of smoke filled the still night air and clung in his clothes. He grinned, remembering the soft body of one of the women, and turned to his men.

"Well, lads," he cried, "we've done well enough. And you, Gayan, and those poor, poor nuns. Whatever would your wife say if she got to hear? Shocked she'd be!"

"Don't you start, captain," replied Gayan, "or I'll be telling how you made them shriek."

The Cymbrians laughed together as they rode south and west down a narrow glen through the hills. Slender trunks loomed out of the twilight and there was not a breath of wind to stir the hanging branches. Stars twinkled in the heavens. The party spurred their ponies on.

Owen lifted a skin to his mouth and deep-red wine spilled from his lips and down the dragon painted on his leather tunic. It looked as if the dragon was bleeding.

"All haste, lads," said Owen loudly. "We want to get back before we're missed or we'll have to share this loot!"

Gayan grinned. "It's been a good night," he repeated to himself.

"Cheer up, Alred ap Gareth," Owen told a young warrior by his side. "They were Feni, for God's sake. They murdered our king and tried to steal our lands. My God, your own father was killed in Dundonald. We've shown them that Strathclwyd is once again a force to be reckoned with! We've become the great nation we once were."

"It was not well done!" said the young man.

"Nonsense, lad," said Owen. "This is war. They were fair game."

"You may scorn," muttered Alred, "but that nun cursed us she did. We should have left the nunnery well alone. It was a house of God. Our God!"

"Nonsense, Alred, they were Feni! Well, Dalrian, anyway. It was there for the taking. If it hadn't been us if would have been someone else."

But Owen suddenly pulled his pony to a halt. "What was that?" he whispered. "Gayan, did you see anything?"

"No, captain, but I could have sworn I heard a woman's voice."

The party sat uneasily on their ponies.

"There you go, Alred ap Gareth," said Gayan, "frightening us all with your tale of curses!"

"Peace," said the captain. "There it is again." He drew his sword. "Ho!" he shouted. "Ho! Who goes there?"

"Captain," said Gayan softly, "is that not the nunnery there?"

"God!" swore Owen. "But how? We've been riding for over a hour. We must have come in a circle."

"Which way now?" said a warrior nervously.

"Dead! All dead!" wailed a voice from somewhere near them.

"Mother of God!" cried Alred. "Mother of God! I told you!"

"Hold your tongue or I'll cut it out!" swore Owen.

"Aieee!" sobbed the voice. "All dead! A curse be on the murderers. Damn all the murderers. Damn them all to Hell! Damn them all to terrible deaths! Damn their King and all his family! Damn them all to Hell." And so the terrible shrieking voice went on and on and on.

"But how?" said Owen, peering nervously forward through the gloom. "All are dead. I made sure myself."

"We missed one, seemingly," offered Gayan.

"Well, we won't make the same mistake twice," said Owen grimly. He dug his heels into his pony. "Spectre or not," he cried, "she'll feel cold steel in her belly."

Owen rode along the track, followed closely by his men. In the distance they could see a hooded figure striding towards them, its arms raised to heaven as if to summon down a terrible curse. Owen's pony whinnied in terror.

"All dead!" screamed the apparition. "A curse be on the murderers. Damn all the murderers. Damn them all to Hell."

"By the Rood!" cursed Owen, trying to rein back his pony.

There was a twang of an arrow string, then a thud.

A shaft of wood appeared in Owen's neck and blood gurgled from the wood.

"Flee!" shouted Gayan. "Flee!"

More arrows fell amongst them.

"I told you!" whispered Alred. "I told you!"

"Shut up!" cried Gayan as the men milled around him.

"Where can we flee to?" Alred moaned on. "We are cursed, by the Dragon! Cursed I tell you!"

"You are anyway!" said Gayan and hewed Alred from the saddle. The youngster fell from his horse and lay groaning in a growing pool of his own blood.

"Come on, lads!" commanded Gayan. "Back towards the nunnery. Come on!"

Two more of the Cymbrians tumbled from the saddle as Gayan led them back down the path.

Then something hit him on the head.

When he came to, he was lying in a bed of bracken. Blood ran down his dark features. Staggering to his feet, he searched the area for his pony, but the beast and his friends had disappeared. Screaming came from somewhere near him.

Gayan gasped. Through the trees came a robed figure, running towards him.

His head swam but he stumbled off into the trees to his right, careering off trunks which loomed up at him out of the dark. Behind he thought he could hear the sounds of pursuit. Redoubling his speed, he came out of the woods and ran across a meadow of springy turf.

Buildings appeared before him and a reek of burnt wood and flesh hung in the still night air. Almost before he had realised it, Gayan stumbled into the ruined church of the abbey. The floor was strewn with charred timbers and smouldering turf from the roof. Barely hidden under the debris were the naked bodies of several women, both young and old: they had been burned alive in the church.

Gayan's eyes opened in terror.

"This one's alive," said Douglas MacGalbrain. The old warrior held a torch in one hand, his axe in the other. The blade was smeared with blood.

Revile looked down at the young man on the ground.

"Protect me!" whispered the youth. "Protect me from her. God protect me!"

Revile and Douglas looked at each other. "From who?" asked Douglas.

But Alred ap Gareth was dead.

Lathspell and Indulf emerged from the trees.

"Did you get him?" asked the assassin. "He was the last. We slew the others."

"No," said Lathspell. "We left him."

A terrible scream shattered the silence of the night, a strange unnatural cry that might not have been made by a man.

"Odin's dick!" swore Revile, the hairs on the back of his neck rising. "What was that? There seems to be a lot of odd things happening tonight."

Lathspell shrugged. "He ran into the church of the nunnery." There was a slight catch in her voice. "We decided not to follow him. I think our choice was the right one. For certain he is dead."

Indulf nodded in agreement, tugging at his beard.

"What did the lad mean by 'Protect me from her'?" asked Douglas, sounding a little nervous.

Aliannia replied. "There was a shrouded figure," she told him, "running towards them. I could just make her out in the starlight. She was screaming."

"Aye, we all heard that," muttered the old warrior unhappily. "I reckon we should get our disguises and leave. The night has an evil feel to it."

"Maybe," said the assassin. "But I think we should make sure that the Cymbrian is dead. If he returned to Dundonald it might disastrous."

"Laddie, if you think after all that has happened tonight that we are going to search these woods in the dark then you're mad." Douglas peered about. "I'm staying here."

"Then stay here!" said the assassin sourly, "and watch out for the bogles. Come, Lathspell and Indulf. Let's go to the church."

"Do you think that's wise?" replied the illusionist.

"Ye Gods!" said Revile in exasperation. "I am surrounded by cowards! I'll go myself then."

Revile strode off into the trees with much low cursing.

Lathspell grinned at her companions and shrugged.

The five companions reached the edge of the woods. Revile peered from round a tree trunk across a small meadow to the nunnery buildings. Although it was dark, the church stood out against the sky, dimly illuminated from within by a few glowing embers.

The assassin drew his sword and padded across the turf to the edge of the church, then peered through one of the shattered windows.

The others remained in the trees.

Revile edge along towards the doorway. Barely across the threshold was the body of Gayan. Somehow the assassin knew the Cymbrian was dead although there was no mark of violence he could see. Dropping to his knees by the corpse, Revile rolled the body over onto his back.

The assassin shivered involuntarily.

Gayan was dead, all right. There was no wound or blow that Revile could find. On his face was a fearful expression of terror. The assassin nodded slowly, then retreated from the doorway back towards the trees. Rejoining his companions, Revile led them back to the path and the waiting ponies.

"Did you find him?" asked Douglas MacGalbrain.

"Aye," said Revile. "Dead as a doorpost. His head had been staved in."

"Who by?" asked the old warrior.

The assassin ignored the question and started to strip one of the Cymbrians. He took the clothing and the man's shield but he left the booty from the nunnery where it had fallen.

Soon they were suitably disguised in the livery of King Ku of Strathclwyd, a dragon emblazoned across each of their chests and shields. They gathered together their possessions, mounted their ponies, and rode to the south towards Dundonald of the Feni.

Indulf caught up with the assassin.

"What did you really find?" he asked. "What really killed the warrior in the church?"

Revile looked grim for a moment. "I found nothing," he said. "There wasn't a mark on him – but he was dead. He did not escape the curse."

"Was there anything else there?"

"Nothing alive," said the assassin with a half smile.

III

The next morning found the five companions many miles south of the nunnery. Revile and Lathspell led the little band, and they talked and argued together. The others were even less happy and Douglas MacGalbrain yawned. He had spent a miserable night in the open, his ears full of mysterious half-heard noises and groans. Aliannia and Indulf had fared little better.

Revile, of course, had slept like a log – or so he claimed.

As the hills heightened into mountains to the east, they came across further signs of the invasion. Farm houses and villages along the road were deserted; others were burned, the bodies of their occupants adorning nearby trees. And here and there they came across single bodies strewn on the road. Not all the corpses were Feni or Dalrian. Over the whole region was a heavy feeling of tension and unease as if there was thunder in the air. Yet Revile and his friends met neither friend nor enemy on the road; nor did they see any birds or beasts except a few carrion crows. The lands seemed emptied.

"With hope we'll reach Dundonald about midday or at least mid afternoon," the assassin replied to Douglas's question. "The road is little better than a track from here on."

"Where is everyone?" said the old warrior, making polite conversation after Revile and Lathspell's heated discussion. "We haven't seen anyone since we left the nunnery – no one alive that is."

"They're hiding," said Lathspell. "Wouldn't you? We're dressed in the livery of Ku of Strathclwyd. Do you think the folk of Dalria are going to come out of their refuges and shake you warmly by the hand? Fool! Let's hope we don't meet anyone. They're unlikely to be friends!"

"I only asked," said Douglas MacGalbrain. "And I don't need any of your sour temper, lassie. I get quite enough from Revile."

"Yes," said the assassin lightly, "sour temper is my area."

"Aye, it is," said Douglas. "And, friend Revile, you are able enough at it without this chit of a girl joining in. Anyway, I'm tired and I'll be glad when we reach Dundonald – although I'm not sure what we're going to do when we get there."

"We've just be disagreeing about it," sighed Revile. "I reckon we should join noble King Ku's army for the present – and that way we will be able to move about freely. Then we'll see. Certainly we won't defeat Ku by strength of arms. Lathspell, here, is all for assassinating Ku. I, too, have a plan but we must get word to Dundonald. Shona must hold out for at least another week."

"And what about these girls?" said Douglas MacGalbrain with a gleam of mischief in his eyes. "Riding into an armed camp with two young, defenceless women might not be too wise."

"I can look after myself," said Lathspell coldly, rising to his bait.

The old warrior laughed.

"They will be all right," replied Revile. "As she has said, Lathspell can look after herself. Aliannia will do as I tell her."

"Yes, master," said the slave girl.

"So, what's your plan?" asked Douglas, lowering his voice.

Revile sighed. "I don't want to discuss it yet."

"Very well," muttered Indulf, "but by the Ring of Boggans I hope it's better than your usual efforts."

All of them agreed to that, even Revile.

The five approached Dundonald from the east even as Revile had done those years before. They had circled the fortress from the north to avoid the main force of King Ku's army and so came to the borders of the forest of Carnmor. They climbed down one last slope out of the trees, and sat there on their ponies, peering at the citadel, town and fortress.

Things had certainly changed since Revile last looked on the place.

The outer town was devastated and in many places the encircling palisade had been thrown down into the ditch. Buildings burned and smouldered; and over the town rose a great pall of black smoke, reaching to the sky like a mighty beacon. Dundonald was burning.

Bodies were strewn about, lying in the many streets, folk slaughtered in their hundreds by the Cymbrians. A reek of rotting flesh stole up to the ridge where the companions waited. Dundonald was reeking.

Only the citadel stood apart from the destruction. It was built on the highest part of the rock and could only be reached across a narrow ravine which split the town from the fortress. The bridge had been thrown down and defenders still stood on the many battlements and towers, firing swarms of arrows and casting rocks on the attacking Cymbrians. Dundonald was bleeding.

The losses must have been heavy. The strength of Dundonald frustrated Ku's siege. Had the Cymbrians had ten times their number they could still not have reduced the fortress by force alone.

Not that they had to. Dundonald was starving.

King Ku's army surrounded Dundonald on all sides – and no greater an army had Revile ever seen. The assassin reckoned there must have been some ten thousand men there, men from all over Strathclwyd and Cymbria. Not even a mouse could have escaped unnoticed from the fortress.

The army was most tightly grouped about the south and west where a huge town of tents and pavilions had been set up. In the middle of the tented town fluttered a massive banner, a great golden dragon on an emerald-green background. Guards and warriors hurried to and fro from a pavilion below the flag.

And even as they looked, the companions saw more warriors, horsemen and wains coming from the south, reinforcements from Strathclwyd to swell the already enormous army.

Revile gazed down and felt depressed. He now understood why King Duff MacDuff MacAiden, Lord of Dalria and overlord of Fenis, Lornland and Cowlsmark had remained in his castle, the

235

Fortress of the Staff, on its rock by the sea. The High King could simply not raise a large enough army to defeat the Cymbrians. The assassin sighed, feeling it would be better if he and his companions simply forgot the whole affair and returned to Llaith. For what could an assassin, a slave girl, an illusionist, a grizzled veteran and a warrior-woman hope to do against so great a force? His friends sat quietly beside him sharing his doubt. Yet Revile still had his plan and the size of Ku's army was not important.

"This is much worse than I'd imagined," said Lathspell softly, breaking into the assassin's thoughts. "There is no hope. We can not help Shona, not even by dying noble deaths. We might as well go."

"There must be something we can do," replied Douglas MacGalbrain, his eyes burning with reflected fire. "I, for one, would not ride all this way to war without one serious fight."

Indulf shook his head. "We can do nothing but die, possibly heroically but definitely point-lessly, as Lathspell here has pointed out. The fortress might hold out for weeks if their food supplies don't run out. But it is spring and they had no warning of the coming war. Only if the High King joined with Ailred of Pentland would there be any hope of Dalria winning this war. Dundonald, Fenis, aye and even Dalria, are otherwise doomed."

"Yes," said Lathspell. "The High King cannot raise enough men on his own – but there will be no alliance with Pentland. Those two kingdoms despise each other. No tears would be shed in Pentland if Dalria fell."

"Which is far from surprising given their history of fighting," said the assassin. "They have good reason to hate Dalria – but that is another story. No. We are the only ones who can help Shona. But what can we do?"

"We could murder King Ku," said Lathspell. "Perhaps with him dead these Cymbrians would go home. Anyway, I thought you had a plan?"

"I do," said Revile, "but it doesn't seem so good as a hour ago. But killing Ku would not work – not alone. The Cymbrians are so close to victory that I don't think his death would send them into retreat. And I dare say we might get close enough to Ku to murder him but I don't think we'd survive to tell the tale." He sighed. "But I do have my plan and I am willing to give it a go."

"So am I," said Douglas, sounding pleased.

The others said nothing.

"Well?" said the assassin.

"I will go with you, master," said Aliannia.

"O very well!" muttered Indulf.

Lathspell smiled. "Come on, then," she laughed, prodding her pony into a trot.

"I am a fool!" said Indulf the illusionist. "I don't know how you do it, Revile. Always you lead me into folly and peril. Next time I think I will refuse the invitation."

"O don't do that!" said Revile, mock seriously. "Don't disappoint me, old friend. How could I possibly survive without your keen wit?"

Indulf was not certain the assassin was being entirely sarcastic.

They rode down the track towards the fortress. They met other warriors on the road but

236

passed without comment: Ku's army was everywhere but there was little discipline. Keeping out of bow shot of the citadel, the little band of riders came to a halt by the remains of the shattered east gate. Several men, dressed also in Cymbrian livery, sat there, eating a meal. The warriors were mercenaries, from Pentland by the looks of them.

"I'm going to get some news," said Revile, and jumped lightly from his pony. He went up and greeted the mercenaries.

"Hullo," said the assassin, "how is it going?"

Revile's companions also dismounted.

"Not bad," said the leader of the mercenaries. "We came round here for a little peace. Things have hotted up today round the other side. Dundonald should fall in a few days – or so the Cymbrians are saying. Us? We're not so sure. I'm surprised you hadn't heard."

"We've been up north, ah, foraging," replied Revile easily. "It's safer and the pickings are better."

The mercenaries laughed. "They are that," one agreed. "The Cymbrians have been throwing men against Dundonald like there is no tomorrow. And even food is getting scarce. It will be better as we go north ourselves."

"Why do you say that?" asked Douglas MacGalbrain.

"King what's-his-name, aye, Ku," said the leader, "means to march on the Fortress of the Staff and trap the accursed Duff in his castle. The Dalrians are in disarray. Badernon, Moryernia and Lochanaber have deserted Duff and allied themselves with our folk, the folk of Pentland. They think that should offer them some protection against the Cymbrians. So only Fenis and Yargllia still oppose us – and Fenis will not last a week. Dalria is finished. Only a miracle will save it. So the rumours go, anyway, although we're not so sure."

"Good," said Revile, "I think we'll go round the other side and take a look. Thank you for the news."

"Farewell," said the mercenaries, "and good hunting." They went back to their food.

The companions rode off to the west. Revile went on ahead and he was joined by Indulf.

"It's not looking too good," said the illusionist.

"Not for Dalria, no," said Revile. "The funny thing is that I am partly responsible for all of this." He waved his arms about the devastation and slaughter. "I caused all this death."

"Really, Revile!" said Indulf with a grin. "Don't you think you are overvaluing your own importance?"

The assassin laughed. "No, not in this case," he said. Indulf raised his eyebrows. "I killed their king," Revile went on, "I killed Eocha ap Gawain, the old king of Strathclwyd, brother of this Ku, with a rope meant for Shona herself. I have caused all this in trying to murder Shona. Anyway, it seems I must save her life and kingdom again. O well, so be it. Indulf, we must talk – but away from the others. I have a plan but I want to test it out on you first. Don't tell Lathspell anything. She has a strong sense of honour and this plan is pretty dirty."

"And I suppose you think I will like it because I have no honour?" asked the illusionist.

"I know you don't," replied his friend, "but if it succeeds we won't have to adventure again for a while. What do you say?"

"As you well know," said Indulf, "I have no loyalty at all – except to my purse and comfort. What have you in mind? Will we betray this Shona to the Cymbrians?"

"Don't think I haven't thought of it."

"You said that once before," said Indulf. "Remember? And do you remember what happened afterwards? You nearly got yourself skinned and boiled in brine."

"I know," replied the assassin, "but I have something quite different in mind this time, something which might even save Dalria."

"But will it put gold in our purses?" asked the illusionist.

"Yes, but it must be kept secret for now."

"Well, you can tell me," said Indulf.

"Not here," replied Revile as the others came riding up.

"What did you say?" asked Douglas suspiciously.

"We were trying to guess how much you weighed, lardbelly," said the assassin, rolling his eyes. "But such things are beyond all imagination."

"Your sense of humour is about as weak as a sparrow's fart," replied Douglas MacGalbrain wearily.

Revile sniffed. "Were you a sparrow," he said.

Night had fallen. A fire crackled and sparked, sending showers of embers into the still night air. The five companions sat around the blaze, talking or dozing or staring up to the citadel. Other groups of warriors lounged about but they left Revile and his companions alone.

Indulf and the assassin sat a little apart from the others.

The illusionist nodded.

"What do you think of my plan, then?" Revile asked him.

Indulf smiled slightly. "I like it – it appeals to my lack of honour. Ah, Revile, we shall be heroes again, at least in the eyes of the Dalrians, if not exactly in those of the Cymbrians. Our reputations will be quite ruined, if anyone finds out. So, like you say, we'd better keep the whole idea secret for just now."

"I can't believe you actually like one of my plans."

Indulf shrugged. "It's a good plan, and after what we've been through in the past, I imagine we can make it work as long as nothing unexpected comes along. You've been to Alclwyd before so we should be able to find our way around. Anyway, how are you going to get into Dundonald? It would be a shame if the Feni surrendered before we had a chance to save them."

"Strangely enough," said Revile, examining his boots, "I've thought of that also. Brother Wilmund will lend a hand. I still have some priestly robes. I shall be on a mission of peace from the Holy Isle. With hope, that may get me in."

"And if not?"

"I'll probably be hanging from the nearest gallows so I won't be caring. However, I think one of the others should come with me, Lathspell I reckon. She can act as bodyguard for Shona and it will get her off our backs. And if we get hanged I'd like her there swinging with me!"

238

The illusionist laughed. "I can't imagine you as a priest," he said.

"It's a part we've both played before," said Revile. "And I can't think of any other way. Dundonald must hold out for at least a week." He sighed. "Shona must be told."

"And what will you tell her?"

"The same as we're going to tell Lathspell – nothing."

"Very wise," said Indulf. "Lathspell would not approve."

The two friends fell silent. The fire hissed in the night air. Then out of the night came a long cry of pain, suddenly cut off. The Cymbrians had caught a Feni spy, perhaps, and were torturing the unfortunate for information – or maybe for fun.

Indulf shivered.

"Aye, my friend," said Revile so softly that Indulf hardly heard him, "there are worse things in this world than murdering merchants and nobles for a little gold."

IV

King Ku ap Gawain was an impressive man. He was by no means tall but something in the way he held himself – and something in his eyes – gave him the appearance of immeasurable stature.

Ku sat on a rough throne atop a slab of granite. He was dressed in plain and unadorned robes and a long dark-coloured cloak. He wore neither crown nor jewellery. Tattoos covered much of his arms and neck: tattoos of dragons and griffins and curling serpents. He had long hair, tied back by a leather thong, and a full moustache.

In all this there was nothing to indicate Ku was indeed the King of Strathclwyd. Yet Revile had no doubt.

The assassin stood in the middle of the pavilion below the great flag with the emblem of Strathclwyd. In front of him sat King Ku, leaning forward with one hand on his chin, all his attention focused on Revile. Around him stood a large number of lords, advisors and captains.

"So," said Ku ap Gawain King of Strathclwyd, "they tell me you have a message."

"Yes, my lord," said Revile, sounding nervous. The assassin was dressed in a worn clerical robe, belted at the waist by a simple cord. On his feet were sandals, on his back a small pack. "I have been sent, with my companion here, as an ambassador from Athelwoodis, Abbot of Saint Aiden's Monastery on the Holy Isle of Bernecia. He beseeches God that the blood shed stops here in Dundonald. My master begs, with the Cymbrians thrice-acclaimed virtues of mercy, justice and compassion, a compromise might be reached with the Dalrians and peace be restored."

King Ku laughed angrily as others of his men grumbled amongst themselves.

"Does this Athelwoodis know," said Ku, "that Strathclwyd, Cymbria and Dalria are outwith his influence?"

"Yes, my lord," said Revile humbly, "and he would not presume to make such an inference. Indeed, my noble lord, he makes no demands on you for he would not have the right. Rather he asks, nay begs, that as children of the same god, you might stay your hand. We are disciples of the same church."

"Are we, indeed?" replied the King of Strathclwyd. "These Dalrians, these disciples of the same church, stole our kingdom. They murdered my dear brother, King Eocha ap Gawain, after holding him in Dundonald, and proclaimed Strathclwyd a province of Dalria to be governed from Fenis. That is what the children of the same god did to us! We can never have peace until they are destroyed! And now, and now you are telling that we should retreat, that we should surrender our advantage? Tell me meddling cleric why I shouldn't have you hanged for your impudence?"

Revile swallowed. "My lord," answered the assassin, "if you find me impudent then I am sorry. It was not my intention. I don't mean to meddle in your affairs – although I am only an ambassador – and that was not the intention of my master. My master, Abbot Athelwoodis, wishes to prevent any further blood shed. He does not question – nor doubt – the wrongs which have been done against you by the Dalrians; nor does he dispute the right to secure your borders against Fenis. All he begs is that you stay your hand, that you reach a compromise. My master does not believe you are a cruel man, rather he believes there may be another solution. We were sent as ambassadors to find this solution.

"My lord, this war is already bitter. Dalria will not be taken easily. There will be battles and skirmishes as you proceed north into the heart of Yargllia. I do not doubt the strength of your army – no man who has seen it could – nor the strength and justice in your resolve. In the end you will have the victory. But at what price? How many of your men will die in this war and never return to the hills of Strathclwyd and Cymbria. How much will your power be weakened in such a war? Will your enemies harbour their strength, then strike when you are stretched and vulnerable. My lord, is there no other way?"

King Ku hesitated for a moment, and then smiled with some humour. "You speak boldly and bluntly, cleric," he told Revile. "Perhaps, just perhaps, these things have occurred to me also and there is some truth in what you have said. Tell me, what other solution is there? We need to destroy these Dalrians and avenge my brother."

"My lord," said Revile slowly, "you have already conquered most of Lornland and Cowlsmark, and Fenis will fall soon. They say that Badernon and the other northern provinces have allied themselves with Pentland. You need no longer fear them, at least for now. Only Yargllia still opposes you but that is where most of Dalria's strength lies. The Fortress of the Staff is a mighty stronghold, a fortress which can supplied with arms, food and men from the sea and the Dalrian allies from Yrelann. The fortress might hold out for months. Who knows what would happen down here in the south?

"Could you not make a treaty with the High King of Dalria, Lord Duff? You could take Lornland, Cowlsmark and Fenis and make them the northern part of your own kingdom. You could do this and so end this bloody war – and at the same time achieve everything you set out to achieve. Strathclwyd would be secure, Dalria would be so weakened as to never be a threat, and you will have gained a mighty wergeld for your brother. Abbot Athelwoodis sent me to plead this of you. I have done so to the best of my ability. My lord, could you not at least consider his proposal?"

"Very well," said King Ku. "Very well. Abbot Athelwoodis is a meddling cleric but I will think about your proposal."

The captains and lords of Dalria started muttering amongst themselves.

"Peace," said Ku, raising his hand. "Peace. Very well," he went on, addressing Revile. "You have one week. After that we will march north anyway – as long as Dundonald has fallen."

"Thank you, my lord," said the assassin, and then licked his lips. "My lord, there is one last favour my master craves of you. In this week let there be no fighting."

"No," said King Ku emphatically. "Dundonald must fall!"

"My lord," said Revile softly, "could I not negotiate with the Lady Shona in her fortress of Dundonald? My lord you are an honourable man. Dundonald will fall in a week. But again to what cost? Say that in seven days the fortress was to surrender? Perhaps the Lady Shona would listen to me, perhaps she would. You could come to an arrangement which would be better for both sides."

King Ku frowned darkly and the assassin feared for his life at that moment.

"You are all the too clever," he said coldly. "All the too clever, indeed. It begins to surprise me that a cleric from Bernecia should know so much about my business and a war which is hundreds of miles away. How does the Holy Isle of Bernecia get news so quickly? Tell me!"

"My lord," said Revile, bowing his head, "there are monks and priests from the Holy Isle leaving and returning all the time. News reached us only four days ago. We took ship and arrived at the Fail Kirk in Calatria that very same night. We travelled from there by horse, boat and foot as speedily as God permitted."

"Hmmm," said the King, "well I don't like you or your meddling master, however important he is in Bernecia. But I will give you a chance. You can enter Dundonald – if the Feni will allow it. But if the cursed Lady Shona refuses to agree to your offer, do not return. If you do, you will die. I hope your powers of persuasion are great. Do I make myself clear? You had better succeed or you will hang!"

"I understand, my lord," said Revile in deference.

Revile, accompanied by Lathspell, walked up through the ruins of Dundonald towards the Citadel. Devastation surrounded them, and a terrible smell, the sweet sick smell of carrion with the stench of burnt flesh stalked through the smouldering streets. Smoke wafted across the road.

The assassin carried a white flag on a short pole.

"I hope this works," muttered Lathspell, pulling the hood of her clerical robe over her nose. "And I don't see why I should stay in Dundonald. What are you up to?"

"Nothing," replied Revile. "It's just better if you stay and look after Shona. If she gets killed then I won't get paid – nor will you."

"Well, I hope this works," said Lathspell again.

"That makes two of us," said the assassin. "I've no wish to be filled full of arrows – whether they are Feni or Cymbrian. Nor to be hanged. I think we should sing. It might persuade the Feni we are really priests. Do you know any hymns?"

"Me?" snorted the woman.

"Just a thought," said the assassin with a curl of his lip.

They approached the Citadel of Dundonald. The two companions stopped at the edge of the ravine which divided the town from the fortress. The gates of the citadel were shut and there was no bridge across. Revile could see Feni warriors hidden behind battlements or walls. He hoped they did not decide he and Lathspell were enemies.

Revile peered down into the chasm for a moment.

He lifted his head. "Hail," he cried.

"What do you want?" asked a gruff voice.

"We have messages for the Lady of Dundonald," replied the assassin, trying to sound important.

"Tell them to me," said the voice, "and I will tell the Lady Shona."

"I cannot," said Revile. "They must be told to the Lady in private. I am Brother Wilmund, and my companion is Brother Peter. We have been sent from the Holy Isle of Bernecia on a mission of peace by my master, Abbot Athelwoodis of St Aiden's Monastery on the Holy Isle of Farne. We came via a tavern in Llaith in Lothland called The Wastrel. Tell the Lady Shona this. I am sure she will speak to us."

"This had better not be some trick," said the voice, "or you will die. We'll give you more holes than a pin cushion. But I will report what you have told me. For your sake I hope she is merciful!"

"So do I," said the assassin softly.

They did not have to wait too long.

"The Lady Shona will see you," said the voice.

A rope was flung from the far wall, and then another. Revile looked at the rope and then down into the chasm.

"You must climb across," continued the voice.

"Great!" muttered the assassin.

A short time later, Revile and Lathspell stood outside the doors of the great hall within the citadel of Dundonald. The assassin was a little hot looking and his breathing was still slightly laboured. Lathspell turned to him and laughed. He found the climb across the chasm, with only a thin rope, difficult and distressing – whereas she had made light of the task.

"I don't think you enjoyed that much," Lathspell told him. "I never knew a brave fellow like you would be scared of heights."

"I hate many things," replied the assassin, wiping his brow. "I hate heights, and the sea, and snakes. But most of all I hate smug little turds like you."

Lathspell laughed. "I'll remember that," she said, "when I'm watching you going back."

Their guide knocked loudly on the doors. There was an answer from within and the doors ground back on their hinges. Revile and Lathspell entered the great hall. The Lady Shona awaited them there. She had changed little in the years since Revile had last seen her save she looked a little older, drawn and thinner.

"Greetings, Sir Maggot," she said to them. "Greetings, Lathspell. I did not think I would see either of you again. I had given up all hope."

Revile hesitated, and then said: "We've got much to talk about, but first, have you any wine."

"Of course," replied the Lady Shona. "I would hardly have forgotten that."

The two visitors joined Shona at the table on the dais. The assassin poured himself a goblet of wine from a bottle, and then drank deeply, sitting back and stretching out his legs.

"I kept it specially," she went on, "in case you appeared."

Revile nodded. "My lady," he said, refilling his goblet, "I came because you asked, bringing with me such companions as I could muster, making five in all." He smiled slightly. "Hardly a great army, yet maybe enough for what I have in mind. I have a plan – and if it works then Dundonald and the Feni will be saved. If not, you've lost nothing. I won't tell you what I have in mind, not yet, and I haven't told Lathspell anything about it either. It's better that way. But I need a week. I know things are desperate. But can you hold out that long?"

Shona thought for a moment. "Possibly," she said. "Am I to understand the High King has deserted me and my people."

"So it seems," said Lathspell, and she told Shona all that had happened since she and her companions had arrived in Dalria.

"This is no more than I should have expected!" said the Lady Shona angrily. "When my father died, Duff tried to force me to marry. I refused all his choices of husband. I made the High King angry. I should have known this would be my reward!"

"What else could you have done?" said Revile. "Besides, he hasn't deserted you – not for personal reasons anyway. King Ku has been clever attacking you and Dalria when you were least prepared. Anyway, there is still hope while you hold out although that must be for another week. Or you must tell King Ku you will surrender in seven days time. Whether or not you do is your own business. How long can Dundonald last?"

"I do not know," said Shona sadly. "We ran out of food days ago although we've still water. I really do not know. The real attack has not yet started – Ku is letting time, starvation and disease weaken us first. But I will agree to surrender in a week if that is what you advise. I will give you a letter to that effect."

She spoke to one of her servants and he hurried off.

"Very well," said Revile, "then we have seven days and let's hope it is enough." He sighed. "I'd better be getting back as soon as the letter is ready. Lathspell is staying here to act as your bodyguard."

Shona nodded. "Well, Sir Maggot," she said, "your stay here has been brief this time. I hope we meet again and under happier circumstances."

"So do I," said Revile with a grin. "I want my gold." He rose to his feet as a servant came in with the parchment and ink. The Lady Shona scribbled her signature, then sealed the letter. "I'll go now," he went on. "I'll see you in a week if all goes well."

He took the letter and placed it in his robe. Turning from Shona and Lathspell, he walked the length of the great hall and disappeared out the doors.

"What is he up to?" asked the Lady Shona, putting her arm around Lathspell's shoulders.

Lathspell sighed. "Better not to know, I guess," she replied, looking a little uncomfortable. "I guess we'll see, but I don't think he wanted me about."

King Ku ap Gawain of Strathclwyd was pleased.

"Anyway, my lord," continued Revile, "it is settled. Dundonald will surrender in a week whatever the outcome of my visit to the Fortress of the Staff and my approaches to Duff – on the condition that its people are spared. The Lady Shona has agreed to your terms. My master, Abbot Athelwoodis, will be pleased."

"Good," said Ku ironically. "What happened to your companion?"

Revile frowned. "The Lady Shona did not trust me as you have, my lord. She took my friend as surety of my faith. I hope that I succeed or he will surely die."

"Well, we would not want that!" said the King of Strathclwyd. "I guess you had better set out for the Fortress of the Staff."

"Yes, my lord," said the assassin, and bowing, Revile left the pavilion.

King Ku waited until he had gone. "Dryff," he said to one of his men, "follow that cleric. Take some men and make sure he goes to the Fortress of the Staff."

"Yes, my king," said Dryff, and hurried after the assassin.

V

"Poor old Dryff!" laughed Douglas MacGalbrain. "Should we bury them?"

Dryff and several other Cymbrian warriors lay dead about the clearing. Most had been shot with arrows but a couple had been hewn down by an axe.

"No," said Revile, "leave them where they fell. If they are found, there will be some confusion. They might have been killed by Feni outlaws. Anyway, we can not afford the time."

The four companions left the carnage, and led their ponies back to the road through the woods.

"So now the race begins," said the assassin. "It should take us two days of hard riding to reach Alclwyd in Strathclwyd – or Dun Breton as Douglas's folk call it. I hope we have enough time."

He jumped onto his pony, turning it round to the south. Aliannia led three more horses out of the trees. Indulf climbed onto one, Douglas onto another, and Aliannia, herself, onto the last.

"We should avoid returning to Dundonald," added Revile. "There's little chance we'd be recognised but it's not worth the slight risk. We can go via eastern and northern Lornland and the east of Pentland."

"And what do we do when we reach Dun Breton?" asked the old warrior. "What is your plan?"

"I'll tell you as we go south," replied Revile, "but not all – that might be dangerous."

The assassin prodded his pony into a trot. The sun was high in the sky and there were still several hours of light. The land about them was mountainous and bleak, and few folk lived in that part of Fenis, although even they had fled. The only people they were likely to meet were refugees, cut-throats or other travellers. The road was narrow and winding, just a country track really, and quickly rose out of the forests of silver birch and rowan and pine towards a high pass through the hills. Gradually the trees thinned, and heather replaced grass, and they passed across a wide, boggy moor. The ground was black and the pony's hooves splashed through the dirty puddles in the peat.

"So," said Douglas, gazing about him and searching the moor for any signs of life, "what is this famous plan? You and Indulf have been very close, and I've even heard you discussing it with Aliannia here. You don't seem to want to keep me in the picture. I hoped that was because of Lathspell. What is it with her, anyway?"

"I'll answer your second question first," replied Revile as he rode along. "I met Lathspell many years ago: it must be ten, in Jorick. We were both young. She was the girl of a captain of the guard, but she and her friends were actually plotting to overthrow the king, and she was only seeing the captain to get information. She was idealistic and honourable. Her comrades had less virtuous motives. Indeed, they decided they needed a martyr, and they chose Lathspell. I stopped her being murdered so she robbed me of all my gold and other possessions. She hoped to use the treasure to further the cause; she did not understand her friends' treachery.

"I was understandably angry. I tried to find her and managed to get beaten half to death by the king's men. They left me for dead."

Revile sighed. "Anyway," he went on, "to cut a long story short, Lathspell led a revolt but again she was betrayed and her little band of peasants and farmers were slaughtered almost to the last. For some reason, which afterwards eluded me, I helped her escape. She has hated me since then."

"But why?" asked Douglas. "If you helped her?"

"I'm not certain," said the assassin. "I think she despised me from the start. We were complete opposites. She is an idealist and believes in truth, justice and honour; whereas, and as you well know, I believe in steel and gold. I was without moral backbone and Hanuman's Holy Dung alone knows what else. Yet I saved her life twice and I showed all her ideals were meaningless and not shared by her friends. She has never forgiven me for saving her life – she would have rather died in battle with her ideals intact.

"That's why we left her in Dundonald. We didn't want her morals or ideals getting in the way. Neither her nor Shona would approve of my plan."

"So what is this plan?" said Douglas. "And how do you know I will approve?"

"Which question should I answer this time?" replied Revile, who was his usual irritable self. "I don't know if you'll approve but then you are getting well paid and that alone should please you. I didn't know I was paying for your approval, lardbelly."

"Neither did I," said the old warrior. "I thought we were all being paid by the Lady Shona. I didn't realise my share came from your purse!"

"Well, think again, blubberguts."

"Sometimes," said Douglas coldly, "I think you grow weary of life, laddie. I think you want your head split like a rotten turnip!"

"I don't want to interfere in your argument," said Indulf lightly, "but why don't you tell him about the plan, Revile. I don't see any need for secrecy now."

"I agree, master," said Aliannia. "Bad temper will get us nowhere."

"Aye, turniphead," added Douglas, "I think that would be a grand idea!"

Revile laughed. "Very well," he said, "since you outnumber me three to one. Very well. We are going to seize Ku's wife and children. Ku loves his family and we'll use that against him. We will force him to retreat from Dundonald. That's the plan."

"That's it?" asked Douglas in surprise. "And how are you going to do all this, laddie, or did you not bother with such minor details."

"I have," said the assassin, "but I'll tell you later."

"Great," said Douglas MacGalbrain.

The four companions rode on in silence. Behind them was the forest of Carnmor and to the west and south was Dundonald, its position marked by a huge pillar of black smoke rising into the late-afternoon sky.

"Master," said Aliannia, "do you think Ku has called off the siege?"

"Who knows?" replied Revile. "But Shona said she could hold out for a week."

The four companions rode east and north until the sun began to sink behind them. They cast long shadows before them on the road, and slowly the miles passed them by. When darkness finally fell, they had already crossed northern Lornland, passed the end of Loch Finn and were in Pentland, a few miles north of the long Loch Lomorard. They spent the night in a sheltered ravine surrounded by a copse of old oak trees.

There were few signs of the Cymbrian invasion over the border but they were wary nonetheless. They had met no one on the road and had seen nothing to alarm then except for a rider in the distance. But whether or not the horseman was interested in them, or had some other business of his own, they could not be sure. So they set a watch and lit no fire.

In the morning they set out again, turning south down the eastern side of the loch. The going was difficult, and often there was no path to follow but the edge of the water.

It started as another warm, pleasant day but by lunch dark clouds had overtaken them on their way south, although it did not rain, just became close and still. They came across a few refugees from Fenis and Lornland, and a party of horsemen from Pentland, but Revile and his companions were left unmolested. And as darkness descended on the second day, they reached the Border Stone, a finger of rock which marked the edge of Pentland and Strathclwyd. They made camp nearby and knew they could reach Alclwyd the next afternoon – if they wished.

"We've made good time," said Revile as they sat around the campfire, "we've been lucky with the weather."

"Aye, laddie," said Douglas, "let us hope it continues."

When they had finished eating, the assassin got up and disappeared into the gloom beyond the illumination cast by the fire. He returned a little later.

"There is no one about," he told his three companions.

The dark hills stood out against the star-speckled sky to the east, and the great expanse of Loch Lomorard lay to the west. The only sounds were the peaceful lapping of water and the gentle rustling of leaves.

"Well," said Revile, "I guess I'd better tell you all what I have in mind. Indulf knows most of it, Aliannia a little more. Firstly, we must split up soon. Tomorrow we'll skirt around the south shore of the loch until we are north and west of Alclwyd. That should take until about midday. Then we'll go our separate ways. Douglas, I want you to go into Cowlsmark."

"Why?" asked Douglas.

"Yours is perhaps the most difficult part," said Indulf, still warming his hands by the fire, "for you must raise a small force from the men, outlaws I guess, of Cowlsmark. Not an army, by any means, but enough men to see off any pursuit from Alclwyd. We will be bringing Ku's wife, Genevieve, and as many of her children as we can. Do you think you can manage?"

"I reckon so," said the old warrior.

"Good," said Revile, glad that he had escaped an argument. "You should try to raise as many men as possible – the more the merrier. When you've done that meet us on the road north where it crosses the border between Strathclwyd and Cowlsmark, beside the Sentinels. In two days time, at sunset. If we're not there, come back again the next evening."

"Very well," said Douglas, "when should I start?"

"Tomorrow will be fine, o eager one," replied the assassin. "We're coming some of the way with you. And, Douglas, I lied to you about your share of the loot. I am to be paid two hundred pieces of gold should we save Dundonald – and you will get sixty-five merks."

"Ye Gods!" said the old warrior in surprise. "That's a fortune!"

"As you once said, lardbelly, it's the dirtiest jobs which pay the best. And this may prove to be a pretty grubby affair."

Douglas grinned, and rolled out a blanket on the ground near the campfire. "I guess," he said, "you're not going to tell me how you are going to enter Alclwyd, never mind get out again with the hostages."

"No, I'll tell you," said Revile. And he did.

"Are we all set then?" asked Revile the next morning.

"Yes," said Indulf.

The assassin prodded his pony into a trot, followed by Indulf, Douglas and Aliannia. The four companions set out on the third day of their journey. The sun was shining down and the clouds of the previous evening had vanished to the east. Slowly they gathered speed, riding by the edge of the loch towards the west and south. It was several hours to midday but the miles passed them by.

There was a dull rumble in the distance and the birds fell silent.

Through the trees galloped four riders, driving their sweat-flecked horses on towards the fortress of Alclwyd. The land before them fell away to the banks of the river and the horsemen turned to the east, following the bank.

"Come on, damn you!" shouted one of the riders. "We must reach Alclwyd before sunset."

"By the Rood!" swore one of his companions. "What's the great rush? There's still hours of light."

"Yes, Arthur," agreed another. "Take it easy! The horses are tired. We'll never get to Alclwyd if we ride them to death!"

"We must hurry!" cried Arthur. "There are outlaws at large in Cowlsmark. John ap Colyn must be told about this mad fellow, Osric. They may slip across the border. He must be warned. And we have messages for the Lady Genevieve."

"So you've already said," muttered another of the men.

The horsemen thundered on, skirting the broken ground in the trees and splashing through the shallows by the edge of the river Clwyd. Before them – still several miles away – stood the fortress, Alclwyd, on its rock. The castle straddled a twin-peaked hill, defended by a high wall of stone as well as the steepness of the sides. Smoke gently rose from the many hearths. Flags flapped against their poles, hiding the dragon of Strathclwyd.

"Come on, by the Dragon!" shouted Arthur again as the others fell behind. "Come on!"

The others grumbled amongst themselves.

It was nearly the last thing they ever did.

Arthur spurred his horse on, digging his boots into its belly. He heard a twang, like an arrow string, and then a strangled cry. One of his men tumbled from the saddle. More strings sang. An arrow whistled past Arthur's ear, the flight scoring his cheek. The young man swallowed, shrinking into the saddle, screaming at his horse. Cries and curses filled the air – and the crash of men and horses falling to the ground. Arthur never looked back and under his breath he whispered a prayer.

His horse pounded on, but the ground was open. There was no cover by the edge of the river.

Then the arrow struck. The young man cried out. He was thrown forward. The pain was biting for a moment and Arthur swayed in the saddle. But he gritted his teeth. The arrow was lodged through the fleshy part of his shoulder. Blood coursed from the wound. Arthur's head swam, for his arm and neck had gone numb.

He clung to his horse. An arrow thudded into a tree just a foot or so from his head. Others whistled past but none found a mark.

Arthur continued to pray.

Suddenly the arrows stopped. Arthur had ridden into a dense part of the woods away from the river. He slowed his horse, but he was still riding too fast for the broken ground. His horse stumbled and he was nearly thrown. Coming to a path in the woods, the young man rode along the eastern branch, gathering speed again. He could hear no pursuit. He hoped and he prayed he was not followed. He hoped he would not lose his arm. His hand was red with blood. But he hung on.

A little later a rider approached Alclwyd from the west. The guards on watch peered down from their posts, shielding their eyes from the westering sun. The rider was wounded and the horse was exhausted. The guards hurried out and led the rider back to the gates of the fortress. Above them, other men pointed and speculated from the walls and battlements.

But Arthur lived, bringing his urgent message with him from the north. Firstly there were outlaws abroad in Cowlsmark, led by one Osric, the brother, it was said, of Lady Shona of the Feni. They could expect no mercy from him. Secondly, the bodies of Dryff and his men had been found. King Ku had sent word south for he feared some conspiracy against his family.

There were outlaws at large and John ap Colyn, captain of the guard and steward of Alclwyd, was to be doubly cautious. John smiled grimly. No strangers were to enter the fortress.

Later that evening, Indulf and Revile sat in the candle-lit common room of a tavern, one of the many they had visited that night. A bottle of clear liquid sat on the table between them. Aliannia was seated to one side and her face held an expression of alarm for her two companions argued angrily. She glanced over her shoulder. They were receiving their fair share of attention. Revile was very drunk, his speech badly slurred, and Indulf was sneering at him.

"Keep your voice down!" muttered the illusionist. "There are people listening!"

"Who cares, by Odin's dick!" replied Revile, taking another drink. "What do you think this rabble is going to do?" He turned to peer at them. They were mostly old farmers too infirm to go to war, or youngsters, lads barely into their teens. "Farmers and peasants all of them!" continued the assassin, sticking his tongue out. The chamber fell deathly quiet. "Weak stupid bunch!" He lowered his voice to a theatrical whisper. "But not as bad as you, old friend! O no! You can't even shoot straight. We might as well return to Dundonald for we've failed. Failed! And it's your fault!" The assassin shook his head. "Aye, we've failed and I promised on my honour!"

Indulf snorted. "By the Cross of Callanish, it was a stupid plan anyway," he told Revile. "Did you really think we could cut of communications between Dundonald and Alclwyd. They were bound to send more messengers. You are the most stupid man I think I've ever met. I ask you!"

"Well, it might have worked," retorted Revile angrily. "Aye, it might have if you could shoot straight. You missed the Cymbrian turd by a mile!"

"I missed?" swore the illusionist. "I missed! The cheek of it! I shot three of the swine. You, on the other hand, couldn't hit a privy door from the inside! You've been drinking all day. Damn you! Damn you and your buffoonery!" Indulf got to his feet. "Well, I have had enough of you! Come, girl, let us leave our friend to his bottle!"

"So now you are trying to take my woman as well, are you?" cursed Revile. "Aye, I should have known!"

Aliannia could contain herself no longer. "Peace!" she cried, looking at her two companions. "Are you trying to get us killed! Keep your voices down!"

Revile and Indulf retook their seats.

"Aye, you are right, I guess," muttered the assassin. "And I am sorry, my friend. I had not meant to anger you. There is a lot still to play for." He smiled slightly. "Forgive my rash words!"

The illusionist sighed and then nodded. "And I am sorry in my turn," he said. "Archery was never my strong point." He took a drink from his mug. "Ye Gods," he cried, "what is this muck?"

Revile laughed. "Good, isn't it?" He finished the bottle. "Anyway, we'd better get going. There is still work to do. We've got another chance to stop the messengers tomorrow – but our whole plan hinges on our success. We will not let any messenger escape this time!"

"Hush," whispered Aliannia.

Revile rounded on her, his eyes flashing. "Hush?" he hissed. "You tell me to hush?" Aliannia cowered back from the assassin, fearing that he might strike her. "Why should I hush? Look at these folk here – not a real man amongst them! They'll not tell on us now, will they? No, because they know what will happen if they do!" Revile stared about him but not one of the other drinkers held his eye. The assassin sneered at them, getting to his feet. "You, girl," he went on through gritted teeth, "I will attend to later."

Revile pushed his way to the door, followed by Indulf and Aliannia. The assassin turned back, laughed in a very cruel manner, and disappeared through the doorway into the night.

Two men who had been sitting quietly at a table near the assassin and his companions looked at each other.

"They were right," one whispered to the other. His voice was slow low that only his companion heard him. "Treachery is afoot in Cowlsmark. We must report back to the fortress. The messengers must be warned."

"Yes," replied his friend, and he smiled. "They will reward us well for this night's work."

They finished their drinks and left.

"Help!" cried a voice in terror. "Help!"

A horse neighed in fright.

"Ride!" said another man. "Ride for your lives!"

It was night. The moon shone down on the clearing, casting a silver line of light glinting from the river. Men and horses crashed through the undergrowth, and their cries and screams echoed in the still night air, wafting all the way to the guards at Alclwyd.

"Argh!"

Three riders broke into the clearing, galloping madly, heedless of root or branch. One of the horsemen was slumped over the saddle, arrows sticking from his back and throat. The other two spurred their horses onwards, shrieking like demons.

Thundering down the track, the riders emerged out of the wood and rode frantically for the gate of Alclwyd, gazing anxiously over their shoulders.

John ap Colyn, the captain of the guard, gave out a great shout and the great gates of the fortress ground open. A large body of horsemen hurried out of the courtyard and galloped towards the woods. The captain had prepared carefully, suspecting that messengers going between Alclwyd and Dundonald would be ambushed. His men passed the wounded messengers and headed off into the woods.

The three messengers rode up and stopped under the gates. They dismounted and went to their companion. He was dead, pierced by many arrows. They sighed and approached John ap Colyn who awaited them.

The smaller of the two messengers stepped forward. His face was masked in blood.

"Greetings," he said, trying to gather his breath. He wiped his eyes. "I am Dragon ap Luther," he said, "courier to our lord, King Ku. We were bidden to ride with all haste, back the long miles to Alclwyd." He paused and then went on: "Lady Shona," and he spat the name, "of the cursed Feni has sent assassins into Strathclwyd to murder the Lady Genevieve and all the children. There are four assassins – three men and a girl. She is particularly noticeable being a Southerner with dark skin and black hair." He went on to give a good description of Revile, Indulf, Aliannia and Douglas MacGalbrain.

"We had guessed something was going on," said John ap Colyn. "Messengers have been ambushed and we have received words of outlaws led by a maniac called Osric."

Dragon nodded. "Yes," he said, "although I don't know how ambushing messengers can fit into their schemes." He laughed. "Do you know these assassins were to be paid two hundred pieces of gold if they had succeeded? By the Dragon, it is a fortune!"

"How could you possibly know that?" demanded John.

The messenger looked surprised. "Then you've not heard?" he said. "Word should have reached here by now."

"Heard what?"

"Dundonald has fallen," said Dragon with a smile. "I thought you were all acting a bit sadly. The cursed Shona," and he spat the name again, "is prisoner of our lord, King Ku. Fenis is ours. You should have had word by now. I take it you hadn't heard?"

The captain of the guard had a blank expression, but then he laughed.

"We're marching north with the dawn," continued Dragon. "There is nothing between us and the whole of Dalria! We have won!"

John ap Colyn smiled. "We've won?" he asked again as if he could not quite believe his ears. The guards at the gates looked puzzled by his question, and there was some cheering and speculation. "When did Dundonald fall?" asked the captain. "The last news we received was that things were not going well."

"Yesterday evening," said Dragon. "The cursed Lady Shona surrendered with the setting of the sun. How is it that you have not heard. My lord Ku sent messengers last night. They did not arrive?"

"They must have been ambushed even as you were."

"I see," said Dragon. "We left with the dawn. I killed two horses getting here." And then he added slowly. "Not all of us made it." He gazed at the body of his companion and shook his head sadly.

"Are you wounded?" asked the captain. "You are covered in blood. Shall I send for a physician?"

"Nay," said Dragon, "I am well enough. This is just a scratch from a branch. It's messy but not deep. No, it's not a physician I need, it is a flask of wine. I'd bless you for that!"

John ap Colyn, captain of the guard and steward of the fortress of Alclwyd, called to one of his men: "Bring wine – and let it be known! Dundonald has fallen. The Lady Shona of the Feni has surrendered. Dalria is ours! Dalria is ours!"

Wine was brought.

"Now," said John to the messengers, "tell me about the victory!"

A little later and the captain and the two messengers stood together on the battlements overlooking the gate.

Dragon yawned. "I grow weary," he said. "It's been a long day."

His fellow courier grunted.

The news of victory had spread like wild fire through the castle of Alclwyd. The celebrations were already well under way. Even the guards at the gate were merry and danced. They had won a great victory.

"We'd better get cleaned up," said Dragon. "And although I am tired I don't think I'll sleep just yet. I'll have a wash for I won't find a woman looking like this."

"It's a great improvement," joked his friend, "over the way you normally look."

The three men laughed together.

"Anyway," said Dragon, "we'll take our leave. Keep us some wine and a warm wench or two if you can find them!"

The two messengers walked from the gate and made their way across the courtyard towards a narrow stair hewn in the side of the hill. Alclwyd soared away above them. The courtyard was protected by a high stone wall with the gates, and housed the stables for the castle. The steps led up into the gloom, up to a door which pierced the defences of the rock. The stair was steep and there was no hand rail. The two messengers felt vulnerable as they began to climb.

They were breathless by the time they reached the top. Guards peered down at them from the battlements and turrets.

"Thank God!" gasped Dragon as they reached the last step. He mopped his brow. The two messengers walked through the door and disappeared into Alclwyd.

John ap Colyn watched them vanish into the castle. He pulled at his beard for a moment, and then turned his eyes to the north and west. Peering into the distance, John ap Colyn tried to pierce the gloom all the way through the mountains and glens to Dundonald.

The pounding of hooves came to his ears but his eyes could not penetrate the night.

One of his men broke into his ponderings. "Captain," said the man, "old Aru would like to talk to you. He said he would meet you in the house of the dead."

John ap Colyn sighed.

Dragon and his companion wandered through the second gate and passed the guards. The doors opened into a courtyard. There were several buildings forming the sides of the yard, and a few trees and flowers grew in a small garden. The two men made for the nearest door and

252

entered a corridor. Chancing upon an empty apartment, the slipped inside, bolting the door behind them.

"Quickly!" whispered the man who had called himself Dragon, and he peeled off his messengers tunic. "We've not got much time!"

"I know," said Indulf, his companion, unpacking fresh clothing from a sack. "But so far so good." He dressed in a clean tunic with the dragon of Strathclwyd emblazoned above his heart.

"Aye," said Revile, feeling cheerful, "I only hope escaping again is as easy. This place is like a prison. There's no way off except back down that stair." He grinned. "It's a grand plan."

In a moment they were ready. They hid their old clothing in the apartment and Revile washed the blood from his features. Listening at the door, they checked the corridor was empty and hurried back to the courtyard with the small garden. The moon shone down and torches flickered in their braziers. A few folk wandered about with bottles or goblets in their hands.

"Where are the royal chambers?" whispered Indulf. "Or hadn't you thought of that?"

"I've already told you I've been here before," replied Revile. "They are up on the south-eastern side. The rock there is sheer and drops straight to the river." The assassin paused. "Or at least that is the way I remember it. Let's hope I am right."

The illusionist grunted.

Skirting the edge of the garden, the two companions came to a tower against the encircling wall. The door was not locked and they climbed a flight of winding stairs to the battlement along the wall. No one noticed them or had cause to. The two intruders were dressed in the livery of the fortress guard.

The walked along the battlements to the east. Below them, some three hundred feet or so below, stretched the mighty river Clwyd. It shone silver as the moon descended westwards. There was a plop and a splash of water from the river.

Inside one of the houses a man laughed and a woman giggled.

"Fools!" said Indulf quietly. "Poor fools!"

"We told them what they wanted to hear," said the assassin. "Strathclwyd is the great kingdom it used to be. They have defeated the Feni and all Dalria is at their feet! Let them have their moment of victory – however brief." He smiled slightly. "Soon we will have to spoil the celebrations."

They went on a little further. Booted feet came marching towards them. But the guards left them in peace after passing a few words. Coming to another tower, the two intruders climbed to the highest turret.

"There!" said Revile, pointing with his finger. "Those are the royal apartments, there, standing a little apart from the hall and kitchen. The Queen's chamber is on the first floor, her children are in the adjoining rooms."

Indulf strained his eyes. "And how do we get in?" he asked. "They seem to be heavily guarded."

"They are sure to be," said the assassin with a short laugh. "Would you be angry if I told you I did not know?"

The illusionist peered at his friend. "We've been through all this once before," he said. "But you were younger then. I imagine you have a plan."

"Maybe I do but it might not work."

Indulf snorted. "When has that ever stopped you?"

The two companions climbed from the turret and back into the tower.

"We put the body in here as you ordered," said the little man. "Aye, in the House of the Dead."

John ap Colyn wrinkled his nostrils in disgust. The sickly-sweet smell of charnel filled the air. The little man laughed.

"You get used to the smell, they say," he told John and sniffed. He pointed to a corpse. "Here he is. I was just stripping him, getting him ready."

"Show me, Aru," said John.

"Touch it," said the little man.

"Why, Aru?"

"Just do it."

The captain bent down and put his hand against the dead flesh. It was cold, cold and stiff. "He's been dead for hours," muttered John. "Hours."

"Exactly!" said Aru.

A guard came running into the House of the Dead. "Quick, captain," he said breathlessly. "Come down to the gate. There is news!"

John ap Colyn sighed. He had the feeling it was not going to be a good night.

Revile and Indulf stood in the tower chamber.

"How long do we wait?" asked the illusionist.

The assassin laughed. "We don't," he said, "we'll raise the alarm ourselves."

"What?" asked Indulf in surprise.

"We raise the alarm ourselves. Come."

The assassin left the tower and went into the square before the royal apartments. Indulf hurried after him.

"Have you gone mad?" cursed Indulf.

"We'll see," said Revile. "Anyway, we're dressed as guards. What else would we do?"

The square was empty. The assassin disappeared into the shadows by the side of the royal apartments. Indulf melted into the darkness behind him.

"What are we waiting for this time?" he asked.

"We need some guards to discover us," replied Revile in a whisper. "Now hush."

There was a jangle of keys and the turning of a lock. The door out of the royal apartments swung open and torch light flooded out onto the ground. Two men chattered together, stepping out of the entrance. One of them turned to relock the door.

The assassin struck twice.

Two men fell with a clatter. The door was ajar. Revile took the bunch of keys from the dead fingers.

"What now?" muttered Indulf.

"I've already told you!" The assassin started to shout. "Enemies! Enemies in the hold!"

John ap Colyn reached the foot of the stair and ran across the courtyard to the opened gates. Four riders awaited him there, four couriers from King Ku. Their horses were flecked with sweat and they were panting, man and beast.

"Greetings!" cried one of the messengers. "We come from the siege of Dundonald. I am Dyllin ap Frian, my companions are ..."

"The siege of Dundonald?" interrupted John ap Colyn in a tone of weary resignation. "Then the Lady Shona has not surrendered?"

"Indeed no," replied Dyllin, "although the end cannot be far away now. Yet I think Dundonald will last a few more days."

John ap Colyn's immediate thought was to have his men slay Dyllin and the other messengers and pretend everything was just as it should be. "Dyllin," he managed through locked teeth, "we will speak later. For now I have rather more pressing business. Guards!" he shouted. "Guards! And, Dyllin," he added, "if this is some even cleverer and more cunning trick then I want you to know I don't give a turd!"

Dyllin looked dumbfounded.

John ap Colyn gathered his men and then started the long climb up the rock of Alclwyd. It was an exhausting ascent as they were in a terrible hurry, and by the time they reached the top they were all sweating and gasping for breath.

They rushed through the gates and into the courtyard with the garden. Running across the grass, they entered a passageway before finally emerging into the small square before the royal apartments. Half a dozen men awaited them there by an opened door. There was much shouting and anger. Two bodies lay sprawled across the threshold. Both had been stabbed in the neck and the ground was wet with their blood. But the door was unbarred and the way into the royal apartments open.

"What happened?" demanded the captain.

"We found them," said one of the guards. "The keys are gone."

"The Lady Genevieve?" asked John ap Colyn. "The children?"

"We know not," said the same guard. "We were waiting for orders."

The captain ran through the opened door, followed by his men. He hurried up a flight of stairs to the first floor and came out onto a landing. Two more warriors stood there, their swords drawn and ready.

"What is happening?" they asked. "We heard the shouting."

"Open the door!" ordered John ap Colyn.

The guard fumbled with the key and then knocked. "My lady?" he called. "My lady?"

"What is it?" said a woman's voice from the other side of the door. "Why do you disturb me?"

"Could you unbolt the door, my lady?" asked the captain of the guard. "It is a matter of some urgency."

"Why?" demanded the woman.

"There are intruders at large in Alclwyd," replied John. "I must check you are safe."

"O very well!" said the woman angrily. The door was unbolted and opened. "Next," she

255

added, "you'll be telling me Dundonald has not fallen!"

"I don't quite know how to tell you this ..." began John ap Colyn.

The captain of the guard entered the Queen's apartments. He apologised profusely while an extensive search was made of the chambers. The Lady Genevieve's children were woken and brought into the same room so that they all might be guarded the more easily. All were safe and well. There were no signs of intruders.

"I'm sorry," said John ap Colyn again after a large sigh of relief. "There are two fugitives at large in Dundonald. They got in by pretending to be messengers from Dundonald. It was they who gave me this false news of victory in Fenis. I'm sorry," he said once again. "I'll leave men with you – just until we capture them. I think the children should stay with you for now. I was very stupid."

The Lady Genevieve smiled slightly. She was an older woman, not very tall, but slender despite her several children. Her skin was smooth except at the corner of her blue eyes where there were laughter lines. She was dressed in a long purple robe, and her blonde hair was loose about her shoulders. She had been preparing for bed.

"No harm done, captain," she said. "This does not need mentioned to my husband. Let it remain a secret between the two of us."

"Thank you, my lady," he replied, "you are too kind. I will leave six men with you and another four outside the door. The door is not to be opened again unless I, myself, am here. You are to bolt the door and not let anyone enter save me or my master. At least until we have caught these cut-throats."

"What do these men look like?" asked the Lady.

John ap Colyn shook his head. "I don't really know," he admitted. "They were both disguised, covered in blood and dirt. They were dressed as messengers – yet no one in the fortress has seen them. They murdered two of my men at the very doors but then disappeared again. In truth, I do not even know if I would recognise them again."

Genevieve smiled, pulling her robe about her, but there was a look of worry was on her fair features. "Then I will do as you say, captain," she told him, and shivered.

"Thank you, my lady."

The Lady Genevieve went to her children. There were six of them altogether. The oldest was by the first marriage. She was a girl of some sixteen years, dark haired unlike the rest of the family. Taller than her mother, the girl had a pale complexion and large cold eyes.

She had four sisters and a brother. The girls were all petite, pretty children with hair the colour of gold. The youngest could only have been a few years old. The boy was a child of some six years or so. He was the Ku's heir, blond haired like his sisters; and the lad smiled at John ap Colyn.

Genevieve stroked the boy's head. "I hope you find these cut-throats, captain," she said. "And not just for my sake."

"As do I," replied John ap Colyn.

"Then let all your hopes be fulfilled," replied Revile. A dagger appeared in his hand, as if by magic, and in a moment he had the Lady Genevieve by the hair, the dagger pressed tightly against her throat.

The guards gasped.

"Leave now!" said the assassin calmly. "Take these men with you."

The captain of the guard hesitated.

"Tell him, my lady," suggested the assassin coldly.

"Go, captain," she said, "and no blame on you."

The guards left the chamber reluctantly until the Lady Genevieve and her children were alone with the intruders.

"Please," she said. "Spare the children!"

Indulf closed the door and bolted it.

"Good," said Revile. "Very good." He hesitated. "Watch them," he added, going across to the window. He opened the shutters and peered out, stretching out over the sill. Indulf drew a dagger, light glinting from the blade.

Lady Genevieve and her family cowered together in a corner.

"Please spare the children," she breathed.

"They'll be all right," said Indulf. "As long as you do what we want. We are not assassins. We are men in the pay of Lady Shona of the Feni. You will come with us."

The assassin had begun to uncoil a rope. He fastened one end to a roof beam and let the other fall out of the window.

"We're going out the window," said Revile. "Asuara, here," and he pointed to Indulf, "is going first with your son and heir. If I do not make it, he will die."

The lad began to weep.

"Very well," said Genevieve.

Indulf took the child in his arms and placed him on his back. He walked over to the window and took hold of the rope. "Hold on," he told the lad, and swung out of the window.

"Now," said the assassin. "We don't need you all. You, girl," he said, indicating the oldest child, "come with us – and you, my lady. The rest can stay."

The children, barring the oldest, all started to weep.

"Thor's scrotum!" said Revile.

"Leave Blwyd," said Genevieve. "Leave her with the others."

"No," said Revile, "she's coming with us."

The candles flickered in the breeze from the open window. Four little girls sat huddled together, crying a little.

There was another knock on the door, louder this time.

"Break down the door," ordered the captain of the guard. "Now!"

There was the sound of pounding and wood splitting. Almost without warning, the door burst open. John ap Colyn stepped into the room, his sword drawn. Other men followed them.

"They have gone," said one man.

"Yes," said John, "but where?"

"The window," replied the first. "There is a rope."

"But we would have seen them," said John.

"Wizardry!" muttered a man.

Checking the little girls were all right, they then searched the chamber and the adjoining rooms, but there was no sign of the intruders, nor Genevieve and the other children.

"Damn!" said John ap Colyn. "They have escaped."

"But how?"

"Does it matter?" The captain of the guard thought for a minute. "We've not lost them yet," he said at last. "I wonder if they have anything to do with these outlaws in Cowlsmark? I wonder. David," he went on, talking to one of his men, "take twenty men. Search the north bank of the river as far west as the Sentinels. And take more men into Cowlsmark. Round up some of the Dalrian scum and then await further orders."

"What are you going to do?" asked David.

John ap Colyn shrugged. "I will stay here," he said sadly, "and make the most of my remaining days. I won't live long when Ku finds out what has happened."

David looked at him. "If Ku ever returns," he said.

John ap Colyn found nothing to say in reply but he shook his head sadly.

"Wizardry," muttered one of his men.

VII

Seven horsemen rode west on six ponies. Revile led the small party, a young lad on the saddle before him. Indulf and Aliannia rode beside him with the girl Blwyd and Genevieve.

"How much further are we travelling?" asked Genevieve. "Thomas is exhausted. Surely we must stop soon?"

"Hush," said Revile. "We will stop later. But we've got a long way to go. And don't worry about the lad here, he's asleep. Maybe at the border with Cowlsmark we'll be able to rest."

On they rode towards the Sentinels, two much-weathered statues which marked the border of Strathclwyd. The statues were carved like demons but who had carved them, or why, remained a mystery. Revile only knew he would be glad to see them again.

It was the middle of the fifth day since Revile and his companions had left Dundonald. Time was getting short. The sky was overcast and it was a grey day, windy with the promise of rain and little cheer.

They had met no one as they went west, neither friend or foe. Revile guessed they would be followed, and that the boat Aliannia had used would be found. For once, one of the assassin's plans had worked well. Without mishap, Indulf with the lad, Blwyd, Genevieve and then Revile himself had been lowered out of the window to the waiting boat. Nobody had seen them thanks to Indulf, and they had travelled west on the river, landing a mile or so from Alclwyd. Here Aliannia had ponies tethered, and they had set out for Cowlsmark with the dawn. Douglas MacGalbrain should be waiting for them at the border, although Revile had said to meet him that evening.

They came out of the woods and into a region of scrub and gorse. The road ran on, straight and true, towards the west. The great river Clwyd flowed away towards the south. In front of them rose the mountains.

The border with Cowlsmark was near.

It has begun to rain by the time they reached the Sentinels. Visibility was poor and the wind had become cold. The weather was worsening but they went on nonetheless. The land about them was grey and featureless, a place of heather and bog and meandering streams, but the road climbed on into the moors shrouded in the low cloud.

At last, the two statues emerged through the rain. A body of horsemen also waited there. Revile could not make out their banner in the gloom. Behind them men he could see twenty or so crosses lining the rode. People were crucified on them.

The assassin pulled his horse up.

"Blwyd," he said to the girl, "go ahead and find out who those men are." And then he added: "And the rest of you get ready to make a run for it."

Blwyd hesitated for a moment. A stubborn expression passed across her pale features. "Go yourself," she told the assassin coldly. "Get someone else to do your dirty work!"

Revile smiled slightly. He drew a dagger and held it against the throat of the lad before him on the saddle. "Do as I say," he replied, "or your brother will die!"

Blwyd laughed. "Go on then," she said, "do it. You're going to kill us all anyway. Why not here? What a brave fellow you must be threatening defenceless women and children."

The assassin sighed and put away the dagger.

"I will go," said the Lady Genevieve. "Ignore, Blwyd," she went on, trying to placate Revile. "She has always been a strange and wilful child. I will go."

Revile peered at both of them. Blwyd's dark eyes were dancing with anger, while Genevieve seemed cowed, defeated.

"Fool!" cried Blwyd, addressing her stepmother. "If we follow this villain it will be the death of us!"

"What choice have I got?" replied Genevieve sadly.

"Well go then," said Blwyd. "Hang yourself and us. Tie your own noose!"

The assassin nudged his horse over to beside Blwyd. Without warning, he slapped her back-handed across the face. Blwyd reeled, tears in her eyes but she braved Revile's glare.

"Don't talk to your mother like that!" he said lightly.

"She's not my mother!" said Blwyd softly. "My mother is dead! What a brave fellow you are hitting women. May you rot in Hell!"

Revile raised his hand again and Blwyd flinched. The assassin smiled thinly. "Go then, Genevieve," he said. "We cannot delay." He looked behind him.

Genevieve nodded, and then rode out towards the Sentinels. She returned almost immediately. "It's all right," she said, "they are your friends. A man amongst them is called Douglas MacGalbrain."

"I thought I could smell him," said Revile. "What did he say?"

Genevieve looked puzzled. "He said," she replied slowly, "you are a brainless turd with a head like a ripe turnip."

"Aye, that's Douglas," said Revile, and he relaxed slightly. "We've done it, Indulf."

The illusionist grinned. "The difficult part, anyway," he added. "The next should be easy – although we better hurry. Time is running short. I wish the weather would improve."

"I am glad you look forward to your deaths," muttered Blwyd. "My father will eat you alive when he finds out what you've done!"

Revile and Indulf laughed together. Aliannia frowned.

They approached Douglas MacGalbrain and his company of men. The horsemen were grouped around the Sentinels. They were a ragged, evil-looking lot, a band of brigands if Revile had ever seen one. There were about fifty of them. The old warrior was quite at ease in their company.

"Greetings," he shouted when Revile was in hearing distance. "Did everything go well?"

"Aye," grunted the assassin.

"Then you have brought Ku's family," continued the old warrior. "Is this them?"

"Yup," said Revile. "This is the Lady Genevieve of Strathclwyd. Her daughter, Blwyd, and this is Ku's heir, Thomas. We left the others. Anyway, I see you've had a spot of bother." Revile indicated the crosses. Each one had a Cymbrian warrior crucified, nailed at the wrists and ankles. The Cymbrians were all dead, pierced with many arrows. More bodies had been placed by the side of the road. These were civilians, farmers and peasants of Cowlsmark, women and children taken from their refuges. "I see," added the assassin, "you've had time for a spot of cross building."

"Firstly," said Douglas with a glint in his eye, "we were expecting you this evening. Secondly, the crosses were built before we got here. We cut down these here," he indicated the bodies of the women and children, "to put up these Cymbrian dogs."

"What happened?" asked Indulf.

Douglas pointed to the Cymbrians. "They arrived last night," said the old warrior, "bringing wood and carpenters. They put up these crosses during the night and with the first light of dawn they rode into the hills. They took all the folk they could find and crucified them – women, children, old people. By then we had had enough! We attacked the Cymbrian swine. Most of them surrendered. Fools! What did they think we would do? They took the places of the innocents they had butchered."

"Very well," said the assassin, "but I think we should get moving. Have you somewhere safe to go?"

"Aye," said the old warrior, "but we'll tarry here for a while. We need to bury the dead. It will not take long."

"Why?" muttered Revile. "Who knows how many people already know of the slaughter here? Word may already have reached Alclwyd. They may be riding here with an army!"

Douglas frowned at the assassin. "I'm not a fool, laddie," he said coldly. "I have scouts out. They told me you were coming so we did not hide. They would also tell me if any of the vermin have issued from Alclwyd."

"Sorry, blubberguts," replied Revile. "I guess you have everything under control."

"That I have," said the old warrior. "And do you know why these poor unfortunates were tortured and murdered?"

"I can guess," said the assassin in a tone of disinterest.

"For those there," said Douglas, pointing to Genevieve, Blwyd and Thomas. "The Cymbrians want them back. The gods alone know what they will do next!"

Revile shrugged. "Sixty five pieces of gold," he said, "eases the conscience."

The old warrior laughed. "That it does!"

An hour later and they set off for the hills, leaving the road behind them. Revile glanced back at the crosses and the Sentinels as they disappeared into the drizzle. There was no sight or sound of pursuit. Relaxing a little and glad they were moving again, Revile rode through the band of brigands towards Douglas. He passed Genevieve and her two children and noticed they were well guarded. Blwyd turned to him and glowered.

The assassin rode along beside Douglas MacGalbrain. "So," he asked the old warrior, "how did things go with you? Did you have any trouble raising the men?"

"No," replied Douglas. His voice was carefully pitched so that only Revile could hear him. "I rode into Cowlsmark, as planned, and almost immediately ran into these outlaws. I saw the smoke. They were burning a Cymbrian captain and his men. They didn't like me much at first but after I'd knocked some sense into a couple, they took me for one of their own. They've got a refuge in the hills. That's where we're going. How did you get on?"

The assassin told him everything that had happened since they had parted. "I didn't think you would have any trouble," said Revile when he had finished his tale. "Everything has gone well – so far."

Douglas nodded. "Anyway," he said, "the leader of the band calls himself Osric. He claims he's the rightful king of Cowlsmark after the last one, Malcolm, died at Dundonald."

Revile smiled slightly.

"I'm not so sure," continued the old warrior. "I reckon he's been an outlaw, and not a very good one, for quite a few years – long before the war with Strathclwyd. He's the biggest bandit I've met." He lowered his voice further. "And if I was given the choice, I reckon Cowlsmark would do better under the invading Cymbrians than under good old Osric. Both him and his lieutenant, Bredric, are nasty pieces of work."

"Will they do what we want?" asked Revile. "Will they hold Genevieve and the other two?"

"Aye, they'll do that much," muttered Douglas. " But I don't know how safe they will be. Osric has no love for Ku or the Cymbrians."

"I guess we will have to take the risk," replied the assassin.

Douglas hesitated and then said: "The men are fond of me, I reckon. I could call out old Osric and slay him. Get rid of him and Bredric too."

"No, Douglas," said Revile, "although I don't doubt you could. It's too dangerous."

"Well, never say I didn't offer."

The party wound their way into the hills. The land about them steepened and the slopes rose away into the gloom above them. The glen narrowed into a ravine and the road became difficult. Before long, they had to dismount and lead their ponies. They followed a path which leapt up the side of high waterfall, past pools and streams and showers of tumbling water. The air was full of moisture and the waterfall roared. On the party climbed until they came to the head of the pass.

The ground fell away before them into a small glen tucked between the mountains. There was no way into the glen except up the side of the waterfall. It was a good refuge for any outlaw band. On one side of the glen there was a wood, hugging the slopes; on the other was a large hall house and other buildings by the side of a loch. The waterfall came down from the heights above the hidden glen – and the party passed by the rushing water into Osric's glen.

"We're here," said Douglas. "They call it Glen Dorb."

They followed a well-worn trail into the glen, down towards the hall. Revile saw guards and other outlaws at their posts in the side of the ravine. Stopping by the side of the buildings, the party dismounted, many of the outlaws disappearing into the hall. Revile and the others waited at the doors.

A few minutes passed.

Eventually two men emerged from the door: Osric himself lingered by the doors but Bredric, his lieutenant approached them. "Greetings," he said and went on to welcome most of the remaining outlaws by name, stopping to jest with them. Finally he turned to Douglas. "But I see there are some strangers here," he went on. "Folk I don't know."

Douglas stirred. "These are my friends," he replied, "the people I talked about. He introduced his companions. "This is Deathshade," he said, indicating Revile. "And Asuara." Indulf. "And Isobeau." Aliannia.

"I see, Dourhand," replied Bredric.

Osric's lieutenant was a large man, heavy of girth, with a cruel look about him. He had a full black beard and long unkempt hair. Like Douglas MacGalbrain, he carried an axe. Unlike Douglas, Bredric's axe was an executioner's weapon – not a warrior's – and it was heavy and unwieldy. Bredric was dressed in a black leather tunic, leggings and boots. He certainly was clad like the lieutenant of a band of brigands.

"I welcome you to our house," he continued, bowing slightly. "We don't normally welcome strangers so warmly – but then so few come of their own accord." He laughed. "Who is this woman, girl and child." Looking Blwyd up and down, he grinned. "Are they gifts, playthings for my lord, Osric, and me."

Dourhand shook his head. "No, by your leave," said the old warrior. "This is the Lady Genevieve of Strathclwyd, wife of King Ku; this Blwyd, daughter of King Ku; and Thomas, Prince of Strathclwyd, heir to the throne. My friends have brought them from the very fortress of Alclwyd."

Bredric started to speak, but Osric interrupted him. "Is this her?" he said. He walked forward, a tall man but slender in build, dressed in gaudy finery. He talked with a slight lisp, his tone one of surprise and delight. "Are these his children, Dourhand?"

"Aye," said Douglas. "They are, my lord, Osric."

Osric clapped his hands together. His many rings and bangles glinted in the light of torches. He wandered over to the Lady Genevieve in an exaggerated fashion and peered into her face.

"Welcome, my lady," he said to her, bowing. "Never," he went on with a curl of his lip, "have I greeted such an important guest at my doors." He bowed again. "I shall make you very welcome. All of you. You shall never forget your stay here."

"Thank you, my lord, Osric," replied the Lady Genevieve, but her expression was of alarm. She could not conceal it. "I am in your debt."

Osric laughed, but the laugh was hollow. He turned his back on them and strode back towards the hall house. Bredric watched him go and then grinned. Apparently they had been dismissed.

"Take Ku's folk," he told Douglas, "and put them in the guest house. You, Deathshade, and your friends go with them. Dourhand will show you."

Douglas nodded.

"I don't like Osric," said Indulf, "or Bredric."

Revile shrugged. "I don't see why it matters particularly," he replied. "Anyway, when it comes down to it, we're as much prisoners as the Lady Genevieve. We can't leave unless Osric lets us."

"And he's no fool," added Douglas MacGalbrain, "despite his looks."

Revile nodded. "I am no fool, either, blubberguts," he said. "I know not to take anyone, especially not the chief of a band of cut-throats, at face value."

"O well," said the illusionist, "it looks like were stuck with him. At least he should hold Genevieve and the rest until we're ready to release them."

"Maybe," said the assassin, "but we've no choice – now. We need his help."

Revile frowned as the others voiced their concerns.

"Odin's frothy beard!" he said. "There is nothing we can do. Besides, time is running out."

Revile and his companions and captives shared a large chamber in an adjoining building to the hall. The accommodation was cramped and uncomfortable, but it was warm and they each had a space on the floor they could use as a bed. The assassin was tired and he settled down to sleep, Aliannia by his side.

"I am glad we made it, master," she told him. "I was worried when you entered Alclwyd. I thought I might never see you again."

"We were all right," he replied. "I'd been there before, I knew the layout of the place. It's by no means the most perilous place we've been together. Anyway, you were in as much danger. You had to steal the boat and look after the horses."

"I was safe, master, I was careful." She hesitated and then continued. "This way of life is too dangerous. I do not see how we will survive very much longer. And then where shall I be?"

Revile yawned. "What do you want me to do about it?" he replied. "How else can I make a living. I can't do anything else."

"Master," she said, "you made a fortune when you were adventuring in the Merse. Yet within a week it was all spent; you needed to come Dundonald to make more money. If you were more careful ... sorry, master, if I am talking out of turn."

"That's all right," said Revile tiredly. "You're right in one way, I guess. Except I hadn't run out of gold. I came to Dundonald because I wanted to. Anyway, I will give it some thought when I've got time."

"You will put it off, master."

"Aliannia," said the assassin, "if I wanted nagged, I'd marry you. Please remember you are a slave and please, please leave me alone."

"As you will, master."

"There is one thing," added Revile.

"Yes, master?"

"Do you think what we're doing here is wrong?"

"I do not care one way or the other," said the girl with a mischievous gleam in her eye. "I am a slave. I do not need to worry about what is right or wrong. I just do what you tell me."

The assassin laughed.

Revile settled down to sleep. Just as he was starting to doze, Blwyd came up to his bed. Aliannia prodded him.

"What is it?" muttered the assassin, becoming irritated.

Aliannia pointed to Blwyd.

"O," Revile went on, "what do you want?"

"Can I speak with you?" asked Blwyd. "Alone?"

"Go ahead, but keep it brief."

Blwyd hesitated. "Alone," she said again.

"Very well," said Revile. "Aliannia, give us a minute."

The slave girl snorted, but got out of bed, wrapping the blanket about her.

"You must not leave us here," whispered Blwyd. "We are in grave danger."

"What concern is that to me?" replied Revile.

"I don't believe you wish to see us suffer," said the girl. "If you leave us we will die."

The assassin shrugged slightly. "There is no other way," he told her. "We are as much prisoners here as you. What do you think I can do?"

"Stay here with us," replied the girl, "you will protect us."

He shook his head in answer. "I have got to see your father," he said. "I cannot stay here."

"Then you will not help," said the girl sadly. "We are doomed."

"Then I am sorry," said the assassin, "for that is not what I wanted."

"I could make it worth your while to stay," she said, lowering her voice still further. "I am not ugly and ..."

"Hush," said Revile. "That will not work either: you have nothing that I desire. Go now."

Blwyd wandered away and Aliannia lay down again.

"What did she want, master?" she asked.

"She reckons you are too nosy for your own good," replied Revile. "I agree and have arranged to have you beaten."

"That is not funny, master."

"No, it's not," admitted the assassin.

Revile woke with the dawn and roused his other companions. They had been granted an audience with Osric in the hall, and – as they had to leave for Dundonald with all haste – it was arranged for first light. The assassin, with his friends and prisoners trooped out of the sleeping chamber, and across to the hall.

Knocking loudly on the door in the grey light of dawn, the assassin pushed his way inside. They marched up the hall to where Osric and Bredric awaited them.

Douglas MacGalbrain stepped forward and cleared his throat. The main chamber of the hall had a low ceiling without windows. It was filled with smoke from the central hearth. Many other outlaws still slept in their furs at the sides of the chamber.

Osric was dressed in a colourful robe and cloak, sewn from many different hues of coloured fabric. He wore a large fortune in jewellery: rings, bracelets, amulets, chains, brooches and belts; the plunder from a hundred robberies and murders. His face was covered in a white powder, and although he tried to present an image of youth and flamboyance, he was well past his prime and only succeeded in looking gaudy. Nevertheless, there was something supremely dangerous about him.

"Greeting," said Douglas MacGalbrain cordially, "We are sorry to have to bother you so early in the morning. But we must depart immediately."

"We forgive you," said Osric with a thin smile. "Now, what else have you to say?"

"My lord, we ride for Dundonald, hoping to reach there before it surrenders or is destroyed. Our plan depends on speed."

"Very well, Dourhand," said Osric, "you have my leave to go. Will you bring Ku back here."

"Aye, that we will," replied Douglas, "if all goes well."

"Will Ku believe you have his family?" asked Bredric.

"He will believe us, my lord," said the old warrior, and then he hesitated. "My lord," he went on, "it is vital – for all of us – that the Lady Genevieve, Blwyd and Thomas are well looked after and treated. It would be a shame if they sickened, or whatever, while we were gone. Therefore I beg you to take care of them."

"Perhaps I will," muttered Osric, his face cracking into a frown. "Yet what is there in this for me?"

"My lord," said Douglas, "if we succeed then you will be the King of Cowlsmark in reality as well as in name. The Lady Shona of the Feni could do this for you but she would need the Lady Genevieve and her children to bargain with the Cymbrians. Do you agree, my lord?"

"Aye, I agree," said Osric. "Come back and make me a king!"

"It will be a pleasure, my lord," said Douglas with a warm smile. "You will be the King of Cowlsmark!"

"Good," said Osric. "The Lady Shona and me will be like brother and sister." He laughed for a moment. "Very well then," he added. "This audience is over. You may go now."

When they were outside again, Revile peered at Douglas MacGalbrain.

"Well," he said, "I had not thought it possible of you. You did not lose your temper."

"Aye, laddie," replied the old warrior, "not with all that gold at stake."

They took the Lady Genevieve, Blwyd and the lad back to the chamber, leaving them in the care of some of Osric's outlaws. Genevieve looked stricken. She stood there, holding the small hand of Thomas, an expression of anguish on her face. The lad pulled at his mother's skirts but she ignored him.

"Don't do this," she said to the assassin. "Please!"

Revile turned away from her, and began to pack his belongings.

"It is no good, mother," said Blwyd coldly. "We are damned. This coward is running away, leaving us to Osric's pleasure."

The assassin peered at her for a moment, took his pack, and left the chamber, followed by Douglas MacGalbrain, Indulf and Aliannia.

Bredric had come outside to bid them farewell. "Take care," he said. "We'll see you soon with our good friend Ku."

"Good-bye," said Douglas MacGalbrain.

They led their ponies away from the buildings and up towards the pass. At the top, Revile looked back into the glen. Blwyd stood there but she did not wave.

The assassin shrugged and made his way over the pass beside the waterfall, disappearing from the view of the hall.

Blwyd still stood there. She could hear Osric laughing with his men.

VIII

Battle raged. The Cymbrians swarmed up and over the wall and fell upon the Feni with daggers, axes and clubs. For a moment the defence was dismayed and fell back, allowing more Cymbrians onto the battlements. Men screamed and cursed as they were forced towards the tower.

"Enemies in the fortress!" cried a Feni voice. "Enemies ..." His cry was cut off as a Cymbrian cut him down.

For a moment more the Cymbrians surged forward, bellowing war cries and slogans, nothing stopping them. Then, at the tower door, appeared two women: the Lady Shona of the Feni and Lathspell. Neither of them wore armour but both held swords.

"It is Shona!" said one of the Cymbrians. "We will take her head to show Lord Ku. By the Dragon, at her lads!"

Shona grinned, her eyes burning. She pushed forward, her sword weaving delicately through the air, slicing through bone and flesh and armour with each easy stroke. Beside her, Lathspell did terrible damage with her two swords, hewing left and right. The Cymbrians fell back as she advanced, the leading warriors slain or maimed where they stood or lay.

"At her, damn you!" swore the voice. "They are only women, by the Dragon!"

More Cymbrians pushed forward. Feni streamed from the tower into the fight. The battle was fierce, but such was the skill and might of Shona and Lathspell, the Cymbrians were slain quicker than they could be replaced. The battlements were covered in corpses and severed limbs. The two warrior women were splattered with blood, their swords dripping when they stopped for a moment to gather their breaths. Other Feni pressed forward past them, forcing the last of the Cymbrians from the wall.

The battle was over.

"We were lucky," said Lathspell, breathing hard. "It was well we were alerted."

"That it was," said Shona lightly cheerfully, putting one arm around her shoulders of her friend. "We make a good team, you and I. I am not as singular as I once imagined. Never have I seen one – never mind two – swords wielded so skilfully – or so deadly." She clasped Lathspell tightly, and then released her. "But as you say," she went on, "we were lucky."

Lathspell smiled, then cleaned her swords on the clothing of one of the fallen Cymbrians. "What happened?" she asked. "How did they penetrate the defences?"

Shona turned to look at her. She had grey eyes, as grey as slate, and her expression was speculative but unfathomable. Lathspell shivered slightly under the inspection, something making her feel uncomfortable. In her turn, she looked at Shona, her gaze guarded.

The Lady Shona was a tall woman with long flaxen-coloured hair. Her build was compact but strong and she had handsome aristocratic features. Her tunic was tight, clinging about her hips and her rising breasts.

Lathspell drew her eyes away in surprise and swallowed.

"They must have shot the sentries," said Shona lightly, "and then thrown ropes across from the ruins. We made it just in time." She smiled but Lathspell did not smile back. "Anyway," she went on, "we can get back to our meal."

Lathspell nodded and sheathed her swords. They turned to go, stepping over bodies. They reached the door back into the tower.

Whirling around on her heel, Lathspell whipped out her swords. Standing on the wall of the battlement was a Cymbrian archer. He had an arrow fitted to the string and his bow was bent.

"My lady!" cried Lathspell, leaping forward.

The archer fired, aiming at Shona's back. But Lathspell jumped in front of Shona and took the arrow. Lathspell staggered backwards and fell to the ground.

The archer frantically tried to fit another arrow to his bow. Shona took hold of her sword by the blade, aimed carefully, and the threw the weapon at the archer. It took him in the chest, slicing through his rib cage and emerging out his back. He stood, looking at the hilt, then toppled backwards from the wall.

Shona fell to her knees and examined. "Not only do I spend my people," she muttered, "now I spend my friends also."

The arrow had pierced Lathspell's shoulder. Shona scooped her friend up in her arms and, grunting with the strain, got to her feet. She carried her into the tower, shouting for a surgeon.

Blood dripped from Lathspell's wound.

"Well, here we go," cried Revile. "Another race."

They had climbed down the last slope from the waterfall and were back on the open road. Their ponies gathered speed as they headed north on the road to Dundonald. The hills were dark and shadowed for the sun had not yet risen above the eastern ridge. The four companions seemed cheerful enough. The outcome of their venture was not assured; yet the most difficult part was completed.

"We seem to have been doing a lot of riding," grumbled Douglas. "I hope it's worth it."

"Aye, let's hope it is," agreed the assassin.

The old warrior grunted.

And so the miles sped by and the four companions rode through the middle of Cowlsmark towards Lornland. By midday, they had crossed the border. There were more signs of the invasion: deserted villages, burnt farm buildings, dead peasants. Twice horsemen thundered by on the way south but they did not stop. Other than this, the company met no one at all. They were dressed in their ordinary clothing, having discarded King Ku's livery for now.

Stopping briefly for a meal, they set out again and continued on until evening fell. Again the journey passed uneventfully, and when they rested again, Dundonald was only a couple of miles away. They lit no fire but made camp in a hollow, sheltered by a wood. Revile sat a little apart, munching his food and brooding. The others chatted for a while. Indulf walked over to where the assassin sat.

"Well," asked the illusionist, "how are things going?"

"All right," replied Revile and went back to his food.

"What is wrong?" said Indulf tiredly. "Anyone would think you were feeling guilty."

"Maybe," said the assassin. "I don't know. This whole thing has become messy. I wish we hadn't met Osric."

"We couldn't have known," said Indulf.

"No, but I could have guessed. Anyway, what's done is done."

"Will Ku have heard his wife and heir have been taken?" asked Indulf, "Will word have reached Dundonald?"

"It is bound to have," said Revile. "We are here ourselves, aren't we? It won't matter as long as Ku doesn't run all the way down to Cowlsmark."

"We would have met him on the road if he had."

"Maybe." Revile sighed. "But we should be careful."

"I think that goes without saying. What's the plan?"

The assassin paused. "I want you to take Aliannia and Douglas into the camp of the Cymbrians. Spread rumours about how demons have stolen poor old Ku away. That he's dead. That the Dalrians are marching south with a mighty army. That men are deserting in droves. Anything like that. You should go now. Take care of Aliannia for me. Meet me back here tomorrow. I will have Ku with me. Can you do that?"

"Aye, just about," said Indulf. "Douglas will not be happy."

"Just make sure you get back here – don't let Douglas argue with the whole Cymbrian army. If I am not here, I may have ridden on with Ku. Ride after me with all haste. I'll wait for you."

268

"Very well," said Indulf.

"Then go now. I'll see you with the dawn."

Indulf nodded, and left the assassin. Revile could hear Douglas MacGalbrain complaining but they soon set off, waving their farewells, and quickly disappeared into the twilight.

The assassin sat with his back against a tree, waiting for fullest night. That was when darkest deeds were done.

It was gloomy in the chamber. Lathspell lay on her bed, having just come from her bath. She was wrapped in furs and blankets, and had not bothered to get dressed. Although her shoulder was stiff and tender, she felt comfortable. A goblet of wine stood at the side of the bed with a plate of sugared preserves. She took one of the fruits and nibble at it, using her left arm. She burst it between her teeth, letting the rich juice run over her lips.

There was a knock at the door.

"Who is it?" asked Lathspell, although she thought she knew.

"It is me, Shona," replied a woman's voice. "Can I come in?"

"Sure," replied Lathspell, pulling the furs further up around her neck.

The door opened and Shona appeared, carrying a candle and a goblet. She was dressed in a plain shift and her hair was free about her shoulders. Sitting down on the bed beside her friend, she put the candle and the goblet on the floor.

"How are you feeling?" asked Shona. "For a while this morning I thought I had a very brave, but dead, bodyguard."

"I am fine," replied Lathspell, feeling relaxed. "I was lucky the arrow missed the bone."

"You lost a lot of blood."

"I know – but I am all right." Lathspell reached down for her goblet and took a deep drink. Some of the wine spilled down her chin. "I was lucky," she repeated. "I wonder how the others are getting on?"

"God knows," said Shona, taking a drink from her own goblet. "Revile or Worm or Maggot – or whatever her calls himself – will be up to something, of that you can be certain. Probably old Ku is already entangled in the spider's web. I almost feel sorry for him. I pity anyone with Revile as an enemy." She sighed.

Lathspell nodded, her expression thoughtful. "He saved my life, you know," she said softly. "Twice. I never even thanked him. It's funny, I was thinking that after I had been shot. I felt guilty."

"Aye," said Shona, "but I must thank you. You took an arrow meant for me, you saved my life. I know you are getting paid but it could never be enough for what you did."

"It was nothing," said Lathspell. "How did it go today? Did we lose many men?"

"Only a handful to King Ku's army, more to wounds and disease and hunger. We've too many folk in the Citadel, far more than this fortress was ever intended for. The wells are drying up, other water has turned green. I don't know why. Of all things, this I had never envisaged." She paused. "I suppose I should have been more ruthless at the beginning, I should have limited the number of townsfolk we let in." She shook her head. "But there were so many: women, children, old folk. I could not leave them to the Cymbrians. How the tide has turned! Here I sit, Dundonald under siege, the lands of the Feni devastated, most of my people dead or enslaved or dying. A few short years ago, Strathclwyd paid us homage, their king acknowledged my own father as his overlord. How arrogant we were! How arrogant! Old Nechtan got his revenge after all!"

"Things may still work out," said Lathspell.

"Not for the Feni or Dundonald," replied Shona. She laughed and then said more cheerily. "Aye, they may I suppose. I get lonely with no one to share the burden. I am feeling sorry for myself. Anyway, it doesn't matter. I came to thank you – not to share my doubts and depression. So, thank you, Lathspell. Thank you for saving my life."

She stood up and leaned over Lathspell, kissing her forehead, then moved down to kiss her nose, and then finally her lips. The kiss lingered, gentle, delicate. Lathspell did not try to break away.

Dundonald frustrated Ku's siege. Still it stood on its rock, high above the army of the Cymbrians.

There were not as many defenders as there had been, they had been reduced by arrows and disease and starvation. Dundonald had had little or no food for several weeks. Smoke still spluttered from the town and outer defences. And a terrible smell hung over the whole area as the dead of the fortress rotted.

The Cymbrian army was frustrated and it, too, was beginning to starve. The lands of the Feni were not rich arable regions such as Strathclwyd or Lothland. Food was scarce. They had exhausted fresh supplies for miles in any direction and were having to venture further and further abroad to find meat. Supplies of clean water were also running out and disease was spreading amongst the warriors and their new army of camp followers. Yet there was nothing they could do about it.

The Cymbrians had no great siege engines, nor the skill to build them. The rock and stone wall and slated roof of the citadel thwarted any attempt to burn the fortress. Arrows and spears were all but useless. And the Cymbrians died.

Not many at first, just a man there, a friend here. But their numbers grew day by day as their attacks became more frantic. Morale was low and getting lower. Their march through Cowlsmark and Lornland had been so easy: all Dalria had opened at their feet. But that had been almost a week ago. Now a trickle of men deserted, skulking away by night with any loot they had found.

King Ku ap Gawain, Lord of Strathclwyd, was frustrated. Although he had promised Revile the siege would be lifted, it had gone on without pause. Ku had lied. The words of the priest came back to him – and he wished he had stood by Shona's offer of surrender.

"Mind you," said Ku out loud, "the priest that called himself Wilmund had turned out to be a Dalrian spy."

His men looked surprised and alarmed by his sudden outburst.

Ku knew that this priest, who called himself Wilmund, had murdered Ku's men. The bodies of Dryff and others had been found where they had fallen, shot with arrows and hewn with an axe, without any attempt to hide the slaughter. Ku still did not understand the point of the

270

whole affair.

"No doubt it will make itself clear in time," he muttered, feeling gloomy. He peered up to the walls of Dundonald and cursed. Why had it not fallen!

Sighing, he turned from the Citadel and made his way through the tents back to his own pavilion. A few stars twinkled above him, and campfires and lanterns cast flickering light across his path. The great banner of Strathclwyd was furled to its pole. Ku had not ordered it so and he spoke angrily to his men. The soldiers tried to free the flag but it could not be opened.

It was not a good omen.

Ku entered the pavilion, having come to a decision. He would continue the siege of Dundonald for one more day. If the citadel had not fallen by then, he would march north, leaving just enough men to contain the Feni within the walls. But his thoughts were cut short.

Messengers waited for him.

"What do you want?" demanded Ku, who was not in the best of moods. "What news have you for me?"

"My lord," started one of the messengers, his expression grave, "I have ill tidings ..."

The Lady Shona of the Feni stood on a battlement, looking out over the camp of the Cymbrians. She thought she could make out the figure of Ku by the great banner of Strathclwyd, but he entered the pavilion. For some reason, the banner had been furled to the pole. Shona had watched men try to free it but they had no success. Smiling slightly, she turned to peer at her own flag. She could not see the emblem of the Feni – and the flag was tattered and dirty – but still it flew. Maybe it was a sign, she thought. It if was, it was too late in coming.

Lathspell emerged from the tower. She was wrapped in blankets. "My lady," she said, "come down. They will see you and shoot you from the walls."

"Let them!" replied Shona. "What difference does it make?"

"Please," said Lathspell, "if you were to die now all would be lost."

The Lady Shona shrugged.

"Anyway," said Lathspell, "we may yet be saved. Revile said to give him a week. Tomorrow is the seventh day. We said we could last out that long."

"Saved?" said Shona. "No, I do not think I will be saved. I am damned by what I have done, and my people with me. It has gone beyond salvation. How many of my people have already died because I was too proud to surrender? How many are starving? This fortress maybe defeats the Cymbrians but we have still lost. I have led the Feni to ruin in my corruption and folly."

"There is still hope," said Lathspell.

"For what? That we will live? I do not hope for that. Only my people are important now. Yet if we surrender, who knows what will happen. Will any of my people survive?"

"Well, they won't get me. I will not surrender. I will fight – and so will you if you have any sense. We're not finished yet."

"Brave words," replied Shona, "but words alone are nothing. Aye, I destroy everything I touch. You took an arrow meant for me, you nearly died so I might live – as so many other friends and companions have died for me. I am not worthy of their sacrifice."

"Perhaps not," said Lathspell, "but that sacrifice will be worth nothing if you throw you life away or surrender this fortress."

Shona nodded. "Maybe you are right at that," she admitted. "I wish this had all happened differently."

"We cannot always make that choice," said Lathspell evenly. "Now will you come down, my lady?"

It was a heavy night. Great dark clouds rolled up from the south but it did not rain. Instead the air became sultry and humid, the wind warm with a rotten smell like the breath of a carrion crow.

Hannar stood with his brother, Igris, sniffing the air, wondering at this change of weather.

"We'll not get much sleep, this night," said Hannar. "I reckon there will be thunder later. By the Dragon, it's heavy."

"Yes," agreed Igris. "The omens are not good."

"So you have heard the rumours, then?" asked Hannar.

"No," muttered Igris. "What are they saying now? Has a giant turd engulfed Alclwyd now?"

Hannar laughed. "No, not yet," he said, "but they are saying that the Dalrians have raised a great army and are marching south." And then he lowered his voice to a whisper. "They also say Ku has made a bargain with the devil!"

"Really?" said Igris, sounding surprise. "By the Dragon, what for?"

"For good fortune. So that we would have victory over Dalria."

"I thought it was too easy," said Igris.

"Anyway, they say that Ku angered the devil and he will have his revenge."

"That doesn't sound right," scoffed Igris. "How could anyone possibly know that?"

Hannar peered about him to make sure no one else could hear. "One of the guards by the pavilion heard Ku and this other voice. Swore there was no one else in the tent. Anyway, Ku was arguing with whatever it was." And he shivered. "And it said it would have its revenge, that Ku not fulfilled his part of the bargain. The guard said the voice was pretty evil and he saw no one leave."

"Hmmm, that doesn't sound too likely."

"Look at all the bad luck we've had today," said Hannar, and then he went on, sounding wise. "Anyway, we'll see in the morning."

And so the rumours spread until the whole camp was rife with speculation.

King Ku sat in his pavilion, knowing nothing of the rumours. Perhaps if the devil had been there then he would have happily made a bargain with it. Having ordered out the messengers and his servants, he sat alone on the stone throne, staring into nothing. He felt like weeping but he was too hard a man to permit himself such a luxury.

His wife, son and daughter had been taken from him.

It was a pain in his chest, a pounding of his heart.

Were they alive? He did not know. In some ways he wished that they were slain for it would free his hands, allow him to kill and maim and destroy. He did not know what had become of them.

No one knew.

"My lord," said on of Ku's advisors from outside the pavilion. "My lord?"

"What is it, damn you!" Ku exploded. "I told you I was not to be disturbed."

"My lord," said the voice again, "there is a man to see you. A messenger."

"Have him boiled in oil!"

"My lord, I think you should see him first."

"O very well!" cursed Ku. "But God help you if this is not important."

A man entered the pavilion. He was a tough-looking character with an eye patch and a scar and was dressed in a leather tunic. Daggers were strapped across his chest."

"What do you want?" demanded Ku. "Who are you?"

"I am Deathshade," replied the visitor. "An adventurer and traveller."

"What do you want?" repeated the king.

Deathshade smiled coldly. "I was sent," he said, "by Lord Osric of Cowlsmark. He calls himself king. Myself, I don't think he is much of a king but in his own halls he can have any title he chooses. So he is king and Ku is king. I was paid money so I came. He gave me a message to give to you."

"And what was that message?" breathed Ku. "Does it concern Genevieve? And the lad? And Blwyd?"

"Aye, that it does," replied Deathshade. "This fellow Osric said that you must go to Cowlsmark. He will exchange you for your loved ones. Aye, and you must withdraw your army from Dalria — or your family will die, in torture. That is his message."

Ku opened his mouth to say something but no words came.

"For myself," went on Deathshade, "I would not go. I would stay here. But then I am not a family man. But you must choose. Swiftly. I rode here as quickly as possible but we have only got until midday two days from now. Then Osric said he would ... well, you know."

"Who is this Osric?" asked Ku, and his voice was perilous. "Who is this man who would dare harm my family?"

"I know little of him," replied Deathshade. "I was wandering in southern Cowlsmark when me and my friends were taken by his outlaws. I thought I was dead. But he gave me a bag of silver and sent me north with his message. That I have done. He offered me gold if I brought you back to his refuge. Alone, of course."

"And my wife?" swallowed Ku. "Is she all right?"

"She was when I left — but I reckon this Osric is a dangerous outlaw who follows no law but his own. I will be honest with you. I don't know but I fear the worst." Deathshade shrugged. "That's not much comfort, I guess. But it is all the more reason to hurry."

"I will go to Osric," said Ku, "with an army!"

"If you wish. But this Osric had me followed and the entrance to his refuge is tightly guarded. He would be alerted as soon as you entered Cowlsmark. Perhaps with a few men you might take him unawares!"

"How do I know any of this is true?"

"You don't," replied Deathshade. "Should we go, do you think? It is dangerous for both of us. Most likely, it will end in our deaths. But you have you wife, and I have my gold."

"Very well, Deathshade, we will go, you and I."

Deathshade nodded.

"If anything has happened to Genevieve I will have this Osric disembowelled and feed his entrails to the crows."

"But will you withdraw from Dundonald?" asked Deathshade.

"Yes," said Ku. "We were getting nowhere. I will withdraw for now."

Deathshade nodded again. "We should leave as soon as possible."

King Ku of Strathclwyd grinned, his eyes burning. Yet he did not recognise Deathshade for the priest, Brother Wilmund, who had stood before him only seven days before.

Douglas MacGalbrain, Indulf and Aliannia waited in the hollow. Hours had passed but Revile had not returned from the Cymbrian camp with Ku. The first light of dawn was glimmering in the east.

"Maybe he's been captured," said the old warrior cheerily. "Should we go back?"

"No," replied Indulf, "I think it's more likely he's gone on without us. Yet he was strange before we left him last night."

"Aye," said Douglas. "What do you think he's up to?"

"Knowing Revile, I can't believe it's anything to our good." Indulf paused. "He's probably run off with our share of the gold," he went on, "that at least would be in character. Maybe I misjudge him." He laughed. "If I didn't know better, I'd reckon Revile is feeling guilty."

"Maybe," said Douglas, sounding far from sure.

Suddenly there was the braying of horns, echoing away in the hills, then the roll of a deep drum.

"What was that?" asked Douglas, standing up.

Aliannia appeared worried. "The Cymbrians are on the move," she said softly. "They are retreating. But where is my master?"

"Gone with Ku, I'd reckon," said Indulf.

It was then, in the first light, they noticed a note pinned to a tree with a dagger.

"What does it say?" asked the slave girl.

"'Follow to Osric's hideout'," read the illusionist. "We heard horses in the night."

"That was hours ago," said Douglas.

"Aye, we had better get moving." replied Indulf.

The three companions quickly mounted their ponies and set off south.

Lathspell moaned in her sleep. Her shoulder still ached and she had been awake for hours before finally drifting into a troubled slumber.

The door of her chamber was suddenly thrown back. Shona hurried into the room.

"Wake up!" cried Shona. "Wake up!"

274

"What is it?" said Lathspell wearily.

"The Cymbrians are leaving. We're saved! We're saved, after all!"

A wave of relief washed over Lathspell.

"Then Revile did it," she said. "But how?"

"Who cares?" replied the princess. "All I now is we are redeemed from the very jaws of defeat."

Lathspell looked thoughtful.

IX

It had started raining again. The air was heavy, and the sky seemed lowered as if was only feet above the ground, weighing all below in heavy gloom.

Low cloud had engulfed the hills, turning the glen grey and shifting. Revile peered out, watching the rain, chewing his lunch.

"Well, Deathshade," said King Ku, "how much further do we travel today? Can we reach Osric's hideout before dark?"

"Maybe," replied the assassin, "if we rode hard. But the weather is against us. It would make our journey even more perilous. Besides, we must wait for my friends to catch up. They are some miles behind."

"What friends?" demanded the Cymbrian. "Who are they? You've not mentioned them before."

Revile turned from the window and grinned. "O, I am sure I did. Anyway, we need them."

"Why?"

"Because, Ku, if we ride into Osric's camp, just the two of us, neither of us will escape again. My friends have special skills we need."

"I don't know whether to trust you, Deathshade. Perhaps I should slay you myself and save this Osric the bother." He peered at his two-handed sword, propped against the ruined wall of the house.

Rain dripped from the ceiling.

Revile laughed and then turned back to the window. "That would do you no good," he told his companion. "Then your wife and children would certainly die. You would have no heir."

"They are maybe dead already," said Ku.

The assassin sighed. "Aye, that is possible," he admitted. "Likely even. In fact, Ku, you are a fool even to think of going to Osric's hideout. I warned you before. Anyway, the choice is yours. But remember you have withdrawn your armies."

"What difference does that make?" asked the king. "They can easily return to Dundonald. That is the order I left if I don't return to Alclwyd."

"O well, never mind."

"You still have not told me why I should not kill you." Ku edged towards his sword. "I might like to see the colour of your innards."

"Then you would die before your time, King Ku of Strathclwyd," muttered the assassin. Revile spun round, his sword drawn. With a flash, the blade whistled through the air towards Ku. The sword stopped short, its edge held tight against Ku's throat. "But that is not my plan," Revile went on. He lowered the sword. "I don't desire your death."

"Very well, Deathshade, I will come with you. If you wanted to slay me you could have."

"Aye, that's true."

The assassin finished his meal and disappeared outside for a moment. "We won't have long to wait," he told Ku. "My friends approach even now."

"Good," muttered the king, "I'm glad!"

The sound of hooves approached the ruined house. The riders dismounted with the clink of armour and harness. There was some low talking, then Revile and his friends entered the building. The assassin introduced his companions.

King Ku nodded.

"Well, Deathshade," said Dourhand. "I reckon it's time we got moving again."

It was raining more heavily than ever.

Ku sighed.

They went on for some hours after their break at midday. It continued to pour and the road became muddy and covered with puddles. The many fording places were treacherous for the burns were swollen with water. Progress was slow, and the travellers were soon wet and miserable. As evening fell, and the grey twilight failed, they searched for shelter and a place where they might spend the night. With some relief, they found a burnt-out hall house. Although the roof had partly collapsed, there was still shelter to be found amongst the fallen beams and walls. Douglas lit a fire, and they sat around the blaze, eating and quietly talking. They set a watch and settled down to sleep.

When Revile awoke the next morning, he found that Ku was keeping watch. The fire was tended and the assassin guessed he had not slept all night. Revile watched Ku for a while, then gently extricated himself from Aliannia.

"How's things?" Revile asked him.

King Ku turned to look at him. The assassin frowned. Ku's face held as bleak an expression as Revile had ever set eyes on: an expression without hope, of one who knows he will die in torment. The Cymbrian's eyes were bursting with pain.

Revile was too hard a man to feel much pity for Ku. Besides which, the Cymbrians were responsible for the deaths of so many men, women and children. How many of Ku's victims had looked like this before they were slaughtered? Nevertheless, the assassin had no wish to be needlessly cruel. He took a bottle from his pack and handed it to Ku.

"The water of life," Revile told him. "*Uisge beatha*. We could both do with it."

Ku took a drink from the bottle and swallowed down some of the clear fiery liquid. With the bite of the liquor, Ku gained his colour. He took another mouthful, then passed the bottle back to the assassin.

"The only good thing Dalria has ever produced," said Ku.

Revile nodded. "If we are to die," he said, "we should do it properly fortified."
He took the bottle.

Still it rained, without let up, without respite for the travellers. It was about two hours after dawn but it was as dark as the grey of evening. The hills of Cowlsmark were hidden in the clouds as they neared Osric's hideout. A burn splashed away along the edge of the path; and beyond, the waterfall disappeared into the mist above them. It roared in the narrow gorge like a mighty lion.

"Is it passable?" asked Indulf as they approached the waterfall. The illusionist looked doubtful. "Should we wait until the rain eases?"

"We might wait until the summer," replied Douglas. "I say we should go on."

Revile nodded. "We cannot afford the delay," he said. "We must take the risk of the falls. Yet I reckon drowning or falling are the least of our worries." He tightened his sword belt. "We must go."

"Very well," said Indulf, but he frowned. All of them looked gloomy.

"We will leave the ponies here with Aliannia," Revile went on. "And any gear or belongings we don't need. We shouldn't burden ourselves. Besides, I'm not sure we'd get our ponies up there in this weather."

"Master," said the slave girl, "please do not leave me. I will come with you."

"No you won't," said the assassin. "You will stay here. We need someone to look after the ponies."

Aliannia's head dropped.

The companions unpacked such gear as they thought they would need. Revile took his bow and quiver of arrows. He also took out a long black knife, and hid it under his tunic. Ku watched him with interest.

The King of Strathclwyd hesitated for a moment, then took his own sword. It was an enormous two-handed weapon which must have weighed a score of pounds. Sending the sword whistling through the air, Ku grinned.

"Let them take me alive!" he said. "Just let them!"

The assassin looked at him.

Douglas MacGalbrain tested the edge of his axe. It was as keen as a razor. The old warrior tied the axe about his mighty frame and then strung his bow. He tested the bend and grunted with satisfaction.

Only Indulf ignored such weapons. He was armed with a plain staff of unfashioned wood.

"You are a strange lot," said Ku with a thin smile.

When they were ready, they gathered together at the foot of the waterfall and prepared to climb the steep path. Revile took Aliannia aside.

"Master," she whispered, "please take me with you. I am lost if you are killed and I can help you against Osric. Please."

The assassin sighed. "It's too dangerous," he said to her in a gentle voice. "Far too dangerous. After what we've been through, I would not get you killed now. We can't get the ponies up

277

the gorge, one of us needs to stay here. Who else could we spare? It must be you, I am afraid."

"I can help you," she said. The rain ran down her face and her long black hair was plastered to her back and shoulders. She was a vision of loveliness and even the assassin could not remain unmoved. "You know I can."

"Only a fool takes his treasure to the house of a thief," replied Revile. "And there is no time to discuss this. You must stay and we must go. Take the ponies away from the waterfall, find shelter, and be careful if you can. Cowlsmark will soon be full of Ku's army and scouts, not to mention bandits and brigands. Return to the foot of the waterfall this evening. Wait one hour. If we don't come, go to Dundonald and seek shelter with the Lady Shona." He put a heavy purse of gold into her hands. "Here is fifty pieces of gold. With it you can hire bodyguards and a ship, and can travel back to your home. There should be enough there if you are careful."

She nodded. "Take care," she said.

"I'll do my best, Aliannia."

They embraced for a moment.

Revile returned to the others. "Right," he said to them, "let's get started."

They started the climb up by the side of the waterfall. Revile led, Indulf and Ku following, and Douglas MacGalbrain making up the rear. The path was slippy, a river of water running down the roughly-hewn trail. The four companions were soaked through to the skin and Revile's boots squelched.

"At least they shouldn't see us coming," mentioned Douglas.

Revile climbed on a way more and then turned to gaze back through the mist. Aliannia and the ponies had gone.

He sighed.

Rocks loomed out of the rain. The path wound up the ravine, disappearing into the gloom above them. And all the time water fall down on them. There was water, rain and mist everywhere – on the path, on the rocks, in the air, seeping down Revile's back.

The assassin wiped his eyes, peering upwards again. But he could see nothing more than the narrow sides of the gorge and the white water of the swollen waterfall. All sounds of their ascent were drowned in the roar.

"Come on!" he shouted, trying to make himself heard. "Come on!"

As he spoke, Ku slipped sideways, his foot turning on a polished stone. Little stones went dropping away to the pools below. Douglas MacGalbrain shot out his hand and caught the Cymbrian king as he fell, stopping him from tumbling to his death in the torrent.

"Thank you!" cried Ku, getting to his feet. "Thank you, Dourhand!"

"Don't mention it!" replied the old warrior.

On the four companions went, on towards the head of the pass. Revile drew his sword.

They reached the top of the gorge. As far as they knew, they were had not been seen so they inched their way past the waterfall along a narrow ledge. The river came gurgling down. The four companions came out onto the head of the pass and peered down into Osric's glen. They

278

could just make out the hall house, the woods, the rain-splattered loch.

Four figures stole through the trees. Nobody saw them, nobody knew of their presence in the glen. The figures approached the side of the hall house along a well-used path. They went warily, expecting guards, but met no one.

The assassin sniffed the air. There was a smell he could not quite place, yet knew so well. They came to a branching of the path. The track directly ahead led to the hall house, but Revile followed the left branch, following his nose. He came out into a clearing in the woods.

In the middle of the clearing were two wooden posts. Tied to the posts were the bodies of two people, a woman and a young lad. The bodies had been mutilated. The woman's head was missing, it had been severed from her body.

King Ku of Strathclwyd hung his head, putting his hands over his eyes. His breath caught in his throat as he turned away from the bodies of his wife and his son.

Revile nodded slightly as if what he saw was what he had expected. Douglas and Indulf stood beside him, huddled together, whispering together.

Ku sank to his knees. "Genevieve," he groaned, "what have they done to you? Dead, all dead. A curse be on me and my House!"

The assassin went over to Ku and put his hand on his shoulder. The Cymbrian flinched.

"Why?" asked Ku. "What had they done?" He looked up at Revile. "Why did they have to die?"

"I don't know," said Revile, "but this is not the time for grieving."

"Yes," said Indulf, his knuckles whitening around his staff, "we need to finish this."

"Aye," said Douglas, "and finish it we will. This is the time for death, for death and slaying and revenge!"

Ku bowed his head. Without looking at Genevieve or Thomas, he got to his feet and left the clearing, following the others.

X

They splashed through the rain towards the hall of Osric. Nobody emerged to meet them. From the building came the sounds of music and merry laughter. A feast was in progress it seemed. The four companions stopped by the door and checked their weapons. Revile looked at Douglas MacGalbrain and shivered. The old warrior's eyes were shining with blood lust. Douglas licked his lips.

Revile smiled slightly. "Right," he said, and lifted the latch, opening the door for his three companions. They entered the hall. The sounds of merriment went on unchecked – for a moment.

Once inside, they found the hall dark and warm. The only light came from the fire blazing in the central hearth and a few smoky candles. Tables had been placed in the hall, surrounding the fire, and many men and their slatterns sat around, eating and laughing and drinking. There was perhaps sixty outlaws in all.

Laughing and conversation stopped as Revile and his friends walked up the hall towards the dais. Osric's mouth gaped before he could stop himself; Bredric looked wildly around. He recognised Ku. Blwyd also sat there, by the side of Bredric. She, alone of the three, masked her feelings. Dressed in a rough tight-fitting dress, the young woman ran one hand through her long black hair.

Ku could not contain himself. "Blwyd," he cried, "you are alive. God be praised!"

Blwyd glowered down at him. "Yes, father," she sneered, "I, too, am glad to see you again." She smiled thinly. "And the rest of you."

Osric stood up. He was clad in a brightly-coloured tunic and a long golden cloak. His hair was powdered as was his face, and his thin pale fingers had painted nails. His face cracked into a smile. He stood up, sweeping back his cloak in a grand gesture.

"So," said Osric, "this is noble King Ku of Strathclwyd. You're quite a brute, aren't you? Long have I waited for your arrival. What a welcome I have prepared! What a welcome, indeed!"

"My lord, Osric," said Douglas MacGalbrain, "I give you greetings from me and my companions. We have brought King Ku ap Gawain of Strathclwyd. Of course, this is Ku. My lord, Osric, where are the Lady Genevieve and Thomas, Prince of Strathclwyd?"

Osric licked his ruddy lips, considering for a moment. He was, after all, in his own stronghold with his own men. What had he to fear from Dourhand and his friends? He was going to lie, but then he shrugged, relaxed and said: "They are indisposed to see you."

This brought laughter from the outlaws, loud laughter which filled the hall. Men slapped each other on the back, grinning at Ku.

"What became of them?" said the old warrior. "Why all this laughter?"

Osric stared down at him. "Genevieve, and her brat, are dead!" he said distinctly. "I had them put to death!"

The outlaws laughed again.

"Then," said Douglas, "explain why you did so?"

"Why?" said Bredric, heaving himself to his feet. "Why should we explain ourselves to you?"

"I had them put to death," repeated Osric, giggling away to himself. "I had the post placed and had Genevieve and the brat nailed there. That was after the men had played with them first. Poor old Genevieve! How Bredric made her squeal! Myself, I preferred your son, Ku. Such a sweet child, although I preferred him before his innards spilt across the floor." He turned to Dourhand. "I suppose you have come to collect your reward, Dourhand. I'm afraid I failed my part of the bargain. What would you ask of me now?"

A silence fell.

Douglas stirred. "My lord, Osric," he said in a conversational tone. "My lord, Osric, we ask nothing of you. There is nothing that you could give us that we could not take. My lord, Osric, Bredric, all you men. This is the day of reckoning, the time has come, and we are your witness, judge – and executioner."

"What do you ..." began Osric.

***

G od," cried Fergus. "O God!"

Revile fell silent and listened.

Booted footsteps approached.

While the assassin had talked, it had grown lighter although the cell was still dimly lit. Somewhere a cock was crowing and welcoming the new morning.

"What is it, Fergus?" asked Revile. "What is wrong?"

The footfalls came even nearer, but then passed by, not even hesitating at the door of the dungeon.

Fergus sighed and Margaret smiled slightly.

"Go with your story then," said Alwyn softly. "What happened next?"

"I can't stand this," muttered Fergus at the same time. "I can't stand the waiting."

The assassin sighed. "I'm not sure I can be bothered," he said to Alwyn. "I'm getting tired."

The farmer went on muttering away to himself.

"Peace, Fergus," said Margaret softly. "Let Revile finish his story."

"Why?" cried the farmer. "Why should I? Who cares about Ku and his stupid family? What about me?"

"No one is going to tell stories about you," said Revile. "I don't believe they would find anything interesting to say."

"What makes you think you are so interesting then?" demanded Fergus. " Tell me that!"

"Listen, Fergus," said Margaret tiredly, "if it becomes a choice between hearing the end of Revile's story or hearing you moan, then I think we'll take the story."

"Yes," said Alwyn. "Anyway, I want to find out what happened. Did Revile and his friends get revenge on Osric?"

"Well," replied the assassin, "I, at least, survived so there is no mystery there."

"We don't care about you!" said Margaret. "What about Indulf and Douglas? And poor Aliannia who is alone with the ponies? Or Ku with all his family dead? I want to know what happened to them. And did cruel old Osric get the terrible death he deserved."

"Very well then," said the assassin, "I'll finish the tale."

"Good," said Alwyn, trying to sound cheerful. "I hope it has a happy ending."

"I guess that depends who you are," replied Revile.

W hat do you mean?" demanded Osric. "Or do you want to join Genevieve and her brat on the post? That is my design for Ku – that he should join his family in death – and could be for the rest of you rabble. I say again, explain yourself, Dourhand!"

"Fool!" spat Ku. "Don't you know death when you see it?"

Ku's sword sang throw the air. Two slashes and two outlaws were cut down, blood spraying from their wounds.

Revile opened his mouth to say something, but Douglas MacGalbrain beat him to it. The old warrior threw the heavy dais table backwards, toppling Osric and Bredric and several other outlaws from their bench. His axe bit into flesh and bone. Swinging left and right, he did terrible damage. Ku joined him, and the two men waded into the outlaws.

Indulf swung his staff. There was a heavy concussion as it struck an outlaw, shattering his head like a rotten turnip.

The assassin hesitated only a moment more. "Shit!" he muttered, and swept out his sword. Revile and Indulf stood together facing the outlaws. Douglas and Ku hewed those on the dais, cutting down any who opposed them, any who stood or crawled or lay stunned on the floor. Osric pulled himself from the confusion and ran towards a door at the back of the hall; but Bredric was trapped under the table. He fought to get to his feet.

"Help me!" he screamed as Douglas's axe came within a whisker of splitting his skull.

Blwyd smiled. Bredric put out his hand. Ducking inside his grasp, she sliced him with a carving knife, opening his belly to the backbone. Bredric watched stupidly as his entrails spilled out. He screamed and screamed.

The dais area was rapidly clearing. The floor was covered in mangled bodies, upset furniture, plates, food, drink, and blood, much blood. Most of the outlaws on the dais had been slain but a few had managed to escape. Amongst these was Osric.

Douglas and Ku had run out of victims so they jumped back down from the dais into the fray, fighting beside Revile and Indulf. Blwyd joined them.

"Did I do wrong, father?" she said, and then swallowed. "I did not want to die."

Ku never heard her.

The fight raged for a moment more. It was fierce as the outlaws surged forward. But there they died. Revile had slain several and maimed many more; Douglas had half a score to his credit; and Indulf had fractured many skulls. But it was Ku who did most damage, his mighty sword swinging left and right to cleave through weapon and armour and skin and muscle and bone. He was covered in blood; but his eyes were terrible. Men fell back before his face. Outlaws lay piled at his feet.

When many men were dead, and more lay dying, the outlaws fled. Not one of Revile's companions had received more than a scratch. The assassin let the outlaws go, mopping the sweat from his brow. Ku would have chased them but Douglas MacGalbrain restrained him.

"We must go after Osric," said the old warrior.

Ku nodded slightly.

They climbed onto the dais and hurried out the door through which Osric had fled. It was bolted but they soon had it open. They entered another smaller chamber. Its occupants had all fled. This room had been Osric's bedchamber.

Another door led outside. Revile approached one of the windows and peered out. There were ten or so outlaws waiting in the trees. Each had a bow with an arrow fitted to the string.

There was a smell of smoke. The hall was burning.

"Shit!" said the assassin. "Osric has escaped!"

"We're trapped," said Douglas, "trapped like rats."

"Bar the door," said Indulf. "Bar the door from the hall."

The old warrior shut the door from the hall and wedged it with a bench. An arrow hammered into the wood by his hand. Douglas cursed.

The smoke became thicker. There were cries from within the hall as the flames spread.

"We must flee," said Revile.

Indulf nodded. "What should we do?"

They peered round the chamber. It was furnished with a bed, table, stool and chest.

"The table," said Indulf. Douglas MacGalbrain nodded. He and Ku picked up the table and carried to the door. Revile opened the latch and yanked back the door. Bow strings sang. Arrows thudded into the upturned table; others embedded themselves in the door frame and wall.

Ku and Douglas sprang forward with the table, followed by Revile, Indulf and Blwyd. More arrows were shot off but none found a mark. The outlaws threw down their bows and swept out their swords just as Ku and Douglas crashed into them. The outlaws broke and fled, although several were too slow and were soon sprawled out between the trees.

Osric was not one of them.

Revile and his companions ran off into the woods. Arrows whistled over head. One passed between Indulf's legs as he sprinted.

The assassin smiled slightly. He had not expected to live.

Five shadows crept through the forest. They knew they were pursued but the outlaws were still far behind. Climbing down the steep sides of a water course, they edged their way down towards the loch hidden in the trees. They went on quietly.

"I can't guess how many of them are left," whispered Indulf. "Perhaps they will flee?"

"Not while Osric lives," said Revile in a low voice. "We should not have let him escape. And I reckon the pass will be held against us. I think we may have to kill Osric."

"We will kill all of them!" said Ku, his eyes shining. "Death find them all!"

"Peace, father," said Blwyd. "We must go quietly."

He turned to her. For a moment it was as if he did not recognise her and his expression was harsh. But then his face softened. "Daughter," he whispered. "Blwyd. My heart rejoices that you live."

She nodded slightly. "I never doubted you would come for us," she told him. "Would that what has been done could be undone." She threw a look at Revile. The assassin smiled back.

Ku brushed her cheek.

"Father," she said, "I did wrong. I was Bredric's ..."

Ku put his fingers over her lips. "It does not matter," he said softly. "It does not matter. All that matters is that you live."

"Let's go," said Douglas who was getting impatient.

The rain still fell from the sky. The light was failing even though it was only late afternoon. Mist was descending from the higher slopes of the hills and the high woods were eaten up by grey clouds of drizzle.

"There they are," whispered Indulf, pointing to the far side of the loch. A group of outlaws emerged from the trees and walked cautiously along the rushes by the water's edge. The outlaws were clearly nervous and they went slowly.

"Good," said Revile, "I think we've lost them. They followed the wrong path."

The two companions crawled backwards towards the others.

"One day you must show me how you do that," the assassin went on in a low voice. "How you make people see things which are not there."

The ground was marshy and their knees sank into the mud.

"It is not as simple as that," replied Indulf. "They are seeing things which they want or expect to see. It's almost like suggesting, putting something into someone's mind. Like what you did in Alclwyd, telling the captain of the guard they won the war. It was what he wanted to hear so he trusted you."

"Hmmm," said Revile. "As you say it's not that simple."

"We all have our own magic," said the illusionist. "Even you, Revile: Ku does not recognise you as the priest in his pavilion."

The assassin nodded. "I hope Blwyd doesn't tell Ku what happened in Alclwyd – or we could be for the chop."

They crept back to where the others waited.

They settled down for the night in a copse of trees. They lit no fire and the assassin took the first watch. It was pitch black and Revile sat with his back against a tree trunk, his ears trying to pick out any untoward noise in the black.

Someone approached from behind him. The assassin was almost certain it was Ku but he vanished into the shadows, a dagger in his hand.

"Deathshade," said a voice quietly. "Deathshade."

"What is it, Ku?" asked Revile from behind him.

The Cymbrian started. "By the Dragon!" he whispered nervously. "How do you do that?"

The assassin laughed. "What do you want?" he asked.

"I want you to promise me something."

"What?"

"Whatever happens," Ku said softly, "make sure nothing happens to Blwyd. Do not let her be tortured like Genevieve and poor Thomas. And if you do escape, take her back to Alclwyd, make sure she arrives there safely."

284

Revile did not reply.

"Please," said Ku. "Please do this for me."

"Why?"

"Because I ask it of you," said Ku in a whisper, "because you have done my House wrong."

"Has Blwyd been talking to you?"

"No," said Ku, "she has said nothing on the matter. She doesn't need to. I am not stupid. You have destroyed me and you owe me this much."

"I destroyed nothing," muttered the assassin. "Was it my decision to invade Fenis and Cowlsmark? Was it my wish to besiege Dundonald and slaughter its inhabitants in their hundreds? I, perhaps, have had a hand in your ruin but no more than others. I did not desire Genevieve's or your son's deaths."

"Perhaps," said Ku, "but you at least owe me this much!"

Revile snorted.

"I charge you," said the King of Strathclwyd, "I charge you with seeing Blwyd safe, seeing her to the gates of Alclwyd. If you fail me, I will call down a terrible curse upon you. You will be struck down."

Ku turned from the assassin and made his way back to the camp.

Revile held a thoughtful expression.

Revile took the watch for the rest of the night but nothing unusual happened. In the grey light of dawn he returned to the camp to find the others asleep.

"By The Seven Serpents of Set!" swore the assassin.

Ku was gone, his sword with him.

Even as Revile cursed there was a terrible cry of pain, shattering the peace of the quiet dawn.

Blwyd heard the cry and rolled over. She smiled slightly at Revile but he frowned back. She rubbed her eyes and then looked for Ku. "Where is my father?" she asked. "Is he on watch?"

The assassin peered at her.

There was another long cry of pain.

"O no!" she said. "O no, not my father as well."

"I am afraid so," replied Revile. "I should have guessed from what he said last night." He sighed. "What do we do now?"

Indulf appeared beside him. "What's going on?" he asked.

"Ku's vanished," said the assassin. "I think Osric's captured him."

"I thought I heard someone screaming," said Indulf. "I wasn't sure if I was dreaming or not."

"It's enough to wake the dead," whispered Blwyd. "Why? Why did he go himself, alone?"

There was the awful cry again.

"Enough to wake the dead?" said Revile with a thin smile. "But not enough to wake Douglas MacGalbrain." He went over and poked the old warrior with his toe. "Come on, lardbelly."

Blwyd hung her head.

"We should move," said Indulf. "Immediately."

"Why?" yawned Douglas MacGalbrain.

"They will make Ku talk," replied the illusionist. "They will make him betray our camp."

The assassin sighed. "I fear he already has," said Revile in a conversational tone. "There seem to be outlaws in the trees all about us. Don't Douglas. We'd be full of arrows before we got a few feet. It's ironic in a way."

"Why?" muttered Indulf.

"Well," said Revile cheerfully, "we betrayed Ku's lot, and now he's betrayed us."

"I am sure he didn't mean to," said Douglas.

"As I was saying," said Indulf loudly, "I do believe Osric is an excellent fellow ..."

Revile and his friends were led through the trees, back towards the hall. They had been thoroughly searched and their hands were bound behind their backs. Blwyd had an expression of defeat and misery across her pale young features. Douglas, Indulf and Revile, however, laughed and joked: it was what was expected from them.

The woods thinned and they came into the open place before Osric's hall. The buildings were burnt for the most part, and smoke drifted upwards to the sky. A few outlaws poked through the debris, searching for anything of use or value that the flames had not consumed. More outlaws stood in a rough ring, surrounding a post set in the middle of the area. Ku was tied there, Osric beside him. The Cymbrian king was limp in his tethers and he sobbed with pain. On a spike near Ku was the severed head of Genevieve. Her hair was carefully brushed, her face powdered, rouge on her lips.

Osric turned from Ku and hurried forward to meet his new captives.

Blwyd hung her head and started to weep. She had lost her stepmother and brother, and now it seemed she would lose her father as well. Ku had been horribly tortured. Beside him was a large fire and a pot of salt. In the fire were irons and pokers. Ku was naked and his squat body was covered in burns, scorch marks and cuts.

The assassin looked bored, but he was wondering what terrible end Osric planned for them.

Osric bounded over and peered into each of their faces. He laughed and joked with the rest of his outlaws, prodding or touching his captives like a man prodding a chicken to see how tender it is.

Revile gave him a thin smile.

"Well," said Osric at last, and his tone was more congenial than ever, "I am glad to see you all again – especially you Blwyd." The young woman shuddered. "Aye, Blwyd, my dear friend," he went on. "Bredric is dead. Poor fellow had his entrails spilled all over the place. Took ages to die and even then it was the fire which got him." Osric shook his head sadly, but there was a smile about his red lips. "Poor fellow. Anyway, I am glad you are here now. You see, your father sold you to me, he sold you so that the pain might stop. Mind you, he gave me his kingdom and much more besides. Come, I will show you."

Blwyd and the other prisoners were taken towards Ku. Osric went up to him and raised Ku's head by the hair.

"Tell her," he said into Ku's face. "Tell her or I will get the salt."

Ku's eyes opened. They were dull with pain.

Osric took an iron in his hand and waved it before Ku.

"Your daughter is mine," said Osric. "Remember? You told us where they were camped. You gave me Blwyd – even though you know what I will do to her."

"Yes," said Ku. "Yes, take her."

Osric let his head go.

"See," he said to Blwyd, coming back over to her. "You are mine. Pah!" he went on, snapping his fingers in her face. He went back over to her father, taking out a dagger. Blwyd turned her head away. Osric stabbed Ku, slicing his neck, blood spurting out.

Blwyd cried out.

"Cut him down," commanded Osric. Outlaws hurried over to the post and freed Ku's body. The ground was wet with his blood. "Bring the girl over here," he went on. "Have her put in his place."

"You craven dog!" cried Douglas MacGalbrain. "Leave her alone!"

"Or what will you do, Dourhand? Mmm?" Osric's smiled faded. "You were once our friend. You came to us and asked for our help. We gave it to you. We gave you everything you wanted. Why did you become our enemies? You betrayed my trust and slew my men. Tell me why, Dourhand!"

Douglas shrugged.

"Why did Genevieve or her brat matter?" Osric went on. "What did Ku matter? I do not understand why you turned against me."

"Perhaps because you are a sick old ponce," replied Revile.

Osric laughed. "So you, too, think you are brave," he said. "Well, I broke poor old Ku and I will destroy you."

"Try me," said the assassin.

"Perhaps you would like to kill me?" said Osric with a gleam in his eye. "Maybe you would." He put a hand to his hip and nibbled one of his fingers. "Would you like to try?"

"Perhaps I would," said Revile.

"Then we shall let you."

The assassin could not believe his luck.

The outlaws gathered themselves into a ring around Osric and Revile. Douglas and the others were taken to the side and there guarded.

"Free Deathshade's hands," said Osric, "and give him his weapon."

Revile's bonds were cut and he took the hilt of his sword. The assassin was thrust forward into the centre of the circle of outlaws.

Osric minced in front of him. The outlaw chief was not even armed and he wore no armour. Revile feared a trick, but he edged forward. Osric circled.

The assassin smiled coldly.

Osric pounced. Revile swung after him but his sword bit nothing but air. The assassin staggered back. Osric had ducked inside his guard and punched him full on the chin. The assassin shook his head. The force of the blow had left him dazed. He stumbled.

Again Osric came at him. Revile thought he was ready this time – he had been exaggerating the effect of Osric's punch – but again his sword whistled harmlessly through the air. A knee landed in his stomach with tremendous force; a fist slammed into the side of his head.

Osric danced away, out of reach again.

Revile staggered, this time for real.

The rain tumbled down.

The assassin straightened up with difficulty.

"You see," said Osric, "I gave Ku the same choice as I gave you. He lost too. I have fought thirty-two men and have never even been injured. I need no weapon but my hands and feet and head. You are going to die, Deathshade, but not quickly. No, I will destroy you piece by piece."

Revile spat.

Osric came bounding towards him.

The assassin slashed left and right. Osric weaved past his sword and struck Revile on the chest with the heel of his hand. The assassin stumbled backwards, falling and landing in a muddy puddle. He clutched his chest.

"Mithra's arse!" he wheezed. "Mithra's golden arse!"

Osric smiled as his men clapped and hooted. Revile lay for a moment in the mud, letting the rain fall on his face to revive him. But Osric did not wait for him to rise this time. Revile only just had time to roll out of the way as Osric's boots danced towards him. The assassin took the full force on his shoulder. His arm went numb and he let go of his sword.

Revile managed to get to his knees before he was struck again. A kick sent him sprawling face down in the mud. Lights flickered and danced before his eyes. Blood spewed from his mangled mouth.

Osric whirled away again to great applause. Douglas and the others flinched. The assassin did not move for a moment, but he slowly rolled onto his back.

Staring at his opponent all the while, Osric started to circle.

"I think you have met your match in cunning," said Osric. "Aye, that you have. Did you think I would fight you if there was any chance you could kill me?" He laughed. "And I've saved my sister a fortune. Shona will be pleased with my work. I've rid her of Ku and his brats. We shall rule side by side, her in Fenis, me in Cowlsmark."

"Sister?" whispered Revile. "Sister?" He tried to get to his feet. "Are you Shona's brother?"

Osric minced. "Yes," he told Revile, "I am. They disowned me, cast me out of Dundonald. Now I will be accepted back! I have saved Fenis, Lornland, maybe all of Dalria. I am a hero and men shall praise me!"

"No they won't!" said Revile. "Men will know you for the painted old whore you are."

Osric snarled and advanced on the assassin. Revile grinned through the pain. Osric was about a yard away. Without warning, a dagger appeared in the assassin's hand. Its blade was black. Osric's eyes opened wide. The dagger whirled towards him with deadly accuracy.

Yet somehow Osric stepped out of the way. His reactions were unbelievable. Yet not even Osric could wholly avoid the dagger. The blade sliced his shoulder, cutting through his tunic. A little blood ran down his arm but the wound was not deep.

"That, I fear," said Osric, "is your last throw." He rubbed his arm. "Prepare to die, Deathshade!"

"It burns," whispered Revile. "It burns like acid."

Osric rubbed his arm again and then looked at the assassin.

"Venom," the assassin told him and then whirled out of the way. "The sting in the scorpion's tale!"

A contortion took Osric. "No!" he gurgled. "No!"

Another spasm flexed his body backwards. He staggered around the ring of outlaws. He danced, danced in a strange rhythmic hypnotic way, danced the death dance.

Revile retrieved the dagger and his sword, wiping blood from his mouth.

Osric pranced about, first dancing one way, then dancing another, going round and round and round again. His body jerked as if he was controlled by a mad puppeteer – yet there was timing and precision in his contortions.

The outlaws watched Osric, struck dumb. It was the most outlandish and fascinating thing anyone there had ever witnessed. Even Douglas, Indulf and Blwyd stared and gaped.

Revile freed his friends. The outlaws never even noticed him. The assassin led Douglas and the others into the woods towards the pass.

The ring of outlaws still stood motionless, watching Osric perform the death dance.

"What poison or venom did you have on that dagger?" asked Indulf when they were a safe distance away. "I've never seen anything like it in my life."

The assassin shrugged.

The four companions disappeared into the trees.

Still it rained.

XI

The waterfall lay behind them. They had made the descent without difficulty and had seen no outlaws.

"Well," said Revile as they neared the bottom, "let us hope Aliannia has disobeyed my orders and is waiting for us."

They all agreed on that.

Although the footing was treacherous and they were all soaked through, they were so glad to have escaped from Osric that climbing down by the waterfall in torrents of freezing water was an absolute joy: one they had not expected to be able to appreciate.

Aliannia waited for them at the bottom. The assassin smiled and hurried to meet her.

"Did everything go well?" she asked. "Where is Ku, master?"

"Dead," said Revile. "As are Genevieve and Thomas."

The slave girl nodded.

They climbed onto the ponies and rode away from the waterfall towards Dundonald. The afternoon waned and evening shadows spread themselves across the south of Cowlsmark. The rain clouds rolled away to the north and the late sun lit the tops of the mountains red as with blood.

They rode on until they reached the Sentinels. Here they briefly stopped.

"Well we did it," said the assassin. "Not the way I expected or hoped." He sighed. "I'm going to take Blwyd back to Alclwyd. You go on to Dundonald. I'll catch you up."

"She can make her own way," muttered Douglas.

"I promised Ku," said the assassin. "He said I would be cursed unless I did this for him. And we've seen what curses can do."

The others pulled their horses around to the north and west, while the assassin with Blwyd went east. Douglas, Indulf and Aliannia rode off.

Revile sighed again. "Come," he said, "there's still a few hours of light."

They had made camp for the night. Revile lit a small fire in a hollow out of the wind and then ate a poor meal of stale bread and cured ham. Even the wine was sour.

Blwyd did not eat. She sat staring into the depths of the small fire, her eyes unblinking.

"What do I do now?" she whispered. "I am all alone in the world."

"There are your other sisters," replied the assassin, chewing his food. "Anyway, you are queen now. You will rule in Alclwyd."

"I know," said the girl, "you murdered the rest of my family."

Revile shrugged. "Not intentionally," he said. "Anyway, what is done is done."

"But why?" she asked, turning to stare at him. "Why did you do this to us?"

"That's easy enough," said Revile. "I did it for the gold."

"I saw that girl with a purse stuffed with gold," said Blwyd coldly. "You did not need any more gold.

"All right then: I felt like it," said Revile.

"So you had my whole family murdered on a whim?"

Guilt was not a feeling that Revile had had much experience of – and he had decided not to start then. True, he had had moments of doubt. But in the end was he any worse than anyone else? He went on munching his food.

Blwyd paused. "Do you think I did wrong?" she asked him at last. "I was Bredric's woman. I lay with him and pretended I liked it."

"Getting yourself tortured to death would not have been a better alternative," said the assassin. "Look, Blwyd, if you want me to lie I will say I am very sorry for what happened to you and to Ku and the rest. For a while I almost did. But there has been so much murder and torture and betrayal in this war – well, in every war – that the death of one man and his wife and son really is not worth bothering about. At least you live. Your people have a queen, queen of a powerful nation. Think of them if you must. They have more need of your concern than the dead. Bernecia and Dalria or even Pentland may look to take advantage of your House's misfortune."

"I will!" she said angrily. "I will when I reach the gates of Alclwyd. But for now I am all alone in the world." No tears welled in her eyes. "You do not know what it was like seeing them suffer.

And," she went on, "I cannot bear the thought that I might carry Bredric's child."

"That is not likely," said Revile. He took another drink of wine.

"I tried to hate you," said Blwyd, "for all the things you have done to us. But I cannot."

The assassin laughed and rolled out a blanket. "Then you've not really tried," he said. "Other folk have not found it so difficult."

Blwyd continued to stare into the fire.

The next morning, two riders approached the gates of Alclwyd. One of them stopped just beyond the fringe of the forest and sat there as the other went on. The second rider rapidly approached the gates of the fortress.

John ap Colyn, captain of the guard and steward of the fortress, stood on the battlements – as he had stood for the last days and last nights. He jumped down and ordered that the gates be opened.

The rider rode up. The breath caught in John's throat.

"Blwyd," he cried. "Blwyd!"

"It is me," she said, jumping lightly from her pony. "I have returned."

"Where are the others, my lady?"

"Dead," said the girl sadly. "All dead."

"It is my fault," said John ap Colyn. "You should have me put to death, my lady!"

"Nonsense, John," replied Blwyd, and touched his arm. "I need you. Now, we must raise a small force. We've got to ride into Cowlsmark to get the bodies of the King and Queen."

The captain of the guard nodded.

"The rider is waving," said a guard.

Blwyd stepped out of the gate and waved back. The rider turned back into the woods.

"Who was that?" asked John ap Colyn.

Blwyd shrugged slightly.

Revile caught up with his friends as they neared the border with Fenis. Two days had passed since Revile had left Blwyd in Alclwyd. There were more people about and the folk of Lornland and Fenis were emerging from their refuges in the mountains. More had fled than had been slain – but that was still a great number of dead. There were few, if any, homes which had escaped the ravages of invasion and would offer anything more than the most basic shelter.

And it was not certain that the Cymbrians would not come north again. The sun did shine, however, and it was spring, and Revile the assassin had his pay to get.

The four companions neared the end of their journey. They could see Dundonald ahead, on its rock. Yet they smelt it long before they saw it. The reek of carrion and rotting flesh hung in the air. Hundreds had died at Dundonald and they had been left to rot.

Revile and his friends met soldiers and scouts from Dundonald as they went on. The Dalrians were travelling south to spy on the Cymbrian armies. A force had even arrived from the Fortress of the Staff. It was not to offer battle to the Cymbrians but was to provide men for the garrison of any strongholds still defensible.

When the party finally reached Dundonald much work was already under way. Folk gathered wood from the nearby woods to build pyres and burn the dead. Work had also started on rebuilding the defences of Dundonald. The palisade had been replaced and Cymbrian prisoners were digging the ditch. Some folk wandered about the shattered streets looking for anything which could be salvaged – or looking for the remains of relatives or loved ones. It was a scene of terrible destruction.

They rode up through the ruins towards the Citadel of Dundonald. Revile was glad to find they had replaced the bridge across the chasm. He had no wish to repeat his hair-raising climb by rope. Speaking briefly to the guards at the gates, they made their way to the hall to find the Lady Shona of the Feni and their companion, Lathspell.

The doors to the hall ground open and the four companions, the four heroes who had saved Dalria, entered the chamber and made their way towards the high table. Shona and Lathspell sat there. Lathspell still had her shoulder bandaged.

"Greetings," said the assassin with a warm smile. "How goes it with you?"

"Take your money and go!" said the Lady Shona angrily. "Do not look for praise or thanks, for you will not find them in Dundonald! How could you, Maggot? How could you make war on women and children?"

Revile opened his mouth to speak, but no polite reply came to mind.

"How could you?" Shona went on. "Thomas was just a child, Genevieve a noble queen. Even Ku. He was the King of Strathclwyd! You slew them in cold blood, you a common, low-born adventurer. Not even the beasts of the wilds make war on their young!"

"We did nothing," protested Douglas MacGalbrain. "Nothing wrong that is. What do you mean?"

"By the Rood!" said Shona, glowering down at them. "Do not lie to me! Word reached Dundonald three nights ago, from Cowlsmark. Guards! Throw them out!"

"That won't be necessary," said Revile with a thin smile. "We will take the gold and go." He paused. "One thing," he added, "was this news from a fellow called Osric?"

"How did you know?" demanded Shona.

"It doesn't matter," replied the assassin. He took the heavy bag from the high table. He opened it. The gold pieces were dipped in blood and entrails. When Revile removed his hand from the bag it was sticky with congealing gore.

"Nice touch," he said. "Gives deeper meaning to 'blood money'. Anyway, we had better be off. I had rather hoped for a nice celebration banquet but I suppose that is out of the question now." He took the bag of gold and turned to go. "Well, Shona," he went on with a bright smile, "I guess we will not meet again – unless of course it is professionally. Good-bye, Lathspell, although I had hoped you would come with us."

"I am coming with you," said Lathspell, getting to her feet. "I knew nothing of this!"

Revile smiled and his expression was quite warm. "Then I am glad to have you," said the assassin.

He walked away from the high table towards the doors of the halls.

292

The Lady Shona still sat there, deep in thought.

Revile stopped in the doorway. "My lady," he said, "was your brother called Osric?"

Shona appeared surprised. "Yes," she replied. "How did you know?"

"We met him," said the assassin. "I expect you were close."

"When we were children," she said. "I have not seen him for some years. He is down in Cowlsmark."

"Was, my lady," said Revile. "Your brother is dead. It was Osric who put Genevieve and Thomas to death, not us."

"I do not believe you!" cried Shona.

Revile turned on his heel.

The Lady Shona of the Feni sat, her face pale, her heart in anguish.

Her kingdom fared little better.

***

There was a long pause.

The dim light slowly grew and Revile smiled. His companions looked at each other through the lessening gloom, suddenly aware that he had stopped speaking. Neither Margaret nor Fergus had been listening to the story.

"I do not know what to make of that," said Alwyn.

The assassin shrugged slightly. "Make of it what you will," he said. He yawned. "It should not be too long now."

"How long before they come for us?" asked Fergus.

"An hour, maybe," replied Revile. "Maybe a little longer"

They could hear activity in the streets above as the people of Bamburg went about their business.

"What will we do?" asked the farmer in despair.

Revile ignored the question and rested his head against his shoulder.

"What can we do?" asked Alwyn sadly. "We can do nothing."

"Nothing," whispered Margaret. She swallowed.

"An hour," repeated Fergus. "Only one hour."

Margaret closed her eyes and tried to calm herself. She was tired – not so much through the lack of sleep as through fear. She was tired with fright. Breathing slowly and deeply, she tried to relax. But her heart thumped in her chest. She tried to be brave, brave at the last. It was too much: too much waiting and too much fear. She no longer had the strength to contain it. Yet she tried to keep quiet.

She did not have the courage.

No one spoke.

And slowly, imperceptibly, the time passed and the light grew.

Seconds dragged into minutes.

But the time passed and nothing would prevent the coming of the new dawn.

As the silence lengthened, the waiting became unbearable. The prisoners found nothing to say. They were terrified as they had never been before. During the long night, Alwyn, Margaret and Fergus had each found courage. But now, now as light poured into the Pit through the shaft, they were numbed by fear, numbed by shame, numbed by the dawning of the new day and the long wait.

Alwyn's body shook. Her head was between her knees, her hands clasped round her shins. She tried to shut out the light and deny its existence. Yet she could feel it through her clenched eyes.

Fergus stared at the wall, his eyes unblinking. Unwittingly his shoulders would hunch, only to be relaxed again. Every part of his mind was devoted to calculate the time by the angle of shadow; and how many minutes and seconds before the jailer came for them.

Margaret sat rigid in her chains, staring vacantly ahead. Her breath came from her body in short gasps. She had been brave before – but no longer. Tears welled in her eyes.

Only Revile was relaxed, his breathing deep and untroubled. His head was resting against his shoulder and the wall.

He was apparently asleep.

Suddenly Revile's eyes flicked open and for a moment he tensed. Then he relaxed again when he realised where he was. Rubbing at his numb bottom rather pointlessly as he had no feeling, he turned and looked at Margaret.

"You are a better-looking woman than I had thought," he told her lightly. "Much younger."

"What?" said Margaret.

"I said," he repeated, "you are a much-better looking woman than I had thought. I can see you now, properly, for the first time. I thought you would be older from your talk. I take back what I said before, about you being an old hag and a grandmother." Revile smiled as he peered at Alwyn and Fergus. "It is strange to see you all. I had built up a picture in my mind and only Fergus is as ugly. Uglier, maybe. But Alwyn, I can see why Bregorin wanted you if your knees are anything to go by."

"For God's sake," said Fergus. "Leave us alone! You are mad!"

"I am not mad, o noble peasant," replied the assassin and he yawned. "I will just be glad when all this is over. I will be happy just to stand, for my arse is so numb I can't feel it." He wriggled about in his chains. "I thought you would have a beard, Fergus. You should have. It would hide your hideous features. How long was I asleep?"

"You were asleep?" asked Fergus.

"Yes," said Revile. "I fear I grew bored. You are a gloomy lot and it becomes wearying after a whole night."

"In that case," muttered Margaret, "why do you talk to us? Why won't you leave us in peace?"

"He cannot," said Fergus with a glint in his eye. "He is as terrified as the rest of us. He only talks to bolster his spirits."

"You are wrong, Fergus," said Revile. "But who cares? It is the beginning of a new day – and anything might happen under this sun. Your lives have been so unrewarding you should be glad that they are coming to an end. No more worrying about the weather and soil, or washing dishes or tending fires, or whether you've caught the pox. No more worrying about anything."

Alwyn started to weep.

"O Mithra's golden arse!" said the assassin coldly. "Stop that noise, Alwyn! Do you wish all of Bamburg to know you are nothing by a wailing baby! Pull yourself together!"

She raised her head slowly and her expression was pitiful. Her pained gaze was caught by the stare of the assassin.

Revile had a hard face. His face was caked in dirt and he had an old scar running from the corner of his mouth to his eye. Yet in this he was unremarkable – he might have been one of a thousand bandits or villains or mercenaries.

Alwyn managed to break the stare and wiped the tears from her eyes. "Why do you treat me so?" she asked in a low voice.

The assassin shrugged. "Weeping and wailing will get us nowhere," he said gently.

"Whereas acting like a cold-hearted bastard will?" muttered Margaret.

"Why?" said Fergus. "Why should we be brave? What does it matter what we do? Why won't you leave us alone?"

"Why does it matter what we do?" added Alwyn.

"It doesn't!" replied Revile. "Weep and wail as much as you want and drown your sorrow in tears. Why did I bother with you? Dull, stupid, witless peasants! Go to your deaths as you have lived your lives: terrified, terrified of anything and everything, terrified of your own shadows! So be it!"

Fergus laughed but it was tinged with hysteria. "You are right, of course," he said, "the brave adventurer is right. For the first time in my life I will be free, free from the wife and the children and the life that I hate. I envy you, brave Revile, more than anyone I have ever met. How clever to be so brave, how clever to despise the rest of us. How ..."

"Hush," said Revile softly.

Fergus opened his mouth to continue but then thought better of it. He swallowed.

"Good," went on the assassin, "maybe now we can get some peace."

"Will it be painful?" whispered Alwyn.

"Will what be painful?" muttered Revile.

"The gallows," she replied, lowering her voice to a whisper.

Revile sighed. "It depends," he replied, sounding bored. "If the executioner is kind, and knows his business, your neck will be broken instantly and you will have only a second of agony. If not, then you may take some time to choke. Your tongue will hang out, your face will become blue, your features contorted, fighting against the rope for every breath. It may take quite a while to choke. Depends on your weight and much more besides."

"God protect me!" she said. "Is there nothing I can do?"

"Aye," said the assassin softly, "call for Bregorin. Ask to be forgiven and tell him that you will be his mistress. Otherwise pray to your god and hope he exists."

"I will go to my death," she said in a whisper. "A shameful, pointless death."

They fell silent for a moment.

The could hear movement in the streets of Bamburg and the hollow echoing of footsteps and voices in the passageways and chambers of the great tower. Jolly laughter filtered its way down to the prisoners.

"What keeps them?" muttered Fergus. "It must be getting late."

"Nothing keeps them," said Revile. "Why should they hurry? They have food to eat, work to do, and bowels which need emptied. To them, this is a morning alike any other, save it is sunnier than most. Today you will liven up their day and give some folk the only entertainment they ever have."

Fergus's expression darkened, and he buried his head in his hands.

"Ye gods!" said Revile. "That's right, you too have a good weep about it all. You'll feel so much better, so much more like the brave warrior who stood on that beach in Cymbria and awaited the onslaught of the Norsemen."

"Leave me alone!" cried Fergus. "That was different: there my bravery might have a reward, there I had some chance to escape and live. Here I will die whatever I do. Why should I be brave?"

"Have you no pride?" asked the assassin softly.

"Let us be cowards if we want," said Fergus.

"Very well, then," said Revile. "I will say no more."

Another uneasy silence fell.

There were booted footsteps in the passageway outside the Pit, and hush fell, broken only by the harsh breathing of those in the dungeon. The feet hesitated outside the door; but then receded further down the corridor.

Revile's companions breathed again.

The ringing of keys and the harsh voice of the jailer reverberated around the dungeons. A cell, further along the passageway, was unlocked and opened. The pleadings of the prisoners were ignored by the jailer and his men.

"Get up, damn you!" echoed the voice of the jailer. "Up! Nothing will save you now!"

The clinking of chains followed.

"Damn you, Gelfand!" cried another man's voice. "We used to be friends! How can you of all people do this to me?"

"I am friend to no traitor!" replied the jailer. "And you of all people, Oswald, should know better than to take bribes."

There was a pause and then the sounds of a struggle.

"You of all people," Gelfand the jailer went on, "should know better than to beg for mercy!"

Footsteps returned past Revile's cell, and then the dragging of something heavy.

"I've done nothing!" cried the voice of a woman.

"Save your breath!" spat the jailer, a retort he had used often. "You will need all you can get before long!"

The noises disappeared into the distance to be ended by one last wail of anguish.

Margaret relaxed slightly and Fergus crossed himself.

"Don't get your hopes up," said the assassin distinctly. "We'll be next."

"Bastard!" cried Margaret. "Do you delight in torturing us?"

"I might, given the opportunity," replied Revile lightly, and then lowered his voice as faint cheers came to their ears. The crowd, the good townsfolk of Bamburg, were welcoming the appearance of the first group of prisoners to the scaffold. Revile looked at the faces of his companions and his expression became bleak. "There would no point," he added grimly, "you torture yourselves more than I ever could." He shook his head.

An evil pause followed for they knew they would be next.

"What are they waiting for?" muttered the farmer as the crowd fell silent.

"Us, you ass!" hissed the assassin.

Alwyn's breath caught in her throat and her face went a deathly pale.

"For Hanuman's sake don't throw up!" said Revile. "Ye gods, it is bad enough being hanged without being vomited over!"

The young woman retched but nothing came up but a thin bile.

Footsteps returned, maybe four or five sets. Each heavy footfall was another nail hammered into their coffins.

The footsteps stopped outside their cell. Keys rattled, armour clinked. The bolts were withdrawn. The lock was turned. The door of the Pit ground slowly open. In the doorway stood Gelfand the jailer and several tower guards.

"Ah," said Revile brightly, "breakfast at last!"

"Very amusing," said the jailer. "Most original. Never heard that before."

The long wait in the Pit was finally over.

Several guards entered the cell and began unshackling the prisoners from the wall. Others stood ready with swords drawn.

"On your feet!" ordered Gelfand. "Come on, you slime, your audience is growing impatient!"

The prisoners stood with difficulty, their legs stiff.

Each in turn was released from their manacles, then bound with hands behind back and hobbled. It was done efficiently and quickly, giving the prisoners no opportunity to escape.

Margaret was first, followed by Alwyn. They were quickly ushered out of the cell into the passageway. Neither of them protested nor struggled. Fresh tears welled in their eyes and Alwyn stared about wildly as if seeking some refuge.

"Seems a pity to hang these two," said a guard. "What did they do?"

"Does it matter?" replied another.

Fergus was less easily, but no less quickly, bound. He swore and fought against the hold of the guards, yet soon he too stood outside the cell, bent double and spluttering for breath.

Gelfand grinned at Revile. "The celebrity," said the jailer, exposing a mouth filled with blackened teeth. "You'll be glad to know you are the main attraction. It's not everyday we get to hang an assassin."

"I am honoured," replied Revile. "Have I drawn a good crowd?"

"Yes, some," said the jailer. "Yes, some. Folk are curious to see what you look like, though I am a bit disappointed myself. They've come from all over – or so I'm told."

"Good," said the assassin and he smiled.

With great care, Gelfand undid Revile's manacles. Four of the warriors stood by, their knuckles whitening around the hilts of their swords. The assassin allowed himself to be bound without comment – to the obvious relief of his guards.

"That was easier than I thought," said Gelfand.

"I would not wish to miss my own show," said Revile easily.

"No, of course not," said Gelfand feeling baffled. "Why would you now?"

The prisoners were led, dragged, or prodded along the passageway, their guards watching them carefully. It was the longest walk Margaret, Alwyn or Fergus had ever had to make. Finally they reached a flight of stairs after miles of featureless corridor. They climbed for an eternity until they saw the clear light of day above them, heard the anticipating roar of the crowd. The steps came to an end and they shuffled through a small chamber, an opened door before them. Walking through the doorway, they came out into the blinding rays of the sun and the enormous cheers of the widely gathered audience.

Revile walked onto the scaffold last, smiling and nodding at everyone.

The hangings took place in the town square of Bamburg. Behind the scaffold soared the mighty tower, rising many storeys towards the sapphire blue sky. At every window and battlement were pointing, cheering people.

Surrounding the gallows on the three open sides was the crowd. People fought for a better vantage of the scaffold and scuffles broke out. The Gallowsgate Tower, the main gate into Bamburg, stood to the left, but on the other sides of the square were houses, taverns and shops. The buildings were filled with folk, hanging out of windows, standing on balconies, or finding some precarious viewpoint from roofs and chimneys.

Revile had drawn a large crowd and he was cheerfully impressed with his new-found fame and notoriety.

The crowd shouted again as each of the prisoners were taken to their respective gallows. The assassin's companions looked terrified, while Revile himself rather enjoyed the attention.

Eight hanging trees had been built, eight hanging ropes had been strung, eight hanging nooses had been tied. A huge man in a theatrical black hood stood behind the prisoners, positioning them to his satisfaction. The executioner's eyes glared out of his hood.

"Nice day for it," Revile said to him.

The executioner pulled on his grey grizzled beard beneath his hood.

When the prisoners were placed to the executioner's taste, there was a long roll of a drum and the braying of a horn. To this flourish appeared the lord and lady of Bamburg at a balcony directly above the gallows.

The King of Bamburg, Lord of Chevia, raised his hands to the sky and an approximate silence descended. When the royal party was seated, Prince Bregorin amongst them, a herald unfurled a piece of parchment.

"Hail and greetings," cried the herald, "from our thrice-ennobled lord, King Ferecund of Bamburg and Chevia. We are assembled here to witness the executions of these villains who have all been found guilty of breaking the laws of Bernecia and God.

"First, Fergus, son of Fergus, a man of Bamburg, found guilty of theft."

There was a loud cheer.

"Miriam, daughter of Cedric," the herald continued, "a woman of Bamburg, found guilty of theft."

Another cheer.

"Margaret, a woman of Bamburg, found guilty of theft."

The cheers continued.

"Beoriff, a Cymbrian, found guilty of theft, pillage and murder."

The herald paused until he could be heard.

"Also," he went on, "Alwyn, daughter of Whiteadder of South Caerwinnion, found guilty of assaulting the royal person. Know also that Whiteadder is cast out, and his lands, properties and revenues are forfeit to the Crown. Whiteadder is named outlaw and there is a price on his head of ten gold pieces."

Alwyn was stricken. "I have brought ruin on my father," she said, but then a great anger welled up inside her and she peered up to the balcony searching for Bregorin. She caught his gaze but the prince sneered down at her.

"Also," said the herald, "Oswald of Bamburg, formerly Executioner of the Tower, found guilty of corruption and bribery."

The crowd hissed and pelted Oswald with refuse and rotten vegetables. The executioner had become an unpopular fellow with the townsfolk.

"Also Yad, a woman of no town, found guilty of foully murdering a priest and stealing his belongings."

Revile peered at Yad. She was a tall, strong-looking character, clad in a priestly robe. She had a patch over one eye and a scar across her forehead. The assassin nodded at his fellow adventurer, and the woman nodded back.

The herald went on. "And finally," he said, "finally, Revile of Llaith, found guilty of the cold-blooded assassination of Rule, a freeman and merchant of Bamburg, and his wife and servants."

There was considerable applause and acclaim for Revile. Rule had been despised for he was a miser. The assassin bowed low.

"Let the executions take place. May God have mercy on their souls!"

A priest mounted the stairs to the scaffold. He was a short man, dressed in a grey robe with a long hood which hung down over his face. The priest walked along the line with prisoners, and stopped before Fergus who was the first.

"Have you anything to say?" he asked Fergus.

Fergus went deathly pale, but then courage took hold of him and he regained his colour.

"I have, father," he said in a loud voice. "I do not repent for I have done nothing wrong. It is not what a man does but why he does it. I stole so that my family might eat while these fat lords in their fine halls have more food than they know what to do with. That is the true crime. I have fought bravely for my lord, I have paid my dues, but my reward was to starve and then to die. Is that justice? I ask you, father, is that justice?"

The priest looked uncomfortable. "Go in peace, my son," he muttered. "God is kind. He will not judge you so harshly if what you say is true. God have mercy on your soul!"

"Thank you, father," said Fergus softly, and then closed his eyes. The executioner placed the rope around Fergus's neck and then looked to the balcony for a sign.

Revile stared at his feet.

Fergus was heaved into the air and there was a dull snap like the breaking of a dry tree branch. He hung and swayed in the wind. The other prisoners flinched.

The crowd was silent for a moment, then broke into half-hearted cheers.

The priest and executioner moved on to the next victim, a middle-aged woman.

"Have you anything to say?" the priest asked her. "Do you repent Miriam, daughter of Cedric."

The older woman looked appalled after the hanging of Fergus. "I'm sorry ..." she started but then faltered, staring at the corpse beside her. She dragged her eyes away. "I am sorry, father," she said, "truly sorry. I don't know what came over me that day." She shook her head. "But I beg you, please see that my children are cared for, father. My husband is a cruel man and bears them no love. Please, father, I love them dearly."

"Be at peace," said the priest.

The executioner hung Miriam high, efficiently and without thought, until she hung limp in the noose.

There was an uneasy quiet. Spectators muttered amongst themselves. They had come to see the executions of villains not old women and farmers.

The priest and executioner moved on.

Margaret stood there, her face pale and sad. Tears welled in her eyes and there was held such an expression of anguish that some of the crowd turned away. But she stood proudly. She looked down into the spectators, looking for the faces of men she had lain with and had come to see her die.

"It is you I despise the most," she said.

"Do you repent, my child," the priest asked her gently.

"I am sorry, father," she replied bitterly, "sorry that I have wasted the life God gave me, sorry that I have achieved nothing more than a dog's death. There is nothing else to say. Is that enough, father?"

"It is enough," said the priest and touched her shoulder tenderly. "You will be saved, my child, you will be saved."

Margaret nodded and swallowed.

The executioner paused for his signal and again it came.

Revile shook his head, his expression grim, his eyes still glued to his boots.

There was a snap as her neck broke. Margaret, daughter of Kenneth, swayed gently on the rope.

The assassin sighed involuntarily.

The priest and the executioner moved on.

Beoriff the Cymbrian spat at their feet.

"Don't bother to ask, priest, I don't repent!" he said angrily. "Not a bit of it. Too long has Bernecia and its thieving minions lorded it over us in the west. Our day will come." And the Cymbrian spat again. "You will be crushed between the hammer and the anvil, between Cymbria and Pentland. Then I will have my revenge – when your lord hangs from his own noose. Curse you all!"

This was what the crowd had come to witness and enjoy. They threw more fruit and rotten vegetables at the Cymbrian; and with one voice cursed Beoriff.

Roughly placing the noose, the executioner gently lifted Beoriff from the ground. The Cymbrian danced and kicked, fighting for every breath, another breath to make a strangled threat or curse. The crowd hooted and clapped and jeered as Beoriff's face went purple and blue and black, as he struggled against the rope.

Gradually his cries lessened as he grew weak, and finally Beoriff went limp, his tongue hanging out, an expression of hatred frozen on his face. The crowd sighed, disappointed that the Beoriff was dead.

The priest and the executioner moved on.

"Don't bother to ask me either!" scowled Oswald, the former executioner, a grim expression darkening his cruel features. "I have done nothing but obey my lord's command and execute who he ordered. You have accused me of bribery and corruption, and of those I am innocent."

"Do you repent?" asked the priest.

"Repent?" said Oswald in surprise.

"So that you will be accepted into the kingdom of God."

The former executioner laughed, a madness in his eyes. "Accepted into the kingdom of God?" he laughed. "Me? Do you joke with me, priest? I am damned, damned to an eternity of suffering by the deaths of all those innocent people, all those people I have killed down the years."

"You shall be forgiven," persisted the priest as the crowd started to mumble about the delay. "If you repent and find remorse in your heart. All shall be forgiven."

"Pah!" spat Oswald. "Save your breath for these other poor fools!"

The priest opened his mouth to continue but then he shrugged. "You have my blessing anyway."

In a few moments, Oswald the former executioner was strung up on one of his own ropes on the gallows he had designed and carefully built. There was a fearful expression on his face as if he had indeed met all those who had died there before him.

The crowd enjoyed the spectacle.

The priest and executioner moved on. Revile could not watch.

Alwyn was trembling, but whether it was through fear or anger was difficult to say.

"Do you repent, little sister?" the priest asked her. "Do you have anything to say?"

"What good are words?" said Alwyn sounding sad. "What good are words? My father is an outlaw and has lost everything because of me. He will mourn me but who will grieve for him?"

"I will spare him a prayer," replied the priest, wiping his brow. "What is his name, Alwyn? I will light a candle for him."

"Whiteadder, Lord of South Caerwinnion," she said proudly. "Kin to the men of Pentland."

Bregorin rose to his feet and stood glowering down at the gallows.

"Why do you delay?" he demanded. "We grow impatient. Get about your business!"

"I am in the business of saving souls not time," replied the priest to the cheers of the crowd. He lifted his head to the balcony and his hood slipped from his face.

"Father?" cried Alwyn suddenly. "Father!"

"Yes, daughter," said Whiteadder, and swept out a dagger. "Did you think I would leave you to die? Alone?"

Bregorin swore.

"Aye, it is me," the old man shouted up to him.

The crowd fell suddenly silent. Warriors and guards surrounded the gallows.

King Ferecund looked wildly about.

"I thought you might appear," said Bregorin coldly. "So I laid on this little reception. Take the old man and hang him with his daughter. Now."

"Bregorin!" said Ferecund. "What is going on?"

"Silence, father!" ordered the Prince.

The five corpses swayed gently from the scaffold.

There was a long pause.

"Damn you, take Whiteadder and hang him!"

But the warriors looked to Whiteadder and took no heed of Bregorin's command. They were men of Whiteadder's household.

Bregorin swore and reaching inside his clothing he produced a dagger and sent it whirling towards Whiteadder. With a thud it sank into Whiteadder's chest. The old man sank to his knees. Alwyn hugged her father.

"I love you, child," said Whiteadder as he died.

Bregorin laughed. His own men pushed their way forward through the crowd towards the gallows. Archers appeared at the battlements and windows of the great tower.

"Kill the girl!" ordered Bregorin. "Kill them all!"

Alwyn was still bound and tried to run. She was run through several times by Bregorin's guards until the front of her dress was wet with her blood. She staggered to her knees, and died by her father. Whiteadder's men were also quickly slain or driven off.

Then, suddenly, there was a huge explosion and flames suddenly tore through one of the buildings to the west of the square. People screamed as they were caught in the blast and the fire. Palls of black oily smoke billowed across the gallows. The crowd panicked, running from the blaze, surging towards the Gallowsgate and taking Bregorin's men with them.

Arrows loosed from the battlements fell on those on the scaffold and the front ranks of the crowd. Many found a mark, causing more panic.

For some minutes there was furore.

More billows of black smoke blew across the gallows, and Bregorin could see nothing of the scaffold. Then the air began to clear.

When Bregorin looked down again, the gallows were devoid of life. Five corpses hung there, and at their feet was the body of old Whiteadder and Alwyn, along with several of Bregorin's and Whiteadder's men.

The Prince searched the scaffold with his eyes. But there was no doubt – Revile was gone: he had vanished along with the smoke.

Bregorin peered round dumbfounded, took one worried look over his shoulder, and fled for the refuge of the tower.

THE END

What Happened After

There was mayhem in Bamburg after the escape of Revile (and, indeed, Yad) from the very gallows. Many necks were stretched amongst the garrison and the guard of the tower as bribes were suspected. Prince Bregorin devoted considerable time, gold and energy into tracking down the assassin and any who had aided him – but no word ever came to him of Revile's whereabouts. Bregorin forgot about Revile after a while and, when old King Ferecund finally died only a few months later, the Prince became the King of Bamburg and Lord of Chevia. The town did less well under Bregorin's despotic rule.

Margaret, Alwyn and Fergus were buried in unmarked graves in the cemetery just beyond the walls of Bamburg. Nobody went to their burials: apparently there was no one to remember their passing.

About a year to the day after Revile had escaped from the gallows at Bamburg, King Bregorin sat in his chamber, drinking good wine from a golden goblet. Thoughtfully the King toyed with his quill, then shrugged and signed the death warrants. There had been so many executions in Bamburg that he did not bother to read the names of his victims.

When his servants had gone, he stripped off his clothes and, after quickly washing, lay down on his furs and extinguished the oil lamp. Before too long his breathing deepened as he slept peacefully.

In the morning they found him hanging from a beam in his chamber, swaying gently backwards and forwards. His toes were just off the floor, and his face was black and his tongue was lolling out. Bregorin was naked and around his bare chest was his own signed death warrant.

King Bregorin, too, had joined them, dancing at the end of the rope.